TEMPTING PROVIDENCE
AND OTHER STORIES

HIPPOCAMPUS PRESS LIBRARY OF FICTION

Edith Miniter, *Dead Houses and Other Works* (2008)
Jonathan Thomas, *Midnight Call and Other Stories* (2008)
Ramsey Campbell, *Inconsequential Tales* (2008)
Joseph Pulver, *Blood Will Have Its Season* (2009)
Michael Aronovitz, *Seven Deadly Pleasures* (2009)
Donald R. Burleson, *Wait for the Thunder* (2010)

TEMPTING PROVIDENCE
AND OTHER STORIES

Jonathan Thomas

Foreword by Sherry Austin

Hippocampus Press

New York

Acknowledging Angel Dean for love and sage counsel,
S. T. Joshi for the reanimation, Barton L. St. Armand for old and
new encouragement, and Micke Maksymenko, Gitte Lilja, and
Amba Esselius for Nordic advice and svensk-amerikanska vänskap.

When the cities change, the memories find a way to hide.
—*Juan Carlos Rulfo*

Published by Hippocampus Press
P.O. Box 641, New York, NY 10156.
http://www.hippocampuspress.com

Cover art © 2010 by Thomas S. Brown. Cover design by Barbara
Briggs Silbert. Hippocampus Press logo designed by Anastasia Damianakos.

First Edition
1 3 5 7 9 8 6 4 2
ISBN: 978-0-9844802-0-3

Contents

Foreword

When literary scholar S. T. Joshi introduced me to Jonathan Thomas's previous collection, *Midnight Call and Other Stories* (Hippocampus Press, 2008), I could see that Thomas was already an accomplished writer of what Robert Aickman, a master of the form, called "strange stories." The strange story is my favorite kind of fiction, one especially suited to the short form, and not easy to do well. Some readers might judge any work that touches on the fantastic or the occult or "worms unknown to science" as strange, but I believe such fantasies must have a subtle strain of peculiarity that quietly but surely perforates our illusion of the ordinary. In the best stories—and Thomas's, like Aickman's, are surely among the best—the surreal is artfully grafted to the real. We have the bizarre sense of a carnival without the carnival glare. Utterly real-seeming characters, in the most ordinary settings and circumstances, find themselves wandering through Kafkaesque day-mares, or trying to reason their way out of bizarre conundrums like the bewildered narrator in a tale by Julio Cortázar or Jorge Luis Borges.

We learn to expect the unexpected in Thomas's adventures, as we do in those of an O. Henry or Roald Dahl, but we are never manipulated toward the kind of slick endings those writers are known for. Thomas's stories keep us grounded in a reality so solid we feel we can reach out and touch the furniture, yet they maintain the unpredictable, fluid, wandering essence of dream. Thomas always evokes a sense of the uncanny rooted in what Poe called "mere household events," yet he succeeds at this better than either Poe or Lovecraft, to whom the title story pays due homage. Jonathan Thomas is a far finer artist of the particular than many writers recognized as giants in the field. I find his weird world so convincing—so organic—I need not bother suspending disbelief.

Myth and archetype, as well as the influence of masters of the Gothic tale, seep in from the groundwater in Jonathan Thomas's world, but the landscape is wholly his own. The stories amuse, challenge, and unsettle. Like the best tales in any genre, they succeed first as yarns, then tempt the reader to go back and uncover the layers, reexamine the nuances, reflect on the very human issues the odd events bring to light. The most familiar face is a mask, Thomas assures us. Underneath the most mundane matters of everyday life, ready to break through in the unexpected moment, lies the deliciously, exquisitely strange.

—SHERRY AUSTIN

TEMPTING PROVIDENCE
AND OTHER STORIES

Dead Men's Shoes

In the remote hills of that country, his steep hiking path descended blindly through thickets and converged with a dusty dirt road. There he found himself in the middle of a trudging funeral procession. The black coffin draped in cowhide and the four pallbearers in sackcloth robes and hoods were a gentle stone's-kick ahead. He was anxious not to offend these people, and tried sidling to the edge of the road without bumping into or cutting anyone off. His sweaty T-shirt and grimy shorts and beat-up backpack and scuffed-up shit-kickers were a disgrace amidst the black velvet and rainbow streamers and red fox trim of the tightlipped mourners. But the men shook their heads peremptorily and waved him back among them, and some clapped him on the shoulder encouragingly. A few women favored him with shy smiles.

So he attended the funeral, planting the backpack between his feet. The cemetery occupied a tableland in the shadow of a great sore thumb of bare rock, with lower, greener, rounder hills all around. Each gravesite encapsulated the landscape: a pale obelisk at the head of a broad oval slab of kale-green slate. No stone bore inscriptions. And despite a working knowledge of the dialect, he could scarcely follow the burly clergyman, who drew heavily on religious archaisms and officiated from behind a lace veil affixed by crepe headband. At numerous pauses in the apparent eulogy, the bereaved all cast hopeful looks at the stranger. But what could any of this have to do with him? Self-conscious, he lowered his eyes to the coffin, divested of cowhide, at the bottom of loamy shaft, awaiting the first shovelful.

The clergyman waved a tarnished cross over the open grave in a tortuous gesture. That was the general cue for weeping and the patter of soil upon the coffin one clod at a time. Many hands, in fact all hands except the outsider's, made quick work and left the gravediggers little more than to tamp the ground flat. An obelisk stood over the new burial, but there was no capstone yet.

Marching back to the rickety village fence of verbena stocks, the men sang lyrics with which they were evidently out of practice, because one man or another was always halting midline till he could pick up the thread from his neighbors. The outsider found these words as cryptic as the clergyman's, and was again uncomfortable when everyone regarded him hopefully at certain junctures. The men clasped his arm reassuringly and patted him on the shoulders, to leave dirty handprints. A formidable old woman was swinging open the wobbly village gate. They wanted him to go inside. He saw no graceful way around it.

The layout of the place was apparent at a glance. From a meeting hall at the hub, with corrugated-tin hipped roof and whitewashed plaster walls, radiated several crooked lanes flanked by irregularly spaced, shanty versions of the hall. Judging by the number of houses, the population ranged between fifty and a hundred. Cobblestones occasionally broke through the lanes' dirt surface.

The village's few children, under the stern watch of a lantern-jawed grandmother, were waiting in the hall. To the reluctant guest, the children, who seemed as confused as himself about what was happening, qualified as kindred spirits. The feeling wasn't mutual. They frowned at him suspiciously, till he attempted eye contact and they flinched aside. The air of mistrust only thickened whenever an adult knelt and whispered in the ear of a child, while motioning at the newcomer. No, maybe it was more an air of disbelief. He left his backpack beside the fluted doorpost. Theft was unlikely to be an issue here.

Group mood had meanwhile lurched toward jubilation. At one end of the clerestoried hall, several graying men rummaged homemade string instruments from a varnished chest bound in iron spirals, and without the formality of tuning, launched into a manic, repetitious dance tune. At the opposite end, an equal number of sturdy crones loaded bundles of kindling onto red embers in a cavernous fieldstone hearth.

Then in the stranger's hand, as in every adult hand, was set an earthenware bowl brimming with a tart black wine, tasting of some unfamiliar berry. A plump, fair-skinned girl must have been clairvoyantly informed of his last swallow, for as he lowered the bowl from his lips she was refilling it with richly spiced ale from a grinning-faced pitcher.

The drink in his veins now urged him to join in the loud talk and laughter and dancing, and he was grateful to behold the crones wheeling a geared framework of skewers and spikes, packed with fat sausages and chunks of meat, to stand amidst the expansive blaze. Raw potatoes and hoecakes went directly into the hot ashes skirting the flames. Knots of hunger had been tightening in his stomach, and he was among the first to approach a trestle bench set up within the hearth's warmth and decked with horseshoe-shaped rye loaves and pucks of flaky white cheese.

Between eager mouthfuls, the guest understood, and was understood by, the natives, but they seemed locked into talking at cross-purposes all the same. He spoke of a summer in the countryside to clear his head and enjoy some freedom before tackling serious employment. They asked if their wine was not indeed splendid. He referred to working his way through grad school as a gofer for the ethanol lobby. They wanted his assurance that a man could get used to eating such excellent bread. He deplored the growing need for a master's in political science when applying for entry-level work at non-governmental organizations. They wondered if he could guess how they flavored the ale. He wanted them to know that higher-paid positions had been available, but his conscience had herded him into a socially responsible company. They nodded appreciatively and urged him to agree that he was in a place he should get to know better.

Many potent bowlfuls along, he saw no harm in nodding and was moved by their unabashed joy at his casual gesture. In the coming weeks, his efforts to reconstruct the rest of that day produced brief fragments of stumbling around the dance floor, laughing it off when he bit down on a sausage and squirted hot grease into his ale-numbed eye, hunting after fingernail clippers in his backpack for some inaccessible reason, and flirting skittishly with the plump serving girl.

Merciless sun, through a narrow window like an arrow loop, stung him awake. He lay fully dressed, but not in his own clothes. He wore a white linen shirt with a row of little red primroses embroidered up each loose sleeve. His knee-length breeches were of gray broadcloth, fastened with a yellow cord belt, from which hung a red leather pouch containing a few coins. The buckles of his low brown boots were rusty. The bare mattress on the floor was packed with soft grasses and aromatic herbs, and rustled as he lunged up and across the room, and across adjoining room with its table and two chairs, and out the unlockable string-latched door.

Men were tromping by the house, most of them bearing hoes or pitchforks over their shoulders, presumably en route to crops or hayfields outside the gate. Their clothes were identical to his, except that some shirtsleeves had a row of blue mayflowers, or a green serpent, or a line of stooping brown wrens. The men answered his blinking, open-mouthed disorientation with affable nods and salutes, and some greeted him as what sounded like "Jad." A wispy cloud of dust floated between him and the last of the men before he regained the presence of mind to ask, "Where are my clothes?"

A voice from beyond the dust, without sarcasm or irony, shouted, "You're wearing them!"

"He's right, you know." The voice at his back recalled the sonorous, arresting diction of a John Carradine or Walter Huston. He was startled, but yesterday was still pressing down on him too hard for his body to show reaction. The speaker's expression was unreadable behind a coarse brush of a mustache that verged on comical, like something from a silent movie, and correspondingly weighty eyebrows. The young wayfarer was surprised he hadn't noticed this extraordinary man at feast or funeral.

His thinking or his body language must have been woefully obvious to these people. The serving maid had homed in every time he'd finished a drink, and now this imposing, rugged man was saying, "You did see me before, at the burial. But custom required me to wear the veil. My leadership here is both lay and pastoral. In accordance with our sacred writ. There is a great deal to explain. Please, let us go into your house." And to be perfectly clear, he waved grandly toward the hovel from which the traveler had just stumbled.

The door stayed open after they went in, to dispel the windowless murk of the room. They stood in awkward silence and eschewed eye contact. So why didn't the headman speak, if he had such a lot to explain? At last the traveler discerned him studying a chair and softly clearing his throat. Aha! In this fluky game, it was incumbent on the young man to offer his elder a seat. He beckoned at one of the straightbacked maple chairs and said, "Please." The headman made himself at home.

Once the young man had joined him at the table, the headman remarked, "Your coming has been a wonderful blessing. We are no longer numerous. When you arrived the way you did, it was clear right away that the death of Jad did not mean we would be one fewer. You were meant to become him, if you understand."

The words were plain enough, but he couldn't believe his ears. "You expect me to live here from now on? You want me to fill a dead man's shoes?"

The headman affected a florid shrug and squinted under the table. "True, those are not in very good condition. You can have a new pair. I will see to it."

"No, no, that's not it." Did this man mean to be obtuse, or exasperating? "I have a life back where I came from. I have things to do."

"What are you doing here, then? You must be looking for something." The headman leaned in too close, like a recruiting officer. "And you must be dissatisfied with what you had. People yesterday heard you say as much. Or else why make such a difficult journey here?"

"I didn't know I'd end up here, exactly." The traveler was hard-pressed to keep frustration out of his voice.

"We are skilled at reading people, you know. So I look at you and I can tell, you are not somebody who believes anything happens by chance, are you?"

Up to that day, actually, he hadn't been. It had been a comfort to imagine that every turn of event served some loftier purpose, inscrutable or not. But in view of the confounding, the absurd upshot of these last twenty-four hours, he was having a change of heart.

These people wouldn't force him to stay, of course. They weren't criminals. Yet it seemed prudent to avoid ruffling feathers. He tested a roundabout exit strategy. "Well, let's say nothing happens by chance. But how do you know anything means what you think it means? I don't know, maybe I ended up here to distract you for a while from feeling bad about losing this Jad person."

The headman snorted and shook his head briskly. "Now you're splitting hairs!"

No, he wasn't, but no matter. Obviously he'd never get any-where along this line. Awareness of how badly he needed a bath-room suddenly overtook him, and his tact began to fray. "Listen, you can't be serious. I don't know anything about your customs or your beliefs. I don't know how to do anything you'd need doing here."

"You can learn," the headman insisted. "Whatever we can do, surely you can do, with all your education." To judge by his eye-brows, he was astonished to hear such a flimsy objection.

"But how do I just become somebody I've never met? How could I be anything like that person to those who knew him?" The young man's heel by this time had taken to vigorously tapping out his need for relief.

"We will help you. It should be simple. Jad had no wife. No chil-dren, either. Take your time and learn his trade. Few others in your position had much difficulty."

Others? Had others like him, abductees in effect, been at the fu-neral, in the hall? What had convinced them to stay? No, he pre-ferred hearing nothing yet about any such particulars. He'd been able to cope with this situation by refusing to make too much of it. He didn't want to know if he were in worse trouble than he realized. All he wanted was a toilet.

"So what do you say?" The headman was performing an appar-ently casual adjustment of his cord belt. As he centered the knot closer to his navel, a sheathless bone-handled dagger, in a black leather loop sewn to his trousers hem, flashed in the shaft of sun through the open door. The possibility that here was a veiled threat occurred to the young man while he was in the middle of asking, "Does this house have a bathroom of some kind?"

The headman rose and clapped delightedly as if the traveler had sensibly given in. "No bathrooms here! You have all of outdoors. More privacy, maybe, behind the house."

The last few minutes may have been rife with implications, but the young man left them all behind as he charged outside and around back. A cobble-lined runnel bisected the alley of weedy earth between the hindsides of houses on his lane and those of the lane adjacent. A sluggish trickle on the runnel's mud floor betrayed a subtle downhill grade toward the village fence. He positioned himself, toes on the brink, and then pawed at his breeches in dismay. The broadcloth was devoid of zipper or buttons. Without wasting time unknotting the belt, he frantically shimmied his pants down to knee level, as if peeling stubborn cellophane.

A lanky woman in a smudgy gray smock emerged from between two houses on the other side, precisely when he'd let fly and couldn't stop. Once again, villager timing was uncanny or else suspect. She was lugging a wooden pail and paused to giggle at the grimacing sight of him. She tipped her slops several feet downstream, delicately to avoid spattering him, and smiled archly. "Hello, Jad!"

He managed a sheepish wave and smile, and grasped an instant too late that he'd been caught in more ways than one. She was already striding away, swinging her pail in carefree arcs, bearing the news that he'd answered to their name for him. He was Jad, according to consensus, and self-admission, and, arguably, the headman's knife.

The young man who was now Jad had no intention of remaining, but harbored no illusions of getting far by simply walking away. He also sensed that failed escapes would meet with general resentment if not punishment. Nor was he ready to forsake his passport, credit cards, money, driver's license, and cell phone. He put as happy a face as possible on biding his time.

Jad was a chandler, or so he was told. Nothing at home seemed relevant to manufacturing candles. For that matter, he could add nothing substantial to the inventory he'd glimpsed on first awakening there, apart from a chamber pot and a tripod stool in the bedroom. The village lacked workshops of any description. Everyone chuckled dismissively at the question of how he was supposed to learn his trade. What would people do with candles now anyway, during the long days of summer? Sundown was bedtime. No examples of Jad's craft, in fact, were apparent anywhere. One jumbled impression from the funeral feast may or may not have involved wrought-iron, trident-headed stands crossing and uncrossing in a mock-combat dance before red candles were lit at the hearth and impaled on the tines.

In lieu of chandlery, he went wherever need arose from day to day, tending cattle, reinforcing the fence, harvesting peas, chopping wood. Jad, according to periodic assurance, had worn as many hats every summer, as did everyone outside the season of their habitual employment. He felt exploited but not exactly oppressed. Nobody relegated him as the "new guy" to the heavy or nasty jobs; all did their share. He wondered if he worked beside de facto cousins or uncles or siblings, but received no introductions, as if such knowledge should be obvious, now that he was Jad. Meals and Sunday worship were communal affairs in the hall, and to skip either was unthinkable. Bathing took place in a very cold brook in nearby forest.

Even during naked ablutions, he never felt self-conscious among the villagers. They really did, he marveled, have preternaturally attuned sensitivity and tact at their disposal, perhaps because they were subject to so few modern distractions, from electrification onward. In the performance of liturgy or manual labor, on a hundred points of etiquette, everyone gently guided him past hesitations and mistakes with bottomless patience, as if each had been an understandable slip of Jad's mind. Pernicious Stockholm syndrome may have been setting in, but he felt his cravings for freedom less acutely the longer he played at the slower, simpler life. And then one afternoon, while patching holes in house walls with fresh plaster, he heard something that jolted him into dropping his trowel. Those he assisted studied him with guarded concern, until he snatched the trowel up and attacked his work more purposefully. The men smiled briefly at what they took for fresh enthusiasm.

Had Jad ever heard a truck before? It came roaring ponderously toward them from below the village, on the road that ended at the cemetery, as if out of another world, another era. That said, the truck sounded ancient, asthmatic, straining against its load or the up-slope or both. It was, in any case, reminder enough of everything out there to rekindle his will to escape. He narrowed his eyes to the exposed laths and thistledown fill of the broken wall before him, while his ears tracked engine racket past the village gate, where the driver honked needlessly, and on amidst grinding gears up the hill, and across the flat ground among the graves. Only after the ignition cut off did Jad realize he'd been holding his breath.

Before he'd contrived good excuse to beg off work and go assess this potential getaway vehicle, the headman, in lace veil and sable-cuffed vestments, collected the plastering crew along with all other able-bodied men. Jad mumbled along with the hymn they chorused on the ascending trail of diesel fumes.

The men gave a solemn cheer as they advanced onto the table-land, and Jad weakly followed suit. The target of their acclaim had the effect of making sacred ground look more like a junkyard. It hulked as large as a garbage truck but otherwise defied classification, a vehicular Frankenstein with dented, scratched, and rusty parts of different makes and colors. Even the headlights were mismatched. The tires rested on broad planks that saved them from sinking into the loam. The driver, as Jad had surmised, bore no resemblance to the villagers. He wore a beige beret and brown tweed jacket and baggy khaki pants. He was short and flabby and needed a shave. At the villagers' resounding arrival, he stubbed out a cigarette against the passenger-side door and pocketed the butt.

The driver shook hands with the headman and nodded at every-one else as they gathered around. He undid the bolts on either side of the back gate and hopped back as it fell open and clanged against the fender. The sun shone down on the roofless bed of the truck and brightened silvery flecks in an oval slab of kale-green slate. The slab weighed down a trio of wooden rollers, and the driver worked loose a half-dozen chocks wedged under the near end of the stone. Behind the slab was a rope-bound stack of wooden rollers, a shallow-angled ramp honed from a single block of giant oak, and other items in blankets. The truck had been parked facing the road, so that the slab could be sent down the ramp and straight along rollers onto the gravesite marked till now only by an obelisk.

The headman climbed atop the cab of the truck, and his lace veil billowed with the commands he shouted as pastoral overseer. Jad had the least muscular arms in the village, man or woman, but did his best to pitch in, levering the stone till it budged, anointing the ramp and the rollers with urns of walnut oil, and crowding in with those who strained to push the stone, while two other teams hauled ropes ending in iron crooks that fit over the broad end of the oval. The headman clambered from the cab to lend his brawn to the rope pullers, for the chanciest part of the operation was at hand. Success depended on steady momentum to propel the greater portion of the capstone beyond the last roller, to run aground directly over the grassless plot.

When the stone cleared all but the last two rollers, Jad knew he deserved neither credit nor a swig from the wine jug that the headman, in a Eucharistic spirit, was passing from man to man. All the same, the headman thrust the jug at him, and gestured as if abstaining would be ridiculous. Meanwhile, others were on their knees, toiling to free the roller half trapped under the edge of the slab, or chopping with hatchets at the ends of the roller farther in.

Jad had been swept up in the esprit de corps, or during quick respites had dwelt on how to speak with the trucker in private. He'd given no thought to whose capstone the men were grunting and hacking at, until the wine warmed his throat and jogged his mind. His stomach began to ache. In more ways than one, perhaps, this was his grave. The situation was making him jittery. "Should I be doing any of this?" he quavered, in case anyone was listening.

"Aren't you feeling well?" asked somebody within the commotion, without raising his eyes.

"Don't you see, it's Jad you have buried down there. But I'm Jad, right? Are you sure there's no taboo or something I'm breaking?"

A few men paused and looked from Jad to the impassive headman, as if trying to figure out what the problem was.

"You're Jad!" exclaimed a native with upheld hatchet, who received an approving nod from the headman.

"But this is Jad's grave," the young man remonstrated.

"Do you see a name on it?" another villager pointed out.

"Okay, then who's under this rock?" Jad demanded.

"Please, Jad," the headman cut in, "let us not dispute for the sake of disputing. It does not become you."

Whether by dint of lace veil or the knife below his vestments, the headman's soft-spoken input squelched further talk. Everyone promptly, gratefully set their shoulders to attacking the rollers again, except for Jad, who could not have squeezed in without risk of injury. The headman ordered arbitrary stops to share out more wine and cajoled Jad into partaking. The trucker had his back to them, off to one side of the cemetery, absorbing the view and discreetly finishing his cigarette. After Jad's pensive frown had shifted between the idle outsider and frantic workgang several times, the headman observed, "You don't seem like yourself today. Relax. When the work here is done and we have gone, maybe you can clean up the pieces of wood. Throw them down the side of the hill. And return whenever you're ready." Jad nodded listlessly. Inwardly, though, it amused him to think that if he were never ready to return and acted accordingly, he would not, technically at least, be flouting the headman's authority. Ah, he would miss that splendid wine!

As afternoon shadows of obelisks lengthened fingerlike across the tableland and the headman led his flock away, choiring a hymn whose syllables they often slurred, Jad finally heeded pastoral advice and began to relax. The driver apparently preferred not to mingle with the villagers in their cups and only now came over to retrieve the oily rollers and empty urns. Jad had formed a pouch with his shirtfront and was dutifully filling it with the scrap wood. He scurried to the edge of the cemetery and flipped the splinters and shavings out into unconsecrated air, and began helping the driver while work enough remained for two.

The driver didn't seem to know what to make of Jad and declined to acknowledge him, apart from some shifty glances. Not until all the urns and rollers were stowed in the flatbed did he see fit to speak. "This ramp is so heavy. Help me get it in the truck."

Jad suppressed a groan. If only, in the twilight, the backbreaking ramp had faded out of sight, out of mind. What to do now, in his supplicant position, but comply with a semblance of good grace? He blamed the wine in his blood and the oil that had spilled all over everything for his failure to handle his full half of the weight.

The driver gave no sign of expecting anything better. He fished his keys from jacket pocket and had half-turned away before pausing to ask, "You want a ride back down?"

"Yes, all the way back down!" Jad was a little shaken at his own vehemence, but it made no visible impression on the glum trucker. Jad heard himself blurt, "I've been kidnapped! These people are forcing me to stay with them. Please, you need to get me away from here, so I can go back home!"

The trucker stared a little more morosely but effected no other change of expression. After a long moment, he nodded and told Jad to crawl under one of the blankets in the flatbed. Beneath mildewy wool, Jad lay on his stomach and peeked from under moth-eaten edge out the back. Only when the driver had planted his feet well apart and bent to flip the gate up did Jad discern that he wore low brown boots with dull steel buckles. The young man gasped, even as the gate slammed shut and the bolts rasped into their sockets. Should he scramble out and rethink what to do next? The truck rumbled to life and jerked forward. Well, maybe it was premature to read too much into simple footwear. It hardly proved that the trucker was one of them. In these backwater economies, some peculiar wares made the rounds of trade networks. The driver's cigarette certainly hadn't been a product of his native territory, so why assume that the boots were? Nothing else on him matched the village wardrobe. Anyway, they were moving, and Jad's only cause for regret so far was the truck's utter lack of shock absorbers.

Then the bumpy, bruising ride was at an end. Muffled by the blanket, lively music and socializing drifted over from someplace indoors, as soon as engine din faded from his ears. Had they arrived in the driver's village already? Between the condition of the road and of the truck, hard to tell how fast they'd been going!

The blanket was gone as if whipped off by a gale, and the tailgate clanged open. The headman, back in secular garb, was glowering down. Jad till now had been able to find some lingering traces of farcical rustic in the headman's whiskbroom mustache and woolly-bear brows. In the cold blue moonlight, though, they recalled to him the grim, baleful funeral mask from that old English pagan tomb at Sutton Hoo. While the driver sneaked puffs on another cigarette and tried to look nowhere special, the Dark Ages thundered viciously at shell-shocked Jad.

"So this is how you repay us!"

Yes, for kidnapping me, thought Jad, but knew better than to say so and energize the tempest. He continued to lie on his stomach, the headman's belt in his line of sight, letting the uproar roll over and past him.

"Did you honestly think you could bleat a little nonsense and turn one of our own against us? Well?"

"One of our own?" Jad echoed, without lifting his eyes.

"Of course, one of our own!" The headman's abdomen twitched in conjunction with the idea popping into his mind. "So you believed him an outsider because you'd never seen him before? Are you under the illusion that we stay here all winter? How would that be possible? There is no way to heat these houses, no shelter for the stock. These are the summer dwellings only, until the hay and crops are in. Then we herd the cattle back down the valley, to the winter quarters. But some of us must stay below all summer, to guard against thieves and squatters. For someone with such intelligent airs, you have pretty stupid ideas about us."

That wasn't altogether fair. As soon as the headman had vouchsafed Jad a few particulars, he realized what was going on. It was called transhumance. He understood the concept perfectly well. His eyes hove slowly to the left of the headman, in time to watch the trucker slouch through the village gate, in the direction of the boisterous hall.

"We made you one of us," the headman railed on. "You have acceptance here, a place where you belong. What would you be going back to? What is so important out there?"

My life, Jad reflected with some acrimony, a life without i.d. or credit cards if I'm any good at second-guessing these people. The headman, with the spooky acuity that no longer came as a surprise, angrily confirmed, "Anyway, that world is closed to you now. Those little scraps of plastic and paper that made you a part of it, we destroyed them, and your old clothing too. Those things trapped you in a selfish life, doing everything for your own sake, and not for the common good, as we do here. Or are you still as selfish as ever?" His voice rose dramatically. "Do you want us to die out? Do you want our traditions to disappear forever?"

Jad, staring earthward, was obliged to shake his head, but felt his worldview shift again, much as it had when the headman proposed that nothing happened by chance, so many weeks ago, or was it months?

He never used to question that cultures everywhere ought to be preserved. Their rich variety, their very outlandishness had cast a gemlike allure into his own drab reality. He'd attended lectures galore by anthropologists who had spoken glowingly, if paternalistically, of "their" people, whose myths and folkways afforded them a stable niche in the universe and full, happy lives.

Jad doubted nobody's word, but saw the wisdom now in saving cultures on a case-by-case basis. The music in the hall was getting faster and sloppier. It was monotonous and grating and he didn't like it. The hall itself was shoddy and charmless, as was the architecture here in general. The apparel lacked color and personality, except at funerals. The standard footwear could have passed for cheap imitation flamenco boots. Mandatory hours of droning tedium every Sunday seemed the extent of local spirituality. What did the village have going for it beyond a sense of community, and what was that on its own but the urge of any social organism to perpetuate itself? Did he sincerely care if all this was gone in fifty years, or tomorrow?

"I know there is good at your roots," the headman declaimed, "so this transgression is forgiven, and talk of it ends here. If word of what you did accidentally came out, people might resent it, so you had best go home rather than risk a slip of the tongue. Our driver will not reveal anything. Too bad you are missing our feast of laying the capstone! You would have been a guest of honor. If anyone asks, I will say you fell ill at the burial ground. Maybe with the same thing that was fatal before." Was that a joke? Jad lifted his eyes, but extravagant mustache hid any chink in the severity.

Jad climbed out of the truck, taking care not to sigh, or betray any expression, or look into the headman's face again. He was halfway to the village gate when the headman called, "One more thing!"

Jad ground to a halt, one foot in the air. He didn't turn around. He heard footsteps, the truck door creaking open, some rifling around, the slam of truck door, and the approach of footsteps. Jad's breath stuck in his throat when the headman's shadow passed over him, as if a huge raptor were singling him out. Then the headman loomed before him and tossed something toward his feet, with the attitude of wasting a promise on an ingrate. Jad warily lowered his eyes. The buckles on new boots gleamed softly in the moonlight. "The cobbler stays below, too," the headman reported. "Put them on now. Leave your old ones there." The headman stalked away, and was gone before Jad had fastened the second buckle.

A restful evening of home confinement sounded fine, actually. After a miserable day of sweaty labor and dashed hopes and brow-beating, did he need the company of drunken, overwrought yokels? The merrymaking was loud enough for him to follow logy attempts at conversations from in bed. The noise began to recede as he dozed off, and he assumed he was dreaming when she sat on his bedside and cradled the back of his head in one hand. She sat him up from there, and he realized that here was the plump serving girl, in the flesh. "I felt bad for you, while everyone was having a good time to-gether. Are you too sick for this?"

The girl pressed a bowlful of wine on him and gripped his hand in hers to ensure he didn't drop it, while groggy Jad tried to say, "What?"

She brought up his hand and the bowl within it to his lips, as she might feed a balking child. She tilted the bowl slightly, and at the first taste Jad held the bowl more firmly, and the girl let go. Her other hand still fondled the back of his head, as if he might tip over otherwise. "Now you feel better, don't you?"

"Very nice of you," he murmured, while the heat of alcohol re-vived him. He was newly appreciative of her easy smile, her lively eyes, her generous proportions, for which the best term was volup-tuous, wasn't it? He hadn't deciphered whether she was gazing at him with solicitude or something more, but he could picture himself sinking into her soft, lavish body, and the way it would enfold and squeeze him. At the same time, he was coolly appraising her and his horny self as if they were images on a screen. A kind of detachment had been stirring in him since that instant of crisis when the head-man had yanked the blanket away. From his dissociated vantage, he connected his bona fide lust for this girl with an escape plan that had yet to attain conscious form. And he knew he would follow that plan, foolhardy or not, as faithfully as a train stayed on its tracks. Nobody ever accused a train of going in the wrong direction.

The girl released the back of his head, to pour herself a bowlful and drain it at one go. That was promising, especially on exhibiting signs she'd had a few beforehand. "You need some more, or you might become sick again," she warned in singsong tones. She peered into the face sculpted into the pitcher and grinned back at it. She gingerly tried refilling the bowl, got nothing, violently upended the pitcher and shook it. The dregs streamed out and splattered against the bottom of the bowl. She giggled when a drop hit her in the nose.

She put a conspiratorial finger to his lips, rolled off the mattress, and staggered to the paneless arrow-loop window. She thrust a hand below the sill, into the wall, halfway to her elbow. She pulled out a dusty little jug made of thick glass. Had she been in here before, or was there a false bottom to every local bedroom window? Jad had never even gone over and looked outside. She uncorked the jug and smiled sweetly as she poked it under his chin. Vapors sprang from a clear liquid and stung his nose. The bouquet was reminiscent of white lightning and brandy. She was kneeling beside him, her knees touching his thighs, and apparently ready to hold out the jug until he took it. "That's it," she coaxed him as he raised his hands. He wondered, in passing, who was seducing who, but didn't want to lose the moment to idle speculation. He had to get on with this.

Instead of grabbing the bottle, he kept reaching and lightly clasped her face between his palms. She lowered the jug and set it at arm's length off the mattress without turning aside. Her smile widened when he kissed her as if she couldn't be more pleased, and she was exactly as he'd fantasized. The onlooker Jad nodded in shadowy approval. The plan was taking shape.

Jad had bought into the received wisdom that privacy was nonexistent among these old-style peasantries. Hell, people had no locks on their front doors. The serving girl knew better. She found him alone gathering cloudberries or filberts, or at the brook filling creels with crayfish or watercress, and led him beneath forest ledges or behind hunting blinds or into ancient brick foundations. They made furtive but manic love, and then Jad reverted to the role of model villager. He never complained or argued, and always pitched in, whatever the task, with a gung-ho smile. He was neighborly to a well-regarded fault. He did nothing in front of anyone in which anything could be suspected.

His interior springs, meanwhile, were winding tighter and tighter with his ongoing resolve to flee. He wasn't deaf to the potential for happiness in this simple, close-knit setting, for all its cultural shortcomings, and the sex was at least as exciting as it would be anywhere else. What he ultimately had against the country life was that he hadn't chosen it for himself. As for the girl, she was foremost a term in an equation that he was still struggling to frame, and whose result would be freedom. She hadn't broached marriage or any specific future with him, but based on the bloodless bed after their first liaison, she was no deflowered victim. Technically, she was one of his captors. Anyone in his shoes would surely use her with as little compunction.

A haystack under the harvest moon concealed their final tryst. Was she tired, or coming down with something? They, like everyone else, had been working dawn to dusk at reaping and picking and culling, in preparation for the move downhill. She wasn't her former uninhibited self, in any case. He never knew what to say after they'd coupled, and usually they lay on their backs, staring at the sky. Today, she rested his hand on her stomach and confessed, "I'm with child." Jad couldn't feel the difference, but didn't expect to, through her abundant flesh. He subdued a grossly inappropriate smirk. I'm with child? Had they strayed into a Robert Burns ballad?

No, wait, this was it! This was how she fit into his equation! "That's wonderful!" he exulted. At his raw outburst and the cold shine of moonlight in his goggling eyes, she shrank away a bit, as if only now realizing she didn't know him at all. Then she lay back, clenching her teeth and examining the stars. A more sensitive Jad might have intuited that she was afraid and not above believing that if she could restore the silence of a moment ago, then he would go back to who he was before she had spoken. Or at least she could create a lull in which to slip homeward before whatever had hold of him said or did anything scarier.

But Jad's mind was already racing over the hills and far away. Somehow or other, this unwed motherhood was what he'd been blindly working toward, his outbound ticket. The village wanted foremost to replace its dwindling membership. What did it matter deep down if he were the replacement, or if he produced a replacement? Why not let him depart, as long as he was giving them what they wanted? The headman, in their first conversation, had mentioned that the deceased had no wife and "no children either," as if a little bastardy among friends was no big deal. And if it were, then according to all the anthropology under his belt, rural primitives, in the absence of police or a court system, got rid of incorrigibles by banishment. Go ahead, he cackled to himself, kick me out of Eden and the company of decent folk!

A vestigial part of him frankly wondered if this scheme made any sense, or if it might take an unforeseen disastrous turn. He scorned to listen. The detachment he'd been harboring for weeks, which he associated with his higher subconscious powers, was calling the shots. Granted, as tacticians went, it was on the inscrutable side, but he didn't feel qualified to judge it. He was, in fact, having trouble seeing his way clear to anything these days. He couldn't recollect the name of the corporation where his job was waiting, or the name and the face of the man subletting his apartment. He blinked as if he'd been napping and found that his hand lay upon cold ground instead of the girl's warm stomach. The wind had already erased her impression in the loose hay and scattered yellow leaves in its place.

The morning after next, the truck rumbled by the village, and Jad was in the crew that followed it to the same field where he and the girl had last been together. The headman issued pitchforks and oversaw the transfer of haystacks into the flatbed. As soon as each was razed, he slapped the side of the truck, and the driver, who stayed behind the wheel, started up and drove to the next stack. There was no hurry, and the headman frequently doled out wine. Jad went through the motions of swallowing, but wanted nothing to blunt his wits later, when he engaged the headman in a private chat. To Jad's delight, the headman, for a change, was guzzling right along with everyone else. Was he trying to get soused for some reason? In any case, by the sunset hour his movements were on the slow side, and he swayed minutely like an oak in strong wind. Otherwise, he staunchly held his liquor.

The truck would have to return for the last few stacks tomorrow. The headman dismissed the gang with a benedictory wave, though he was in lay costume. The truck barreled off and the men separated into cliques and sauntered away over the next few minutes, some singing, some in palaver, pitchforks over their shoulders in soldierly fashion.

Jad took pains to wish people good evening so that they'd see him untie his belt and hustle behind a haystack for an ostensibly long piss, to preempt notions that he had any more personal motive for lingering. When he emerged, only he and the headman remained on the stubbly field. The headman was eyeing Jad intently, who surmised that the headman was also anxious to have a talk. Well, Jad couldn't afford to worry about that, or about his pitchfork, now perched on the headman's shoulder. He had to stay on message. The headman gestured grandly toward the road.

As they set out, Jad inhaled to launch into his opening arguments, but the headman was a breath ahead. "It was brought to my attention that one of the girls is with child. I put on the veil and she made confession to me." His glare bore down on Jad till Jad peered back at him. "I should have known. And you should have known better."

Was the plan showing signs of derailing? Jad refused to panic yet. "Don't you want more people here?"

"She is your second cousin!" The headman's legs were shaking, whether with wine or stress or both, and his previously superb modulation kept sliding up and down the scale.

"What difference does that make?" Jad, because he thought it went without saying, neglected to add that they both knew she really wasn't any such thing.

"Too close! Still too close to be lawful! What they would call, over in your schoolrooms, taboo!" The headman's veneer of dignity was cracking. Nor would it likely matter that nobody had informed Jad of his "family ties" with the girl.

On second thought, Jad bristled at how she'd so frivolously abused his trust. "And what about the girl's responsibility in all this? Didn't she know what she was doing?"

Could Jad say anything that wouldn't rile the headman further? "She is only a poor stupid girl," he bellowed, "and does not understand any of this!"

That had to be the headman's most absurd claim yet. Did he sincerely believe it? Maybe he had to, or else the community in his charge, and his authority, would become a sham.

"She and the child will bear no blame." The headman was reining in his temper and weighing his words more carefully. "If she had been blessed with any wits, she would have learned by now."

By now? Could she have had anything to do with whatever had

happened to Jad's predecessor? While he considered that, the head-man was asking what the girl stood to gain by acting so foolishly. The answer was straightforward, but wouldn't have brightened the headman's mood. Anyway, the clever girl had earned Jad's grudging admiration for exploiting sole means of influencing the course of events, of enjoying the only kind of power available, under a patri-arch like the headman.

"So you see how it is." A hint of entreaty put Jad on his guard. "I am truly sorry, but you will have to die. The law here is plain."

No doubt the headman was sorry. It explained the drinking, the nervous legs. And the death sentence explained the appropriation of Jad's pitchfork. There was a heat in his throat as he gaped at the pitchfork, rocking back and forth in march time. Then he had the sensation of snapping out of something, and a vivid perception of watching himself and the headman as in a dream, as a third person walking beside them, with the capacity to advise and rescue himself.

The headman followed Jad's riveted eyes. "No, not here, not with this. It would not be fitting." Yes, the headman was a great one for observing the niceties. "Let us go to your home." Jad nodded, and the dagger at the headman's belt came to mind.

Without warning, the headman veered to the roadside, where a path snaked upslope between thickets. Leaf mould clogged a shallow drainage ditch along the road to either side of the junction with the path. The headman caught himself at the edge of the path and stood over the ditch. "Wait, I need a minute." He leaned the pitchfork against the wall of vegetation and huffed with annoyance as he undid his belt and worked tight trousers below thigh-level. The man was all right at holding a day's worth of drink, but his bladder was an-other story. He sighed, and Jad heard piss slam into dead leaves, and gawked incredulous at the pitchfork standing within reach. Relief had made the headman unmindful, and his confidence in his own au-thority was badly misplaced. The detached part of Jad that was look-ing on from outside, that did whatever it had to do, snatched the pitchfork with nary a jostle of shrubbery. In the instant it took the headman to blink and twist around, pants around his knees, Jad had the tines aimed point-blank at his midsection.

"No, Jad, you are good!" the headman pleaded, hands naively upheld. "I know you! You have not acted this way in all our years!" Jad could see the reward for being good, fastened to the headman's bunched-up trousers and reflecting dull sundown glimmer. He drew audible breath as if to reply, and in that tiny interval of false reprieve plunged the points through dingy white shirt, deep into abdomen, with laudable force for a mere city boy. The headman squealed like a puppy under stomping foot. Jad hadn't expected that! The headman gripped the pitchfork handle as Jad let go of it. So Jad had misread the subconscious master plan! This was where the affair with the serving girl inexorably led! To get back home he had to kill the headman, who toppled into the ditch and landed on his side, convulsing and groaning, his two hands unequal to dislodging the pitchfork. Its handle extended beyond the lip of the ditch and smacked it weakly while punctured stomach muscles spasmed.

Jad tarried a moment to be sure the headman was going to stay down. Maybe Jad was doing this poor stagnant village a favor. A healthy culture was not a specimen in aspic. Under new leadership, it might evolve into someplace less hermetic, less fragile. Or it might degenerate into a ghost town in short order. Jad didn't care one way or the other, and the villagers, of course, would be anything but grateful to him.

The uphill path called. Just move, cover some distance while a modicum of light remained! Plenty of time to worry about food and warmth when he was hungry and shivering. As he took to his heels, he wondered how soon people would miss the headman and, after the initial shock and confusion upon finding the body, how soon they'd suspect Jad. The headman, after all, had asserted that the Jad everyone knew would never impale anybody. Jad was short of breath before he recognized that he was on the same path that had thrust him into the funeral procession in the first place, subjective eons ago.

He pushed onward. In the last of the twilight, he heard hallooing and heavy footfalls, but from ahead rather than in pursuit. Hah! How to comport himself? Whoever this was, Jad had to disown village identity. He practiced introducing himself, but went no further than, "I'm not Jad, I'm . . ." Was it the strain of the preceding hour, or had he overstayed a day too many out here? He was in appalling ignorance of his own name.

From around the next bend, with excessive breakage of twigs and branches, a young backpacker caromed clumsily into sight, out too late in the day, too late in the season. He flapped his arms to right himself as he reeled to a standstill. The former Jad smiled in wordless greeting. A renewal of faith surged through him like a second wind. Maybe nothing happened by chance, at that!

"Thank God I ran into you!" the backpacker gasped. "I can't find my campsite. Is there any kind of town or hostel or farmhouse up this way?" The hiker's face was pasty and, whether by dint of gloom or the escapee's frame of mind, as vague and generic as a storefront mannequin's.

"Keep right on the way you're going. There's a village close to here. They'll make you very welcome." What with its population down by two, that seemed a pretty safe bet. "You ought to take it easy. The trail gets pretty steep all of a sudden."

The hiker thanked him and pressed on. The former Jad quietly picked up an egg-shaped stone and with cold-blooded accuracy winged it into the back of the hiker's head before he'd advanced ten paces. The hiker pitched over and sprawled motionless.

The former Jad sprinted over and wrenched off the backpack, snagging wallet and wristwatch for good measure. The hiker moaned. The former Jad paused to listen for a disinterested second. Then he hurried away, shoving wallet into backpack, and putting on wristwatch, and digging into backpack contents, all in midflight. Extra layers of clothing, and with any luck, food and water—check!

If worst came to worst, maybe he could be whoever this guy was. For now, he had no concept of being one person or another, no awareness of a name present or past. He was nobody in particular, only a random point of consciousness crossing dark hills. In him, one last ember of hope still dimly glowed, that if he could retrace his steps far enough without anyone stopping him, then whoever it was that he used to be might come back to him.

Into Your Tenement I'll Creep

Lorraine, that fool, has been so kind. Dressed for temp work, she comes in, teases me a little with the tip of her tongue, tells me to feel better for later. What a lovely place to lie sick abed! Rather, the situation is lovely. The place is a dump. Dark, rubbishy East Village roach nest. But rent, food, and love come free for the foreseeable future.

And they say it's tough getting started here! Says who? I blow into town, take a cheap room off Union Square at the Scandinavian Sailors' Home, where you don't really have to be a Scandinavian sailor, and two nights later I'm in one of those Avenue A bars, the No-Tell Motel or Downtown Beirut, can't remember which anymore. But no matter. Lorraine is there. Trying to think slinky, ever slipping into wide-eyed li'l angel mode. I charm my way into her bedroom, and the simple application of furrowed brow and brave beleaguered smile turns one-night stand into something more beautiful. Do I need a place to stay? A hand till I find some source of income? And with a mere nod, I'm in like a virus.

No fault of mine, coming down with something a few days later. Not that my plans included looking for a job, but really, I did get sick. Sore throat, swollen glands, headache. Cold or flu.

All in all, though, my luck inspires me to make bedsheet into burnoose and sing, despite sore throat,

> I'm the Sheik of Avenue B
> Your ass belongs to me
> While your reason sleep
> Into your tenement I'll creep

Self-styled worldly girl, you'd think, would see a leech like me a mile away. But naïveté, unto utter cluelessness, seems to have more staying power here, as if it rolls happy-go-lucky into the countless sheltering cracks this city affords. Spandex does not a cosmopolite make. Try to freeload like this back in Ohio and your legs would be sticking out of a snowdrift in no time. Ah yes, this is like collecting unemployment. Good for six months at least.

That Lorraine may be one sweet sucker of a slum angel. But what a slob! I roll over and face the wall. My profile overhanging the chasm between wall and bed. Start coughing. God, what a lot of dust! Down I squint, leeringly. Ugh! Hair and dust cohere as a mat, looking as solid as that coarse, fibrous layer they lay under carpets.

I may be a weasel, but I have my standards. Sick or not, I shamble to the kitchen. Grab broom and dustpan. Setting dustpan on floor at the mouth of the chasm, I stand on the bed and trawl bedside detritus into dustpan. Carry dustpan to kitchen wastebasket. Creating airflow enough to billow particles from loaded dustpan up at my face. Roiling spores of squalor.

But wait, more is moving in the dust. Brown worms stand out in the gray. Many are dead, but several poke up curious heads. Worms no bigger than fingernail parings, there among the fingernail parings and hair and seborrheic flakes and snot and God knows what other bodily jetsam, forgotten but not gone. Petite burrow holes in surprisingly regular matrix riddle the human fabric.

The worms are hard and segmented, with tiny beebee heads. Maybe like the worms reputed to feast on our remains. Which, in a piecemeal sense, they were doing here. By whatever means they'd arrived on the fifth floor. John Donne and friends called sleep "counterfeit of death," and I shuddered at the idea of these worms working on me and Lorraine while we slept, albeit on dead and detached parts of us. Rest comes easier to me with the worms consigned to tightly knotted garbage bag.

Lorraine comes home and opens me a can of soup and makes love to me and otherwise dotes on me. And all the while I think, Maybe lucky for her that I'm here after all. Jesus, worms in the boudoir. This kid does need someone to keep her place from becoming a charnel house. Sure, I'll handle her like putty, but at least it'll be clean putty.

I never mention my housekeeping efforts. If she's lived this way all along, it probably fits her definition of cleanliness. No point testing how sensitive my little gift horse is.

Then I see her going out in the cold November rain with nothing but flannel shirt and slippers. Afterwards I ask if she's trying to catch what I've got. She laughs like I'm silly. She only went across the street for a newspaper. "And besides," she suddenly shoots from the hip, "our bodies are mere tenements, and we are not the only tenants, and we are never the last."

This gearshift toward profundity, even if just a bombastic riff on "ashes to ashes," spooks me a minute. Then, with a trippy smile, she reverts to type. Folds a sheet of newspaper into a bib. Tucks it between my shirt collar and undershirt and announces, "Soup's on."

Congestion, headache, weakness linger into second week. Am I going stir-crazy? I'm definitely sick of being sick. Maybe Lorraine is sick of it, too. How else to explain why she said what she said, and my response?

We're snuggled up in bed watching the archaic portable TV on the dresser. During an ad for tightass blue jeans she blurts, "You know you weren't the first. There were others here before you."

What makes her say that? Not that I ever presumed otherwise. But why rub it in? To make me feel bad, after all my care never to loose a discouraging word? Provoke me, will you? With no more premeditation than a frog leg twitching at voltage, I snarl "Bitch!" and smack her across the face. Her look dares me to do it again. No idea where this hostility comes from, but my hand complies with it. Right. Left. Right. Left. Have to catch my breath. Lorraine tries neither to run nor shield herself. Sits there, a blubbering martyr. A wordless minute passes and my heat fades. Lorraine goes to the kitchen and makes us herb tea. Our eyes return to the TV like nothing has happened. Women! Who can figure 'em?

The next morning I feel lousier than ever. Bad conscience, or exertion of bruising the girlfriend? She comes in before going to work. Thick oases of makeup on face are as telltale as any black and blue. She sounds down but not angry. Says, "I never finished what I had to say last night. It's true, there were others here before you. But you've swept them away, and it's like you've emptied them from my heart."

So she's upset over falling for me too hard? My heart leaps despite my overall weakness. "Why didn't you just say so?"

"I didn't want to admit it. Please don't be angry."

"No. Of course not." On the emotional hook and dying to be reeled in! And reel I will. Whisper the right sweet nothings, and when she swallows them, I'll be free to sleep around, slap her around, whatever, with impunity. Till more pleasing prospects offer themselves. But for now, just let me sleep a while longer . . .

The room is black when I awaken. Night already? I blink, dazed and disoriented, as Lorraine enters and turns on the overhead. Blink is all I can do. Can't move. Can't speak. Numb. And no less odd in its fashion, for once Lorraine's office clothes really seem to fit. Like she means business. Stands arms folded at bedside. Keeping her distance. As if I am among the unclean. No longer in her class. Nobody with whom anything could be personal. "My pets, my little loved ones, you've killed them all. But that's all right because more are on the way. You swept my pets away along with the others who were here before you."

Her pets? The worms? Between whom and herself Lorraine put me? And if carrion worms accept hair and dust as proxies for the dead, why reject the meatier proxy of sleepers counterfeiting death?

A lot of people let their pets curl up at the foot of their beds. But feeding your pets in bed, now that's gross. What kind of slob would do that? Letting them crawl down boyfriend's snoring throat or lay eggs in his ear or wherever? Munching deep down, disconnecting nerve ends, leaving me like this. No wonder I've felt sick!

"The look on your face tells me I don't need to explain anything. I'm glad you said this morning that you wouldn't be angry. Remember?"

And as if things needed to be clearer I sense, dully as through Novocain, an eruption on my cheek. Right below the eye. Before which a tiny worm is swaying back and forth, looking very big indeed from my point of view, seemingly dizzied by the expanse of light and air, the sensory overload around it. I know how it feels.

Unceremoniously Lorraine rolls me over, my face smushed against wall, to fill the crack and sink slowly into it as my dead weight forces the bed to give creaking way.

Lorraine says, "You may be out of sight, but this isn't good-bye, is it? Unless someone later on is as cruel as you."

And ever since then there's been nothing more to tell. Except sometimes, I come around enough to catch that rhyme still running through my head, "While your reason sleep, Into your tenement I'll creep."

Tempting Providence

Justin, till a month ago, had never expected to be here again, but over three decades and several dead-end careers later, he was back as an "honored alumnus," no less. The room, true to memory, was on the scale of a hospital ward, and the walls were a dull aseptic white, typical of countless other gallery spaces. His photos were of "The Beautiful and the Condemned: Parting Shots," and were on a two-week sojourn in Providence between exhibits in Boston and Philly.

From humble beginnings as snapshots of lopsided red barns, his work had evolved into highly polarized, finely etched silver nitrates of charming landscapes, buildings, or neighborhoods about to be bulldozed for development. Their pathos had touched a mainstream nerve somehow and earned him grants, and articles in the *New York Times*, and NPR interviews, and calendar contracts. Meanwhile, the irony of displaying these images in a place that stood atop a former charming site was evidently lost on the faculty, homecoming alum, and students at the opening, bless their uncritical hearts. If his alma mater wanted to show him off as a successful graduate, he guessed he could live with that much boosterism. No, nothing much had changed about the List Arts Building since grad school, except he strongly doubted he'd run into the ghost of H. P. Lovecraft tonight.

Justin, in fact, had never set foot in the building after that incident. He'd been offsetting his tuition as a night watchman for Campus Security and had refused any further assignments there, and what's more, he'd admitted why. And why not? He saw what he saw, and youthful principles dictated he "tell it like it is," in the parlance of the day. True, he'd been reading up on Lovecraft for his comparative literature thesis about local-color fantasists, so he knew that Lovecraft's Early American home had been uprooted and towed over the hill to make way for the List Building. Untrue, however, were rumors he'd been on acid, as fabricated by those intent on "common sense" rationale for any brush with the supernatural. Luckily, suspicions of drug use rendered nobody a pariah at the time, or the entire university population would have been on the outs with itself. Vexing enough that LSD and "some space cadet" figured in every recap overheard at parties, or worse, thrown back in his face by unknowing raconteurs.

In any case, the unvarnished facts had remained in Justin's drug-free head, and one of the more remarkable was that the ghost had behaved exactly as he would have anticipated. Justin, in baggy blue uniform, had been on midnight rounds in the building and had entered the room where his work would someday surround him. Track lighting with dimmers set extremely low barely alleviated the darkness; there were no windows.

From out of the murk burst someone pacing rapidly, who nearly collided head-on with Justin before performing a last-second about-face and pacing away. Justin had time only to gasp and stumble to a halt, heart thumping, while the trespasser paced toward him and away once more. At second glance, Justin took note of short hair parted on the left above a high forehead, a thin-lipped mouth that seemed small because of a substantial chin, and a gaunt physique in a 1930s suit replete with white shirt and black tie. The similarity to Lovecraft in off-register photos on yellowing newsprint was unmistakable.

In keeping with his fitful stride, the revenant's expression was of confusion and distress, readily understandable in anyone who found himself in a bleak hall where his snug parlor should be, and in someone so skeptical of the spirit world who was suddenly one of its denizens. Trembling Justin drew flashlight from belt holster and asked meekly, and sympathetically he hoped, "Can I help you?"

The ectoplasm must have been too delicate to withstand spoken vibrations. The agitated Lovecraft failed to re-emerge from the shadows. Darting flashlight beam detected no one anywhere in the gallery. Nevertheless, Justin hightailed it out of there, pausing only to lock up behind him with unsteady hands. Thus began and ended his sole occult adventure.

None of his instructors or classmates were at the opening. Good! Chances were minimal of having to endure urban legends about himself. By the grace of free wine, though, numerous alum, whether staid and middle-aged or impossibly young, saw fit to buttonhole him on ever more familiar terms. He extended cordial thanks for generic compliments, even when some cranelike dowager pumped his hand and actually exclaimed, "Nice captures!" And what harm in disclosing that he lived in the Catskills, and that he wasn't going to the "big game" tomorrow against Princeton because he hated football? Or that he was staying on Benefit Street at a Victorian bed-and-breakfast, yes, every bit as quaint and genteel as it sounded, maybe a little rich for his blood in fact. Did he travel with his family? He'd been twice married in haste and divorced at leisure, thanks for asking. "Irreconcilable differences of standards and values," he explained, "but everyone's amicable. The exes are too humane to try squeezing alimony from a stone. Anyway, no children, thank God!" Was Justin coming off as brusque? No matter, if it kept tipsy parents from bragging about their overachiever kids. He'd been hitting the wine himself, after all, and was at the point of wishing Lovecraft's ghost would reappear, if only to light a fire under this whitebread crowd.

Aha, someone with whom Justin needed a word was crossing his line of vision. Dr. Palazzo, head of the Pictorial Arts Division and a darling of *ARTnews* and its slick-paper ilk, was homing in on a few equally overdressed attendees. Sturdy Dr. Palazzo exuded brash corporate airs in powder-blue three-piece suit, yellow tie, and wavy silver hair too majestic to be real. Despite art-world prominence, had he ever in his life so much as handled a crayon? He came across as governor of a military occupation, but Justin steeled himself and essayed an engaging smile. Reimbursement for lodgings had been a condition before Justin agreed to wedge this fortnight into his itinerary at the last minute. The exhibit would otherwise have gone into storage at his Boston or Philadelphia venues, and he'd have been home resting up days ago. Typo-laden e-mails from the gallery director promised that only the formality of Palazzo's signature stood between Justin and repayment, but he had yet to hear a straight answer about that after a full day in town.

Justin flagged Palazzo down and introduced himself. Palazzo congratulated him on the show without acting especially impressed. He was clearly en route to more important conversations. Justin presented his case with all due tact, while ruminating that the sum in question wouldn't have bought one of Palazzo's shoes. Palazzo's curt advice was to discuss petty cash with the gallery director.

"She referred me to you," claimed Justin, a shade archly.

"I can't do anything right now." Oh? That much "petty cash," and then some, was probably wadded up in Palazzo's back pocket.

"Why don't I drop by your office Monday morning? What time is convenient for you?" Justin swallowed a belch an instant before it was too late.

"You'll have to call my secretary." Palazzo rushed off before Justin could say anything else.

The gallery director had been across the room all along, but Justin didn't want to make her evening any worse. She looked like hell. Curly brunette strands were stuck to her clammy brow, her eyes were bulging, and she was dividing frazzled attention between a cell phone and the micromanagement of slowpoke undergrads in catering uniforms. Dr. Palazzo, meanwhile, was hobnobbing with the impeccable few, as if nobody else were around. Justin downed one more plastic goblet of Chablis and slunk out and down the hill to Benefit Street.

He awoke in a sweat under fleece comforter. Between the cushy down-filled mattress and the hiss of radiator going full blast before Columbus Day, he felt decadent as much as overheated. He also felt he might have been a bit uncharitable toward last night's attendees, and even Dr. Palazzo. He couldn't, in fairness, object if the lives of others led them to perspectives different from his own.

According to bedside digital clock, it was earlier than he thought. He could still catch the tail-end of breakfast. He rolled out of bed and into the bedraggled, off-balance aftermath of more plastic goblets than he cared to tally. In the dining room downstairs, the other guests had come and gone, and the staff had yet to clear the self-serve table. Justin grabbed three cups of coffee to be sure they'd be there when he wanted them, along with croissants and orange juice. The second cup was lukewarm but did the trick. His frilly surroundings became sunnier, and he gamely conceded that even if they were overly precious they attracted the clientele without whom this address might devolve into one of his silver nitrates. Justin had been pleased to find the East Side pretty much as he'd left it, thus far at least, including Geoff's Sandwiches, still in business across the street. Or did it use to be Joe's?

Justin had wisely packed an okay digital camera, to make the best of imposed leisure. The b&b counted homecoming as a "special weekend" and obliged him to book three nights, which was just as well, in view of Monday morning business. At a whim, he headed south on gloriously unchanging Benefit Street, and at the first major intersection he spotted a white cardboard rectangle taped below a "No Left Turn" sign. Big black letters proclaimed "Alumni Tent," with an arrow pointing up the curve of Waterman Street. The phrase put Justin in mind of a circus, and despite the low odds of reality bearing him out, he opted to go see what was what.

The street skirted the drab, postwar School of Design campus and the List Building again and the venerable Main Green of the university, and at the corner of shopping-strip Thayer Street, another white placard directed him one block farther, where an arrow sent him north. He winced at vinyl siding on historic walls in a neighborhood that should have known better, and then smiled. A circus tent indeed dominated the little urban meadow of Pembroke Field. Clusters of red, white, and brown balloons bobbed at the tent entrance and along the chain-link fence around the field.

The illusion of a Big Top dissolved as soon as Justin trudged amidst a gaggle of merry old graduates through the gate. Demographically, he was back at the gallery opening, only with a much stronger turnout here, and the addition of many babies in strollers. A guy in a cartoonish bear costume was posing for photos with happy couples. Justin was mildly amused at his inability to look upon jaunty mascot without thinking "narc." Name tags adhered to the majority of sweaters and jackets, and sociable Babel emanated from a dining area where a pregame box brunch was under way. The "Alumni Pub" was doing a lively business, and Justin vetoed the passing thought of a beer to wash down breakfast.

These people were having fun, and more power to them, but black loneliness latched onto him and gnawed deeper the longer he steeped himself in the festivities. He had a master's degree from this school, and every right to be here, and had come at departmental behest, hadn't he? But he wasn't feeling particularly "honored" and suspected that the gallery director's invitation to him had somehow fueled bad politics between her and Palazzo. He also suspected that somebody sooner or later would notice him languishing in solitary discomfort and ask him to leave. He needed no outside confirmation that he didn't belong. Out on the sidewalk, he breathed easier.

He retreated to Thayer Street, and his eyes widened in immediate dismay. Damn his vivid recollections! A dorm complex with red and green brick façade, like a dull-witted kid's Lego project, had replaced a row of classic Victorian mansions, mansard roofs and gingerbread eaves and all. He continued down Thayer and wished he could stop himself. He remembered a second-hand bookshop notorious for buying stolen collections, and a locksmith whose illegal dupes of dorm keys abetted countless student flings, and a hole-in-the-wall deli where a grouchy octogenarian sold expired yogurt and treated the customer like a sissy for not eating it, gray fuzz included. These and other upwellings of robust personality had no latterday counterparts. Clothing and restaurant chains were in ascendancy, some chichi, some tacky, but all with deep pockets to absorb the likely sky-high rents. Something he didn't recall was the excessive number of trust fund babies out making fashion statements. He had meager faith in the survival of a record store, a pizza joint, and a few other mom-and-pop operations beyond their next lease renewals. To discover a new generation of panhandlers in front of Store 24 was heartening, though he wasn't about to waste any cash on them. A little scruffiness, a little waywardness remained of the Runyonesque street of his less uptight era. That was the kindest spin he could manage.

Thayer outside the commercial strip was even more appalling. His mental map contained a neighborhood with attractive houses, and a popular breakfast place, and a clothier who specialized in dated formalwear, and a corner grocer's, Boar's Head Market, wasn't it? Progress, or science, or capitalism, if any distinction applied in this context, had rolled over it all, and on its dust the university had installed gigantic barracks of lab facilities and gussied-up bunkers of congested dorms. Regrets about hanging his work anywhere on this overreaching campus were weighing more heavily on him. He was glad Lovecraft couldn't see any of this pox of oppressive architecture. Or could he? What was a ghost, and what was the extent of its awareness, its powers of observation? Justin's mind wandered aimlessly in and out of these meditations, while his feet led him back to the solace of Benefit Street. He was sure now only of what he had been sure of all along: he had not been on hallucinogens, that night in List.

He ordered lunch at Geoff's, where sandwiches bore the names of local celebs, none of whom rang a bell. He took his Antoinette Downing a few blocks north, into the secluded old graveyard behind the stately Episcopal cathedral. Poe had courted Sarah Helen Whitman here, and Justin thought he'd read somewhere that Lovecraft had done likewise with his fiancée, Sonia. He tried reviving the tradition one night while dating his first wife-to-be, till a humorless geezer cradling a yappy pug appeared at a window overlooking the churchyard and threatened to call the cops on them for "scaring everyone half to death." Today Justin sat on a tabletop sarcophagus off to one remote side and ate in peace. For all he knew, the humorless geezer was buried somewhere in here.

At the b&b again, he slept all afternoon under the fleece comforter, without breaking a sweat. His eyes opened to the waning hour when the outlines of things softened, though he could still navigate by natural light. He retained no contents of any dreams, yet was firmly convinced he'd been dreaming. Or more precisely, he had the sensation of something external impinging on his sleeping self, which, according to received wisdom, had altered the course of those dreams he'd otherwise forgotten. Room service? Intruders? He gave the bedroom a wary once-over and switched on the bedside lamp. Neither his duffel nor the items on top of his bureau showed signs of disturbance. He was picking up none of the eerie vibes he imagined would accompany a haunting. If he couldn't shake the feeling of having been watched, then he'd sensibly ascribe it to pigeons on the windowsill.

What he needed now was to get out and walk, preferably in the direction of supper. He had done nothing to work up an appetite, but hunger pangs and a nervous energy were prodding him toward the door. The East Side had depressed him enough for one day. Grabbing the camera, he headed west, confident of eating well on

Federal Hill.

A Holiday Inn on the far side of downtown doubled as a gigantic, informal welcome sign to the Hill, luckily for Justin. Traversing the business district, he felt like a rat in a watermaze. His most substantial old landmarks were proving ephemeral. A puny three decades had obliterated railroad trestles, Civil War monument, a huge department store, the bus station, and a sprawling annex of the state university. He peevishly navigated around the multiple sore thumbs of upstart high-rises and was never happier to be making steady headway toward a shamelessly boxlike hotel. He hadn't planned on going in, but there he was at the desk, asking an aloof clerk about the availability of rooms on Monday. Not a problem, allegedly. All the college types in town for girls' hockey or whatever were checking out tomorrow. Justin said he might be back, and the clerk grunted and re-entrenched himself in a Sudoku book.

Like a great X marking the spot, a four-membered arch now spanned the beginning of Atwells Avenue. By way of keystone it featured an outsize bronze pinecone, or maybe a pineapple. He rejoiced at recognizing the Old Canteen and Blue Grotto, evocative fixtures from yesteryear and still prosperous. But on his budget, he was more delighted about the warm light from the windows at Angelo's. Inside, the tin ceiling and white enamel tables and the menus nailed like eye charts to big square support posts conceivably looked the same as in 1971 or 1931. And at 5:30, he had his pick of the seats. A chipper waitress called him "sweetie" as she placed his order for sausage, peppers, and French fries, with a glass of the house red. No knots of fat or gristle were hiding in the sausage, the clear outer skin sloughed right off the peppers, and the fries had entered the kitchen as fresh potatoes. The burgundy wasn't bad, either. Justin tapped the bottom of the glass to coax the last drops into his mouth and pushed away from the table, contented, and thought, This is the good life for me. Should that be so hard? Plus, Justin had beaten the dinner crunch! He left a nice tip and continued up Atwells.

Bewilderment made his steps drag at times. What had happened to the solidly Italian enclave of yesteryear? Chinese and Caribbean takeouts, a nouveau hippie coffee house, an Indian eatery felt incongruous, as if plunked down by some cosmic joker. And where to go from here? The night was in its infancy. If he wasn't mistaken, one of the Lovecraft sites mentioned in his thesis was a few blocks away. Maybe the Historical Society had bolted a commemorative plaque to its door by now.

Justin gradually sped up from minute to minute, till he identified the silhouette of a church across a tiny courtyard. He peered more closely and harrumphed. No, this wasn't it. Too recent, and too wholesome for a horror yarn. And he had gone too far. He was well over the hilltop and halfway down to Olneyville, if memory served. This, unlike the locale in the story, wouldn't be visible from Lovecraft's address on College Hill.

He backtracked. How had he missed an entire church? He had a bad feeling about an open space at the corner of Sutton Street. The sidewalk widened into a modest plaza, with an ash-gray disk embedded at its center. He glossed its incised text by streetlight, and by the third line was too incensed to follow the rest. Since its founding in 1875, the Catholic church of St. John had been important to "many ethnic groups" and in local working-class history. Then in 1994 it was demolished. Just like that. Persons unknown to him had designated the resultant vacant lot a park and relinquished it as a "gift to the city."

Disgusted Justin glared past the plaza and the remnant church steps toward a curb-bound circle of dirt with sparse patches of defeated-looking grass. On the outer perimeter was one park bench, paintless, with a number of broken slats. To its left, springing mushroomlike from the soil, was a pair of cement tables with inlaid checkerboards, flanked by three and four cement chairs, respectively. These furnishings wore a thick coat of rust-orange paint, which reinforced an appearance of being salvaged from a fast-food chain. So even in 1990s Providence, a repository of clear-cut neighborhood and literary value could come to this. What good would it do, though, to bust a blood vessel over other people's disordered priorities?

A wire fence behind the bench denoted one edge of the property. Beyond were three tenements: beige, with flat roof; blue, with pitched roof; and green, with hipped roof. A powerful security light between the uppermost windows in the blue house cast a surprising level of brightness on the park grounds. From stark shadow in back of the checker tables, somebody was careering straight at him. Getting mugged would be the perfect finish for a day like today!

Justin was too stunned to utter a sound and grew faint at a face-to-face glimpse of his assailant, who suddenly U-turned away into the darkness. He stood motionless as the restive ghost of H. P. Lovecraft strode out of the shadows again and beckoned earnestly at arm's-length perigee before withdrawing once more. On Lovecraft's third approach, Justin's professional reflexes nudged him into raising his camera, popping the lens cap, and shooting a rapidfire sequence. His hands were trembling, but at least the automatic flash didn't instantly scare off Lovecraft the way his voice had. In fact, the apparition paused longer and beckoned more demandingly. Maybe verbal communication would work this time. His hands became steadier as he continued to shoot. He gazed through the viewfinder upon Lovecraft's forlorn expression, and felt sorry for him, and was at a loss for words. Nonetheless, he wasn't about to follow anyone's ghost into blind obscurity. Lovecraft, a little sadder it seemed, turned on his heel and did not return a fourth time.

Justin lowered the camera and self-consciously checked hither and yon. No other pedestrians were around, and the occasional motorist had tooled by as if nothing unusual was going on. Moreover, the inner-city scene was getting to him now more than when a ghost was flitting through it, because the security light, which must have had some finicky sort of motion sensor, had gone out, to swamp everything beyond the church steps in uneasy mystery.

Justin was shaken, of course, and perplexed, but as he stooped to grope against the paving stones and miraculously find his discarded lens cap, he realized he was also famished as if he'd never had supper, and more antsy than ever, as if some long-awaited desire were near fulfillment. But what did he have in the offing that wouldn't pale beside the sight of a spirit? He had no conscious inkling and concluded he was too hungry and overwrought for his mind to be doing right by him.

The dinner crunch was just ending as he re-entered Angelo's. His previous table was available, and the chipper waitress remarked that he must really like the food here. He chose the gnocchi because nothing else would be as filling, with sides of rabe and eggplant parm and a half-carafe of the red. The waitress beamed as if gluttony were admirable and called him "sugar." If he looked like he'd seen a ghost, she didn't make anything of it.

And what about the ghost? Justin was in the hapless middle of an emotional pileup, dazed, indignant, intrigued, anxious, excited. Still, his thoughts kept looping back to certain vagaries of what he'd witnessed. He attacked his food and pondered how the ectoplasmic Lovecraft had successfully crossed town but upon arrival was confined, with a single variation in gesture, to performing exactly the same motions as in the List Building. Ghosts might be prone to stereotypy, but that seemed too glib an answer.

Nor was Sutton Street where Justin would have staged a rendezvous if he were in Lovecraft's position. True, the church of St. John had some importance as a story setting, but to Justin's knowledge Lovecraft had only seen it from a few miles' distance. Any number of places closer to home must have been more meaningful to him. Why not materialize at one of those? And why Justin? Twice? Whatever the unquiet spirit wanted, countless others had to be better qualified to help! Yet he'd never heard of Lovecraft haunting anyone else.

He regarded his three clean plates and empty decanter. Everything had been tasty, and he'd swear to that, but he couldn't remember consuming any of it. He'd eaten like one possessed. Fortunately, none of the other customers were staring as if he'd been boorish about it.

He got a cannoli to sweeten the return trek through downtown. The ricotta filling burst through cracks in the pastry casing, so his hands were a mess when it finally hit him that he could review all his occult images in-camera this very second, while walking down the street. Going digital was about to pay off already! He stopped himself an inch away from smearing expensive technology with sticky fingerprints. Back in the b&b, he fastidiously washed and dried his hands, but afterward scarcely had the energy to undress before toppling into bed, as if someone somewhere had thrown a lever and cut off his jitters of the last few hours. The pictures would wait.

The heat in his room next morning bordered on stifling, and an unpleasant hint of scorched mold laced the air, a byproduct of antique steam pipes, Justin reckoned. He also awoke with a heightened perception of being an outsider, of not belonging, an echo of what he'd felt at Pembroke Field yesterday, but he connected it now in some dreamtime logic with the excessive heat. Was the management trying to drive him off with too much of a good thing? He opened the window somewhat and discovered that the radiator beneath it was cold. So was the one in the bathroom. Had the warmth wafted up through the floor? These old buildings usually had their anomalies. On the positive side, he was up in plenty of time for breakfast. How fortuitous, seeing as last night's insistent hunger was homing in on him again. And the sooner he was out of the room, the better. Camera in hand, he noted that the corridor was downright chilly. Happily, he'd left the fungal scent behind.

On the last flight of stairs before the foyer, the distinctive rumble of an oil truck reached his ears. A mature woman with bobbed reddish hair and bulky green sweater turned to him from the partly open front door. Justin guessed her to be one of the owners, because she apologized for the furnace running out of fuel in the night. "Not a problem. Please don't give it a thought," he replied without slowing down.

He staked out the table nearest the breakfast bar and pounced at the eggs and sausage and bacon that rewarded early risers. He may have cut off rival guests when going for extra platefuls; he could only vouch for moving faster than whoever else was en route at the same time. To discourage any challenges over his right to multiple helpings, he scowled needlessly at the goateed kid on inattentive duty.

Between every course, he re-examined his new series of shots, as if enough squinting would flush out what he wanted to see. According to his feckless camera, Lovecraft was purely a hallucination, invisible in blurry and sharp exposures alike. The security light upon the blue wall, however, exerted an inordinate presence. It consisted of three bulbs in an upside-down triangle, and though he'd gazed into its glow last night with impunity, in pinpoint reproductions it was burning bright, painfully so within seconds. More inexplicably, it remained in tripartite clarity even when the rest of the frame was smudgy. And toward the end of the sequence, the bulbs were plainly larger, or perhaps in the process of sneaking closer. They weren't playing by the rules of optics in any case, but there his patience for analysis ended. His eyes roved dully over the dwindling contents of chafing dishes. He could always consign more servings to the bottomless pit, but had felt no more satisfied after the last couple. He was becoming too fidgety to stay any longer.

Today's morning walk differed markedly from yesterday's. It proceeded north along Benefit Street and wasn't recreational. Justin wasn't sure yet what it was, but he was averse to letting nostalgia or disappointment enter into it again. Four cups of coffee did not in themselves account for the high-strung nerves that required he range across the landscape, and half a mile of Georgian and Federal elegance was behind him before he understood he was in pursuit of something. Where Benefit merged with North Main, and only dreary new shopping centers and prefab apartments and "professional buildings" lay ahead, he swerved right, up Olney Street. He wasn't out to take stock of his surroundings, but the wrong ones, he sensed, would ill-suit his purposes, whatever they were. At the hectic intersection with Hope Street, he marveled that Tortilla Flats, the one Mexican bistro in town way back when, had survived a third of a century. For other than old time's sake, he tried the door. He was now willing to have another go at breakfast, but they weren't open yet.

He forged on, into neighborhoods of Colonial Revival mansions and wedding-cake Victoriana and prim bungalows and rundown triple-deckers that still had more character than anything constructed in Justin's lifetime. Not till he was deep in a terra incognita of broad avenues and manorial pretenses did he grasp that Lovecraft, or his unbodily likeness, had some bearing on this obscure mission. Much keener was his awareness that it must have been lunchtime, and he in a gilded wasteland as far as restaurants were concerned.

Subjective, hungry ages elapsed before he chanced upon a busy artery, with the brackish Seekonk River to the east, and westward, a cluster of businesses. It was dimly familiar, and on its outskirts the words Wayland Square popped into his head after thirty-five years of disuse. Historically it had been an "exclusive" retail hub for the old money, but Justin at present had eyes only for the black and yellow sign that read Minerva's Pizza.

At the cash register, a gray, spindly gent with a gravelly voice told Justin to sit where he liked. A table up front afforded him a view of the sunny street through an expanse of plate glass. Apparently churchgoers didn't come here for Sunday dinner, and none of the homecoming set were in evidence either. Some kids from a prep-school track meet, to judge by the uniforms, were lunching with their families, and that was about it.

He scanned the menu for whatever promised to contain the most meat, and under Subs he gravitated to steak and cheese. His cravings and his restlessness were no more subject to free will than were his eyes, drawn irresistibly to the movement on the screen above the mirrored bar. The sound was muted, and the kitchen crew had forgotten the TV was on. How else to explain why nobody changed the channel? Outdoorsmen were fishing in some Deep South cypress swamp, and Justin couldn't imagine a more tedious contest of man against nature. Nonetheless, he had to watch until there was a sandwich to devour. He didn't notice who brought it. But while he bit off and chewed mouthfuls, his mind's eye kept harking back to close-ups of the bait in taunting play, back and forth, back and forth, just below the leaf-strewn surface. He knew he'd seen the like somewhere lately, and it nagged at him and eluded him and made him put down his sandwich and think.

Then the revelation pitched him into momentary vertigo. His putative Lovecraft had shared in the abridged range of motion, the repetition, the agitated beckoning. If ghost he really was, he was under some duress, but of what nature and to what end? Lovecraft, or his puppeteer, had coaxed Justin to follow. That same hidden agency was implicated, coincidentally or not, in firing up Justin's feral appetite and joyless wanderlust. He dared not conjecture further without more to go on. He was in too vulnerable a mood.

His hands had raised the steak and cheese halfway to his mouth. He forced himself to put it down again and stared out the window to take his mind off food while he tried to concentrate. Justin's one conceivable source of information to tie together Lovecraft, and the two places where he'd seen Lovecraft, and some background on those places, was the novelette by Lovecraft himself. But how to get hold of it on short notice, and what was it called, anyway? His eyes were scrutinizing storefronts across the street, as if that would help. Then he laughed out loud, wolfing the rest of his sandwich and handful of chips with a rush of new determination. In what was once a branch post office, a fanlight spanned masonry façade. Fanciful lower-case letters in each of its trapezoidal panes spelled out "Myopic Books." He strode to the cash register without waiting for anyone to bring the check, and was almost out the door before he reversed course and stuck 20% in singles under his water glass. If this manic energy refused to let him alone, maybe he could at least channel it for his own good.

He reined himself in after sprinting up Myopic's front steps. No point in alarming people with a dramatic entrance! The layout was uncommonly airy for a used bookshop. A fetching girl with long black hair and disarming eyes was online at the desk, presumably filling mail orders. She escorted him to the horror section, a freestanding bookcase in a far corner. What jaw-dropping luck! A Lovecraft omnibus stood on top of the case, beside a slipcovered set of Tolkien. "Looks like you found what you wanted," she said.

He had her ring it up and asked if she'd mind him reading it on the premises. She shook her head. "We're open till six." At second glance, she was simply rendering realpolitik its due. A couple of bearded duffers were ensconced in comfy chairs by a coffee table, noses deep between covers. They gave off a vibe of barnacles. Toward the rear wall he settled into a barber's chair, upholstered in chiffon green. He strove for a semblance of composure, though inwardly he was on a breathless hunt.

His hunch to skim through last stories first proved correct. An allusion to Federal Hill guided him to the title "The Haunter of the Dark," and he resolved to peruse carefully, to stay on track from word to word, despite his jumpiness. In barest outline, a Midwestern visitor to the East Side blunders into mental linkage with a hostile alien while inspecting vestiges of a grisly cult in a deserted Atwells Avenue church. Justin had read the tale before, but so long ago that this amounted to the first time all over again. His reactions, too, were bound to be different now from when his interests were merely academic.

He had to stop sometimes and bathe his eyes in the calming brightness around him, to divert his racing thoughts from premature conclusions. The protagonist's dread of "something which would

ceaselessly follow him with a cognition that was not physical sight"
reminded Justin of those hypothetical unseen trespassers during yesterday's nap. And concerning the "unholy rapport he felt to exist between his mind and that lurking horror," why wouldn't that express
itself as the insatiable hunger and compulsive restlessness which even
now tried to unseat him, and in which he was no willing participant?

He pushed on through the text. More stubborn efforts led only
to graver intimations. The victim's despair at "a strengthening of the
unholy rapport in his sleep" reminded Justin of how displaced and,
yes, alienated he'd felt first thing that morning, and when the hero
later stirs from a mesmeric daze in the church and inhales a "stench
where a hot, searing blast beat down against him," Justin recalled the
heat in his room and the stink of burnt mold, after a night without
oil in the furnace. He felt hemmed in by the pages and looked out
the narrow window in front of him, but it was half blocked off by
foreign-language dictionaries, and beyond the glass was an antitheft
steel latticework, with a claustrophobically nearby brick wall filling
the view. Justin dove back into the book on his lap.

The narration laid increasing emphasis on the malign entity's in-
tolerance of sunlight, and Justin had to nod in tentative agreement,
since both his Lovecraftian experiences had occurred after dark. Finally he reached the diary excerpts recording the hero's semi-
coherent desperation as his nemesis closed in. The climactic image of
"the three-lobed burning eye" turned Justin's stricken musings to the
camera hanging from his neck, and its documentation of the church
site's security light with its three glaring bulbs and disregard for the
way objects should take shape in photographs. And in retrospect,
how disquieting that the lights had gone out after Justin had been
working his flash a while. He twisted his head away from the book,
toward a wider window to his left. The shop had a flagstone patio
out back, where the blooms on a hydrangea and the leaves of a vir-
ginicus were already brown. Must've been nice here in summer! He
wondered if he'd live to see it, then grimaced at himself for turning
morbid on such a flimsy basis.

The sunshine happened to fade before his eyes. How long had he
been in that chair? Had the overhead fluorescent been humming like
that all along? He stood too fast, and everything spun for several

heartbeats. Stiff and creaky legs carried him to the desk, and he started framing an apology for loitering till the last minute. The barnacles had vacated their comfy furniture! A bad sign, but the wall clock above the desk was a tad shy of 5:15. He relaxed a bit and thanked the fetching girl for being very helpful, hoping his long-term occupancy hadn't been a problem. "As long as nobody heard you snoring," she assured him.

Out on the sidewalk, he slid his purchase into a big inside pocket of his denim jacket. Desires to eat and roam plagued him again. Minerva's was right there, and a large meatball calzone stood out as the shortest wait for the most protein, with the added virtue of portability.

He headed down Angell Street and wondered how far he'd get before tearing the wrapper off dinner. Past the first bend in the road, the green and white sign for a Newport Creamery loomed over him. One more youthful hangout he'd forgotten for decades! Too bad he hadn't scouted ahead; a burger plate and sundae sounded good. Then he saw that nothing was left but the sign. Streetlight penetrated sheet glass sufficiently to indicate an interior gutted of booths, counter, stools, freezer cases and all.

But in the distant recesses, people were moving around, unhindered by gloom, animated, at arm's length from each other. The more he studied them, the less shadowy they became, as if Justin must have been wrong about the dearth of illumination back there, and they seemed closer than at first. Momentarily in lambent glow he beheld a frail, gaunt oldster presiding over a table of deferential young men. He wore a dark suit of '30s vintage that seemed on the verge of falling apart at the seams, and he retained enough thin white hair to part on the left. His chin projected well ahead of his delicate mouth, into which he was spooning a banana split with laudable gusto when he wasn't offering an opinion. His audience had shoulder-length hair and turtleneck shirts and flared jeans, and were patently not the youth of today.

Back when researching his thesis, he'd woven trivia about Lovecraft and this stretch of Angell into wistful daydreams centering on this restaurant. At seeing them converted into three dimensions, he fought a lump in his throat. Opposite the Creamery hulked a typi-

cally boring apartment complex of the '50s and, to add injury to in-
sult, for its sake the beautiful birthplace of H. P. Lovecraft had been
destroyed. In the young Justin's reveries of a better Providence,
Lovecraft had not been struck down in middle age, overdue royalties
had let him regain his ancestral home in the nick of time, and his
legendary taste for ice cream frequently enticed him, in his fragile
but genial eighties, to cross the street and hold court in the Creamery
with Justin's horror-fan contemporaries. Justin still cherished that
daydream, and to gaze into its world, not only parallel but long defunct, made him weak with yearning, and his lower lip trembled.

He blinked away tears. The kids at the table were regarding him
with anticipation, as if he had agreed to come palaver with them,
and the ancient Lovecraft was graciously waving him in. Justin
gulped. Who, me? But the door ought to be locked. He stepped over
and tugged at the handle. He saw and felt it start to heave open, yet
could see through it, at the same time, to a door that wasn't budging,
as expected.

Justin let go, shuddering, and his melancholy reddened into anger. What would have happened if he'd set foot across that phantom
portal? Lovecraft and the boys were still hopeful of his company.
Justin grabbed his camera, stowed the lens cap, and turned on the
flash. Not now, not ever had he seen Lovecraft's ghost, but only this
soulless effigy. Absurd to suppose a spirit would age posthumously!
And what about this coterie of ghost hippies? Whatever was pulling
the strings here either thought little of Justin's intellect or had major
limitations in its own.

Justin raised the camera. The tableau most likely wouldn't leave
a record, but why not see what would? And if something sinister,
and photophobic, were trailing him, this was the least he could do.
He aimed and shot a sequence. When he lowered the camera, the
interior was dim and empty again.

His appetite, however, was unabated. The calzone was reduced
to grease on his fingertips, for all the restraint he could summon,
blocks away from Benefit Street. Furthermore, knowing that his surplus energy derived from some ominous, furtive source was of no
help in suppressing it. He could, at best, shut himself in his room and
ride the frazzling current toward a better understanding of whatever

was hounding him.

He washed his beefy-smelling hands, flopped into bed, plucked the remote off the nightstand, and turned on the TV. He used whatever began yakking at him as a subliminal anchor to normality, while he examined his series from the Creamery.

Naturally, his was the only human form throughout, camera masking his face, as reflected in the brilliance of the flash upon plate glass. Inside, trackless dust between bare walls showed faintly. All the way back, a rear door opened onto the Deco brick row of Medway Street. That he had to take on faith, because a substantial area within the vague doorway contained three scorching orange discs in triangular arrangement. The security light had followed him to Wayland Square!

After a bout of hot sweat and nausea, Justin noted with perverse satisfaction that a meager five minutes in bed were yielding valuable insights. Lovecraft and anyone with him were figments planted in his mind. The "three-lobed burning eye" was not. And the sentience behind that eye and those figments had even more invasive access to the mind of man, or to Justin's at least, than it had in the story.

As he spooled through the sequence, the "lobes" hovered unwavering, as if in wait. On finer inspection, though, they weren't exactly framed by the door but overlapped it, so that they seemed to shine from vastly farther away than the door, yet were inside the building at the same time.

In the last image, all that changed. The eye, in predictable reaction to too much flash, had departed, but in its place was not the formerly hidden portion of doorway. A circular hole was floating there, and not a vacant one. A pattern informed the murky grayness, as of braided strands of dirty smoke or striations in muscle tissue. The printed page had implied a winged and cloudlike entity skulking in the church. Here was a glimpse of detail, intriguing, disturbing, but equally uninformative in practical terms. It was, in fact, petrifying to linger over that fingerprint-sized window onto inexpressibly remote and strange conditions. Justin started feeling dizzy, as if on the brink of physically tumbling into that tiny gateway.

Look away! On television, a silver-whiskered park ranger was calf-deep in reedy wetland, lecturing on the ecology of the Blackstone Valley. A local cable production, Justin surmised. The visuals switched to fishermen flycasting from a grassy riverbank. They jogged his thoughts back to the TV in the pizzeria, and to the bait wiggling on the hook.

Different bait for different fish, he thought, then thought further, Depending on the neural circuitry and genetics and much else of which the fish had no clue. And yes, depending also on the mood of the fish. Was his predicament the upshot of being the right person in the right mood, in his case of withdrawal and loneliness, broadcasting a signal from the right place at the right time, perhaps "when the stars were right," as Lovecraft put it? Was there a species of angler, a predator whose range was of dimensions rather than miles, receptive to that signal? In that angler's continuum, had that first incident in List happened scant moments ago? If only he could recapture what his mood had been before he'd first sighted Lovecraft. Had he been troubled, depressed, tense? He drew a total blank. In respect to emotions, it may as well have been a stranger in that baggy uniform.

But in common with his younger self, and with Lovecraft too, there was Providence. Justin had never encountered ghosts and aliens elsewhere. And perhaps he could also share with Lovecraft the distinction of being the same kind of fish, in a manner of speaking. Minutiae cluttering his brain for half a lifetime were paying their rent at last! In letter or essay, Lovecraft had reported seeing nymphs and satyrs under the oaks in his backyard during his childhood, and at this time of year. If he'd tried to join them, would he have met the fate Justin had narrowly escaped tonight? Plenty of people disappeared forever, without motive or signs of foul play, from their home streets or front porches. Wasn't there an author, Charles Fort, who based his whole career on compiling hundreds of such cases?

The angler had most definitely made an impression on Lovecraft, subconsciously or not, and a line or two in his mountain of correspondence might testify to that. In one aspect, Lovecraft had been among the lucky ones, insofar as timing and placement and mental state had never combined to block his path with irresistible temptations and a hole in space. How much longer would that luck have held out if Lovecraft hadn't died at forty-six? Had a "Damned Thing" of sorts eventually ambushed the elderly Ambrose Bierce in Mexico?

Would even Charles Fort have gone out on that limb to explain Bierce's disappearance?

Justin had to blame the driven presence in his head for the ideas bubbling up so furiously. He'd generally be nodding off by this stage of the evening. His skin, meanwhile, crawled at visions of what had fastened on him. He felt violated, unclean, as at louse or ringworm infestation. Not that he was in immediate danger, for what consolation that offered! As if the barrier between his world and the angler's were a surface of ice on which it impatiently trod, the angler could only lower bait and lure its prey through openings at fixed earthly locations, and at fixed earthly times. As for the sleepwalking toward doom that afflicted the story's character, the entity had needed weeks, and not paltry days, to impose that much influence, if those episodes were ever more than Lovecraft's dramatic invention.

Justin would be leaving town by Tuesday, one way or another. Though his worries had ballooned to a grander order of magnitude over the weekend, he did have business tomorrow with Palazzo. It had seemed so pressing Friday night, without entering into his considerations since. Better late than never, he tried mapping out a plan of attack, how he'd parry attempts by Palazzo or his secretary at the runaround. But the aggressive current was rapidly ebbing from his body, and before he could exploit its sputtering last, he was asleep, fully clothed on top of the blankets, TV nattering through the night.

His eyes opened at the customary 7 A.M. The room temperature was normal for once. However, he needed a minute to remember his age, and what year it was. The public access channel was airing a community bulletin board to the accompaniment of jazz fusion. The remote control still rested on his stomach. He flipped to a so-called morning news program, for the short while he could stand the medley of fluff and atrocities. He gave up during reportage of one more missing pregnant wife and of unfaithful husband under suspicion, when he couldn't tell in which category it belonged. Nagging hunger and raw nerves were in remission, as if they'd been a weekend-long dream. The entity had relented, or the stars had ceased to be right. Either way, Justin could tackle his last b&b breakfast strictly for the sake of returning well-nourished and caffeinated to the List Building.

He ate, packed, checked out, and hastened to the parking lot behind the inn. The management probably wasn't sorry to see him go. His dingy '85 Dodge van could only detract from any ambience they intended to cultivate. Yet for all the patches of gray undercoat where cobalt blue paint had flecked off, and rust damage like a row of ragged buttonholes between the front and back wheels, and other cosmetic shortcomings, the old Ram refused to die, and it wasn't in him to junk it. But at his first eyeful of it in days, he winced with the shock of seeing it as others did. Blessedly, that passed as soon as he was in the driver's seat. He was out the gate at a commendable 8:45.

Some forethought before confronting Palazzo would have been preferable, but last night he was too exhausted, and now he was busy navigating. Resigned to winging it, he parked alongside the List Building. So where in all this cement did the division head hole up? The gallery attendant dislodged her designer-punk self from a semiotics primer and answered him audibly the second time. There was an elevator, but climbing the fire stairs to Palazzo's floor possibly delivered more oxygen to Justin's brain.

The door beside the room number was open. Into the breach! This could have been the anteroom of any dentist or accountant, save for the pricier art on ivory-white walls. The trophies included Lichtenstein, Ben Shahn, David Hockney. Justin stopped there. Conspicuous enough consumption for his blood. The receptionist wore tortoiseshell glasses and her brown hair in a bun, and would have looked bookish apart from an ingrained pout. He requested an appointment sometime that day with Palazzo. She didn't know if he'd be in or not and didn't bother asking what his business was, which made him suspect that Palazzo had warned her about him. Through the closed door behind her, he could hear someone tromping around and the scrape of a wastebasket across tiles. Neither of these people seemed to have a very high opinion of him.

He smiled broadly and said he'd wait, that he had all day. He took one of several squeaky leather seats along the wall, and she began typing with unnecessary force at her computer. She sighed a lot. Justin zoned out, to conserve energy. He owed all he had to his refusal to go away, and today was shaping up as no exception.

Half an hour crawled by. He approached the desk, cleared his throat, and asked the frowning secretary for a blank reimbursement

form, in case Palazzo had misplaced the one from the gallery director. She claimed not to have any. The door behind her opened silently a hair's breadth, and Justin's eyes chanced to meet the eye that
peeked out. The door closed swiftly but silently.

The receptionist's phone chirped several seconds later, while
Justin was still watching the door. She swiveled away from him and
whispered. She hung up, and the inner door swung wide as if pro-
claiming, Hail fellow, well met. The ever-impeccable Palazzo briskly
invited Justin in, but didn't proffer a handshake.

Justin hadn't finished taking the liberty of sitting down when Palazzo launched into preemptive strike. "You've come back at a very
exciting time! Great things are under way all over campus. And
we're a part of that too, you and I."

Justin greeted this with the polite reflex of a weak nod. Misgivings were already fluttering in his stomach.

"This university is gearing up for the biggest phase of growth in
its history, thanks to a hugely successful capital drive. And we're going to be enlarging this department too."

"Enlarge it how? Where is there room? What are you going to
do, declare war on the library next door?" The prospect of even
more demolition of his beloved old Providence made Justin queasy,
and outraged, and remorseful at displaying his work here.

"Oh, we leave that to the professionals." Had Palazzo actually
chortled? "So you see, we have tremendous amounts of funding tied
up in all this. I don't find any record of contributions from you,
though."

That smelled much more like guesswork than the results of re-
search, and not terribly astute guesswork either. Justin's misgivings
were fluttering harder.

"If I remember what you're up here for," Palazzo ventured, "I'd
consider it a personal favor, and an appropriate gesture, if you'd regard the money in question as a donation to the future of our department." Justin was amazed at how ghastly an ingratiating smile
could look.

Easy, now! "Listen, I had an understanding with the gallery director. A deal. There are e-mails to that effect. I put a lot of time and
effort into installing the exhibit here on short notice, and I'm getting

nothing out of it myself. I really need what you owe me."

"I don't owe you anything." How quickly the worm turned! "She didn't consult with me first. She went over my head, and not for the first time. You made your deal with her, not me. There's plenty I could have done with that wall space for two weeks."

Justin shrugged and spread his hands. "That's not my problem. I came to town in good faith."

"Well, you invested your faith badly. And yes, it is your problem." With the tiniest adjustment of facial muscles, Palazzo would be gloating.

"You can't be serious. Where is the gallery director, anyway? I'd like to hear her side of this."

"She's called in sick."

Justin wouldn't put it past Palazzo to lie, but he conceded the point. "And I suppose you're going to fire her as soon as she gets well? If you haven't already?"

"Oh no, that would be crude. Her contract is nearly up. We won't renew her, that's all." God forbid that any whiff of discord emanate from Pictorial Arts!

Palazzo had inadvertently helped Justin plot his next move. *Si le geste est beau*, as the French said. But in good conscience, he had to brave the direct route as last resort. "So are you going to pay my hotel bill or not?"

"How simple do I have to make it for you? No!" Justin had pushed the decorous Dr. Palazzo into quaking like an aspen. Maybe that short fuse had propelled Palazzo's rise to the bureaucratic top, Justin speculated.

"Fine, then." Justin stood up unhurriedly. It behooved him to take the high road, though he'd have been more satisfied, and eminently within his rights, to vent a resounding Fuck you. When Justin began to speak, Palazzo lost his cool altogether and shouted at him to get out and stay out, but Justin doggedly followed through on the grounds that he'd always hoped for the occasion to say what he was saying, whether Palazzo was listening or not. "You know, Doc, for some people, the present represents an accumulation of everything past, like it's all there to some degree as a source of inspiration. For others, the present only represents as clean a break from the past as possible, and the less history there is to get in the way of business, the better. It's just too bad a city like this has you, or anyone like you, in the position you're in."

Palazzo, red, heaving, goggle-eyes hurling malice, was temporarily out of steam.

"Did a word of that sink in?" Justin asked.

Palazzo gathered breath for another tirade, but this time Justin had the drop on him. "Anyway, fuck you," he summed up, ambled out, and closed the door with overweening deliberation till it clicked, amidst new barrage about how vulgar and unimportant he was. The receptionist was gaping at Justin as if he'd blown up the dam. "Boy, he's going to be fun for the rest of the day," Justin forecast. Only when he was on the fire stairs did he realize how much he was shaking.

In his van, a cursory mental survey located reasonably clean blankets and towels, for art-swaddling purposes. He'd removed and stacked three 18" by 24" frames from the gallery wall before the attendant was at his elbow.

"It's all right, I'm the artist," he told her.

"Are you sure it's okay? Isn't this show up for a week or two?" A good do-bee in spite of spiky pink hair!

"If you're worried, call Palazzo. In fact, I wish you would."

She said no more and was nowhere in sight when Justin set another frame on the pile and debated carrying four at once. He was out to the van and back and had voted against more loads that size, when Palazzo and the attendant arrived at the doorway. He barked at her to come back in an hour. He stormed in, but halted judiciously out of swinging range while bellowing, "What do you think you're doing? This is unacceptable! What are people going to say when there's nothing on the walls?"

Justin begrudged him a morose glance. "Call it a matter of trust. I don't feel safe leaving my artwork with you. You've already expressed a rather dismissive attitude toward it." He was also, admittedly, loath to stay or return where a grotesque death was in store, were the stars ever "right" again.

"Have you any idea how unprofessional this is?"

Justin shook his head impassively. "Maybe some token on your part would help. Something tangible. Otherwise, I don't know."

"You want money? This is childish! This is blackmail!"

"Well, that's not how I'd describe it." Justin reached for another picture, but stopped as Palazzo charged from the room. Would he enlist campus security? And make a scene strong-arming an exhibiting artist and "honored alum"? Justin doubted it.

Then the gallery lights went out. Brightness from the doorway made negligible impact in the mineshaft blackness. He anticipated Palazzo would let him stew a while and was reconciled to waiting in the dark. If the stalemate dragged on long enough, how would Palazzo respond to inquiries about the gallery blackout and Justin alone inside? Justin was conversant with feeling ridiculous, but he'd wager Palazzo was not. A drawback in these circumstances!

The dark was coming to seem less absolute. Were his eyes adjusting? No, not exactly, because he still couldn't see his pictures on the walls. Just the same, a glow was spreading through the room, as if someone were almost imperceptibly upping a dimmer switch, to reveal surfaces at right and acute angles to each other, which dwindled to a vanishing point miles beyond the rear gallery wall. And as if it had never been absent but only lurking below a subliminal threshold, ravenous appetite welled up in him again. Nor would it scruple to take a bite out of Palazzo at the least provocation.

He also hungered for what had attained depth and sharp outlines in soothing twilight. He was standing on a mossy slate terrace, facing west. No List Building surrounded him, no high-rises rudely interrupted the scarlet horizon of western hills, and even the massive Colonial Revival courthouse on Benefit Street had reverted to rows of antique gables and gambrels. The tallest structure by five stories or so was the bracket-shaped Hospital Trust bank across the canal. A few electric signs lent primary colors to the bricks and masonry of downtown, but only the one for the Old Colony Hotel was within reading distance. Sunset made the gold dome of the Congregational church on Weybosset Street gleam softly. The streetlamps ought to be on in a minute.

Here was the unmodern Providence of his dreams, and of heightened poignancy after a weekend in the brave new Providence. Lovecraft had not emerged beckoning, but that would have been impossible really. This was the Providence of Lovecraft's schooldays, and since Justin couldn't imagine Lovecraft as a child, that version of him couldn't materialize. In any event, it was very beautiful over there, and Justin could have it for the rest of his life, if he simply walked into it.

He was aware at the same time of how short such a life would be, and that the cosmic angler's hidden eye had to be glowering down at him. He also belatedly recognized how cunning the angler had been, to give the fish all the line it wanted, and an illusion of freedom, while that fish spent its strength and the hook stayed embedded in unfeeling lip.

None of this stopped Justin from shuffling his feet eagerly. His hankering for that place was inseparable from the hankering of something that regarded him as food, and he had no means to pull out psychic hook, any more than a fish could sprout hands to save itself. How covertly active had the entity been after the line had gone slack? What kind of orchestrations had been involved for Justin to end up back at List, in the dark?

A phrase from Lovecraft's story echoed at Justin, even as left foot rose in defiance of better judgment: "I am it and it is I." Did the "it" in question feel or understand any of Justin's yearning for the mirage it created for him, the way he suffered its hunger pangs, its anxiety, because Justin wasn't in the net yet, and meals were few and far between? Did Justin want to help assuage that cruel hunger? All he had to do was be eaten!

"Now will you please come out and behave reasonably?" Palazzo's outburst confused Justin and threw him off-balance. It sounded so clear and immediate, but how could that be? Justin was virtually a world away. "What are you doing in there?"

Palazzo was too worked up to be observant, or else from outside, the gallery was still in darkness. But Justin soon learned that it wasn't necessary to be him to see what he was seeing. Palazzo was beside him, directing eyes wide with horror north and south, east and west. "Where are we? What the hell is going on?"

Justin, despite everything, smiled wryly. "It's Providence."

Palazzo became even more distraught. "Where's our building? Where's everything that's happened in the last hundred years? All that progress gone! Everything we've achieved! This is terrible! Why are you smiling, you little son of a bitch?"

Justin had been about to tell Palazzo it was all in his head, but stopped himself. Not after that abusive tone!

Palazzo wasn't doing especially well at coping with the situation. He began babbling about what they could do to fix all this. Justin could have suggested leaving the room or taking some flash photography, but why put himself out? And would Palazzo listen to someone as unimportant as him? Remarkable, in any case, that Palazzo was so susceptible to psychic influence, taking the reality of their vista at face value. Maybe he had too much else on his mind to think critically about this. Dotted lines of streetlamps were beginning to incandesce hither and yon.

Justin understood what happened next, because it was also happening to him by dint of celestial meeting of minds. Traveling across any surface obviously entailed the risk of slipping on that surface, particularly at stressful moments. Those who fished through a hole in the ice were always one misstep away from an unfriendly medium. And now Justin's idyllic Providence descended instantaneously from mellow dusk to heavy gloom. Big and low in the gray northern sky floated the denser black of what first seemed the moon in eclipse. But pale stars, and not craters, were scattered across its surface, in a range of sizes from pinpoint to grapeshot. Here was the angler's native sky, as glimpsed through the hole in space where three-lobed eye had glared down and dispensed visions till brief clumsiness dislocated it. If Justin had blinked, he'd have missed it, for there followed a thud that shook the unseen gallery floor and rattled the unseen pictures on the walls, and the hole in space was jammed with frantic, ciliated tissue that bulged like a bubble into the room. On contact with the atmosphere, it shone pink and then hot red.

In that span of seconds, a mounting stench of scorching mold and incinerated carcasses made Justin choke, and he reeled at a protracted, inhuman wail that was as much between his ears as in them, and that also spewed from his own mouth. It distorted as if channeled through cheap microphone. The surroundings, meanwhile, kept flickering between darkness and dim simulation of bygone Providence.

Then further sound impinged on him. Palazzo was still babbling in the same rhythm, at the same tempo, but the syllables had devolved into baby talk, and their volume had drastically risen. Callously or not, Justin felt a burden melt from his shoulders, and a release of tension in his chest. Palazzo going mad had saved Justin from doing the same. This chaos wasn't simply an expression of Justin's lone delusion. He needn't doubt, or abandon, his own sanity!

The entity broke free of vacuum seal between dimensions, and in its wake left unmediated the passage between here and there. A sonic boom knocked Justin off his feet, and the walls in the dark room rumbled, and all his artwork plummeted with a crash of shattering glass. The sour air began to whistle by his face. He lay as flat as possible, and his lunging hands bumped and clung to the cold steel siding of the attendant's desk. Praise the Lord, it was bolted down!

A hole in space, left on its own, couldn't be stable. It had to collapse soon! But the leakage between dimensions was still accelerating, lifting Justin off the concrete floor, when Palazzo flopped onto his belly and grabbed Justin's ankles. Justin's sweaty handhold on the sharp edge of a slick metal panel began to loosen. He couldn't hang on much longer in this wind tunnel with patrician dead weight doubling his own. He kicked out as if swimming the Australian crawl, once, twice, and screaming Palazzo lost his grip. Had Justin done what was needful to save himself, or had he outright killed a man? The keening airflow was already beginning to tug less fitfully at him, and with a moral issue assailing him on top of everything else, his overtaxed consciousness gave way, though his fingers knew better than to let go.

Justin opened his eyes to bright gallery illumination. The attendant was standing beside him, studying him fretfully. She evidently knew where to find the circuit-breakers, or at least the janitor. Justin was lying on his right side, and had unhanded the desk. He and the girl gawked at each other a minute. He didn't feel impelled to say anything yet.

"You okay? You want me to call the infirmary?"

Infirmary? The word dredged up long-lost campus lore of subpar doctors burning warts off the wrong hand. Last thing he needed now. "Oh no, not those butchers."

She shrugged. "A friend came and got me from upstairs when she heard a noise and saw the lights were out. Was there an earthquake in here or something?"

"Something, yeah." He raised himself on bruised and achy elbow. By the grace of whatever laws governed pressure or gravitation or aerodynamics between worlds in tangent, little had been scooped up from the edges of the room. Most of his photos lay face-up on the floor, though a lot of busted glass had crossed over. "I'm a lucky bastard," he mumbled.

"What?" The girl wasn't going to freak out, was she? "Where's Dr. Palazzo?"

"I don't know." Not the lie it sounded like! "Pretty sure the earth didn't swallow him up."

She assessed the damage with a few birdlike turns of her head. "There's not much glass." She crinkled her nose. "Do you know what that smell is?"

Pleasantly for her, most of the stink had been funneled into the void. Justin started to get up, but one foot skidded out from under him when he put his weight on it. He sat awkwardly with leg outstretched. The attendant had skipped back several prudent steps, and waved toward his less trustworthy foot. "What's that?"

He shifted the foot aside, drew his leg in, and huddled forward for a closer squint. The item on the floor had the circumference of a pancake, and was related to humanity somehow, but was hard to define because it was so out of context. Aha! Palazzo's majestic head of wavy silver hair really had been a toupee. "It's Palazzo's," he told the girl, who persisted in her puzzled stare. "Looks like he flipped his wig," Justin hinted. Comprehension dawned. Understandably, she made no move to pick it up.

He managed to stand. He might be in shock, but theorized that if he chose not to think about it, he could function indefinitely. "Look, if you're not busy, help me load the rest of my stuff in the van, will you?"

"Are you sure it's all right? I thought Dr. Palazzo wanted everything to stay."

"He left it up to me." Was that less than a half-truth? Did it matter? "Now come on. I want to be in the Catskills by nightfall."

She wavered as if tossing a figurative penny, then with a fraction of a nod capitulated. What the hell, why not? A bigger relief than Justin dared let on! Sooner or later, Palazzo's disappearance would be police business, and they might well talk to the girl and go from there. Justin gave her two frames to carry at a time, and dawdled so that she always went out by herself. The more trips she made, the more chances she had to snoop around the van, fore and aft, and ascertain that it contained no *corpus delicti.*

He thanked her afterward, but she only made a noncommittal sound and scurried for the shelter of the List Building. Was he really such an unnerving presence? Just as well she was gone, anyhow. A bothersome soreness and itch below his left ribs called for investigation. He untucked his shirt. Thank God the psychic link was compromised when careless alien faltered onto the hole! Otherwise, instead of a puffy, flaming red welt, wide and round as a CD, he'd have an empathic third-degree burn to explain at the emergency room. He was a lucky bastard all right. Even if he was stuck with the bed-and-breakfast bill.

He hit the road. Minutes later, according to a sign on the median strip, Massachusetts welcomed him. He'd made a scot-free getaway, or had he? Ten days went by, in which the angry red welt faded, and he e-mailed the gallery director an unacknowledged apology for yanking the show, and he reframed his photos, and then the phone rang. The Providence police wanted to have their inevitable talk, and he obliged them on the way home from his Philly opening. They recorded the diffident, submissive Justin for posterity. His account contained no untruths and hoisted no red flags. He did omit any nonsense about nostalgic hallucination, hostile alien, hole in space, and kicking Palazzo into that hole. In the official version, he fell unconscious during a local tremor that interrupted an argument with Palazzo, and when he came to, Palazzo was gone. The police didn't ask about Palazzo's toupee. It must have landed in the trash before anyone realized what it was, before Palazzo was numbered among the missing. And the gallery attendant had forgotten or hadn't troubled to mention it. Justin owed her for that!

The police let him go. He was undeniably the last man on earth to see Palazzo alive, but only he knew that for a fact, and Palazzo must have had longer-standing, uglier imbroglios with others. Hopefully Justin was shut of Providence forever. Foolhardy to second-guess when next the stars above town would be "right" again!

Behind the wheel, it gave him pause to consider how blithely he was sidestepping any remorse about his role in Palazzo's demise. Technically, he'd killed the guy, unavoidably or not, willfully or not. But what about the hundreds of more cold-blooded, premeditated murders on the books that went unsolved? Plainly a crowded field of killers had learned to live with themselves, and go to work every day, and get married, and raise kids, and collect a pension. Justin wasn't even asking as much of life as all that. He too would learn to live with himself, just as he had learned the ropes of so many careers in his checkered adulthood. That malaise seeping up from the bedrock of his conscience would settle down if he ignored it, and stay down for months or years like any of his other wellsprings of guilt. What good would confession do himself or anybody? He was under no illusion that a jail cell or padded cell would "cleanse" him. To be honest, wasn't the world better off minus one arrogant yuppie?

Next afternoon, he was in his sunny, cluttered parlor, with its rugged mountain view that had seemed so breathtaking, prior to his glimpse of interstellar gulf. He was finally unpacking the duffel bag in which dirty clothes had accumulated since homecoming weekend. He should have emptied it before stuffing in more to wear in Philly, but if he'd arrived at a greater appreciation of anything lately, it would be that he wasn't perfect.

From the bottom of upended sack, his digital camera plopped onto a cushion of stale shirts. He couldn't figure out what it was for a second. He started picking it up, then slung it across the table as if it were electrified. In it was documentation, unique in human history, immensely valuable, of alien life, of alien interaction with this unwitting planet. Personally, on the other hand, it was a reminder of near-death experience, a preamble to homicide. If his eyes lingered on the camera for any time, that dizziness from back in the b&b, when he thought he would topple into that viewfinder miniature of a cosmic gateway, overtook him again. Would he always be a fish with immaterial hook in his lip to draw him into that hole?

He went on with life, as he trusted he would, crisscrossing the world on photo shoots, exhibiting his work, making enough money, and he let the digital camera gather cobwebs where it lay, religiously averting his eyes from it. He never felt or acted particularly crazy, to the best of his knowledge, not even when visitors were apparently looking at his dusty camera on the table, and he startled them by roaring, "There's your murderer, right in there!" Nobody ever dared inquire what he meant, and he always seemed fine after a minute of probing lower lip with upper incisors, as if for a foreign object.

A Different Kind of Heartworm

Because Paula had waited so long for marriage, her expectations were high. At thirty-five, surely satisfaction came due with interest. Conversely, the available choices compelled making more of less. Still, courtship with Phil had never lacked for the flowers, the wine, the candlelight, the sweet talk, the smoochy strolls on tree-lined boulevards, the heavenly sex. They never argued, and she couldn't believe then that they ever would. Granted, Phil was neither Adonis nor Einstein, but his mind was admirably, refreshingly his own, and Paula felt she had the rest of their life together to get a handle on it.

She made nothing at the time of that one rough patch on the road to betrothal, large though it loomed in hindsight. They were camping in the state park, miles from anyone. Mild days gave way to chilly nights, ideal for love play in the tent. The tent sat in the shadows of pines, amidst boulders that blocked the wind, on the edge of an embankment cut by a rushing brook. Directly behind the tent, the brook formed a little spinning pool, just deep enough to be black. Boulders to either side of the pool made for a natural booth.

Sunday morning, Phil was up first, presumably to take a piss among the pines. Wondering what he could be doing after so long, restless Paula ventured out. In pre-coffee blear, she stumbled down the bank and threw her arms around a boulder to slow herself down, momentum swinging her halfway around it. Breathless, she turned her face from the rock and there was Phil, sitting with feet just above the pool, in the instant after snapping something from between thumb and forefinger. His look of slack abstraction, encasing his eyes as if they were eggshells, dispelled her first impression that he was casually picking his nose. And she thought she glimpsed something long and white spinning out of sight in the current, resisting it with vain zigzag constrictions.

"Phil? What are you doing?"

"Nothing," said Phil, and his eyes, briefly bright with surprise, clouded over again. But now there was a cagey, sheepish ring to his voice. "I meant to pick you some flowers. I guess I must've spaced out looking at the water. Sorry." Paula nodded, preferring to take his word for it that she'd seen nothing.

A year later, married life had settled into creaky, lumbering rhythm. Had anyone asked, Paula would have sworn that love was the medium sustaining that life, but this went without saying for so long that Paula became no more mindful of her love than her gloxinias were of the sun. To abet the show of intimacy, conversations and actions generally ran within channels of safe habit. Always seeing eye to eye was impossible, of course, so for her part Paula rerouted talk whose obvious terminus was a no-win battle. How could fighting about needle exchange programs, voting rights for felons, or cartoon violence help each other or anyone else?

Paula termed their relationship normal, despite some doubts after the incident at the kitchen sink. It had been one more lazy evening of watching TV from in bed. During an ad, Phil got up, apparently to fetch a snack. The show came back, but not Phil, not even after the next commercial break. What the hell was he doing, baking a pie? Paula went to check on him, despite a reluctance that paged her insistently from parts unknown.

The kitchen was dark. Phil was silhouetted against streetlight from the window. He was leaning over the sink, hands cupped to his face as if eating a juicy mango. But between thumb and forefinger he seemed to be kneading, or twirling, something. The faucet was running. She turned on the doorway light, and his hands plunged into the sink as if on fire.

She walked over to him. He looked taken aback but stood his ground. Surprise faded from his eyes like light bulbs cooling off. Was his steady gaze trying to hold hers, to divert her from something in the churning water? Her look darted toward the sink. Something white, like the end of a piece of spaghetti, was spiraling down the drain.

"Were you eating something?" she asked quietly, still focused on the drain. He stopped the faucet.

"Had you wanted me to bring you something?"

"What were you doing in here?"

"Why?"

She was in no mood for Ask Me Another. "What were you do-ing?" She felt waspish, as when sirens roused her from deep sleep. "We have nothing to hide from each other, do we?"

"What I'm doing has no bearing on the two of us."

"What's that supposed to mean?"

"Two people can't know everything about each other. In any case, they shouldn't." Paula found herself backing off from Phil's un-nerving matter-of-factness. "Too much honesty is like too much oxygen. Things blow up to no good purpose."

Clearly, a no-win fight was brewing, and true to habit, Paula started seeking an out. But hold on a second, were Phil's words meant to get her mind off whatever he'd been doing?

Then Phil exclaimed, "Jesus! Is that show still on? I probably have no idea what's going on by now."

"You really haven't missed much," Paula said dully.

Afterward, the question sprang up at unpredictable moments, "How can we really be together if we're not open with each other?" But mouthing the words to herself, they sounded naïve, and all the more so in the face of domesticity's ticking regularity. The confession she finally wrung out of Phil brought her no happiness but, to her initial bewilderment, no regrets, either.

They'd made perfunctory Sunday love, and duly switched off the lights. Silent minutes crawled by. Deciding she'd go to the bathroom, Paula turned on the bedside lamp. Phil, no doubt, had thought Paula was asleep. He was lying on his back and, in the instant before the shock of illumination, wore an expression of pure contentment, as both hands intently unreeled and unreeled something white and wriggling that was already wound thickly around one index finger. Paula was fixated like a fawn in high beams. She felt no urge to scream or bolt. Instead, in a monotone frightening to herself, she asked, "What is that?"

Phil spoke as if still in dreamland. "I don't know," he mumbled, and blinked, and with more alertness added, "Really, I don't know exactly." At a sharp jerk of his free index finger, the white strand snapped. The loose inches retreated up his nose like ribbon into a tape measure. Phil got up and went into the bathroom. Paula heard the toilet flush.

She didn't budge a muscle, as if he had to return to the spot where she'd caught him in the act and tell all, as long as she stayed right there to retain that power over him. Nonetheless, once back in bed, Phil seemed perfectly amenable to saying nothing.

"Well, where is that thing from? How long have you been hiding this from me?" Paula demanded.

"Please, just lighten up." Phil had the audacity to sound put upon! "It's nothing I care that much about. It didn't appear under any dramatic circumstances. Sometime when I was twelve maybe, I noticed this little white thing poking out of my nostril. It wasn't mucus, it broke off easily enough, and it didn't show up again for weeks or maybe months. Whenever it did, sometimes in the right nostril, sometimes in the left, I just broke it off again. I never gave it a great deal of thought. I mean, around that age your body goes through a lot of changes that adults don't necessarily explain to you, so I kind of took this thing for granted."

"But aren't you at least curious about it? How do you know it's not doing something to you? Jesus, Phil! It's a parasite and you don't even know what parts of you it's living in!"

He shrugged. "Is it a parasite? What's it taking up in me besides space? I think I'd have felt any ill effects by now. I have no idea where inside me it originates, but when I feel it in my nose, I just pull until it stretches tight. Then I snip it off with my fingernails, and the tag end retreats back into me somewhere. Whatever it is, it seems to appreciate the pruning, even if the detached part puts up some reflex struggle. Who am I to question? Anyway, it's kind of satisfying to get all that extra worm out of me. It's like a comforting little sense of accomplishment."

"Aren't you afraid it's contagious?" Paula felt herself growing squeamish. Every so often, it was hard to hold still.

"Never has been. Not as far as I know. It's mine."

"*Are* you going to do something about it, now that I know it's there?" Paula felt herself losing ground, in some way she couldn't quite define yet. It wasn't that she was losing Phil to this thing, but some idea of him, yes, that was slipping fast.

"Do something about it? Why? Get rid of it so you never find out about it? A little late for that."

Paula's failure to make argumentative headway was beginning to infuriate her. "The fact remains, you've been deceiving me all this time!"

"What was I supposed to tell you?" At last Phil's sangfroid was fraying a little. "Are you happier now for knowing?"

"It's just not fair!"

"We can't gain anything by fighting. You've already got three or four issues muddled together. Everything's fine. You'll be fine. Now I wish you'd turn off the light. We both have work tomorrow." Phil rolled over and pulled the blankets over his head. Paula was at a loss for words, even as she felt the need to clutch the sheet into big bunches, so as to keep from sliding off some sudden edge. Something akin to bedspin harried her all night, leaving her too unsteady even to turn off the light. In his makeshift cover of darkness, Phil was snoring softly.

He proceeded as if nothing was wrong, as if Paula had seen nothing, which intensified her sense of isolation, of dreamlike daze. Her sleep was as shallow as her wakefulness. Routines of eating, talking, sleeping, and making love with Phil went on nervelessly, as if she were seeing it all as an out-of-body experience.

But she looked on with ever growing horror, and ever darker musings. She felt resentment at being cheated. This package of a life with Phil, this assumption of being better off married than single, had been a lie. Instead, every time he'd been inside her, this parasite, this monster had been inside her too. Even if Phil were right and no ill effects surfaced, she felt violated, unclean. There was no name for Phil's category of pervert, but now the prospect of having children with him, which she'd meant to broach soon, made her weak with nausea.

Then they fell prey to one of those mornings that guarantee nothing but trouble all day. Someone had forgotten to set the alarm, the coffee pot broke and flooded the counter, the gas company meter reader rang the bell, and while Paula let him into the cellar, Phil's office phoned, making him dash half-ready from the bathroom to explain why he wasn't at the staff meeting. He was out the door as

Paula was trudging back up, and to herself alone, safe to say, he seemed like Dagwood Bumstead as played by Christopher Lee.

She shuffled into the bathroom, dropped the seat, and was about to sit down, when she saw that Phil had forgotten to flush. And down in the yellow water, circling with deliberate speed, was a length of whatever that white thing was, one end almost touching the other and forming a hoop. Paula shivered to the marrow, wondering if chasing its own tail would have sufficed if her potential host body had come any closer. She flushed and straightened up and let out slow breath. Passive rancor had reached the breaking point. Paula resolved to do whatever promised to salvage this life she had invested in, to neutralize this wormlike spoiler of the way things were supposed to be.

Paula's ostensible new closeness to Phil, the long gazes, the doting attentions, belied how balefully she sought a way to get at the worm.

Channel-flipping gave her the answer, during one more idle evening in bed. She paused at the local animal shelter's cable show. Though she knew better than to burden herself with any of the adorable strays and foundlings on euthanasia row, they always induced a lump in her throat. Then the animal shelter emcee gave a spiel about the importance of canine heartworm medicine. Overtaken by brainstorm, Paula gaped unblinking at the screen. Worm medicine! After all, what infested Phil but a different kind of heartworm, so to speak?

Phil asked what was so spellbinding about heartworm pills, seeing as they didn't have a dog. Well, she reflected, they did have an exotic pet of sorts because of him, didn't they? She changed the channel rather than voicing her reply. Let *him* sit in the dark this time.

Paula's mind was made up. She could no more harbor second thoughts than a wheel could stop itself rolling downhill. Why be deterred by Phil's inevitable objections, or even by the potential harm to him from a worm rotting or convulsing inside? Not that the medicine would necessarily have any effect! Anyway, the Phil she wanted, for whom she'd bargained in good faith, was lost to her. Damage to the bodily Phil, now that her image of him was ruined, involved a risk of a lower order, or so it seemed within her haze of desperation. As long as he was infested, nothing around her felt consequential or even real.

She was thrilled at how easily she could abuse the online honor system and order something conceivably dangerous. She had the parcel shipped to her work address and stowed the contents in her purse. The meds were packaged in single doses, in the form of knuckle-sized bricks of ersatz burger. One a month was the allotment. Paula opted for three.

In deworming Phil, she saw justice in practicing deceit on him, just as he had deceived her about having the worm. Moussaka was his favorite dish. She didn't know or care about what he made of having it set before him, without pretext of any special occasion. It was no secret that she hated the bother of making it. He seemed to take the meal happily in stride, along with all other recent semblances of endearment.

From the kitchen Paula brought Phil's portion of choice, the corner with the darkest crunchy crust. He lit into it without a second glance, and why not? A food with layers so easy to lift offered no indications of careful tampering.

Halfway along, he did remark, "That last bite wasn't hot at all. You sure this is cooked through?"

"I let it bake the same amount of time as always," she replied honestly. "Just what the recipe says."

What was left to discuss? Toward bedtime, Phil complained of "gas pains or something" and gave her a probing look, but forbore mentioning supper. In bed he asked if it was hot, and she turned on the air conditioner. Half-asleep, she heard him get up and assumed he was bathroom-bound. After a minute of hearing nothing more over the grind of the air conditioner, she drifted off. She squirmed and groaned all night, but until the alarm rang, nothing shook her from the dogged sleep of those who want badly enough to avoid the waking world.

She turned off the alarm. Phil wasn't there. Twin streaks of blood on his pillowcase resembled nothing worse than the outflow of two abused pimples. Nonetheless, they distressed her, and her eyes shied from them as she rolled out of bed. En route to the bathroom, she turned off the air conditioner. The house was silent.

She nearly stepped into an overlapping pair of sloppy red spirals on the white flocked bathroom rug, like the imprint of carelessly tossed coils of wet rope. She cried out and slipped a trembly foot under the rug to flip it halfway over and hide the unpleasantness. Whatever it betokened, she refused to think about it yet, beyond resolving to dispose of the bathroom wastebasket without peeking under the lid, in case it contained further unpleasantness.

All too soon, she was sidling slowly past kitchen doorway, letting one eye make its appraisal before she ventured in. It looked as if a dog had run amuck. The fridge was wide open, and its yellow light shone in the pool of meltwater around it. The utensil drawers beside the sink were pulled all the way out. The wastebasket lay on its side, and trash and torn liner bag were strewn across the linoleum. The wrappers that Phil had found in the trash were taped neatly to the side of the fridge, along with a note. He wasn't around.

Paula had to stretch way over to pluck off the note without stepping in the water. Phil's hypocritically dispassionate block-printing was vexing, in view of the emotionality manifest around her. He wrote:

> I won't be coming back. Marriage is a piece of paper. I won't let it stop me from doing what I want. I advise the same for you. I'm not leaving because of something you didn't accept about me. No two people can accept everything about each other. I'm leaving because you couldn't leave alone what you couldn't accept. Apparently we can't trust each other.

Paula eventually shut the fridge door. The mess on the floor could wait. First she had to get a handle on her feelings. Whatever they were, she couldn't condemn them outright, for feelings weren't right or wrong, they were just a part of oneself, weren't they? Denying them wasn't healthy, any more than tying a tourniquet on an uninjured limb. And Paula had to acknowledge something hidden in her all along, only now breaking surface.

Suppose she raised her arm, would imagination show her doubly thick and coarse black strands projecting from the fine, flat auburn hair? Would they radiate from a center and wave in a crawly rotation, like a spider embedded in flesh? That was how she envisioned her feelings, in apt complement to Phil's infestation. Something was monstrous about her feelings, absolutely, but she could no more picture regulating them than regulating her heartbeat. Shaking drops of water off one foot and then the other while backing away from the creeping pool on the floor, she let herself gloat, basking in the satisfaction that he was gone. She had won.

Gumball Man

Gumball Man put in his first appearance when Lewis was looking for a new place to hide. On the front porch, in the cellar, up in his room, behind locked bathroom door, he could still hear the stupid arguments in the kitchen. This time, Dad was yelling because Mom couldn't butter the toast right. Might as well be a plateful of goddamn pieces and crumbs! Good thing Dad didn't know he hadn't tasted butter in years. On Mom's skimpy grocery allowance, she'd confided to Lewis, they were lucky to afford margarine. Anyway, their arguments were always screaming contests over nothing. For as far back as eight-year-old Lewis could remember. Real adults were like that, he'd concluded, and not like those nice phonies in TV show families, like on *Father Knows Best*. He swore, the same as every day, that he wouldn't grow up to be like Mom and Dad.

They had a barn for a garage, from back in the 1800s when the house had been a farmhouse and the backyard had been part of a farm. Until the town got bigger, and ate away the original property lot by lot. Lewis stood in front of the bulkhead to the barn cellar. Not as if he'd never seen it before in his life. But this was the first time he'd given it any thought. Nobody had ever told him not to go down there. He turned toward the house again. As if giving it one last chance to produce more pleasant sounds.

"Why do you always have to be such a goddamn bastard?" That was Mom.

He pulled open the big wobbly old slat door till it was all the way up and it caught. Nasty, tattered spider webs on the underside of the door twitched in the morning breeze. Ancient, dusty shale steps took him into a dim wasteland of cobwebs and scrap wood. Farther back, it was too dark to tell what was in some piles of junk. Several square load-bearing posts made it feel like this place was from the Middle Ages. Like where the coffin would be in an old Dracula movie. Kinda cool-looking down here, but mostly creepy.

As soon as Lewis began to explore, he almost stepped on a dead cat. Outstretched, with bulging eyes, mouth in rictus, sunken body, a few bones showing through coarse fur. Lewis thought he might puke. Had to turn away, toward the staircase. A little kid, or so he thought at first, was standing on the bottom step. One of the Morin kids who'd just moved in next door, he assumed. So he didn't jump out of his skin. And even after he realized he was wrong, he had the funny feeling he knew this whoever-it-was from somewhere.

Or was it a whatever-it-was that stood there grinning? Trying to act friendly, Lewis guessed. A friendly jack-o'-lantern, maybe. A head too big for the body. Eyes too big and mouth too wide. And a crummy little nose, the way the nose came out on a jack-o'-lantern when you couldn't think of anything good to do. "Hello, Lewis." The oversized eyes, with little black irises, stayed focused on him.

In the bright daylight from behind, the weird trespasser, hairless and naked except for a loincloth that matched his skin, was a deep, worrisome gray like a thundercloud. Rubbery, too, and greasy with something that shone when the light hit it right. The skin gave Lewis the idea that there might be no bones underneath. This could have been one of the little plastic creatures come to life from one of those gumball machines at the plaza. A bug or a monster, squeezed into a two-piece plastic capsule, that popped out when the capsule opened. Lewis couldn't see him fitting into something that small, but maybe he could scrunch real tight into the gumball machine itself. A Gumball Man.

"How did you know my name?" Lewis asked.

"I've been around, on and off, for a while." This Gumball Man never blinked.

"How come I never saw you before?"

"Oh, I think you have." It was starting to bother Lewis that he'd thought so too.

"Are you a leprechaun?"

"No." Gumball Man answered gruffly, and Lewis decided against more questions along those lines. "Lewis, do you know what 'vulnerable' means?" Still no blinking.

"I know that Superman's invulnerable. I know what that means."

"Don't you want to be more like Superman?"

"What do you mean?"

"You hate to hear Mom and Dad fighting, don't you?"

Lewis nodded a bit. He didn't understand how one question was leading to the next. Gumball Man's arms hung straight down, limply. His fingers were wiggling, though, as if each had a mind of it own.

"Wouldn't it be better if you didn't care what they did?"

"I don't know." Lewis was suddenly nervous.

"Well, you just think about it." Gumball Man was shuffling his feet from side to side, and the air between him and Lewis was getting cloudy. Something went up Lewis's nose. He sneezed. Gumball Man was gone.

Lewis bounded up the steps and into the August sunshine. He wouldn't be going down there again! He jiggled the door free of the catch and let it thud shut.

The yelling from the kitchen had stopped. In the quiet, Lewis thought of a dream from when he was a little kid. He was in the house by himself, except that wherever he went, a little monkey man, with a long tail and a bellboy's cap, would show up. It tipped books off shelves or smashed teacups against the linoleum or clawed the stuffing out of armchairs, and leapt away when Lewis started hollering at it. It wasn't doing anything to Lewis. Not yet anyway. But Lewis was sure the monkey man was bad, and he finally went outside to get away. In the sky between the house and the barn, there was a dark gray cloud, getting lower and bigger. It was higher than the barn roof, yet seemed to be right on top of him all the same. In his dream it made sense that this was the way the monkey man had followed him outside. The cloud was turning into a giant unsmiling face, wearing something like a Napoleon or navy admiral hat from old cartoons. The face kept growing and coming closer. Lewis knew that if he stayed there, something bad would happen to him. He tried to run into the house but could only go in slow motion. That's when he woke up.

The same summer Lewis had that dream, his mother, upon discovery of some precancerous cells, underwent a double mastectomy. The doctors called it a matter of life or death. After her discharge from the hospital, the most trivial disagreements with her husband escalated into bitter donnybrooks. He, at the same time, began bringing home a new kind of magazine, which he hid in bureau drawers and under the bed, with only mixed success.

Lewis kept his distance from that bulkhead door and had no repeat visits from Gumball Man. Problem solved. Seasons passed. When Lewis thought of Gumball Man at all, it was as something he must have imagined. Harder to picture under buildup of later memories.

Meanwhile, Mom and Dad got louder and meaner with each other. Every time Lewis thought the arguments were as bad as they could get, they got worse. Dad never hit Mom or hit her with anything, maybe because she made it clear that if he did, she was out of there.

Lewis needed a hiding place more than ever and had to leave the homestead to find it. The Morins next door had a bunch of kids. Girls of different ages. He was never sure how many, because they always had friends over and he could never figure out who was who. And one son, Marcel, a year or two older than Lewis. The girls ignored Lewis, but Marcel was friendly enough, so Lewis started hanging around over there. The Morins' kitchen often smelled weird. They ate stuff like baked pumpkin and soft-boiled eggs and had a baby whose diapers always stank. Lewis never heard Mr. and Mrs. Morin fighting, but knew they must have, when he wasn't around. Of course they did! Who did they think they were kidding?

Usually he and Marcel just played catch or walked around the neighborhood or saw how deep a hole they could dig in the weedy backyard before Mrs. Morin made them stop. Other days, Marcel acted like a bully, mostly in the house when his sisters were in another room. Marcel and Lewis were watching wrestling, one Saturday morning, and Lewis said that some move looked really fake, and Marcel, who'd also said a hundred times that wrestling was fake, now said it wasn't, and to prove it put Lewis in a headlock till Lewis yelled that it hurt and Mr. Morin came in and broke it up. Lewis knew other kids at school but they lived too far away to go see, so he took for granted that other kids had cruel streaks once you got to know them well enough. Not Lewis, though!

One hot July afternoon, Lewis and Marcel were in the Morins' attic. In a big empty room, except for a few wooden chairs. And several big brown wasps that made Lewis nervous. They droned through the air once in a while, when they weren't crawling across the sealed windows that faced out on the street. Sometimes the wasps came and went through an open door to a walk-in closet.

Marcel wanted to show Lewis what had happened the other day when Marcel was up there with his big sister. He had a rusty old key, the kind that had a little ring at the grip end and a pair of buckteeth at the keyhole end. He shut the door to the room from the inside and turned the key in the lock till it clicked, then pulled out the key. See, the door had been locked just like that. He went to the middle of the room, where there was a round knothole in a floorboard. His sister had the key and was fooling around, and pretended she was going to drop it in the hole there. Why would she do that? You know, because she was fooling around. And then you know what she did? Just like that, she really did drop it in the hole. Marcel demonstrated by dropping the key into the knothole for real. And how'd you get out of here, Lewis wanted to know. Well, they had to scream until Pa came upstairs with the spare key. So that's what they had to do now? asked Lewis. Uh-uh. That was the spare key Marcel had dropped this time. What the hell did Marcel do that for? Marcel guessed he just wanted to see what Lewis would do when he was locked in.

One of the wasps gave up butting its head against the window and came buzzing right at Lewis and Marcel. Lewis was scared and skipped backward into the locked door. He turned and pushed against the door and then tugged on the doorknob with all his might until it broke free and he heard the knob on the other side clunk on the floor. He started yelling for help.

Marcel came over and punched him on the arm and told him to shut up. If Pa caught them up here, he'd kill them. Marcel looked at the doorknob in Lewis's sweaty fist. "Boy, now you've done it!"

Lewis had done it? What about what Marcel had done? And they were gonna get stung sooner or later! "Okay, okay, don't get hysterical!" demanded Marcel. "What do you want me to do?"

Lewis bounced the doorknob off the floor. The wasps were getting in through the closet. There must be a hole in the wall or something. The least Marcel could do was go shut the closet door.

Marcel looked at him like he was a big baby, but went over to the closet anyway. And right behind him, from out of nowhere into Lewis's field of vision, tiptoed Gumball Man. Before Lewis could cry out, Gumball Man turned his stiffly grinning face to him and put a long finger to his lips. Then he bent his elbows back sharply and shoved with both hands at the small of Marcel's back. Marcel tottered in, and Lewis heard him smack into the rear wall and topple to the floor.

"Quick, hand me that chair!" commanded Gumball Man, pointing to it with one hand and slamming closet door with the other. Lewis was too dumbstruck to disobey. As if this were only a dream.

"Who are you talking to? Let me out!" Marcel hollered. But Gumball Man had already propped the chair under the doorknob. Marcel banged on the door, but that hardly made the chair tremble.

"Lemme out of here! It's full of bees! I got stung! Shit! Help! Help!"

"They're not bees. They're wasps," Lewis said, but he doubted Marcel heard him between the banging and the screaming. Much louder than Lewis had been before Marcel punched him. Lewis, though, hadn't had wasps all over him.

Gumball Man, on the other hand, with folded arms and the same steady gaze as before, had been listening. "Very good," he nodded. "Imagine, making a stupid mistake like that. You're really nothing at all like him, are you? Don't you think you'd be better off, if you never had to put up with anyone like him anymore?"

Lewis couldn't think of what to say with all the noise, and then Marcel's father was beating on the locked door and swearing and bellowing at them to let him in. Then the pounding on the door grew steadier and harder, like a battering ram. Wood splintered. Lewis hastily kicked the chair from under the closet doorknob. Mr. Morin staggered in at the same time Marcel reeled out, brushing and slapping off wasps real and otherwise.

Mr. Morin wanted to know what the hell was going on. He was red-faced and breathing heavily, and looked as if he were about to wallop someone.

"He locked us in here!" accused Lewis, even as Marcel was wailing, "He locked me in with the bees!" Gumball Man, of course, had not stuck around to be gawked at.

Mr. Morin kicked Lewis out of the house. A week went by before he was allowed back.

That was the summer when Lewis's Dad, ill-content with glossy magazine photographs, bought a kiln. Lewis was convinced that Dad's interest in ceramics came from watching him make dinosaurs and spaceships with Play-Doh. Dad's first attempts at crude heads and nude figures were too thick and went off like bombs in the dead of night, halfway through firing. So he invested further in molds and slips and paints and glaze, and he mass-produced busty harem girls, flimsily veiled or topless, to stand on their own or recline on the edges of ashtrays. Mom vowed to divorce him if he didn't turn his talents elsewhere. Dad vowed to divorce her if she ever baked one of her awful meatloafs again. They were both in earnest.

Lewis never treated their yelling about divorce seriously. It was only one more thing for them to turn the volume way up about. He knew better than to blame himself whenever they threatened to split up. What had he ever done that was so wrong? He also refused to believe they were staying together only because of him. He expected they'd go on forever the way they had been, except for maybe getting louder with time. As they always had done.

Mom and Dad never took out their foul moods on him, or else the long drives during family vacations would have been unbearable. By age ten, he'd become quite the expert at tuning them out. In the back seat, he read monster magazines, which he liked even if he didn't understand all the jokes in them, or superhero comics, the one kind of reading material that made Dad ask Mom why he bothered going anywhere if the kid was just going to look at those damn things and ignore the scenery.

They rented a cottage on the Cape every summer, and though the time always zipped by, Dad never failed to rub it in that a week out here was too long because the lease cost him an arm and a leg. Still, it was the one occasion all year when Dad went to the movies with Lewis and Mom, and to restaurants, and to fireworks shows.

What's more, the beach was only a two-minute walk, so that was something to do every day. A jetty made of boulders was at one end of the private beach for the rental cottages. The other end merged with the town beach, as marked above the high water line by a weathered Keep Out sign that everybody from the town side ignored. At low tide, the water went out as far as the end of the jetty, and a sand bar came to light. It emerged from the tidal flats over near the Keep Out sign and curved away into the bay, deep water on both sides, back toward the jetty.

Lewis and Mom were beachcombing after breakfast. At ripe-smelling low tide. Mom must have been feeling adventurous, because she said that if they started that minute maybe they could explore all the way to the end of the sand bar, and back, before the tide came in again. She sounded sure, so Lewis swallowed his doubts.

At first he let himself be carefree. Glad to just follow along. Walking with Mom, but each of them alone with their observations till one of them saw something worth mentioning: hermit crabs, horseshoe crabs, little green crabs, blobby little jellyfish, or see-through minnows, and then dark red sand dollars, purple starfish, a few spiny sea urchins, a skate, some flounders, out farther in the bay where the steeper sides of the sandbar disappeared into black water.

Another year, Lewis had spotted a really big, disgusting sea worm in the mud around here. It looked like it could bite or sting. Thank God he and Mom were on dry sand. He wished they could go on and on, but he noticed, before Mom did, the sand getting soggy and a film of water underfoot in places. He, the mere kid, had to be the responsible one and announce it was time to head back.

The rising water couldn't be too deep yet. So why was Mom frowning in the direction of the beach? The tide must have been coming in faster near the land than out here, because the sandbar had become an island. But that water toward which they hurried looked like nothing more than the film of water behind them. Or like a heat mirage of water on the highway. Maybe that's what it was, only a mirage.

Lewis felt kind of shaky, but didn't want to admit he was scared. He had to show a brave face. Nothing to be afraid of yet. Two steps ahead of Mom, he charged off the shoreward end of the sandbar and into knee-deep water. And into sand that squished up between his toes, and that he'd sink into if he stopped for long. Mom was yelling for him to let her to get in front. But could he rely on her, after she got them into this mess? With no telling how bad it would get? While he debated what to do and she skipped ahead of him, his eyes rested on the sunny surface that masked the unknown depth beyond the sandbar. A few inches down, right where the sunlight gave out, Gumball Man was leering back at him. Drawing a finger across his scrawny throat, a finger that changed into a darting minnow as soon as it was past his neck.

Mom was shouting at Lewis to come on. He needed no encouragement. All thought of acting heroic had fled without a trace. He had to pull hard before the sand released his feet, and each time they touched bottom he remembered the sand worm, and the skates and crabs and sea urchins he knew were down there. Every step when nothing pinched or punctured his toes only made it seem likelier that at the next step something would. But if he didn't push onward, Mom would leave him behind, and the water that was over his knees would soon be over his mouth. Maybe that's what Gumball Man's dramatic gesture meant, that Lewis was screwed either way, and it was Mom's fault! Or had Gumball Man been some kind of mirage? Lewis couldn't think straight. Or see straight. The sun was really beating down. Everything around him seemed to be made of flashing, rippling movement, the same way the sea looked with the wind and sun upon it. It made him start to cry.

Mom turned around for a second. Annoyance on her face. Or disappointment in him for crying. How dare she! Whose fault was all this? The water was almost up to his trunks now. Would she be careful about staying in the middle of the sunken sandbar, so he could follow her without getting in deeper than he had to? He wanted to say something, but couldn't put the words together.

The beach was still a long ways off. Dad had shown up and was watching them from the water's edge. Shielding his eyes with one hand. From here, the size of a green plastic soldier. Not even waving. As much help as a plastic soldier. Something slid out from under Lewis's foot. He yelped and cried harder. By some miracle, he hadn't been stung or bitten. Mom checked to see if he was still moving along, but didn't stop or say anything.

The pointy little waves had sloshed water all over his trunks. In no time, he was in up to his waist. The current was trying to throw him off-balance. And then the tide wasn't pushing against his ass exactly as hard, and the water was back down to his hips. He suddenly realized that he could have started swimming a while ago. No contact with the muck at all. Why hadn't he thought of that? Why hadn't Mom? He might have stopped crying then, but the instant he tried launching into the dogpaddle, a small hand grabbed his ankle. He felt the fingernails dig in. Gumball Man! He screamed and tugged free and swam for his life. He lost track of Mom. When his toes stubbed into firm sand on the downstroke, he straightened up and ran, splashing wildly, still keening and sobbing, through the shallows and onto dry land. Surprised at making it back alive.

Dad had on that stupid captain's cap and was keeping his distance, acting as if this crybaby kid were no one he knew. With sneaking glances right and left to see who was paying this shameful display any mind. If strangers were gawking at him, Lewis couldn't see them through his tears, and didn't care. Mom was telling Dad that her sunsuit was wet and she had to go change. Dad carped about how they were late already if they were going to drive over to some Cranberry Museum. It was nowhere Lewis wanted to go. Then in a lower voice Dad complained about something else, and Lewis made out the words "sissy" and "spoiled." Well, screw Dad! Lewis could have drowned. Or been attacked by a Portuguese man-o'-war. Lewis rubbed his eyes and studied his foot. He wasn't bleeding, but little red scratches were spaced just right for the fingernails of a child or a monkey.

Mom and Dad were having it out like cats and dogs again. How was Lewis crying in public any worse than that? And they were stalking away as if they'd forgotten him, as if they had no son. Assuming he'd just catch up. As if he had a choice! He wiped his runny nose. Straggled, to keep the wind between himself and what they were saying. Lewis didn't need Gumball Man to spell out the morning's lessons: Don't trust Mom. Don't expect any sympathy from Dad. Mom's head was in profile now. She was speaking to Lewis. Something about getting some sunburn lotion on him. He wasn't listening.

That was also the summer when Mom demanded appeasement. Dad had made no more ceramic harem girls. But he refused to toss those that he'd lovingly, painstakingly embellished with gilt and a broad iridescent palette and sparkly glaze. The longer they heaved their shiny breasts at her while she had to dust them, the more self-evident it became that she was entitled to a much heftier concession from him. The nature of which should be up to her.

She made a convincing case, wherein the words "mental cruelty" played a major role. And so, at the top of the driveway, framed by the picture window in the kitchen, her dream came true of a lily pool in the middle of a flagstone patio. Mom plainly enjoyed loung-ing in a deckchair out there, sunning herself or reading *Life* magazine. Lewis was puzzled at times to find Dad glaring out the picture win-dow at her. Lewis shied away from the pool himself, in dread of see-ing Gumball Man sneer back at him, as he had from beneath the ocean surface.

Coincident with growing pains, Lewis entered a phase of needing to get things just right and succeeding only after three tries, if not six or nine. The bedsheet could only come up to a certain point be-tween his shoulder and chin, and it couldn't touch his neck. The sound on the TV needed adjustment to exactly the right volume, a smidgen different from the bad volumes higher or lower. He had to bound up the stairs two at a time, or three when he had the energy, and always set his right foot on the landing first. He didn't know why any of this, and much more, had become necessary. Except that it all protected him somehow from something.

Or did it? Alongside the barn, a nasturtium-fringed path led to a gate in a white picket fence. Beyond the fence was the backyard. One gray October suppertime, Lewis was coming in from out back. He went to close the gate, which meant lifting it a bit by one of its crossbars, while with his other hand he fit a swinging hook into an eyelet screwed into a fencepost. But the hook resisted sitting straight up and down just right, and he had to unhook and lift the gate again and again. On the fourth go, a voice next to his elbow jeered, "Up and down! Up and down!" It sounded sort of like Dad. Lewis un-handed the gate and checked around. Nobody there. Gumball Man! Who else? He fled the scene before further words could taunt him out of thin air. He didn't mention the voice to Mom and Dad, of course, any more than he let people see him laboriously get things right. They would only think he was crazy.

That was also the autumn when his voice first changed, and his social bearings too, though he carried on none the wiser. During a game of hide-and-seek next door with Marcel and some friends from his parochial school, it fell to Lewis to hide. Dusk was in the air, and many of the kids had taken off already. He considered holing up in the Morins' cellar or shed, before the brainstorm hit him. Home! He'd just go home. It was a really funny idea. See if Marcel or anyone else was smart enough to think of that! This was the kind of clever trick Gumball Man might have talked him into, but Lewis had hatched it all on his own. He slipped away and strolled into the kitchen just as Mom was putting supper on the table. Huh! So he couldn't have stayed out any longer anyway. After supper he phoned Marcel, a little put off that nobody had caught on and come ringing the doorbell.

"Where the hell did you go?" Marcel sounded peeved.

"I ran home!"

"What the hell did you do that for?"

"Because it was a really funny idea!"

"We were looking for you for half an hour."

"It was a joke!" Marcel couldn't actually be mad, could he?

"Are you crazy?"

"No!"

"You're a little jerk then." The line went dead.

Didn't Marcel get it? Maybe he wasn't smart enough. Even after Marcel had hung up, Lewis refused to take his anger seriously. He had done lots of worse things to Lewis! Had that occurred to Marcel?

Lewis went to bed with worries at bay. Marcel would be fine tomorrow. Lewis hadn't done anything so bad. Like any other night, he didn't pull the shade in his bedroom. Nobody could look in. Nothing but the barn and trees and sky out there. He fell asleep as usual, once he positioned the sheet and the blanket just right, but woke up much later, after his parents had turned off the TV. Midnight at least. All quiet. Why was he up? Marcel came to mind. Suppose he was genuinely pissed off? And didn't want to be friends any more? Had Lewis done something worse than he'd thought? He was hot and sweating. Stomach full of jumpy locusts. A fine hour for his conscience to act up!

The darkness in the room was becoming darker. Something big and vague like a cloud was moving across his window, which was lined up with the foot of the bed. No, not a cloud, because it felt too close. Maybe between the house and the barn. It blotted out the starlight as it went, but he couldn't see an edge to it or any details. Nothing visible about it except darkness. Lewis sensed it was alive, though, and that he'd met it sometime before. When? No use trying to remember now. He was trapped and helpless and really had to go to the bathroom. It was all he could do to stop from wetting his pajamas.

The darkness was bad. Unmistakably. It gave off a bad feeling. And Lewis knew what it was saying, though it didn't break the unnatural silence with any sound. "This one is vulnerable now. We can have him."

Lewis's fight-or-flight mechanism kicked in at last. He knew what he had to do. Inspiration to the rescue, from out of nowhere. Or at least nowhere conscious. On the child-sized bureau beside his bed was an assortment of stuff he'd found on the sidewalk. Nothing valuable, just whatever struck him as neat. He grabbed a string of DayGlo rosary beads. Balled it up and flung it at the window. Crack! The glass didn't shatter, but it was no longer in one piece. Never mind that for now. The cloudy thing was gone!

Down the hall, Dad was shouting from in bed, "What the hell are you doin' in there?"

Lewis thought fast. "I'm sorry! I was having a nightmare! I'm okay now!"

Good enough, apparently. No more was said.

Lewis stole off to the bathroom, and afterwards, completely spent, fell fast asleep. Come morning, he didn't let himself think about what had passed in the night. Nor was his conscience bothering him. Back to normal!

The friendship with Marcel resumed, only he seemed to think twice about much of what Lewis said, as if it might not make sense, and he wasn't home as often when Lewis came over. That was all right, because Lewis wanted to spend more afternoons reading, mostly science fiction or Tarzan. And to be honest, he was becoming more interested in one of the other Morins, the one he recognized among all the girls at that house, and who was his age, and whose name he knew. Mireille. Had a pretty ring to it. She wore her thick black hair in a short round hairdo with bangs and with upturned points next to her cheeks. She had sleepy hazel eyes and a slinky walk and was an inch taller than Lewis. At first he realized only after the fact that he'd been gazing at her. No harm done, fortunately. She never acted as if she noticed him. Never said a word to him. He was free to exercise his sidelong fascination.

It wouldn't do, though. He had to bridge that chasm of indifference somehow. So that she felt like being with him. How to make a good first impression? How to get her attention at all? He was as likely to come up with the answers as he was of climbing a waterfall. But he dared not let his eyes meet hers otherwise.

Over the winter nights, he did no more than picture her face in his half-moony, half-despairing mind while drifting to sleep. Not till spring did it occur to him that he wanted to kiss her and feel her embrace him. With that, he was two dizzying giant steps ahead of himself, since he still had no idea how to start talking to her. And nowhere to turn for advice. Mom and Dad knew about a lot of things, but love wasn't one of them.

That same spring, shortly after the handyman's special of a wintertime fiberglass cover had come off the lily pond, Dad contributed some decorative accents to the patio. Young specimens of Norfolk pine, orange tree, and hibiscus stood top-heavy in faux-wood Styrofoam pots and blew over during April showers. Coyly peeking from among the flora was a buxom two-foot-high cement lady, wearing nothing but swimming-pool blue paint. A few lime-green blades of tall plaster grass did the work of a fig leaf.

Lewis didn't hear Mom and Dad battle over the poolside statuette. Maybe they held back till he was out of earshot. Nothing to bring up in front of the child! It was no secret, though, that Mom was never in a good mood anymore. A woman of few words, especially toward Dad. The deckchair on the patio waited for her in vain all spring and into the summer.

A heat wave blasted all hope of enjoying July. Brutal, day and night, for weeks. Long before it ended, nobody was thinking straight. Or so someone could plead, when accidents happened. Like when Mom was swinging the station wagon around in the broad part of the driveway so she could park with headlights facing ahead from inside the cool of the barn. Tricky business, that turning radius. After three near-misses that grazed the rose bed, she reversed into the blue nude and demolished it. Smushed the Norfolk pine as well. Oops! Lucky she hadn't backed into the pool! The sun sweltered down murderously for several more days, but that didn't prevent her from catching up on deckchair reading. With a smile of quiet triumph.

Lewis, meanwhile, perceived that Mom's day-in, day-out silent anger had gone to live in Dad. Who had a grouchy disposition at best. Never a display of affection for anyone in Lewis's memory. Hid cheerful moments well if they ever happened. Lewis didn't want to be home when Dad's clenched-up ill will broke loose, the way it had for Mom behind the wheel. He scurried next door for refuge daily, as soon as Dad pulled in from the office. As if his friendship with Marcel had never fallen into disuse. On most occasions, Marcel wasn't in and Mrs. Morin shooed Lewis away with growing impatience. All too seldom he managed to get an eyeful of Mireille. A mental snapshot for him to admire later.

Was he becoming a pest? The possibility never occurred to him. He needed someplace to hide. The Morins were letting him down! He thought of Gumball Man for the first time in ages, and wondered why he had, and made no headway recalling just when they'd last met.

One September afternoon, Lewis beat his usual retreat to the neighbors. He trod up the cement steps, across the screened-in back porch, and through the unlocked back door. He wouldn't have liked it if Marcel had ever come over and just walked in rather than ringing the bell and waiting. But the Morins had different standards. Why should Lewis let that weigh on his mind?

The longer it took anyone to discover him, the longer he could hang around in here. He held his breath and eased the door shut. Gently, till it clicked. He was in a large space, neither kitchen nor dining room. People might stand around or sit at a chipped Formica table along one wall, but mostly they trooped through on their way in or out. Nobody here now, though. To the left was the kitchen, from which he expected Mrs. Morin to charge, fake-throwing a dish towel or rubber gloves while crowing at him to go home because Marcel was out somewhere. Nope, not this time!

A rare moment of peace and solitude in the Morin household! Should he make himself at home? This was actually better than finding Marcel at hand. How long could it last?

Somebody had to be here. Feet were tromping around upstairs. He could hear them through the ceiling. Mireille's, maybe. At the other end of the room, four steps led up to a landing. Then after that was the staircase to the second floor. Lewis moseyed over to the bottom steps. A shadow came and went on the landing like a tongue briefly sticking out. Lewis called, "Hello?" No answer. He correctly set left foot on second step, right foot on landing. Looked up. Saw Gumball Man's backside bolt from view, down the hall. Was Mireille in danger?

He sprang up two steps at a time. Put left foot on the upstairs carpet first. Uh-oh! Not a good sign. His eyes probed the gloomy hall. Nobody there. Light fell from an open bedroom doorway. Halfway to the door, he made out DJ chatter from a cheap radio. He barged into the room. Before he could see that it was Mireille at her white particle-board desk doing homework, he was asking, "Did anyone come in here?"

She didn't startle easy. With one red-stockinged foot she lazily swiveled her chair to face him. "Only you." Even her indifference made his heart race.

Then it hit him. He'd spoken to her, and she'd answered. Steady, now. If he stuck to the subject, who knew how long he'd be able to keep talking to her?

"Isn't anyone else home?"

"Not this minute."

"I saw someone's shadow on the stairs when I came in." Jesus, was that gabby DJ ever going to play a song?

"Who did you think it was?" She was wearing sleek turquoise pajamas in the afternoon. But she couldn't be sick if she was doing homework.

"I don't know." His first lie to the girl he adored! Like he had a choice? Oh, it was just this creature I call Gumball Man running around up here . . .

"How are you at geography?"

"Okay, I guess." Now the DJ was playing squawky commercials.

She had an open schoolbook next to an open composition book. They looked funny, not altogether for real, because they were different from those at his public school. She'd been writing answers in the composition book to questions at the end of a chapter in the schoolbook. "Do you know where Egypt is?" she asked, swiveling away from him to face her desk again. Flipped schoolbook pages to a world map at the back.

Lewis tactfully hid any show of surprise. She didn't know that?

"I've looked all over Asia," she was saying, "and I can't find it anywhere."

"It's in Africa." He tried to avoid sounding smart about it. She frowned at him as if he were joking. "Look, it's right here." He leaned over her shoulder and pointed.

"Oh yeah," she drawled, as if reluctant to believe him or her eyes. "Thanks."

"Do you need any more help?" She seemed to be giving that some thought, so he indulged a quick survey of the room. How could she sleep with all those stuffed animals on the bed? Beside the bed was a vanity with an attached mirror and a lot of makeup containers. Was she old enough for that stuff already?

The DJ finally started playing a song. Remarkable! Lewis had never paid much attention to what was on the radio. Didn't know who any of the bands were. Or the names of any hits. Some songs he liked and some he didn't. The song that was on now he didn't really like. Too shrieky. How else was there to put it?

But Mireille felt differently. The radio was near the corner of her desk beyond the schoolbook, and she reached out to turn up the volume. Lewis hadn't moved after showing her Egypt, so that her cheek was an inch from his while her leisurely hand adjusted the dial.

She had a nice flowery scent, and it went to his head. Why was she dawdling so long right next to him? Then it came to him that maybe she wanted him to kiss her. Why not, when it was what he wanted too? He snaked his head around so that his lips could touch hers. She pulled her face aside at the last second. As soon as she understood what he wanted? She looked inconvenienced at most. Not really mad. She didn't yell or push him away. Said only, "Cut it out."

Lewis held his ground. The urge to kiss her was in charge. He swooped in, till she paddled at the air in front of his face with both hands. "Stop it," she said, in the same monotone. No angrier than before.

Something wild and new in him wasn't about to give up so easily. Like his own inner Tasmanian Devil. He was giddy. Excited such that he dared not let her look below his waist. More enticing than ever, that teasing lack of interest in the way she was watching him. That idle curiosity about what he might do, how long he might try. Like she was getting something out of this, of seeing what kind of effect she was having on him. But this realization prompted no second thoughts.

Maybe he had to hold her before he could kiss her. This time, she snared his wrists and thrust him away. "Stop it!" she repeated. At the same half-hearted level of impatience.

He had to be faster. A lot faster, and he'd have her. That shrieky song was somehow goading him on. Kind of like itching powder. He wished it would end. It was forcing his hand before he was completely ready. He held his breath and grabbed at her. Quick like a hawk, but still too slow! She slapped aside right hand and then the left in one motion. He was impressed despite his frustration. "I'm not going to kiss you!" She sounded petulant. But was studying him with the same maddening detachment.

"Why not?" he demanded. Pleased with himself, as if the question represented a strategic breakthrough. A new, almost ticklish sensation began to make him tingle all over. Mireille's foot, in its smooth red stocking, was rubbing slowly up and down above his sock, under his pants cuff. She continued to watch him. Lewis had a disconcerting sense that something mysterious was about to happen below the belt.

Downstairs, the back door slammed. "Kids! Anybody home?" Mr. Morin! Whatever had been about to happen was water under the bridge now. Mireille had withdrawn her foot. "You better get out of here, or you'll be in trouble!" she warned. Without any forethought, he lit out into the hall and down the stairs. No Mr. Morin in sight! He must have gone into the kitchen or a front room. Lewis thanked Lady Luck and escaped out the back door. Well, he shouldn't have expected things to work out any better. He had put left foot first at the top of the stairs, after all.

From the safety of his own side yard, he cast a resigned glance toward the neighbors. His jaw dropped. Was that Mireille, in a gray woolen jacket and matching beret, slinking up the cement steps to the screened-in porch? Was it even possible that she'd gotten dressed already, sneaked out the front, and then come around back? And anyway, why would she? But if that was Mireille going in now, who had Lewis been trying to kiss? His inner gears seized up at trying to think that through, until it dawned that he was really getting what he wanted, wasn't he? Whatever had actually happened in Mireille's room, he couldn't be in any trouble for it, so long as he hadn't in reality tried kissing her. He could relax. Off the hook!

He whistled a happy tune, as opposed to that shrieky one on the radio, till his kitchen was in earshot. Oh shit. Sounded like the silent malice that Dad had caught from Mom was finally making itself heard. Lewis had fled scot-free from Mr. Morin with seconds to spare, but his timing was really rotten after all.

Mom was hollering, "You have no right!" Dad was keeping his voice down. Which made him seem more like the reasonable one. And prevented Lewis from catching every word. The gist involved a done deal with the tree surgeons. Tomorrow morning they'd be out back with chainsaws. The tree had to go. It was too big and the garden hadn't gotten enough sun this summer.

Standing by the back door, unwilling to go in, Lewis couldn't believe his ears. Dad had to mean the huge maple, with two trunks joined at the base, that towered behind the barn. Lewis loved that tree! And so did Mom. Look no further to explain why it must die. Mom, in fact, hated to see anything pulled up or chopped down that she was used to having around. To yank out the daisies or the morning glory vine would have upset her too, but Dad couldn't make a stronger point than with the maple. Nothing bigger was alive on their property.

Sitting on the back stoop, Lewis stared groundward in dull shock. Why did an innocent tree have to suffer because of this fight over a stupid naked statue? The workings of Dad's mind were beyond understanding. That tree belonged to Lewis as much as anybody, but he knew that if he spoke up he'd be sorry. Screw Dad anyway. Someday Lewis would get even for this. Or maybe a sawed-off bough would land on Dad's head and they'd have to stop chopping the rest down.

To Lewis that maple was something majestic and wondrous in his own backyard. Something that had always been reassuring because it would always be there, as if it were too big to die. It was supposed to be invulnerable. This felt like the end of a chapter, the end in some unclear sense of himself. He sat there till Mom made him come in for supper. By then the dusk chill had numbed his fingertips and he had to wiggle them to get any sensation back.

Same hour next day, Lewis, with vacant eyes, sat on the knee-high stump, as big around as the kitchen table. Sorry to say, no falling bough had brained Dad and halted the operation. Dammit! Lewis had hidden in the cellar all that Saturday reading superhero comics, but was unable to get the awful keening of the chainsaws out of his head, then or now. After the so-called tree surgeons had left, Mom made Lewis go outside. But she couldn't make him play. So he sat and brooded, feeling every bit as fallen and dead inside as the tree, exactly as he'd expected.

He heard the gate beside the barn creak. Mom was on her purposeful way, probably to tell him supper was waiting. He stretched his legs, and only then found how cold and stiff his joints were. She must have been heartbroken about the tree too, and he wanted to overcome his leaden state and tell her he understood, he knew how she felt. Maybe throw in some comment about what a tyrant Dad was. But before the words came together, Mom was chewing him out as if everything wrong with Dad now applied to him.

"I just talked to Mrs. Morin. Her daughter came up to her in tears and said you sneaked into their house yesterday. You wouldn't leave her alone and kept trying to kiss her. I'm so humiliated. Well? What have you got to say?" Mom had her fists on her hips. And Lewis had been so sure he was safe! Worse, he was suddenly the bull's-eye for all this anger, after he'd been on Mom's side and had wanted to say something nice. Nor did it look like he'd get anywhere protesting that Mireille hadn't been so tearful yesterday. Mom was apparently going to glower at him until he answered.

"I like her," he squeaked. Shocked that his voice was so puny.

"You little punk!" He could tell she was mad at him for more than what he had just said or what he'd done yesterday, but beyond that he was clueless. "You can just march yourself up to your room. And you can forget about supper."

He wasn't hungry anyway. Decided against saying so in case he came across as insolent. Nothing to gain by making a bad state of affairs worse. He stood and brushed sawdust off the seat of his corduroys. Tromped up to his room without a word. Looked back only once, from the open gate. Mom was glaring at the stump as if he were still sitting on it.

Facing the window from his bedside chair, with dim starlight to outline his surroundings, Lewis's position was plain. Where could he be in this house except here? Dad had done something terrible and didn't care how it made Lewis feel. Mom had turned against him and didn't care to hear his side of the story. He didn't want to be near either of them. On top of that, he gathered that he was beginning to feel toward them the way they felt toward each other. Wasn't that the same as becoming more like them, which he swore he'd never do? But where could he turn? Mireille was pretty definitely a lost cause. Doubtful he'd find a welcome with any of the Morins from now on. He wanted to run away or disappear.

Something was blocking the starlight. From the depths of his brown study, he couldn't tell if the obstacle were inside with him or outside. Lewis blinked, and Gumball Man stood almost within reach. The window framed his slinky form, which gleamed in the starlight. As usual, he was eyeballing Lewis, but his expression was different. As if he were hungry. Or sort of like the way Mireille had been watching him.

"You won't have anything to do with those people, ever again. You're ready now, aren't you? Come on, you little monkey." Ready for what? Gumball Man's meaning was as unclear as it had ever been. And "little monkey"? That's what Lewis had imagined Mireille calling him! "Come on." More insistently.

Then it was Lewis's turn to stare, as Gumball Man changed at the tempo of a movie Jekyll into Hyde. The bald flesh of the top and sides of his oversized head melted into a big rounded hairdo, with bangs, and upturned points next to rubbery cheeks. Alien, lipless mouth blossomed until it was pouty. Kissable. On the deep-gray body, naked as always apart from loincloth, sturdy breasts budded and ripened. Nice little handfuls, Lewis couldn't help but observe.

"I'm going to let you kiss me now," whispered Gumball Man. Or was it Gumball Girl? In either case, the creature minced the little distance between them and opened thin, boneless arms wide to enfold him. Lewis pressed back into his chair, but vetoed any more serious evasion. He was prey to that feeling again that he'd had when Mireille had been rubbing his leg. Whatever was about to happen here, he'd had it with Mom and Dad, with the neighbors, with everything he knew. If he had nowhere to go, he'd be better off not caring. And Gumball Man had changed to meet him halfway. Who else had ever done that?

The thing with Mireille's hair and lips, and better breasts probably, settled onto his lap and slid its arms between Lewis and the back of his chair. The chair groaned. Lewis had never considered that the creature homing in on him with parted lips would have any weight, but it did. Lewis would have had to struggle to stand up. But he didn't want to, and even leaned forward to intercept Gumball lips. It wasn't lips he felt, though. Instead, the thing was pushing slimy, muscular tongue into his mouth. Yuck! And it had the flavor of gumball-machine toy! Lewis began to jerk his head back, but then the tongue was gone, and the weight was gone, and around him was a clammy gray cloud that he was inhaling with the same breath with which he was going to taste his first kiss. The bitter cloud stopped up his breath, which made him gasp that much harder, which drew that much more cloud into his lungs. The grayness before him thickened, and everything went dark.

The brusque and aloof new Lewis, as far as Mom and Dad were concerned, was part and parcel of the bottom dropping out of his voice, and the poor fit of his old clothes, and the spread of hair to novel places, when these developments came belatedly to their attention. He certainly wasn't taking after either of them! One of their rare points of agreement.

It was Marcel who produced the only flash of real insight. A couple of years after that last fateful visit to the neighbors, Lewis was in his side yard, overlooking the Morin property. Lewis was watching from between two witch hazel bushes as Marcel and a snooty new friend hit golf balls up the Morins' driveway. Marcel noticed standoffish Lewis and felt sorry for him in a way he couldn't readily explain. He eased two steps closer, as if trying not to scare off a squirrel. Smiled, and invited Lewis to take a couple of swings at the ball if he liked.

Lewis nodded and mumbled, "Okay." He directed a wary eye at Marcel and friend, even when handling the club. He made a few timid little efforts. Grimaced when he succeeded only in nicking the ball once. Followed the ball with expectant eyes over its course of paltry inches, as if it might show some initiative and speed up at the last instant. Then he handed the club back and departed in silence, his fingers wiggling compulsively, as if they were gelatinous.

Marcel watched him recede between the witch hazels and reflected that Lewis had become a completely different person. As if somebody had knocked the stuffing out of him. One way or another, that jumpy little boy was gone. Then Marcel's impatient friend shouted at him to forget about the weirdo and get back to the more important business of improving their form.

The Silence in the Copse

This flight to Stockholm had put him in mind of the other momentous trip in his life. He wasn't planning on a third. He'd been a grad student, still a gangly kid really, when improbable fortune smiled and he fell in with a girl who idolized Emma Peel, from those *Avengers* reruns on cable, and who even boasted similar bone structure. They tooled up and down the Eastern Seaboard in her apple-red MG, blasting psychedelic tunes and almost constantly high.

In the White Mountains they overnighted in little Wigginsborough, at a formerly magnificent Victorian hotel looming over, and conceivably about to crush, the rest of the town. The mansard roof, at least in nostalgic magnification, could have kept a football stadium dry. A hundred empty rocking chairs straggled the length of the gingerbread portico. He signed in as Mr. and Mrs. Wright. They were the only guests.

What was her name again? He recollected calling her Emma, but that couldn't be it. Anyway, she was up taking a bath, and he tarried in the drafty sitting room, in hopes of chatting with the manager. Once, years earlier, Oscar's father had mentioned uncles or grandparents living in Wigginsborough, or maybe Peterborough. The Wrights were no close family. And unapologetic about it. But why not poke around for missing roots while he was here?

As if on cue, the manager strode in with an armload of wood and offered to make a fire. He bet Oscar didn't know August nights in New Hampshire were so damn chilly. The manager had the build of an understuffed scarecrow, and startling features, giving the impression he'd combed his bluff of sandy hair forward too forcefully and had pulled his brow and face along with it. He sat in the dusty armchair across the fireplace from Oscar and, without coaxing, unlocked his word hoard. Listening to him was apparently the price of a fire.

Oscar nodded patiently on learning the town had seen better days, and how the hotel had battled slow decline since Teddy Roosevelt's second term. Newsworthy events? Only one in living memory. Or had Oscar heard of it already? Nope, didn't think so.

Well, a native son who'd served in the Big One came home to take over his dad's hardware store. Never liked to talk about the time in Germany. A lot of veterans didn't. He passed for normal, aside from spells of spooking easy, till one Christmas, when he took his old Army rifle up to the roof of the store and started shooting people on the street. Nobody in particular, just anyone in range. Killed three, wounded four more. And no crazy laughter, no raving or ranting. Not a word. Calm and collected. Professional conduct, for a sniper. Except that the hardware store was surrounded by higher buildings. The sheriff got some men in through back doors and up onto roofs with a view of the shooter. The sheriff hollered a warning, but the crazy bastard wasn't listening. They all fired at once before he pulled the trigger again.

"Did they kill him?" Oscar asked.

"Yes, they killed him!" snorted the manager. And they never found out what set him off. Oh, there was a note in his vest pocket, but that only muddied the waters. Three little lines: "Tally ho / To the hunt we go / Now we're on the high road." Nonsense, but memorable after a fashion. Became as well-known for a while, locally, as that rhyme about Lizzie Borden and forty whacks.

Some sense of obligation made Oscar ask, despite sudden inner butterflies, what the sniper's name was.

"Orson Wright." The manager had a quizzical gleam in his eye. "Any relation?"

"Not that I know of." True enough. So why were Oscar's jitters worse now than when he'd lied in the registry book?

Up in the room, he treated "Mrs. Wright" to the story and his misgivings about a psycho-killer lurking in the family closet. She was superb at laughing things off. Urged him to roll another joint. Tainted blood? Bullshit. No scientific basis. If the mad marksman was even a relative in the first place. So Oscar shoved his worries to the back burner, to make the most of their traveling days.

This proved wise. By October the relationship had unraveled. He was only surprised it had lasted that long. She'd gone on to other places and people. A year later, she was dead. Blew her brains out on her birthday, from a combination of bad acid, her own unique wiring, and a cockeyed optimism, believe it or not, about advancing to a higher spiritual plane. He never repeated the sniper story to anyone. Her name still escaped him, but her MG, come to think of it, was called "Unrest."

At that tender age, he'd clearly been on the verge of a great adventurous life. And now he was on the verge of a new adventurous life. Which maybe accounted for the resonance between today and that spontaneously vivid past. As for the great life imminent in his youth? While earning his master's, he'd made ends meet as a postal clerk, and afterwards the pay and benefits and security at the PO beat anything he could do with his degree. And a mere twenty-five years later, he was a free man. Literally a pensioner, and shy of the half-century mark! From the vantage of retirement, though, the preceding decades amounted to a regrettable hibernation.

Moreover, with nothing but time on his hands, he started seeing the world as if he'd just awakened. It had changed for the mean-spirited worse since young, stoned Rip Van Winkle had zoomed through it in the passenger seat of a sports car. Civility was deep in an unmarked grave. Look right there at the newspaper in Oscar's lap. One more macho dad had punched out his kid's Little League coach. And luckily, Oscar's student phase was ancient history, or he'd have been a basket case. School shootings had been a sporadic fact of life for over ten years, in a hormone-happy culture where gun control was a laughable dream. As it was, every day in urban America was surely one day closer to Oscar suffering "collateral damage" via road rage or gang-war crossfire or some such idiocy. Then too, Oscar's own iffy legacy of violence skulked in the back of his mind, where he'd banished it a generation ago, but whence something, especially nowadays, might tempt it forth to join in the social breakdown.

For the moment, Oscar was pleasantly miles above it all. At the high point of this journey in more ways than one. Its potential as a positive experience, 100% intact. The sky was still the limit. Nothing to disappoint him yet. Scandinavia had slim allure for tourists in mid-autumn, so he had leg room, and elbow room, and a vagrant desire to prolong this flight indefinitely. If he craved a simpler, crime-free, stress-free life, what could trump riding around on a half-empty airplane, watching the wooly topography of clouds below, while food and drink and entertainment came to him? Barring that, he was moving to Sweden.

He was glad to have no encumbrance of wife or children or even pets. Therein lay another benefit of his postal career. He'd seemed too much of an egghead for any of his desirable co-workers to contemplate him romantically, and to women of his own educational level, working at the PO branded him an obvious loser. This used to bum him out. Lately, though, he'd ceased to care. One of the joys of aging!

Two weeks later, he was beginning to understand how little he understood of his new homeland. Maybe procrastination about applying for immigrant status was wise after the fact. Of course he had yet to explore much of the country, but so far he'd been disenchanted everywhere with how soon his ATM withdrawals dwindled. A decent draft beer cost $7 at least, and even hostels were so expensive that Oscar took advantage of a charming law allowing anyone to camp anywhere for the night, upon notifying the property owner.

He'd bought a rail pass and headed south from Stockholm, and among the vast majority of Swedes who were nice and spoke English he counted the ticket girl at Central Station who looked him over and gave him the senior discount. She also warned him to stick to the shadows underneath the mezzanine gallery and avoid the open floor en route to his gate, because kids spat over the railing at out-of-towners. And to date, the worst sourpuss had resembled a suit-and-tie version of himself who forbade Oscar's tent in his pasture on the technicality that the law was valid for Swedes only.

Oscar paused on his steep uphill path. He took deep breaths and mopped forehead and sparse scalp with a handkerchief. Global warming was a huge calamity in the making, no doubt, but today he was grateful for an aberrantly mild October that let him sweat away starchy meals and sleep outdoors. He resumed his climb among moribund brown ferns and bluish ground cover and the lichen-capped boulders that ensured lebensraum between straight trunks of conifers. Still, the trees were big and numerous enough to form a canopy that trapped humidity and dimmed the light, on what was already a damp, overcast day. The slope was also thickly dotted with rocks like cannonballs, suggesting the aftermath of barrage. Had they been hurtled down at invaders? A sign in the parking lot claimed that on the hilltop had stood an Iron Age fort. Worth a look! No Iron Age forts back in the States, as such.

The sign further stated that Oscar was entering the southernmost National Park in the country, and he'd garnered the minimal Swedish to translate its name as Stone Head. Well, Stan's Promontory might really have been more like it, but couldn't compete with the pithier version. Atop the promontory, he indulged a disappointed grunt. Hardly room here for a bungalow! Nor were there recognizable ruins. Only bare granite and some stunted bushes and weathered rocks. How had archaeologists ever excavated here?

Anyway, the view was outstanding, or would have been if haze hadn't lowered a curtain across half the curve of Baltic inlet that should have been visible in one direction, and half of the green hills in the opposite direction. The afternoon light was starting to weaken. He had to get a move on. The trail had been tricky enough to follow beforehand, without nightfall to handicap him. But first he gazed seaward, getting his wind back, and his mind drifted. In the milky sky, after a while, were hints of a teeming iridescence as when he squeezed his eyes shut. The turbulence became more distinct, and he could almost believe that something sizable was churning forward from deep within the murk. A high, rough-edged sound was too faint to discriminate from the distant surf. An airplane? Oscar had lapsed into a spacey fascination.

He'd seen no other hikers on this off-season Wednesday, or any cars in the parking lot. Hence he was mystified beyond resisting when a hand grabbed his and pulled him along, and he heard, "Kom nu!" Kiss me? No, she wanted him to go with her. Off the summit by some unmarked path. After his last backward glimpse at yellow flecks pulsing in the cloudbank.

Descent was headlong. Avoiding roots and slippery moss left him few chances to glean more than the obvious about his companion. She had a wealth of red hair, long as a horse's tail, and the physique of a runner. She wore a beige, perhaps institutional-issue smock, and calfskin boots. At a guess, he was a head taller than her.

She hadn't relaxed her urgent grip on him, but stopped short and swatted her free hand downward. The gesture, Oscar noted ruefully, to make a dog lie on the floor. Then they were ducking into a low overhang, the outcome of two trees lifting a boulder as they grew. There was scant room to nestle in and squat, which was no help to Oscar as he panted for breath. She brusquely covered his mouth, with a palm dry and cool as talc. Their warren smelled of wet rock and earth. Her skin smelled of juniper. And in the shadows, it had a grayish complexion. They waited in silence. Her eyes were big and her cheekbones were broad. Her chin was small. She was cute. And at the same time, more foreign than anyone he'd ever met. Hard to pinpoint why, exactly, or what her background might have been. Also hard to estimate her age, but they were in pretty deep shadow.

She was staring into space, listening intently. Directly overhead, but muffled by great height, passed a chaotic gabbling. Aha! He knew what it must be. When the noise receded westward, the girl slowly withdrew her hand from his lips, in what bordered on a caress, he thought. By now, he was dizzy from shallow inhalations, but managed to gasp, "Wild geese? Why hide from wild geese?"

The girl wrinkled her thin nose. "You heard nothing but birds?"

"All right, what did I hear then?"

"You from America?"

He nodded, unexpectedly sheepish about coming across as an archetypal Ugly American.

"It's something you have there, but nobody knows about it." At some point she'd stopped holding his hand. While they talked, she slipped from the shelter and continued on her arcane trail, and he accompanied her, at a loss for a polite way to abort the conversation. She said her name was Astrid and eyed him as if gauging whether he believed her. But why shouldn't he?

The woods were in twilight, and he worried aloud that they were veering steadily away from the parking lot and the campsite he'd secured a mile farther down the road. The time of day, like their dark refuge, lent grayness to her skin.

She brushed hair from her eyes and informed him, "You've been out of the park a long time now. You're quite lost. That hill you thought you were climbing is way back in the fog." She shot him the same look as when she'd stated her name.

"So how do I get back to my tent?"

"You don't. Stay with me. I have a place less than a mile from here."

What else could he do? Stumble around in the woods all night? And what, he asked several times, had driven them into hiding? In ersatz answer, she expounded on regional history: about Bronze Age dolmen-builders who venerated the double-axe, about pagan sea-kings and their commerce with England, about violent changes of hand between medieval Denmark and Sweden. Oscar gave up, with the consolation that she sounded awfully knowledgeable to be an escaped inmate. And proud of her heritage, too. At this point Oscar, though aware that distances took longer in the wilderness, expressed surprise that they hadn't covered a mile yet.

Astrid inhaled sharply. "Oh! No, I meant a Swedish mile. About five of your American miles. Not too much farther now." On the positive side, the overcast had dispersed in the night, allowing Oscar to navigate by the moonlit glow of Astrid's red hair as well as the sound of her discourse.

They'd been traversing level ground a while. Oscar was losing a fight against the urge to whine, like a kid in the back seat, if they were almost there yet. And then, thank God! The woods were behind them, and across a modest lawn hunkered a gambrel-roofed farmhouse, no doubt the customary red with white trim, but uniformly cobalt under the stars. Older houses around here had heavy thatched roofs and whitewashed walls, but this was the more generically Swedish clapboard exterior with tile roof, from a mere couple of hundred years ago.

An unlocked side door opened into the kitchen. Astrid flicked the switch for the overhead lamp. "Welcome!" With every surface tiled or enameled or of maple, it was quite the neat and cozy digs. Did she own it?

"I don't own anything. I'm the caretaker." She got him a medium-strength "people's beer," as it was known, from the compact fridge on the counter and poured it into a lager glass. She had something to do in the cellar for a few minutes. She came back before his glass was empty, with potatoes and some frozen hamburger. She made a kind of hash, with a couple of eggs broken over it, and referred to it as what sounded like "Peter Pan." That seemed right to Oscar at this tired and, over the course of supper, ever beerier hour.

Mysterious duty called her back to the cellar. She poured him a people's nightcap first, which he finished in her absence. He sought for a bathroom in vain. Could that explain her sojourns in the basement? On coming back up, she twisted an old iron key in the classic old keyhole in the white cellar door and dropped the key in smock pocket. Bathroom? She handed him a vintage chrome flashlight. The outhouse was behind the barn, at the edge of the woods. Please don't drop the flashlight in!

After her turn with the flashlight, she led him up steep stairs, like those between ship decks, to a bedroom that occupied the whole second story. Its low ceiling followed the angles of the roof, and a long, shallow dormer on one side functioned as a skylight, bathing one of the two single beds in moonshine. The other bed, by the opposite wall, was in shadow. She pointed him toward it, and then gave him a leisurely kiss. "Maybe someday, the same bed for us. Not now." Between being a gentleman and being confused and a little the worse for drink, what could Oscar say except good night?

All the same, he had lucked out here, even if one dinner and a warm bed were the extent of it. She lay on her side, on top of the blanket, in knee-length nightshirt, a hand between her face and the pillow. Under the moon, her hair was copper and the rest was slate, reminding him of a Maxfield Parrish study or maybe Klimt. Twin points of light signaled that she now had her eyes on him, but that was all right. Her look was concerned. Solicitous, he supposed. It helped him doze off.

He dreamed that he was back in the red MG. "Emma" was behind the wheel, only she was the exact likeness of Astrid. They were speeding down a straight dirt road through Maryland cornfields. From well behind them, and gaining fast, came the honking of a flock of geese. Every time Oscar tried turning to see them, "Emma" took one hand off the wheel and squeezed his hand to stop him. Oscar liked the way that felt and started turning just to make her hold his hand. Her look of irritation after a minute warned that he was fooling nobody. Had the car just backfired? No, those were gunshots from somewhere back there. Was a hunting party having at the geese? Then Oscar had to struggle against vomiting because the back of her head was missing, just a bloody cavity flanked by twin cascades of red hair, though he didn't see her get shot. Her driving, miraculously, was unaffected, and she repeated her look of irritation at him.

Oscar woke up. Astrid was gone. And in his ears, was that some species of ringing, or night sounds distorted by his half-asleep brain? Or were those really geese exiting the fringes of perception? Details of Oscar's dream recurred to him. He grimaced. What business did his subconscious have equating "Emma" with Astrid, especially since he'd met her less than twelve hours ago? Or if Astrid were under thirty, was she supposed to be the long-lost girlfriend "come back," as it were? Ah, but those cornfields. Hadn't thought of them in decades! According to local custom, "Emma" insisted, they could eat all the raw corn they wanted as long as they stayed among the rows. Just the same, Oscar was always surprised when nobody chased them out with a shotgun full of rock salt. More surprising now was how wistful he felt, considering he'd been having a nightmare a moment ago. He was pondering this, when Astrid bent over him and pressed her lips to his cheek. As she withdrew, she said what seemed like "Go not." Oscar dozed off again.

Come morning, he expected she'd set him on the road back to his tent. Instead, they breakfasted on a crunchy bread like thick cracker, with cheese and cucumber slices and a sort of caviar that squirted like toothpaste from a tube. They took a nature hike and found a shiny purple beetle, and an orange mushroom about the size and shape of an army helmet. After a lunch of scrambled eggs and fried potatoes, they followed country lanes to a rockbound lake in vain hopes of glimpsing its legendary twenty-foot gar. And every few hours, Astrid conducted cryptic business in the cellar. The day ended with the same bedding arrangement as before.

The next few days fit this pattern. Oscar was content with it so long as she was. That easy, footloose feeling from many summers ago was making a comeback. He chose to be incurious about Astrid's trips to the basement. No filching the key while she was in the shower. He'd be fine around her without knowing if anything sinister was happening, and otherwise, a nervous wreck, trying not to let on that he knew whatever he'd surreptitiously come to know. The golden goose would be dead. Let well enough alone. She was decidedly, if inexplicably, well-disposed toward him.

Monday morning she escorted him to the small barn with red walls of vertical slats. As she slid open the broad black door, she brought up their need for provisions and asked if he could drive. She couldn't. Some Swedes just didn't. A robin's-egg blue jalopy, its nose an inch from the doorway, confronted Oscar. It was something like a cross between an old Citroen and a VW bug.

"A Volvo from the '50s," Astrid volunteered. "An Amazon Sport. The owner left it at my disposal. I can't do anything with it."

Oscar supposed he could handle a standard. Sure, after their woodsy routine of late, shopping in town qualified as an adventure. "One thing, though," he began to ask, and found the words a hard reach, as if trying to channel another, already irrelevant life. Would she mind a detour first to pick up his tent and backpack, providing nobody had swiped them? "Time I had a shave. Plus I could use a change of clothes."

"Me too." She smiled agreeably. That smile took him way back. They'd also gotten a lot of mileage out of one day's outfit in that youthful roving season. Odors? Then, as now, they never noticed.

Oscar's campground, in the vicinity of Stone Head Park, was easy enough to track down. Last Wednesday the owner, a trembly codger with one black lens in his glasses, leaned out the window of his decrepit cottage and invited Oscar to stay in a clump of trees in the roadside pasture. Oscar was miffed now at the apparent theft of all his portable property, till he peered across the field and located the tent in a different copse. He'd set up behind a secondary screen of jumbled rocks, and all was as he'd abandoned it. Probably the old guy had forgotten about him the next day.

They skirted the many postcard villages within a half-hour of home. No good stores out in "the spinach," she complained. As they approached the sign for Gladsax, she asked, "Do you know what that means? Happy Scissors."

"Can we go there?"

"No." So they cruised around grassy hills and along the steely grey Baltic and into prim Simrishamn. They parked in a lot outside the town center and loaded up the trunk at a supermarket and adjacent state-run liquor store. That left Oscar's wallet in crying need of an ATM, and their casual search led them down broad cobblestoned streets between low rowhouses encased in ochre and seafoam green and baby blue plaster. They lucked out at the edge of the main drag, and Oscar pulled the maximum allowed. They splurged on moose steak with new potatoes and lingon sauce at a sidewalk table on the arrow-straight "Great Street," which from their perspective descended heedlessly into the sea.

They took a constitutional in the pedestrian-only commercial district. Stationed at regular intervals in the middle of streets were terracotta planters like hollowed-out blocks of the pyramids. From each of them erupted a monstrous plant with fleshy purple stalks and a riot of great, red-veined, rather cannabis-shaped leaves. Beautiful, if overwrought. "Impressive," Oscar commented.

"Ho ho," rejoined Astrid. "They're castor bean. Extremely toxic. Take a bite and you would die in thirty minutes. Death in the midst of life, as they say. Or else I don't know what message the town fathers had in mind."

They stumbled upon a flea market crammed into several blocks of sycamore-lined boulevard. Amidst the old clothes and beat-up 45s and Sunday paintings and auto parts, a square little plaque of unglazed clay caught Oscar's eye. It was beige, with red-filled carvings of stick figures in processional rows or driving a schematic chariot, and with equally stylized fish and beasts. Astrid squeezed his arm. "I see you're drawn to that. What do they want for it? Ten crowns? Very cheap. Buy it." She was in wide-eyed earnest, putting serious pressure on his arm. "It concerns something I need to show you later." She got hold of herself, softened her grip on him, and tried for a careless laugh. "This is tourist junk, of course." She snaked her arm around his waist, and her more familiar affectionate eyes gazed into his. He spent the ten crowns.

She suggested they head back and claimed she could find the car from there. One of the outlying tables sold World War II memorabilia, from medals to bayonets, German, Japanese, American, Soviet, all in a tarnished heap. Beyond the last booth stood a mustached young man to whom Oscar would never have given a second look were he not seemingly giving Oscar the finger. Astrid observed Oscar's discomfiture and glanced to one side. "It's not you," she said. "This is between those two." She jerked her head toward the dealer. "He definitely started it, somehow." The dealer had a thin face and heavy brows, a hawkish nose, and shoulder-length stringy blond hair. He wore an old green U.S. Army jacket. To judge by body language, he wavered between throwing something or giving chase, but was unwilling to risk any or all of his merchandise as a result. Oscar faced forward again before he could be accused of staring. The mustached young man was gone.

"Especially in the south, people can be on an Aryan trip," Astrid explained. "They provoke the *svartskallar*. Black skulls. Their word for immigrants, guest workers."

"But that guy didn't even look foreign."

Astrid shrugged. "A lot of them come from Turkey, the Middle East, what used to be Yugoslavia. They don't look Swedish." So the famously peaceable, progressive Swedes had a problem with racism! Who knew?

Astrid's sense of direction served them well. Soon Oscar was easing the Volvo out of the lot when a pair of middle-aged men strode from the liquor store. They wore a pastel medley of Izod shirts and sports slacks, and one of them pushed a button on his keychain that made a black BMW at the curb whoop harshly. Yuppies, thought Oscar. The same all over the world. Then the men sighted the Volvo and stared as if at a ghost. Oscar gave them the hairy eyeball in passing. He was about to remark on them when he beheld Astrid scrunched below windshield level, making a point of pawing around for something. "Astrid?"

"There's change on the floor. I wanted to pick it up while I was thinking of it."

"Okay," said Oscar and nothing more, for the sake of happy status quo.

The shelves were stocked for weeks thereafter. The car gathered cobwebs in the barn. Nor did they set foot on any long trails. November days were too short for more than a Swedish mile, she said.

Their relationship also advanced no great distance, though she really liked him, beyond question, and offered promising tokens of physicality every day. Not that Oscar would have characterized her as a tease. She never subjected him to criticism, either, unless he counted her gentle rebuke that the outhouse was really for solid waste only, even if it was hard for him, as an American, to get used to pissing into bushes.

They had grown closer in one sense. After they'd unpacked the goods from Simrishamn, Astrid asked if he wouldn't mind her wearing his clothes. Yes, underwear and all. She managed to sidestep talk of what had happened to her own wardrobe, as she sidestepped all other details of her past. He had long ceased to think about her trips to the cellar. Anyway, for her to be inside his clothes was a mark of intimacy, wasn't it? He, for one, found in it a reassurance of continued togetherness. And he had learned one little thing by this time. "Go not," her customary words before lights-out, was how his Yankee ears heard the Swedish for "good night."

She was also forthcoming with one personal detail, but it almost slid completely by him. On a November date of no overt importance, Astrid started bustling in the kitchen just after lunch and from the cellar procured a few platter loads of ingredients hidden under towels. She shooed him into the parlor when he tried lifting a corner of one of the cloths, and shook her head perfunctorily whenever he stood at the doorway to come back in. He was making scant headway with a year-old Stockholm newspaper and blamed an exotic, diverting aroma as heavy as incense, when she called him to the table, where bowls of soup were waiting, while she hauled what looked like an oversized duck from the oven. "I cooked us the traditional meal for this night," she announced as she carved, "when people accepted that winter could not be prevented from coming." She recounted that for longer than anyone knew, geese, harbingers of cold and darkness, were objects on this occasion of feasting and of something else, a word that sounded equally like "bloat" and "blurt." She translated it as "blood offering" and admitted that modern Swedish had discarded it. "Anyway, you want people to think you're an expert about wild geese, you should know what they taste like." She smiled playfully.

The goose was splendid, even more flavorful than duck, and Astrid had to pester him into sampling the soup before it cooled. "I always loved it better than anything when I was a little girl," she mused, and Oscar found it rich and tangy, a bit like Thai sweet-and-sour, except for an almost metallic aftertaste that made him question if he should really be ingesting this. Astrid had almost finished hers already, so Oscar forged ahead, though he felt obliged to ask, "Why is it black? Are there beans in it?"

"No. It's made from goose." Then she adjourned to the stove for a second serving. Oscar kicked himself at realizing too late that she'd actually divulged a childhood memory, and he hadn't drawn more out of her. And now that opportunity was downstream forever.

By this juncture, Oscar was concluding that Sweden, despite his isolation from most of it, was overall the country for him. Based on what he'd gleaned, lobbyists and litigation weren't calling the shots here to the American extent. There was universal healthcare. People, and not just corporations and the media, were the arbiters of culture. Maybe that held true all over Europe, but Oscar wasn't all over Europe.

He hadn't suffered one homesick moment, and only realized two weeks after the fact that Halloween had come and gone. Thanksgiving was in the offing, but he didn't need to know when. On occasion he missed reading Zippy the Pinhead and Mary Worth. Funnies aside, though, he'd retired from the States as much as the Post Office. The relationship with Astrid might well take a great leap forward anytime. "Marriage" could be his one-word answer to the question of Swedish citizenship. Meanwhile, the more immediate question had crossed his mind, of whether they would ever leave the farm again.

Had she sensed that nascent restlessness? In the center of the rock-maple kitchen table was a thick cut-crystal vase, with dried pods of little Arctic poppies high above the oval mouth. Against the vase leaned the beige clay plaque from the flea market, as it had since its arrival. During breakfast, on a morning of leaden overcast that Oscar equated with a threat of snow, Astrid pushed the plaque onto his placemat. "I need to show you something. But we should go someplace else first, so that what I show you will be more plainly genuine. We should go now to see what your tourist junk is modeled upon." Astrid's earnest tone did nothing to mute Oscar's delight at embarking on a road trip, at last!

They followed the signs north to Kivik. The initial "K" was pronounced as in "cheese," she informed him. Kivik was a mere couple of American miles beyond Stone Head Park. They bypassed the harbor village per se and veered inland. She had him park up a dirt road, where the car would be invisible from the two-lane blacktop. Then they threaded a footpath through the leafless tangle. "This approach is more impressive than the official entrance," she claimed.

Oscar was inclined to believe her. The brush gave abrupt way to a grassy fringe. The first tentative flakes of a snowfall had begun. Beyond the fringe was an immense, saucer-shaped cairn. It seemed low-set because it was much broader than it was high, but at close hand Oscar estimated its height at eight feet or so. It must have been around 250 feet wide, and in its scale if nothing else there was a disorienting, otherworldly quality. The thickening snow, he supposed, put him in mind of that '50s sci-fi flick, *The Thing*, where scientists in the Arctic measure a spacecraft under ice by outstretching arms and joining hands across its diameter. How many scientists would be needed here? This could have been a mockup of that UFO, constructed of countless stones the size and shape of a child's head.

Oscar and Astrid were cautiously negotiating the loose, unexpectedly slick cobbles toward the summit. "This is Kiviksgraven. The grave at Kivik," she explained. "Three thousand years old. From a culture that left different kinds of traces in stone all over this region. Very distinctive, very influential for a long time. Signs are posted in English here that say the same. You need to understand, so you will take seriously what I want to show you tomorrow. Wait here a minute." Astrid continued toward the center, and as the snow began to distort her outline she dropped from sight. Oscar gasped and picked his way over. A causeway curved from the edge of the cairn to its midpoint, where granite lintels framed an iron door. She was at the door. "I'm fine!" she shouted, without facing him. "I'll call you."

Okay then. Oscar's eyes followed the causeway back out, to an empty parking lot and a shack, boarded up as best he could tell through the snow, that presumably sold admission and souvenirs. He casually tried for steadier footing, and that's when he slipped and sat down hard on knobby rock. He struggled to his feet, hoping Astrid hadn't heard him fall. On the ground beyond the cairn an old man, hands folded over the head of a cane that supported his weight, was watching Oscar. Was one lens of his glasses black? Was this the same codger who'd let him camp in the field? How had he gotten here? Impossible to be certain about anything in this flurry! The codger briefly raised his cane at the causeway. "She's no easy one to catch. I know!" he crowed, and grinned. Remarkably toothy, at his obvious age. Feral, in fact, as he persisted in baring his teeth till Astrid gave a yell.

"Excuse me," Oscar mumbled, relieved at the interruption. Averse to seeing that grin again, he stepped to the edge of the causeway and lowered himself where it crooked to the right and no snow had landed.

Before he could mention the old man, Astrid emerged from the darkness of the open doorway and kissed him. "I found the lights!" she exclaimed and reached within, to one side of the lintel. With a click, brightness spilled out on the paving stones. She took his hands in hers and, treading backward, drew him in, beaming unguardedly for an instant. They were in a long gallery, whose walls were dominated by square slabs the size of picture windows, which in a sense is what they were, weren't they? He recognized the original of his little flea-market tchotchke, and as Astrid led him along he discerned more stick figures of men, and horses, and axe heads, and wheels, as well as abstract designs and marks. "Remember the style of these," she instructed, "so you will know it again when you see it, and know that what you see is very old, and authentic."

"What is this place?" whispered Oscar, more spooked by her gravity than anything else.

"The king who was buried here is dust, along with whatever possessions surrounded him. Nameless. Only the stones remain. This room enclosed in white plaster is a modern restoration. Clinical, but it could have been worse. The ramp and the doorway are also new."

Oscar nodded slowly and remembered the old guy skulking outside. She tensed up when he described the encounter, and on word of the black lens grabbed his hand. "We have to go."

She hustled him out, extinguished the lights and slammed the door. In the open air, bass-heavy dance music blasted at them. Oscar

couldn't tell what language the lyrics were in, but winced on principle at the violation of what still, on some rarefied level, constituted a
sacred place. In the parking lot idled a big dark-green SUV, and an
olive-skinned girl in expensive jeans and fur-trimmed leather was
leaning on the hood, barking into a cell phone. Oscar couldn't make
out a word, and in the snow couldn't tell if she were Arabic or Lao-
tian or Chilean or a ridiculously tanned Swede, and didn't care. He
did know that here, in one loud, rude, materialistic package, was
what had prompted his exodus from American culture in the first
place. Fucking hell!

Surely Astrid's expression was more dispassionate than his. She
patted his arm. "Don't move." She sauntered over to the girl, waved
to get her attention, spoke calmly, and gestured toward the woods.
Oscar wished he could hear. The girl only shrugged and went back to
her strident conversation.

Astrid beckoned urgently to Oscar, latched onto his hand again,
and hurried them to the Volvo. She snatched an ice scraper from the
back seat and cleared the windshield, and he brushed snow off the
rear window with his forearm. "I tried to warn her." Astrid shook her
head resignedly.

On the road, Astrid urged Oscar to drive a little faster, and a little faster again. She wouldn't say why, and Oscar feared they were
always one kilometer per hour shy of skidding into a tree. "Is someone after us?" He flinched at his own shrillness.

"Someone always is," she replied. Oscar had no further questions.

He judged they were better than halfway there, holding the road
at nerve-wracking speed, when behind the swish of windshield wipers and the engine's rumble he perhaps detected a far-off dissonance
of squabbling geese or baying hounds. Were they near a poultry operation or a kennel? "Don't look back!" Astrid was now as shrill as he
had been. "Don't slow down! Go!"

Oscar weathered a chill at realizing how closely this moment
echoed his nightmare of last month. But this time, tricking her into
holding his hand was not in the game plan. He glanced at her and
was appalled. He'd never seen her subject to desperation. Her complexion was ashen gray, and she had a piteously haunted look. No,
more hunted than haunted.

They were in the home stretch, and Oscar wasn't any nearer to making sense of the noise, though it verged on loud and clear. It was still easier to take than Astrid's bulging eyes and hoarse breathing. They careened down the gravel drive, and Oscar worried that he was nosing too fast into the open barn. The car stopped an inch from the rear wall, and while the brakes were screeching Astrid leapt out and yanked the barn door closed. She joined him back in the car and they stared straight ahead. The building rattled with what might or might not have been rising wind. In a heartbeat, the racket was overhead, with too many deafening elements for assembly into any coherent whole. Thundering hooves in midair, canine voices in painfully high-pitched excitement, a bellowing chorus that never paused to inhale, all punctuated by clangs and jangling and bursts of discordant horns, threw Oscar into short-term shellshock. The chaos ebbed so rapidly that he heard the sliding scale of Doppler effect, and then the only sound was a ringing in his ears. He groped for reasons to believe they'd simply outraced a nasty snowstorm Swedish-style.

A cool hand was stroking his feverish head. Astrid, with the danger in remission, was her old self once more. "Did you think it was only a bunch of birds this time?"

Oscar judged himself sufficiently shaken to excuse a lack of response. When next he knew, Astrid was heaving the barn door open. The sun was down, the wind was up, and a thin blanket of snow reflected a full moon among the shrinking clouds. "It's beginning to look like Christmas," she mused, with atypical bleakness.

Neither of them made bold that evening to comment on their harrowing afternoon, but come sunny breakfast time Oscar felt less restrained. "So how do you know that one-eyed guy I saw yesterday?"

Astrid, back in form, blithely ignored the question. "We're in luck. Conditions are ideal for our little expedition. If you don't have a winter coat, you have to dress in layers."

Oscar ultimately needed layers as well as coat to meet with her approval. She professed to be fine with his denim jacket over a bulky sweater. From a narrow kitchen closet she extracted a whisk-broom and stashed it in the deep inside pocket of the jacket. Then they were out in the fresh, dazzling cold.

This foray in short order assumed a tone of Alice in pursuit of white rabbit. Astrid broke into the thicketed forest wall at seeming random and plunged down no visible trail. Had everything been in leaf, the underbrush would have been impassable. Every time he fell behind by ten feet or so, she waited, grim concern creasing her brow and making him feel like a doddering patient. To forestall that look, he tromped at foolhardy pace across the treacherous mix of dry snow and dead leaves. He was in wheezing misery long before she stopped, at no less arbitrary a point than where they'd entered the woods.

A patch of ground, roughly the dimensions of a king-size bed, gently sloped uphill. Astrid impetuously embraced and kissed Oscar, and released him. "Just stand watch while I do this."

She squatted at one corner of the area, took out the whisk-broom, and brushed away leaves with an archaeologist's degree of care, methodically working her way around, straining to reach the center without setting foot past the edge. Oscar hoped that "standing watch" was her idea of busy work.

At ground zero again, she went after the remaining snow even more meticulously, with so light a touch that the bristles made no contact with the underlying dolphin-gray rock. Her breathing grew louder as her concentration increased.

Oscar continued to play sentry, with a growing sense of how fearsome the heart of a true wilderness would be, insofar as this mere glorified woodlot was getting on his nerves. Had Astrid unintentionally planted a suggestion that hidden eyes were upon them? If he had to strike homeward alone, which direction would he go? Oscar frowned at his own cluelessness.

The cold was compelling him to dance from foot to foot when Astrid briskly stood and grasped his arm. She gestured broadly across the exposed outcrop. "Here is where you start to find answers." Astrid's painstaking efforts had removed all snow from the blank surface, while sparing it in thin engraved lines comprising several clusters, casting the lines in white relief. They might as well have stayed under the snow, though, for all that Oscar could read into them.

"Nobody else knows about this place." She used a stick off the forest floor as a pointer. "These sets of incisions that might look like combs or centipedes on their backs represent boats. Sometime later this wheel, which stands for the sun, was superimposed on them. This rock was carved and recarved for centuries, to commemorate, or else influence, events. The armless figures with what appear like tails are soldiers with long swords in belt scabbards." Oscar could see what she was describing while she spoke, but on looking back at any of it, disorder reasserted itself.

"Oscar, pay attention now." She poked the stick toward the right-hand corner. "This you've seen before." Oscar nodded. There was no Babel of petroglyphs here. Ancient man had avoided any association-by-overlay with these chisel marks. The schematic chariot and pair of horses were almost replicas of those at Kiviksgraven or on the kitchen table. Here, however, the charioteer had thrust out both his arms, with giant hands that were each the size of the rest of his body. An implication of aggression or menace was borne out by the placement of a figure running two steps ahead of death by trampling. Crude protuberances in its outline connoted breasts. Behind the chariot followed a procession, in which some rode horses, and others hoisted swords, and a few blew horns that dipped in a U-shape down to chest level and then rose high above their heads. "This is what you heard. This could be your undoing. It's the Hunt. In Sweden we call it the *Odensjakt*."

Plainly she was dead serious. He didn't want to injure her feelings. Or antagonize her out in the pathless wasteland. But how to deal with cherished beliefs at pretty strong odds with reality? "Isn't this three thousand years old?"

"Oh, at least." She was borderline smug about it.

"But didn't you say something about Odin? Even if people here today are descended from the ones who did the carvings, what makes you think they had any of the same gods? That was so long ago, wasn't it?"

Oscar was afraid of pressing his luck with too much critical thinking, but Astrid's eyes were full of love, and patience, and condescension. His heart and mind were hard-set to find common ground. And his feet were swollen and numb. "These circumstances go well beyond your experience. One pantheon may supplant another, but the old gods remain in lesser importance. Or the new gods are the old ones under a new name and guise. Even your Christian saints, in their lives and attributes, may reprise divine pagan forebears."

Crazy or not, dammit, Astrid knew more than he did. His resistance to her arguments was buckling, despite their absurdity. How to choose where to start assailing them? Must have been the cold getting to him. He felt obliged to offer one more objection. "If this is Odin, what's he doing in a chariot? In all the myths I've read, he's never connected with chariots. Is he supposed to be leading this Hunt in one to this day?"

"Chariots have fallen out of style. As have those swords, and those horns." Her eyes followed a black leaf rolling across the outcrop. Was this debate beginning to bore her?

A twig snapped. Oscar checked all around, but discovered nothing. It could have been a small animal. It could have been anything. No reason to think that the entity behind unlikely hidden eyes was making its move! He was about to ask Astrid if they could go home before he froze, but she was gone.

This wasn't funny! What was happening? Should he call her, or was there good cause not to? Till a minute ago, Astrid had been his font of rejuvenation, imparting an energy, an adventurousness he hadn't felt since that summer in the red MG. Could that account in full for why he'd been staying with her, lo these many weeks? Yes or no, in her absence he felt all the younger. Like a lost little boy. What to do? He could only produce sensation in his feet by stamping them very hard. Inaction was not an option. Still, he was too lightheaded for making big decisions. "Emma" had also left him, back in the day, hadn't she? He heard himself mutter, "Mrs. Peel, you're needed."

"Oscar!" shouted Astrid. She was an arm's length away, and then she was hugging him and kissing him all over his face. He let out a long breath as warmth, psychosomatic or not, surged through his bloodstream. "I had to turn away. But it's all right now. Isn't it?"

"I want to go home."

"Yes, of course. Right away." Her face was a millimeter from his. The juniper smell of her skin was intoxicating. "But from now on, although you'll finally stand or fall on your own, I really need you to trust me."

Oscar nodded readily enough. What choice did he have, out in the subarctic middle of nowhere, whether she was crazy or something else? Something worse, perhaps?

The days were becoming oppressively shorter, consigning both breakfast and supper to darkness. Worse, by most lunchtimes galloping masses of dense cloud had dimmed the sun and loosed cold rain or a few inches of snow. Astrid's visits to the cellar were getting longer, prefaced by apologetic, half-intelligible mumblings about "more to do this time of year." They never went any farther from home than the outhouse.

Meanwhile, Astrid was showing more and more affection, but this seemed less their "great leap forward" than a compensation for keeping him indoors, a preventive measure against cabin fever, a diversion from some sinister claimant on his attention out there. They might use up a whole morning or afternoon making out, until her shallow breathing and the way her fingertips pushed into his back signaled that her point of no return was near. Then she fell back upon herself and unhanded him. They were always fully clothed.

Oscar had been better at handling her previous token fondness. Rather more frustrating, to apply the brakes after hours of heavy petting, on a daily basis or more. He was usually giddy with a surplus energy that should have discharged sooner or later, he imagined, through his extremities as blue lightning. But he was loath to plummet from grace by doing anything ungentlemanly, and she'd promised to be his if he stayed beyond Christmas. So why would he up and leave now?

Count on Astrid not to run out of surprises! Early on December 12, Oscar awoke when she sat on his bed. Her skin in predawn light was an arrestingly vivid gray, as of beech bark. "I've stretched our provisions as much as possible. We need to go restock once the sun is completely up." She'd used that same weighty tone back in the woods, when entreating him to trust her.

"To Simrishamn?"

"No. Too far today. Kivik."

"What? Out in the spinach? Where they don't have anything?"

She smiled sweetly, stood up, and left the room. Her prepared response to an obvious objection?

They'd lucked into the best weather all month. Bright sun and crisp air stayed with them into Kivik. The "ICA Supermarket" occupied high ground, overlooking choppy, bruised-blue sea in the middle distance. Its counterpart in Simrishamn had been twice as large, but Astrid filled the shopping cart, and emptied Oscar's cash reserves, with similar ease. The state-run liquor system also had an in-store outlet, which ended up with the rest of Oscar's money. Why hadn't they simply come here before, instead of all the way to Simrishamn? Oscar, despite lack of dating expertise, did grasp that skipping some questions was helpful in most relationships.

In the course of shopping he'd noticed special displays for stubby candles, and stylized goats made of wood or wicker, and yellow buns called *Lussekatter*, and pink marzipan pigs in sundry poses and sizes, and a stack of remaindered Advent calendars. Apparently Yuletide with its singular array of artifacts was under way everywhere in Sweden but the farm. Waiting for their number to come up in the liquor outlet, Oscar recklessly asked, "So do people do anything special here for Christmas?"

"Oh, yes. Lots of things," she readily answered.

"What do you like to do?"

"Nothing," she said just as cheerfully.

He didn't know where to go from there. They were still some numbers away from seeing service, and Astrid probably had esoteric, time-consuming requests for the clerk. Oscar handed her the wallet and said he'd go move their groceries from shopping cart to trunk.

As he wheeled the cart out past the automatic door, he stopped and did a classic double-take. Yes, this really was the goon with stringy blond hair from the flea market, in winter wear of pea coat and combat boots. He was ripping down a flyer taped to the plate-glass wall, and furtive didn't suit him any better than aggressive had. No hope of turning aside this time before the guy caught him staring! The goony Aryan stood his ground and put on his best poker face, perhaps wary of causing a scene and making himself conspicuous. Narrow eyes under heavy brows appraised Oscar, and then, holding out the crumpled flyer but not unballing it, he said, "It's out of date." In English.

Jeez, thought Oscar, is it that easy to peg me as an American? Oscar gave a nod and pushed the cart along, without looking back.

When he finished loading the trunk, he went back inside and helped Astrid with the plastic bags bulging with bottles. He saw little point in mentioning the Aryan. No telling sometimes what would upset her.

The afternoon devolved into their most athletic foreplay yet. Meager exaggeration to call it grueling. A marathon. As if she meant to wear him out. And afterwards, no time for a nap. She wanted his help cooking dinner. No, they shouldn't make coffee. It wouldn't go with what they were having. There was a ponderous sausage known as *isterband* that allegedly had no English translation, and pickled beets in a magenta cream sauce, and boiled potatoes, also in a cream sauce. They washed everything down with two kinds of sweet and potent Christmas beer, and shared another as they washed the dishes.

Oscar, with the detached air of a particular stage of drunkenness, wondered why he wasn't feeling logy by now, and theorized the alcohol hadn't hit him yet. Then in the parlor, she poured him a *mumma* as a special Christmas treat, for this was the eve of the first day of the season leading up to *Jul* on the twenty-fifth. The bottle held well over a pint, and the contents seemed to be a fortified beer, spicier and denser and sweeter than the Christmas beers, maybe a long-lost cousin of wassail. Oscar thought he'd never tasted anything nicer and didn't object to a second one.

While he drank, Astrid explained that in older tradition this was the longest night of the year, when the supernatural was most active, amidst the worst dark before the rebirth of light. Whether or not that was true, she wouldn't recommend going out to gaze at the stars tonight in his condition.

Did she reckon that her *Odensjakt* was out and about? Oscar tried to repay that little jab about being tipsy with a light touch of sarcasm.

Yes, the Hunt was out and about tonight! She listed examples down the centuries, from this date alone, of men crushed under hooves or dragged by their feet or dropped from great heights who had stood in the way or were seized unawares from behind. Or they were conscripted into the Hunt, at devilish whim. And then the situation was not so simple.

Oscar wanted to ask what she meant, but she saw the empty glass in his lap and crooked her finger for him to follow. In the kitchen, she took raisins and raw almonds from a cupboard and heated a whole bottle of apparent red wine in a kettle. She set out two glazed clay cups without handles and undertook a procedure with the almonds and raisins that Oscar lost track of every other second. He thought she referred to this as the holiday favorite *glögg*. Could that be right? Anyway, there was plenty for both of them. His fingers and cheeks and teeth may have grown numb, but he could still appreciate that *glögg* had its merits. They drained their cups and replenished them until the kettle was down to dregs. Oscar regarded Astrid lovingly and asked if all this drinking was because she was worried that the Hunt was after her.

Her eyes upon him had such a depth of sympathy and sorrow that he wanted to cry. Jesus, what had gotten into him? "I'll be fine," she said. "Can you walk?"

Such a silly question! But the effort of standing forced him to admit, "With a little assistance maybe."

She put a big antique porcelain item in front of him. A chamber pot, he surmised. "You'll want to piss in here first. The outhouse is off limits tonight." She studied some scuff marks on the kitchen floor while Oscar complied, proud of his near-perfect accuracy under trying circumstances. Supporting him from behind, she helped him upstairs, one step at a time. She was strong for her size, wasn't she? He fell into bed and into a sleep from which nothing was about to stir him till tomorrow. Secure from all alarms. Just before he passed out, he saw Astrid standing with her back to the bed, facing toward the skylight, as if on guard duty.

Oscar awoke to the smell of coffee downstairs. He cautiously sat up and swung his legs off the edge of the bed. He planted his feet on the floor. He was groggy all right, and slow, and a little shaky, but no headache! No nausea. A Christmas miracle already!

The outhouse had better not be out of bounds this morning. He very gingerly trod down the stairs. Astrid wasn't in the kitchen, and the cellar door was open. He moved no closer to the doorway, but whatever was audible from where he'd paused, well, that seemed like fair game. The creak of a bed, the wringing of a wet towel into a pail of water, the dabbing of towel upon flesh, soft talk from her as to a child or as if she were a nurse, and a dry, cracked attempt at a groan by someone with lockjaw, may or may not have been apt interpretations of what he heard. He began to feel himself getting spooked, his mind shrinking back within his quivering eggshell of a body, so he turned on his heel and went out as fast as hungover legs could carry him. Granted, he'd been dishonoring only the spirit and not the letter of his taboo against snooping, but needless derailment of his one approach to love in decades would be stupid.

On the latrine, last night's rich food and copious alcohol caught up to him with a vengeance. He was detained long enough for the cold to get under his shivering skin. Did people actually use these facilities all winter?

He emerged to encounter a weathered, grizzled hulk of a man, who somehow violated Oscar's personal space despite standing a good ten feet away. He wore a bulky black cable sweater and black wool cap, and muddy hip boots. And at second glance, an eyepatch, its blackness merging with that of the cap. People around here seemed unusually prone to eye injuries. Parked in the driveway was a dilapidated white van that may have belonged to a bakery in the 1950s. Now it was badly dented and covered in brown streaks and spatters.

"I'm here to muck out your shithouse." His voice was gravelly but disarmingly hushed. "You have to get it done before everything freezes. Or it'll pile up right to the top till spring thaw. You don't want that." He grinned. Another old guy with healthy choppers!

Oscar hadn't said anything yet. He cleared his throat and asked, "How did you know I was an American?"

"From the way you looked at me!" The outhouse man let out a coarse laugh and started back to the van, but with a semblance of afterthought turned and held out a flyer. "Just in case," he said, and shook it insistently a few times before Oscar stepped forward and accepted it.

The outhouse man disappeared into the back of his vehicle and began banging around. The paper was in Swedish, but laid out exactly like a missing-persons flyer anywhere. The underexposed photo was of the annoying girl with the green SUV, several weeks ago at Kiviksgraven. Huh! She might have been completely obnoxious, but too bad anyway about whatever had happened to her. He folded the paper in four and stuck it in his rear left pocket.

Astrid was in the kitchen scrambling eggs and frying potatoes in a cast iron pan. A cup of coffee waited for him on the table. "I'm sorry to take so long down there." Why did she sound so solemn? "You'll feel better after you eat." She tipped everything from the pan onto his plate.

"Aren't you having any?"

"Maybe later."

Something was bothering her, and that in turn made him anxious about what to say, or not. In due course, the outhouse man came back to mind. Was he paid in advance, Oscar asked, or would they have to scrape together some cash?

Wrong thing to say! Astrid gasped in agitation. "I hired nobody for that!"

She raced out the back door, and Oscar trailed behind, sorry to have opened his mouth at all. The van was gone. Whatever else was afoot, Oscar suspected that nothing had been done about the out-house buildup.

"Was he missing an eye?" Astrid scanned the woods behind the barn, then homed in on Oscar. He nodded.

She rushed back inside. Into the cellar. Up again in a minute. Ashen face downcast, the weight of defeat upon her shoulders, slow-ing her down. She sat at the table and sighed dejectedly. It behooved Oscar, for once, to come hold her reassuringly. He sensed no tension. Rather, she was drained, inert. "They've killed him." She spoke in a deathly monotone.

"Who killed him? Who did they kill?"

"I guess he just wasn't good enough."

"Good enough? For what?"

She sighed bleakly again. Lifted her face toward Oscar's. It re-minded him of a desolate full moon. "You remember in the woods, how you gave your word to trust me?"

Oscar nodded as readily, and haplessly, as on that day.

"You have to honor that now." She had slipped her hands over his, and then she was up out of the chair and holding him. Pressing upon him a long, sad, yearning kiss. "Sit down now and finish eating," she urged. "Your appetite may soon desert you for a while."

Not an auspicious sentiment. Oscar took it at face value and cleaned his plate. At the last mouthful, he surveyed the room. She'd vanished, and from below rose squeaks and thumpings. He entered the cellar with trepidation, as if it were another world. A 25-watt bulb glowed from the ceiling. Shelves of garden and household supplies lined one wall, and a white freezer, in the proportions of an ancient Roman sarcophagus, abutted the opposite wall. In the middle, at the end of a diffuse shaft of light through a dusty rectangular window, was a single bed, from which Astrid had dragged the sheet and the body that had been on the sheet. She eyed him beseechingly. "This is all happening too soon. Too much at once. I'm not ready." Desperation he had seen before, but Astrid in over her head? Could that be? That was as shocking as anything else down here.

The corpse lay in the sheet on the floor, limbs askew, like a dazed victim of hammock collapse. Its bald crown was about a foot from the bottom step. The body was blackish blue, naked from the waist up, sunken and desiccated as from long cold storage. Oscar avoided the face.

"Pick up the end of the sheet near you. We have to carry him out and bury him. This is going to take all day."

Oscar knew he'd help her, but couldn't bring himself to move yet. "I thought you said he'd just died."

"Yes." She brushed red hair from her eyes. "When the Hunt executes them, the body becomes the way it would if it had died the day of being taken. And it's also from being so long in the upper atmosphere."

Oscar stooped and gathered his end of the sheet in both hands. Best to start getting this over with. Then decide what to do from there. Talking to her would not help clarify their predicament.

He'd always heard that corpses were a lot of dead weight, so to speak. Astonishingly, this one was flimsy. As if freeze-dried. And was that the glint of frost on blue flesh, and steam of condensation like tiny smoke signals from the torso? Cold, moreover, had spread across the linen and into Oscar's fingers. He didn't have to be told, on reaching the kitchen, that their objective was the Volvo. The sooner he could let go of this cadaver, and all the riddles its icy condition posed, the better.

Had they really taken the car out only yesterday? And if Astrid were complaining of too much too soon, how was Oscar supposed to cope? It was only 10 A.M.! On the count of three, they swung the sheet and its sickening load into the trunk. Thank God dead limbs folded to fit inside, and without Astrid needing Oscar's help. Neither rigor mortis nor stench had set in, and who cared how unnatural that was? He warmed up the engine while she angled shovels and other clanking tools across the back seat and chucked in some work gloves. They drove off under darkening overcast.

Barely out of the driveway, she sent them down a bumpy, rutted lane almost as overgrown as the path they'd followed to Kiviks-graven. Small wonder he'd never seen it before. "I have somewhere in mind. Narrow roads will be safer," she explained.

Their tangled way ended at an intersection with a twisty ribbon of stony dirt that might have been a cow path. It meandered through meadow reverting to forest. "Maybe you should tell me something about the guy in the trunk," Oscar suggested. He missed "Emma" this morning more than he had since her death, though her real name at this rate would never recur to him.

"I was his caretaker." She looked straight ahead, and her tone was subdued.

"You mean of his house? Or of him?"

She favored him with a brief smile. As if giving him credit for getting something right. First time for that! But in oblique response at best, she said, "A man can be participating in the Hunt without knowing it. In your country as much as anywhere."

"And the man who owned your house? Was he participating, as you say, when you met him? How did he end up like he is now?" The cow path paralleled and then merged with a dirt road into more mature woods.

"After they seized his spirit, it could have ended with releasing him instead of destroying him. Sometimes it does. I helped him as long as I could." She was looking out her side window, showing him the back of her head.

"So now we're just going to dump him in some unmarked grave?" Oscar wasn't angry. He didn't know what he was anymore. Apart from amazed at getting a more or less direct answer from her a second ago.

She regarded him as if he were simple after all. "Hallowed ground would reject him. We will handle him with respect." Their route continued unpaved but had become smoother, with a ditch along both sides. To the left, the terrain resembled Stone Head Park, and to the right, a screen of trees blocked grassy fields. Was this a service road for forest rangers and such?

"You're not worried about what the Hunt might do to you?"

"Me they have given up on." She had returned to watching the scenery out her window. "Slow down now. Pull over. Not too near the ditch."

The fields behind the windbreak trees had begun to seem familiar, but belonged to so typical a landscape that Oscar didn't make too much of it. That is, until they'd crossed the ditch and entered the open ground with their problem invisibly cocooned inside the sheet, and with the items from the back seat crisscrossed on top. Straight ahead loomed the clump of trees where Oscar had once hidden his campsite. Did Astrid know they were on the one-eyed codger's land? He debated saying something, then voted no, for the sake of finishing their morbid business without risk of delay.

Oscar's roaming eye while en route flushed out no lurking enemies, but caught the first flakes of snowfall. Within the copse, they lowered their burden behind the rocks that had shielded Oscar's tent from passersby. Flurries in progress created a third layer of concealment, after vegetable and mineral. So far, so good! Then on went the gloves, and as Astrid flexed the body into more compact fetal position before it stiffened, Oscar attacked the uppermost stones where Astrid decreed the plot should be. Some rolled aside with a gentle push, some took prying apart with a crowbar, and many had to be worked loose from packed soil and levered free with a shovel. Astrid soon joined him, and by the time an inch of snow lay outside their muddy work area they had backaches, sore muscles, clammy shirts under grimy coats, and a pit roughly three feet deep.

"I will place the body," Astrid stated.

"Already?" asked Oscar, uninterested though he was in quarrying any further. "Is this going to work, without digging a foot or two deeper?"

"He'll stay dead," Astrid assured him. "Not a chance he'll try breaking out and giving us trouble."

Oscar opened his mouth to tell her he was more worried about someone stumbling upon the body, but let it pass. In Astrid's world, legal consequences had all the reality that vindictive ghosts had in his. He shut his mouth. Not that Astrid was paying any mind.

"You should rest a while," she said. "Let me be alone here, and when you see me at work again, then you can come and help. A cairn should suit him well."

"I didn't know him." Oscar felt foolish pointing this out and beat a weary retreat to the car. The snow was sifting in over his hiking shoes.

He cleared off a corner of the hood and sat there. The passenger seat would have been too claustrophobic. On the edge of audibility, an angry whine got his attention. Was the Hunt on to them? No, this was different. Where was it coming from? It was already louder, still some distance up the road, from what he guessed was the direction of Kivik. He squinted into the flurry. He identified the squeal of tires and screech of brakes an instant before a juggernaut burst into view, and then Oscar was diving for his life, into the ditch and scrambling up the other side, as the vehicle skidded from one side of the road to the other and clipped the corner of the car where he'd been sitting, spun the Volvo at right angle to its former position, and slid back across the road to hop the ditch and straddle it, stuck there, wheels slowing in midair. The goddamn green SUV! The girl leapt out into the ditch. No obvious injuries. At least she'd had the sense to wear her seatbelt.

"You bloody idiot! You almost killed me!" he hollered, staggering with wobbly knees back to the roadside, grimacing at broken Volvo headlight, before he took inventory of the girl's ravaged and filthy face, hair, and clothes, that same outfit, in fact, as back at Kiviks-graven. He knocked off scraps of snow that clung to his coat and trousers, and in the process nicked a dog-ear of the missing-persons flyer in his back pocket. He pulled it out and unfolded it. She was wearing that leather-and-fur jacket in the bad photo too, but was younger-looking there. Hardly old enough to be behind the wheel.

All at once she was in his face, shaking his arm, jabbing a finger at the Volvo, and making demands. These were in Swedish with some indefinable accent, and in the torrent of verbiage he parsed the phrase "Give me your car." At last, someone who didn't realize right off the bat that he was American! And after he'd bitched at her in English, at that!

"I can't just give you the car." Nor could he invite her to hang around with them while they disposed of a cadaver.

"Give me the keys, you stupid American! I have to get out of here!" Not one to waste time on ingratiation, was she? He couldn't place her accent based on her English, either.

"No. I can't go anywhere now." He didn't like her. She was plainly in a bad way, but that didn't make her any more likable. Nothing to do with wherever she came from. He just didn't like her, dating back to that first brush with her loud arrogance, her sense of entitlement, all those things and more from which he'd fled, and which his adopted country didn't need any more of, thank you.

She grabbed his shoulders and shook him, cursing in her mystery language, and thrust her hands into his coat pockets, rummaging for the car keys. He shoved her away, and one of her arms flew up and scratched him on the cheek as she slipped backward and sat down in the road.

"I sure as hell wasn't the one who crashed your damn SUV driving like a lunatic." He had no idea how she was going to get out of whatever mess she was in. And at present, didn't care. The flyer had somehow remained in his gloved hand. He let it fall and dabbed a gob of blood off his stinging cheek with a handkerchief. She still sat in the road, and they glared daggers at each other. What would Astrid do here? What was she doing this minute? She must have heard the accident.

Oscar snorted derisively and started toward the clump of trees. Just because he put his own crisis at the top of his to-do list, that didn't mean he was anything like the Aryan goon. Absolutely not.

Speak of the devil! With extraordinary stealth for their size, a Buick Electra, a Galaxie, and an Impala, all from the mid-'60s or so, had eased to an expert standstill, the first in line idling where the SUV had started its skid into the Volvo. All three cars were black like hearses and in beautiful condition. The hawk-nosed blond threw open the driver's door in the Electra, and the other drivers and passengers, all blond and scruffy, followed his lead. The girl was up and running. In midflight she shoved Oscar and spat "Fuck you!" Then she was over the ditch and in the woods, lost among the trees. Oscar was about to topple into the ditch on his side of the road when the Aryan goon clutched his sleeve and steadied him. While the dozen or so others streamed around them and into the forest, the goon paused only to say, "Thanks. We'll take it from here." Then he joined the chase. Oscar couldn't help cracking a smile in spite of everything, but quashed it out of a sense of decency. We'll take it from here? Did those oafs memorize vintage American cop shows? Now that the girl was gone, he hoped that she'd escape somehow. Meanwhile, the silence in the clump of trees puzzled him, and he hurried to investigate.

Astrid was sitting on top of a finished cairn, the height of a gazebo. Fixated on his approach. Bottomless disappointment and pity were chiseled into her face. Implacable as a wooden idol. Something in her look stopped him at the edge of the copse. Doubtful that she was in any mood to tell him how that rockpile had risen so fast. What was wrong with her?

"I've tried to keep you from it, but you've been part of it all along." Her tone was unbearably mournful. Her arm rose, and her finger wavered in the direction of his cheek. "I can smell it in your blood from here. I'm so sorry."

Wait, people said that about the deceased at a funeral! In his hour of need, from his own ancient history, sprang the words of the other great doomed love of his life and, at least by comparison, the voice of reason. To the effect that tainted blood was bullshit. No scientific basis. Even if she hadn't totally convinced him. Then or now. But his chance to speak had lapsed, because behind him, in the field, someone bellowed, "Tally ho! To the hunt we go! Now we're on the high road!"

Beaten to the punch by another quote from another voice from that same day! He jerked around with all the deliberation of a severed limb in galvanic shock. Stark against the snowfall, an immense black procession snaked back and forth through the field. It didn't end so much as it became blurrier and blurrier toward the roadside screen of trees, until it faded away into someplace else, outside waking experience. And it was still arriving, still crowding more densely into the field. What you'd pretty much expect from three millennia's worth of conscription.

Some were on horseback, and some on foot, all mobbed together, and though the horses were galloping, the footmen on the slow march were keeping up without difficulty. In the hindmost ranks before individual outlines became fuzzy, a man in plaid flannel stood out from the black breastplates and cloaks and tunics. He looked about Oscar's age, and damned if he didn't look a lot like Oscar. He hoisted a World War II–era rifle over his head in salute, but didn't make a sound. Nobody made a sound yet, right down to the brutish black mastiffs baring their teeth and snapping at each other. Some whey-faced adolescents in gray dusters also looked familiar, maybe from the evening news of the last ten years, but Oscar couldn't be bothered with them now. He was relieved that "Emma" didn't seem to be in the troop. Probably no girls allowed.

At the head of the teeming company was the decrepit landowner with the black lens, and with beanpole arms that shouldn't have been up to the task, he was reining in an ornery black stallion. Then Oscar's eyes repeatedly lost focus or were drawn aside without his input, and at each new sight of the presiding rider, and always as if through turbid water or vaselined glass, Oscar beheld the outhouse man, or someone gaunt, or stout, or hooded, or in archaic helmet and chain mail, or fatherly, or devilish, or with beard and slouch hat, or with crooked neck and dead eyes and black, protruding tongue. Always shifting between one form and another. The rider leaned forward in the saddle, metamorphosing all the while. "Young Oscar Wright! How refreshing you are, compared with your younger countrymen among us, those preening children, always petulant! I'm not sure how much longer I'll be able to stand them. But you're a young man of promise! I see some of your Uncle Orson in you." Was that praise? How to trust these words any more than any one of their speaker's appearances? The rider bared his teeth and leaned so far out that his nose was next to his horse's. "Welcome!"

Oscar was sitting on an unruly black horse, controlling it with the reins as if he'd ridden all his life. Hey, his own horse, and at the front of the pack! He already rated better than his footsore uncle, and how long ago had Orson joined the Hunt? But there he also was, standing on the same spot where he'd last been, and then he saw himself collapse in a dead faint, and Astrid come running to him from the clump of trees. Good old Astrid. He had a place in her heart after all. She squatted over him and cradled his insensible head in her hands, and he wished he could feel her doing that, and she cried, "Why can't you let me have anybody?"

The mutable rider was leering at her. "If I can't catch you, I can still catch them!"

He lifted a spear with a rusty, many-barbed iron head. A deafening, ragged cheer, and atonal fanfare, and canine howling went up from the multitude. They were off, and Oscar with them, though many of the more seasoned and skeletal black-clad huntsmen quickly overtook him.

And so he rides around and around the world, upon the ground or across the sky, without rest or reflection, always spent and always going full tilt. Often at the same elevation as when he'd wished his plane to Stockholm would stay aloft forever. Back when he'd ruled out the prospect of any more major trips. Hell, what had he known then?

No chance to converse with, or even catch sight of, Uncle Orson. And the noise! But he knows better than to complain. Wherever they go, there's violence. Not that there isn't plenty elsewhere, but in their wake, it's worse than it would have been. If they're on the trail of any particular prey, Oscar never hears about it. Maybe there isn't any. Maybe there couldn't be, if it's to be a Hunt in perpetuity. Only a chase without quarry is guaranteed never to end.

Sometimes they swoop over Kivik, and from whatever altitude Oscar can look down and see the Aryan goons, whom the Hunt is pleased to leave on their own, and he sees Astrid caring for him. In the cellar, where he'll stay fresher. Bathing him, grooming him, soothing his outbreaks of fever, chafing his face and limbs when stratospheric cold starts to blacken them. Much as she had for his predecessor. Except that her final words, not quite eradicated by the roar of the Hunt as it spurred forward, return to provide his only comfort, and one that her previous consort hadn't enjoyed. Or so he assumes. "If he releases you, we will be as we were!" Something to look forward to! The one thing that saves him from going as mad as everyone around him! So he tells himself, with an exultant cackle.

And on these occasions, when he happens to face forward, he's both disconcerted and gratified that the lead rider is mindful enough of Oscar to turn amorphous head toward him and vent an exultant cackle, very much an amplified echo of his own, but whether in mockery or approval, it's impossible for Oscar to say.

The Lord of the Animals

The neighbors' backyard I counted as an oasis, and rightly so. Without, for months, understanding in how many senses. Or that this was not an entirely idyllic thing. Most yards front and back around here, including my rented own, are penny-ante Versailles wannabes. Orderly, trim, a lot of unnatural right angles, devoid of personality. A cookie-cutter product of pricy landscape services.

From my upstairs bathroom, on the other hand, the standard 500 square feet behind the Colonial Revival next door looked far more inviting. As densely green as possible, without being tangled or overgrown. Scotch pines, poplars, birches gave the impression of transplanted forest, with dogwood and azalea and honeysuckle bushes getting what sun the trees spared, along with atolls of cosmos and hollyhocks and less familiar flowers. Flagstone paths followed as organic a pattern as any of the branching vegetation, and somehow a couple of grassy runways withstood encroachment. Garage walls and palisade fences were almost lost within rose and clematis and trumpet vines, in which birds and squirrels and bumblebees were only the most conspicuous fauna. A single serving of paradise! At the houseward edge of the yard, a couple of metal lawn chairs, painted white, sounded the only false notes in the orchestration.

I craved that restful view on many an overbooked day and evening, as my eight-month contract at the School of Design ticked away. I was "guest faculty" in their Art History Program. Lecturer in a couple of courses, part-time guide in the museum, co-instructor in night classes, and, to wring the last drops out of the school's investment in me, teacher of pre-collegiates in Summer Sessions. On paper, my workload hadn't seemed so onerous. And even if it had, my quest for solvency would have ensured my name on the dotted line. At least the school was springing for the rent on this house, whose owner, a regular faculty member, was enjoying a year's sabbatical.

The woodsy prospect next door also eased my homesickness, and my concerns about Pam and the twins getting along without me. She had her career, and the kids had their friends and school, from which they preferred not to be uprooted while I did my best toward making ends meet. They had their lives, and I had this.

As for the neighbors per se, I'd seen the lady of the house exiting her front door once or twice in my first week, and the man a number of times in those first ostensibly straightforward months. To the naked eye, nothing noteworthy about him. Average height, average build, middle-aged, short brown hair parted on the left, nothing unusual in the size or placement of any facial features, nothing colorful or eccentric about his clothes.

All sightings of him were out back, starting in late winter, when trees were leafless and the ground was frozen, until spring thaw released pale green shoots from the soil en masse. He was never without a big mutt, black with white blaze on head and chest, and white-tipped tail, and white feet up to boot level. Big floppy ears and a houndish snout. Maybe part Lab, part Dane, part Dalmatian, impossible to peg, but very handsome and alert. The dog was as distinctive as the man was ordinary. They were in ongoing eye contact, and the dog was excellent at communicating, and getting, what he wanted. At canine urging, they played fetch with a well-chewed red plastic ball, and the man was always ready to leave off long before the dog. And when the man deemed playtime over, the dog commenced a more willful game of sitting in the shadow of the back fence till the man tossed a piece of biscuit from the middle of the yard toward the door, and before the man could collar the dog and bring him in, the dog had gobbled the morsel and dashed back out of reach. This went on for four or five rounds, but the man's annoyance wasn't convincing. I sensed a brotherly connection between them, and the dog always acted as if he understood what his human was saying. To this day I don't know the man's name, but I overheard him calling the dog Diesel.

At other times, when the dog was sniffing around or snoozing briefly in the sun, the man would stand there, observing, thinking, spacing out, I supposed. In short order, sparrows, robins, and cardinals would land at his feet and peck at the dirt. Squirrels regarded him fearlessly from atop the picket fence between his yard and driveway and came running close circles around him till Diesel chased them off. Once a hummingbird perched on his shoulder, and a mouse gnawed on his shoelaces. The man betrayed no emotion in these moments, and indulged only tiny adjustments of neck muscles for the sake of a better look. On this little square plot of nature, he accepted rapport with wildlife as matter-of-factly as rapport with his beloved Diesel. I can't remember where I'd heard or read the name, but I found myself thinking of this man as Lord of the Animals. No sarcasm intended.

One April afternoon I was out in my minimal backyard of lawn and pachysandra borders, busting up some deadwood that last night's windstorm had shaken from juniper boughs hanging over the rear fence. Above the barberry hedge between our premises, I spotted Lord of the Animals in a contemplative stance. I hailed him, and we fell into conversation with no sign from him that I'd impinged on his woolgathering. Diesel barked once in a show of territoriality, and then sat and watched me indifferently.

My neighbor worked at home. Wrote ad copy. Wasn't proud of it and did no more than expenses demanded. His wife had a "real" job at the School of Design. Something administrative. He asked what my specialization in art history was, and I told him twentieth-century American. He professed to like Edward Hopper, and we talked about that for a minute. I complimented him on what I termed an "empathy" with the animal kingdom. He shrugged dismissively. Cast diffident eyes earthward. "I don't know, guess it's a matter of keeping still. Surprising what you can see the longer you keep still, and what will come to you when you're seen as no kind of threat." That struck me as simplistic, but I nodded agreeably. Diesel arfed and planted a paw against the man's leg. He asked the dog what he wanted, and I let them get back to playtime.

After this exchange, weeks ensued of no contact with, or sight of, the Lord of the Animals. On-campus demands and half-hearted efforts to be sociable at faculty cocktail parties and the like made for hectic and irregular comings and goings. In my spare time, keeping up with the wife and kids was the top priority. Working the phone, so that absence didn't make their hearts grow colder. I felt compelled to stay on top of developments, and add my input, on the home front. Didn't want them to miss me too much, of course. Or too little, which would have been rather worse. Couldn't tell from a distance if they no more than tolerated my disembodied influence. If they really had to hang up and get going when they said they did. Welcome to breadwinner limbo!

By mid-May I was grading final exams and getting started on student evaluations. Never mind how low an opinion I'd had of the semester so far. This was absolutely the pits. The world was obviously sunnier the farther away I stepped from my desk. I resorted to that upstairs bathroom window. Needing to see the tranquil little wilderness, the peaceable kingdom in miniature, a portrait of nature in harmony. Instead, the Lord of the Animals was pacing obsessively up and down the grassy stretch, crying uncontrollably, calling Diesel's name with no hope of response and howling like a dog himself. I couldn't help shedding a few tears of second-hand grief. Poor guy! Poor Diesel! The dog had seemed fine a month ago, graying in the muzzle maybe. Nothing to warn of death at hand. But what could I do beyond respecting his privacy until he got the sorrow out of his system? Hands-off appeared to be the general neighborhood policy.

A month went by, and no letup on the horizon. He was out back whenever I looked. Carrying on with undiminished force. Back and forth as if caged. Sobbing, wailing, calling Diesel in vain. Even if he never crossed the line and tried hurting himself, this couldn't be good for him. I wasn't sure how long I could stand it, either. Where was his wife? Or had she given up?

At last I had to grit my teeth and admit it was incumbent on me to run the push mower over the seedy grass in my backyard. With fingers crossed that he'd be too bleary-eyed to notice me. But no sooner had I dragged mower from garage than the Lord of the Animals hallooed from his side of the hedge.

"I don't know if you were aware of it, but poor Diesel died," he said, laboring imperfectly to keep his voice from cracking.

I mumbled something to the effect of how sorry I was and hesitated to ask about cause of death, in case that loosed more weeping and gnashing of teeth. But his mind was already off and running in its own direction.

"You never got to see how smart he really was. Once we had some friends over, and one of them had one of Diesel's toys and was playing a little too rough with him. Diesel didn't like it, so he picked up the toy and walked over to his toy chest and dropped it in. I'd never seen a dog do anything like that before."

Me neither, I confessed, and then I could see he was about to lose it again, so I offered hasty condolences and said I had yard work to do. I kept my head down till the lawn was half-mowed, and at sidelong glance over the hedge the Lord of the Animals was gone.

For the first two weeks of summer session, I made a point of avoiding the upstairs windows. Then, as had to happen sometime, my eyes strayed toward motions in the neighbors' sunny yard and, dumb-founded, I dropped my electric razor in the sink. The Lord of the Animals was outside, and he was throwing the red ball for Diesel. As if nothing had ever happened. Or as if time within the yard had skipped back to April. Except that the plants were in full summer bloom. This was more disturbing than the raw, nonstop grieving from which I'd had to retreat. Although, on the face of it, a happy Lord of the Animals and an extant Diesel were better than the alternatives. Had Diesel's demise been some ugly sort of hoax? Had a surrogate turned up at the pound? Something was really askew here. I was more leery of dealing with my neighbor now than when distress echoed from the trees.

Around this juncture, a look at the calendar afforded me the first jubilation I'd felt all year. Three weeks to go! Servitude at an end, family reunited, rightful order restored! No more next-door enigmas! Back to pounding the pavement? I could join the crowd and stress about that when the time came.

In my new, improved frame of mind, I was strolling back from class one suppertime and beheld the rare sight of the neighbor lady out front, tending some hydrangeas and cone flowers and ornamental grasses. I extended a cheerful greeting, praised her gardening, and asked if she'd just returned from some travels.

Her brow furrowed and she shook her head. No, she hadn't been anywhere in a few years. She'd been around the whole while that I'd been subletting.

Oh. I conjectured that we must have been on pretty divergent timetables, then, since we'd never bumped into each other.

Her look became more confused, a little guarded. Why no, she'd waved at me from out back any number of times while I was gaping out the window. But I never waved back, so she gave up, concluding I was distracted or near-sighted. I winced at her casual euphemisms for "rude."

So now she had me at a loss, and after some inner flailing about for anything to say, I stammered, "Well, you must be happy anyway that Diesel's in good health again."

She was profoundly taken aback at this. I'd hit a nerve, hadn't I? "I'm sure I don't know what you mean. Diesel died three years ago."

Her ashen face shut me up after I'd started to blurt, "But I saw your husband—"

"I don't know who you saw. But my husband had very high blood pressure. And he was so upset all the time after Diesel died that he had a stroke a month or so later. I was at the market when it happened. By the time I came home he was gone." Her jaw was tight-set. Hostility in her eyes.

I told her how sorry I was, and no exaggeration, either. Apology not accepted. After a cold stare at me for a little longer, she resumed weeding. Come to think of it, nondescript as both she and her husband were, she differed from him in seeming a bit older. Which made sense if he'd died three years ago. Nothing else was making sense at this stage.

Three weeks was suddenly too long to be sticking around. Did these wheels of the apparent supernatural turn at a constant rate? Or would the remaining time suffice for the whole morbid train of events to enter another cycle? And what about all the sociable critters? All those birds and bees? What were they? The Lord of the Animals had spoken of "keeping still" as his means of drawing them to him. Did "keeping still" account for my own unwanted perceptiveness, in the sense of how I was living, or not living, my life? Right or wrong, I had to answer yes, to stave off the question of why I had to be the one to see that deceased man and his dead dog.

I had an overriding urge to rejoin my family before it was somehow too late, but in the cool of the dusk, I realized that early exodus, and any forfeiture of my stipend, would only mark me as unstable, all the more unfit. An even worse excuse for head of a household. No, I had to tough it out. Not as if I were in any physical danger.

At bedtime, though, I had to spoil everything with a careless glimpse. Halfway through brushing my teeth. The white lawn chairs had always been vacant. But tonight the neighbor lady was occupying one of them. Surveying her beautiful oasis. An oasis for much more than diverse flora and short-lived creatures. If she only knew! Judging by her posture, she was weighed down, inert within herself. I thoroughly regretted whatever I'd added to her present depression. She gave no indication of seeing her husband and Diesel directly in front of her, getting in some last fetch for the day. Husband and wife in the same backyard. But in mutually exclusive worlds.

He pried the ball out of Diesel's stubborn jaws, and slick with dog drool, it slipped from his grasp and bounced toward the widow. She may have waved away a gnat or something while the phantom ball bounced off the arm of her chair. Or she may have caught the ball and tossed it listlessly back to Diesel. Too dusky to tell. The strength went out of me, and I lost hold of myself for a second. My toothbrush clattered against the tile floor.

Whatever was really going on in that house, I decided at that instant to get the hell away from it. Maybe the school could find me other accommodations. If I were extremely lucky, nobody would press too hard for a reason. At worst, living in my car for the duration would be okay. I was fearful mostly that events here amounted to oblique foreshadowing that I was as good as a ghost at home already. For the time being, be it hours or days, I pulled all the shades on that side of the house and emptied the linen closet, nailing bedsheets over all the window frames. The homeowners might well understand. Or else they wouldn't. I didn't care. Meanwhile, I had to envy the Lord of the Animals in a way. There was no one else I could name who, despite heartbreaking reversals, would always be happy again.

The Salvage Saints

He saw the body face down in the tidal pool and indulged a moment's optimism. To strike gold minutes from his doorstep, after ranging all the way out and back! Sand grated between his feet and sandals as he clambered down the dune, across narrow, kelp-strewn beach and onto the slick rocks. He cautiously wedged his ash-wood staff under the body at chest level, and as he levered it over, the water churned violently with little scavengers vanishing into cloudy green algae.

His eyes narrowed disdainfully. No use in further reaction. The white mantle may have been old-fashioned Templar, but crabs had been at the face. This was no saint, no more than any of the water-logged corpses he'd ever found. Emil stalked away before the stench lodged in his nostrils.

A voice from the sky accosted him. "Should you only leave him there?" Its accent was Western and uncouth, its wording less than fluent. He surveyed the landward prospect. Beyond the dunes huddled the flat-roofed, whitewashed village. Beyond the village loomed the blockish fortress of the monastery, whose round cupola with conical roof overlooked weedy plaza and surf-worn jetty. In an eyelet window along the hitherto abandoned top course of cells, a head reduced by distance to almond-size was watching.

"No one pays me for a profane carcass!" He didn't care whether his answer carried to the strident, sharp-eyed inmate. His stipend from the abbot scarcely fed him and fell woefully short of inspiring selfless deeds, let alone honesty. He lowered his eyes to the firm sand above the tide line and trudged on.

His territory commenced at the jetty and encompassed four days' beachcombing south, to the outskirts of the next hamlet. The monks themselves covered the ground a half day to the north, where sheer cliffs blocked further foraging. The fee would be lavish were Emil ever to drag back a saint, though paltry compared with what successive handlers would pocket on the long road to Rome, and compared with the profits after holy flesh was authenticated and maybe divided into relics. But Emil, in almost twenty years, had never known occasion to unfold the ingeniously hinged sledge in his rucksack, and had met only two salvagers to claim better luck, truthfully or otherwise. Not like the old days, which were beginning to assume the wan aura of unlikelihood.

The Westerner must have arrived after Emil had left on his rounds over a week ago. If he had joined the order, why was he in isolation? If not, what was he doing here?

A groaning of wheels and harsh chorus of men waylaid further speculation. From behind a dune some fifty yards ahead, four fishermen with arched backs were doggedly pushing the mangonel toward the jetty. Two more pairs out ahead were as strenuously pulling it by thick cables chafing their shoulders. Their song usually accompanied the hauling of nets from a grudging sea, perhaps an easier business than inching ancient siege engine across pebbly ground and loose sand. That time of year already! The throwing arm with its gaping bowl to hold projectiles seemed wobblier than last year, the frame more brittle. According to village legend, which everyone cherished and nobody believed, heroic General Belisarius himself had bequeathed the people this machine after training it upon the walls of Damascus, centuries ago.

Emil couldn't have returned at a worse hour. Should the men catch sight of him, they'd insist on his help. He hastily dropped onto the beach, squirmed out of his rucksack, and used it for a pillow as he relaxed and listened. He closed his eyes against the day's stinging brightness. It was very warm for late October.

On awakening, he briefly mistook screeches of gulls for the tortured grind of sluggish axles. No, the machine stood alone on the jetty, ready for the priest to load on All Saints' Day with clay icon plucked from church niche by luck of the draw. This trick to appease the sea hadn't worked within Emil's lifetime, and he wondered if his neighbors clung to it strictly out of habit, as they clung to their myth about Belisarius.

Emil's first stop was the monastery. The studded double-gates were ajar and probably had been since the men had dragged forth the siege engine. Most of the brethren were out scything the last of the barley. A pockfaced monk with a nasal Bulgarian twang directed Emil to the stables.

Portly, mordant Abbot Clement was scolding a reedy Greek novice for overfeeding the horses. Emil cleared his throat and rummaged from his rucksack a stale little disk of flatbread. It came from the next village, where sour wine in the dough instilled a unique reddish tinge. The abbot withheld payment pending this proof that Emil had trod the entire route and, by gauging the bread's texture between expert fingers, could tell it had been baked this week and not stashed after a previous excursion. Satisfied, though the matter of any outlay visibly pained him, he produced several reasonably intact bronze *nummi* via some sleight-of-hand and thrust them at Emil, and tossed the bread into one of the stalls.

"A foreigner shouted at me from a window right below the tower. Is he going to be joining you?" If Emil took him by surprise, the abbot might just speak frankly.

There was nothing off-guard about Clement's smile. "You have company." He ambled away, deaf to Emil's faltering confusion over what that meant.

The village streets ran downslope haphazardly like channels of rainwater through dusty masonry. So alike as loaves were the houses that Emil bypassed his own because lazy grey curls were rising from the smokehole. Even if he'd left smoldering ashes in the hearth, that had been over a week ago. Then the word "company" popped back into mind, and he swaggered in, clacking his staff on the earthen floor, contriving to intimidate whoever dared impose on him. But nobody was depleting his shelves of dried apricots or dates, or waking up in either far corner on what passed for beds, each a mass of feathers and moss enclosed by a blanket of homespun and an L-shaped brace of planks, well-greased to discourage vermin. Nor was anyone sitting on the stool by the firepit, whose smoke wafted up the sooty back wall and through the chute in the form of flaring half-cone. Was anybody in here? Someone had built a feeble excuse for a fire.

Four poplar trunks, stripped of bark and sealed with olive oil, supported the roof and held pegs to hang things away from the snakes and scorpions that sometimes scouted the floor. Emil blinked in confusion. Someone had been standing all along beside one of the posts nearer the firepit, who did not blend in with the shadows so much as haunted them. His flat-cheeked face had the pallor of a drowned worm, and his eyes were narrow and colorless. Should Emil test the stranger's solidity with a quick jab of the staff? Why did the man, if man this was, keep staring dumbstruck? Aha, the ghost could speak! "Your abbot told me to be at home here. He said you stayed away mostly." The voice was boyishly high but magisterial at the same time. It made Emil uncomfortable. It also suffered from the same accent as that of Clement's sequestered guest.

"And what are you going to do for me? I own this house, and not the damned abbot."

"What is it you want?"

The question gave Emil pause, as if he were bargaining with some capricious spirit of the air, and care was warranted. He pensively rubbed his stubbly beard while sizing up the foreigner's ankle-length white ecclesiastic robe, of an off-puttingly unfamiliar cut. It reinforced the impression of a visitor from beyond the material pale, as did the fine straw-yellow hair that spread limply across bony shoulders and the outlandish cap wadded up in front where a handkerchief was pinned, folded tightly in semblance of a badge and depicting the face of Christ. So what did Emil want? He'd have to reflect further. "Were you going to cook something at my hearth? Aren't you too hot in all that clothing?"

The stranger shook his head. "I always feel cold. The fire was to warm me."

"And what were you going to do for food? Do you propose to eat mine?"

"I will have meals at the monastery. The abbot sent me here because I think somehow he expects me to spy on you."

Emil knew better than to trust such a big, open admission at face value, but thanked the foreigner as if he did, and added, "I want you, then, to get food for me when you go to have yours. Wine, too."

The foreigner nodded thoughtfully. "That satisfies what you want of me?"

Emil shook his head just as thoughtfully. "No, but we'll have to see."

The foreigner beckoned impatiently toward the firepit. "But for now, please, can you make the fire larger?"

Emil's brow furrowed at the mess of smoldering sticks and tinder. It looked as if it had been assembled by a windy day. "You don't build your own fires at home, do you?"

"Innkeepers and servants of my hosts see to it, mostly."

"Not servants of your own?"

"I have none, no. And no home. I am only a humble servant of God."

There was a claim that never rang true. Emil cracked a scornful grin once his back was to the foreigner, to rearrange firewood and fan a blaze that forced him to retreat behind the poplar beams. The stranger eagerly swooped in and hovered over the heat, cupping his hands dangerously close. He neglected to tender any thanks.

"So you're a priest then?" Dislike for this man was taking firm root.

Without turning from the flames, the stranger shook his head emphatically. "I am a pardoner. Do you understand? I enrich the grace of the poor in spirit in exchange for what is in their purse."

"You sell blessings? Salvation?" Emil was amused to learn of a line of religious work more suspect than his own.

"Indulgences, they are called. I carry relics also, to coax wayward souls away from hell."

Emil expelled a skeptical laugh. "I knew a salvager who went on pilgrimage. All the way to the Jordan for a bath. I'll never know why. He kept count of every leg bone in every shrine to Saint George. He said that if they were all genuine, Saint George must have been a giant cockroach."

The pardoner vented a forbearing sigh. "Maybe the clerics at those shrines lacked virtue. Or maybe they lacked a proper skepticism. Either way, the Church is wise to teach that sacraments received from corrupt and greedy clergy will still do good."

"Like the warmth from a badly set fire?"

Rising to the bait was apparently beneath this humble pardoner. He waved a careless left hand toward opposite corners of the room, his face fixated on the blaze. "You have two beds here. Is there family somewhere?"

"In the ground. Pox came on a ship from Venice, years ago. While I was on my rounds." Emil couldn't say why he maintained that second bed and asked himself why only at times like this, when it led to intrusion and nuisance. The pardoner wasted no breath on token condolences, which Emil found both sensible and offensive.

The monastic iron bell tolled lugubriously, but both men instantly brightened. The pardoner withdrew from the fire and clasped his hands together, like a mantis, Emil thought. A glance out slit window at the shadow on his neighbor's wall confirmed the hour. "Don't forget to fill that," he warned, pointing at a kidskin satchel slung onto one of the beds. "And don't take all night. I haven't eaten since morning." The pardoner's bland, nodding acceptance of Emil's gruff demands rendered him even more suspicious.

The villagers fashioned their oil lamps from the thick blue shells of big crabs seized at low tide. Come nightfall, Emil hadn't long to wait before his lamp's orange light guided half a dozen agitated moths and the pardoner through the open door. Without comment, the pardoner let slide the bulging satchel off his shoulder and onto the shaky little table made of wormholed wreckage. Neither man violated the silence till Emil dumped out a half-moon of black bread and a fist-sized chunk of stew meat wrapped in smeary napkin and, dwarfing those two items, a swollen wineskin tooled with an ornate red Maltese cross. The portions, so conducive to inebriation, were not in keeping with a disinterested provider. "What the hell is it you want of me?" Emil snarled.

The pardoner blinked at this outburst, with no loss of poise. "Or what, you may ask, does your abbot want? The generosity was his." Be that as it may, the pardoner was exhaling the fumes of one drink at most. Another cause for mistrust! Emil attacked the food while warily eyeing the pardoner, who waited for him to uncork the wine and wash down a mouthful of salty meat before asking, "The word you have here for the sea is 'hagiophagic,' is it not? Does it mean 'eater of saints?'"

Who didn't know that? "You must have come with that other Westerner in the monastery. For you to be aware of this place at all, how could you be ignorant of the first thing about it?"

The pardoner raised aggrieved eyebrows. "I stepped forward when my bishop called for someone to escort a heretic here, who was to undergo penance until he recanted, as your abbot saw fit. To help absolve the fallen, it is my vocation. What did I need to know of this place beforehand?"

"Why not jail the heretic in his own land? Why go to all this trouble?"

"I was not privy to that. Who am I to question His Eminence? Maybe the merciful bishop thought to redeem the sinner but send him where dangerous error could work least harm."

Gulping wine was easier than bristling at this tactless churchly assessment of his village as expendable. The pardoner watched him drink, affecting the same blank expression with which he'd first regarded Emil. "Did it really happen," he asked at length, "that the sea somehow ate saints?"

"Used to." Again, resorting to the wine was easier than berating the pardoner for posing questions whose answers he must have known. "It was said the waves, once upon a time, washed over the sides of ships and tasted holiness in certain seafarers, and liked it, and swept them overboard. But people only started saying that after the bodies started casting up on these shores. The clothing on them was old, from the Crusades or before. Roman sometimes. And always good as new, except for a few loose stitches. And nobody would have blinked if those bodies had sat up and asked for a towel. No trace of rot on them. They even gave off a fragrance."

"Ah, the odor of sanctity." So the pardoner knew about that, did he? Yet he stood fascinated as if all this were revelation, as if nothing more telltale than a delicate burp had left his mouth. "Then it behooved Roman and Greek Church alike to declare these corpses saints," he murmured, "because they were incorrupt hundreds of years after drowning, and bestow names on them and feast days. Yes, that much is clear. And no saint ever survived a voyage across your sea? Quite a penalty for godliness."

Petulant Emil shrugged. He slumped forward on the stool, and his unmindful grip squeezed a trickle of wine up from the spout. "Saint Nicholas was supposed to be the last to cross this water before it got hungry. A monk somewhere wrote that."

"And the sea still gives up saints for you to salvage? That is your vocation?"

Emil snorted. Vocation? It made him sound like a member of the clergy. "I don't know. The sea's appetites changed before I was born. Nobody can say yet what kind of people it's acquired a taste for. As for saints, the surf spits out so few nowadays. I've never found any."

Emil hadn't noticed the pardoner moving, but there he was, between Emil and the lamp, his face an unhealthier gray in the dimmer light, and with distracting shadows of frantic moths on the wall behind him. For no plain reason, the pardoner's demeanor seemed more severe, as if Emil were holding something back. His words, though, were at variance with his look. "It is my hunch that your luck is due to change. And when it does, let me ask you, does your labor not merit more than a handful of bronze coins and a satchel of scraps?"

Emil had no wish to dispute that, but the idea of luck on the rise sounded like such a hollow jest that he only cleared his throat and let the shadows of moths draw his gaze.

The pardoner carelessly signed "pax vobiscum" and leaned closer. "By the way, did you ever learn to counterfeit the red bread?"

"What kind of stupid question is that?" If he'd been holding anything except a wineskin, he'd have thrown it in the pardoner's smug face. "Do you think I have no shame?" Of course he'd daydreamed about just such fakery, but no, he was hardly clever or ambitious enough.

"Your Abbot Clement bid me ask. To justify giving you the food. Now, please, the fire has died down. Can you rebuild it?"

After a miserable night's sleep, Emil was en route to inform the abbot of his immediate departure on salvage rounds again. Worse than all other vexations about the seemingly delicate pardoner was the very substantial racket of his snoring. The shepherds' hive-shaped stone huts along the foothills above the shore would be especially squalid in this season, but quiet and seldom used, and he also had his choice of bedrooms in a couple of villas unpeopled by that pox from Venice.

Lean and waspish Father Theo was in front of his church, coughing fitfully into the sunny air till he spewed a gob of blood into the dusty weeds. The white plastered church was barely larger than the chapel of a cathedral and had the only pitched roof in the village, and an off-square belfry at the far end that hadn't housed a bell since Emil's childhood. As Emil clacked by, the priest stuck out an arm to detain him. "Ask the abbot if he means to go through with it." The priest's whisper was as conspiratory as it was sickly. Emil acknowledged it by meeting Theo's swollen eyes and pushing on, mystified that some plot had been brewing in his absence, and that he was allegedly wise to it.

Most of the men, making the best of lingering summer, were reduced to the scale of fleas in their bobbing splinters of fishing skiffs, remote on the bright water. Out on the flat roofs, their formidable wives, hanging lines of silver herring to dry, stopped and glared down as Emil passed, as if he were en route to cheating them somehow. Several fragile grandfathers were slowly tugging at the mangonel arm and kicking its wheels to determine its sturdiness, while dirty children stared vacantly.

Emil retraced the mangonel's path of flattened, broken weeds across the plaza, to avoid getting burrs on the brown wool of his knee-length tunic. He scowled before he'd gone halfway. Were midmorning devotions in progress already? From monastic nave echoed the brisker first of forty kyrie eleisons, after which the prayers and psalms were far from over. And today the gates were shut.

He stood in the shade of the wall, hands on hips, peevish, when a crockery bowl exploded against a stone right beside him, and a spatter of pottage struck his naked calf. He skipped backward into sunlight, cursing, craning his neck, ready to dodge, but only words rained down now.

"Do not leave! I feel sick and thought you might not hear me call."

"What do you want?" Emil shouted. The Westerner sounded hale enough.

"Thank you! You did not leave the dead man on the beach after all."

Emil had to think a moment. Oh, the Templar. "High tide took him away! I didn't!"

"Come up to me, please! They pulled the gate but I heard nobody bar it. You can open it."

Nobody intercepted Emil as he climbed the dusky stairwell, monkish chants reverberant in the stones and through his soles. Five flights up, the foreigner obviously waited in that cell with an oaken beam snug in new cast-iron brackets. The square window in the door was only wide enough to admit the bowl that had almost brained Emil. Behind the window loomed the face of the pardoner's countryman, ruddier and better-natured, but with deep blue eyes perhaps too eager for talk. And instead of sensible gray linen and a narrow band of tonsure, he wore smothering black and less barbered hair that clung to the back of his neck. No doubt he was feeling sick in his baking oven of a cell.

"The abbot was charged to cleanse me of error, but he brings food and then goes, and no one else passes here. There may be fear that others will take my revelation to heart. Can I tell it to you?"

Emil gave a half-hearted fraction of a nod, but the stranger trembled with jubilation.

"God does not want us to make sense!" Had Emil heard right, or were Eastern words failing the Westerner? "He does not wish us to be beasts of reason! Do you need an instance? Behold a cathedral. If God desired us to be rational, why is He pleased when we reserve our biggest and most beautiful buildings for Him? He needs no shelter and will never claim the keys to His houses. He has no body of flesh to enter them. Why lavish all the gold and labor on places so useless to Him?"

Emil shook his head obligingly. Here was a giddy madman all right, but was there any reason in what he said? As far as Emil went, all theology was conducted in Turkish.

"The Church teaches that too much curiosity and learning can harm faith and foster the sin of pride," the lunatic expounded. "I only go one more step and reduce reason from a gift to a burden. So why am I here?"

Yes, why banish a mere lunatic when chaining or shunning him would do? Did he know the wrong people in high places? Or did family connections save him from a bloodier end? "I don't know."

True enough! Politics and theology offered equally gristly food for thought, and Emil was relieved to see Clement huffing toward him.

"Your friend here threw a bowl at me. I wanted to tell him what to expect if he ever went outside." At least the madman had the presence of mind not to contradict him.

Clement peered sternly at Emil and pulled him to one side of the door. "Did he try talking to you?"

Emil peered back gravely and tapped his forehead a few times. That seemed to put the abbot more at ease, and then Emil broached his traveling plans.

"Just as well," observed Clement. "Your guest should be gone in a week. By the way, did you take a poke at my friend, as you call him, through the window with that blunt weapon of yours?"

"No, but I came close to bruising my guest, as you call him, when I mistook him for an evil spirit."

Clement nodded serenely, as if that didn't upset him at all. The discussion had run its course, and the abbot, as customary, closed his eyes to ponder worthier matters, without any formal farewell. Emil had put most of the corridor behind him when an afterthought sprang to mind. The abbot was still lingering by the heretic's cell. "The priest wanted to know if you were going through with it!" shouted Emil across the echoing distance.

Clement grimaced toward the listening inmate. Then he spread his arms in a show of perplexity, but his eyes were baleful. "Please ask him what he meant."

As always, Emil squandered too many coins on provisions for the southward patrol: flatbread, salt fish, raisins, almonds. He crossed his threshold, anxious to depart with the least ado possible, but as the pardoner rose from the fireside stool Emil noticed the priest sitting on the left-hand bed. "Why is he here?" Emil asked the pardoner.

"He begged me to come in and stoke the firepit!" Father Theo spoke up. "And now he's full of questions, but how can he stand all that heat? I can't!"

"The abbot is led to believe you are going away? And others think so as well? That is very good for us." The pardoner addressed Emil, ignoring priestly distress. "The wheel of your fortune is already in the ascent."

"Why is he here?" repeated Emil.

The pardoner withheld any emotion from his colorless face. "If everyone assumes you are gone, you can come out of daytime hiding to help me. With your brawn and my knowledge, we can secure opulence for us both, and neither of us will be suspected."

"What the hell are you talking about?" And more to the point, why, Emil asked himself, had he not already turned and left?

"Our reverend father here, with the wisdom of age, should be able to remember lore that seems unknown to you. We, in turn, will share the bounty with him."

Exasperated Emil asked Theo, "Is it too hot inside for you?"

The priest fairly shrilled that it was.

"All right then. We can talk behind the bone hills. If anyone in the monastery is watching, I want to put on the rucksack and start down the shore till I can circle back behind the dunes. Give me some time before you leave, and you shouldn't have long to wait for me."

The pardoner's impassive mask finally cracked with alarm. "But I am comfortable! Why not stay here?"

"Go with the priest, or find other lackeys." As he grabbed rucksack and staff, Emil took smirking satisfaction at the pardoner's whiny objections, audible from the street.

On the approach from the hindside of the village, the four bone hills were high as a house and slowly growing with each day's fresh refuse. On the inland side, though, wind and rain and sandstorm had scooped the terrain to expose more mountainous slopes, whose lower stretches of fish skulls and oyster shells had fused into soft, gritty rock. The afternoon was well under way when Emil finally hiked down the massive, fan-shaped incline that spread out from behind the towering middens. Through cool hillside shade he discerned the priest, sitting on a weather-worn hassock of compressed herring bones, and the doleful pardoner, who beckoned imperiously at Emil to hurry or hugged himself to retain warmth. Emil smiled and trod the shifty gravel more slowly.

"Your priest would say nothing till you arrived!" the foreigner complained when Emil was a stone's throw away. "Can we now move into the sunlight? I cannot breathe next to all this stink of decay."

Emil and the priest shrugged at each other. What stink? "You should say what this is about before you choke or freeze," Emil advised.

"I have the same innocent questions as any stranger here." The pardoner tried conveying indignation, but seemed rather to pout. "Your village must have been busier when the waves more often cast up saints. What was it like then?"

"It was the same all around the sea," said Theo. "In my grandfather's day, when the church first understood it had been losing saints for centuries, it took strong measures, and then stronger." Emil still bet that none of this was news to the pardoner, but Theo plainly enjoyed a captive audience. "The waters were crowded with clerics in hired boats, sprinkling chrism and blessings. But years passed, and the sea kept singling out high churchmen and others of renowned piety to fill its belly. So the church tried exorcising the waters, to no better effect. Both Rome and Byzantium resorted to disinterring candidates for sainthood ahead of schedule, and those who failed the test of incorruptibility were submerged off our coast, in hopes they might taste holy enough. About the same time, our village wasn't alone in trying clay icons weighted with lead chains as easier decoys. Of course, nobody else had a catapult like ours. But catapult or no, the sea wasn't so easily fooled. The chronicler at our own monastery wrote that 'the sound of the surf became as laughter.'"

The pardoner may not have been hearing what he wanted to hear, or perhaps the evening chill was starting to gnaw at him. Either way, his speech had acquired a testy edge. "Saints no longer litter your beaches. Did the sea signal some great change?"

Emil idly kicked the brittle stones, in preference to listening as if he cared. Theo coughed, spat phlegm, and rattled on. "After the prelates despaired of taming or even making sense of the sea, they accepted it as an instrument of divine will, though unsure whether drowning was the trial that fixed someone's sainthood, or if these martyrs were due to be canonized however they died. Reckless aspirants to sainthood went so far as to lash themselves as living figureheads on embarking prows, hoping to whet marine hunger and gambling that their barnacled, otherwise unblemished corpses would someday roll ashore within human sight. Presumably their bindings allowed the waves to seize them while sparing their ships. But then the sea, as if to mock any bid at making it serve human ends, vomited what my father said was hundreds of saints at once, swamping ship decks and quays and dunes. I was too young to remember it, but my father never forgot all the bodies side by side in Coptic and Varangian and Crusader garments. The sea's cravings had moved on. We still don't know what flavor of man it likes now, and because all but saints will rot without a trace, perhaps we never will."

"And where did all those saints go?" The question sounded accusatory, as if Theo may have hidden the saints himself.

"They must have been carted off," the priest speculated, while Emil eyed the pardoner narrowly.

"But to where?" This foreigner was now outright belligerent, and Emil gripped his staff as he would to deal with any bully.

Theo raised a pacifying hand toward Emil. "Nobody thinks about that much," he claimed, without scrupling to mention the pox that had provided something else to think about, and left few people to do any thinking. "I was a little boy when it happened, as I said. Why do you ask?"

The pardoner pursed his lips a moment as if such naïveté deserved no spoken response, and then entreated, "Can we gain entry to the monastery without leave of the brothers? Do you know the way around inside?" He betrayed no awareness of wrenching their talk onto a new path.

"You eat supper there," Emil reminded him. "They've become pretty careless with their gatekeeping. Fluster them somehow when you leave, and the gate might stay open all night." Emil was beginning to grasp the pardoner's scheme, but couldn't tell yet if he liked it or not. As for what the priest made of it all, he was too busy paying for his wordiness with a coughing fit to communicate any meaningful glances. The pardoner ruefully eyed the bloody gob that landed at his feet until the priest gasped, "And the abbot? Is he really going to do it?"

"I cannot promise what my reverend superiors will do." The pardoner was pious and diffident again. "I am but a humble servant of God." The fluty voice shook with his shivering.

"It must be mealtime soon," Emil observed, "and I'm hungry. You two go back, and I'll follow after dark. Don't skimp on filling that satchel, either."

"I cannot procure you food any more," the pardoner objected. "You were supposed to depart this morning."

"Feed me, and I don't care how you manage it, or I 'return' for everyone to see. That's our agreement." Emil leaned on his staff and grinned at chalky Western apprehension.

"But don't you realize you stand to seize wealth too? That you might be putting very much in jeopardy?" The pardoner might have been more convincing, were he not blowing on his hands to warm them between sentences.

"I don't know what will come of what I think you're planning. But I know I'm hungry now. Skip the wine if you must. It's been more for your benefit than mine, hasn't it?"

The pardoner shifted his critical gaze toward the wheezing priest, who needed a minute before finding breath to get up and escort him from the reeking wilderness.

For the next three nights, the gate was duly barred despite the pardoner's contrivances, and Emil had to endure snoring and ongoing protest about sneaking him food. Then by day, Emil had to prevent the least whiff of himself from escaping the house, bodily functions included. Theo discreetly visited with worrisome tidings that the pardoner was wearing out his general welcome, first by trying to sell dubious relics and then, after people laughed in his face, by trying to buy theirs. The pardoner had also become a worse pest at home through his greedy fondness for Emil's short supply of dried figs.

Emil, meanwhile, believed that All Saints' Day must have come and gone, because the mangonel had sat on the jetty for the unprecedented better part of a week. But he hadn't heard the jangling, garishly masked All Hallows' Eve procession to the church for the random selection of a clay saint to catapult. Only the monks had possession of a calendar, so he and the rest of the village had to take Clement's word that it was still October.

Next dusk when the pardoner emerged from monastery gate, fussing about the hat he must have mislaid in the refectory, a crusty bowl and wooden spoon crashed between him and the skittish monk seeing him out. The attacker on high roared, "Roast in hell, you simpering shit!" Had the heretic fallen into frothing mania, or was he lending a hand after three nights of listening and guessing the pardoner's game? The monk behaved as if the sky were falling. He retreated headlong, squealing that the apostate had run amok and must be restrained, with no apparent thought of the oaken bar that kept the lunatic in his cell or of the oaken bar he should have slid across main gates that still gaped open. The pardoner gently pushed them together, praying the brethren wouldn't notice anything amiss till morning.

With the priest in tow, the pardoner bustled into Emil's house and reported this windfall of luck, loosing a trebly exuberance that made both villagers squirm. From the priest he exacted reassurance that monastic schooling had instilled a lasting memory of the building from cupola to crypts. Then Emil clenched and reluctantly unclenched his fists at the pardoner's every high-handed directive to inspect the folding sledge and fuel the crabshell lamp and attach its long-handled bronze holder and stock the green-bark ember box. Best to defer killing the pardoner till he could afford a golden knife! He no longer trusted himself to carry his walking stick. They also retrieved the priest's lamp from the church, while Emil wolfed bread and mutton from the pardoner's satchel. They had discussed neither the broad shape nor details of their business, and speech posed only needless risk as their muted footfalls navigated dim, deserted streets.

They opened one monastery gate by degrees too tiny to yield any creaking and stood hesitant in the deathly-quiet moonlit courtyard. All their earlier tacit unanimity could bring them no farther. The pardoner whispered to Theo, "When you were a pupil here, did you ever smell anything strange? Anything sweet?"

The priest squinted into his past and shook his head.

"To the cellar then. Can you lead us?"

Theo nodded and tramped toward the refectory. The others padded after him, and inside they steered clear of benches and trestle tables by virtue of faint glow through tall, narrow windows that faced onto the cloister. The table for the abbot and his stewards stood on a wide dais, in an even feebler glow from a niche in the rear wall, where a lamp always burned at the feet of a cherry-wood Basil the Great, patron saint of monks and of the local coastline. To the left of the dais was a doorway, and the trespassers breathed more easily within its concealment.

Their eyes adjusted to the obscurity of a T-shaped passage. At the end of one arm was the kitchen, and in the other hung the heavy funk of the latrines. Ahead was a more oppressive darkness from which a cold, unclean draft seeped out.

To no better purpose than hearing his own voice, Theo observed that here was the way to the cellar. Emil put down his lamp, rummaged iron tongs from his rucksack, lifted red ember from the green-bark box with them, and held it to the floating wick of his lamp and the priest's lamp. Stark light revealed the pardoner shaking like a hatchling in a downpour. He began to suggest that his comrades search below while he stood watch in the warmer refectory, but Emil's uncomradely glare stopped him.

Then Theo swallowed grimly at reading the others' expectation that he go first. He tentatively advanced and thrust his lamp into the gulf beyond the landing. From the top step onward, they all had to press forth against sharp chill and the foulness of accumulated death. Nothing saintly in this direction, Emil mused, but who was he not to stand and watch if the pardoner were determined to steep himself in so much nastiness? "I've never been down here," the priest whispered. "But they told me this used to be storage for meat and cheese and carrots, until they needed the room for a charnel house." The staircase adjoined the wall to their right, and to the left gaped much more darkness than two lamps could dispel. Only when their light spilled past the bottom step did they begin to fathom their surroundings.

The full breadth of the floor was lost in shadows, but a multitude of squat pillars supported a low ceiling of stoutly ribbed vaults and instilled a dread of suffocation, as if the monastery's weight might anytime finish crushing the compressed columns flat. Even worse, the air down here was insufferable on account of the corpses side by side, row on row, to the edge of light, in winding sheets stained brown with rot. To all appearances, they'd become oversized likenesses of the worms that Emil imagined were still feeding under the linen.

"The brothers have always entombed their own in the monastery," Theo wheezed, fighting to exhale each syllable. Much longer in this stink, Emil brooded, and he'd have to break out the sledge and haul back a lifeless pastor. "What land is fit for tillage around us must be tilled, and the rest is too rocky for gravedigging. We villagers go to our rest in family cairns, out past the hayfields." The priest coughed as softly as he could.

The pardoner crassly shook his arm. "When they needed room for bodies in this place, where was it that was getting too full?"

The priest blinked a little in confusion at the pardoner's phrasing, and then he gasped, "The subcellar, of course!"

The pardoner rudely snatched away the priest's lamp, raised it high, and set illumination crawling across the chamber. In the outermost vestiges of light, the vague silhouettes of two pillars stood uniquely close together, and an arch, rather than the corners of a vault, surmounted them. Between the pillars was pitch darkness, and in front of them was the end of a path that meandered among gaps in the bundled ranks.

The pardoner lowered the lamp, and his darting eyes picked out the forepart of the path from his feet to the archway. "Come!" He bolted ahead with startling artfulness and never a backward glimpse, as if hesitation on his confederates' part were inconceivable.

By the time they were together under the yellow brick arch, Emil had a lamp in one extended hand, while his other arm supported the priest, now as ghostly as the pardoner had ever seemed. The pardoner, though, had grown substantial with anticipation, and if it wasn't a trick of the light, his alert, formerly pale face was ruddy. The chill no longer caused him visible discomfort, and his fussiness at bad smells had also vanished since his visit to the bone hills.

The roundness of the arch persisted in the horseshoe shape of the stairwell ceiling as they descended. Then the stairs opened onto a cavernous expanse, and the steps gradually widened, like ripples spreading from a stone dropped at lakeside, as they neared the gleaming floor. More bodies in brown winding sheets littered the roomier steps, as if discarded by indifferent waves.

The air was less baneful, and priestly breathing less labored, as soon as the cellar was behind them. Nor was anyone deterred by the noxious vapors from this small clutch of bodies, after fording the horrific cellar. What's more, a new odor gathered strength toward the foot of the stairs, and out on the polished travertine floor it was dense enough to make Emil dizzy, even if Theo inhaled greedily and tottered free of Emil's shoulder, reinvigorated. It was preferable to what might kill them yet on the return trek, but unpleasant to Emil in its fashion, a ripe blend of honey and tidal flats, with a tinge of rosewater. The pardoner was breathless in the throes of a rapture somehow so unwholesome that Emil shied away and followed the pardoner's roving light in its survey of this otherworldly hall and its otherworldly contents.

How could any place as alien as this have existed all along, directly under his feet? Walls of naked auburn bedrock curved into darkness and bore the peck marks, numerous as stars, of excavating chisels. At haphazard intervals and heights in the walls were berths whose upper lips had been carved away to resemble scallop shells or eagle wings or laurel garlands or parading cicadas. Upon the floor, and spaced as haphazardly, were stone chests ponderous as overturned pulpits, crowded with reliefs of people in swaddling clothes or equally outlandish scaly armor, or of oxen under a radiant sun or naked angels or demonic beasts. Holding up the high, craggy ceiling at the center of the hall was a shaft of raw bedrock that had remained unquarried, like the uneaten core of an apple, and rivaling the thickness of a cedar trunk.

In the niches, and upon the caskets, and between them lay the host of sources for the cloying, marine perfume. Aside from a crust of sea salt, they could have been guests sleeping off the excesses of a masquerade ball. Complexions lustrous in the wandering light ranged from Ethiopian to Russian, and the costumes encompassed Teutonic Knights, Armenian bishops, Roman senators, papal emissaries, Cyprian sailors, Serbian merchants, and dozens that Emil didn't recognize.

The whereabouts of the saints spewed en masse by the fickle sea, at least those in the monastery's vicinity, were no longer a mystery. By the same token, Emil understood why the cellar overhead had to accommodate all the deceased brethren. Then with a breathtaking burst of insight, he also understood why the monastery, which neither grew nor produced anything to sell in the world, always had the *nummi* to pay him every other week. A ship from the West could dock in plenty of coves away from village eyes, and Emil was too seldom home to catch foreign comings and goings. Nor were his fellow villagers, as a rule, inquisitive. The delivery of a saint once in a prearranged while, rather than divulging their actual number and destroying the market, might guarantee monastic solvency for several lifetimes. Emil's so-called work served no real purpose beyond helping to bolster Clement's deception.

The priest was sitting on the bottom step with legs akimbo, oblivious to the rotten bodies flanking him, awestruck at the concentration of sanctity at his feet. His mouth hung wide open like a dying cod's, but his breathing was more relaxed than Emil had heard in years. The pardoner had taken to pacing among the beatific jetsam, eyes flashing in amazement as at the exotic wares of an Arab bazaar. In a voice initially hushed with reverence, he announced, "This must be the holiest room in Christendom. More grace here than anywhere else in the world. Get that one! To declare him genuine should not be a problem." He bent low and swept his hand over a fair-haired, sunburnt monk in tunic and cowl and full-length robe of coarse wool. A curious silver brooch, whose pin protruded well past a spiral-embellished semicircle, had prevented the sea from stripping its victim. "He came from Dalriada. A missionary, from a country long extinct. His type of habit has not been worn for at least five hundred years." He straightened up, unabashedly proud of his superior knowledge.

Theo, despite the promise of wealth writ large here, sighed mournfully and drew in his legs, to rest chin between knees. "Here they might molder till doomsday, in limbo, with no one to venerate them. We'll never know what miracles they performed, or what trials they overcame, or even what their names were." Both Emil and the pardoner, in rare solidarity, gave him a look that questioned his mental fitness.

Emil foisted his lamp onto the pardoner, who acted put upon at holding both lights, till Emil grumbled, "I can't carry your missionary and the lamp at the same time! The sledge is useless on stairs." Unfortunately, the saint hoisted over Emil's shoulder was as burdensome as any other dead weight, and the potency of sweet-and-stagnant odor right beside his nose was staggering. He was desperate

to get this part of the adventure over with, but the priest sat entranced, blocking the way, dazed in the mystery and wonder of so
much secret godliness.

In the quiet, waiting irascibly for the priest to move, Emil
thought he heard the lapping of waves, echoing across the ungauge-
able black distance outside the intruders' two circles of light. A
grotto could be hidden amidst the coves and seaside cliffs, couldn't
it? And it could connect with this sanctum. And whatever had arrived here from the shore could go back the same way. Aha, the
misty-eyed priest was swaying to his feet and starting to climb, dis-
pirited as if in retreat from heaven itself.

To avoid losing momentum, Emil had to bump aside the dawdling priest, and he stumbled now and then negotiating the grisly
path through the cellar. Otherwise, the men filed back into the refectory without incident, where Emil brusquely dictated that the
lamps be doused and that his weaker accomplices keep their trophy
and its telltale dew of sanctity away from the floor. Once the salty
ankles were in Theo's hands and the slippery armpits in the pardoner's, Emil unhinged the sledge and despised his fingers for fumbling more than he could blame on the feeble light from the feet of
Saint Basil. Was it fatigue, nerves, hankerings for a life of luxury? He
couldn't tell.

Emil positioned his sledge in the nick of time, to catch the saint
that struggling priest and pardoner haplessly dropped. Ignoring their
plaintive gasps, he adjusted the body, which had thudded almost
squarely onto the hazel basketwork, and its costume, which had
nearly brushed the floor. He reminded Theo and the pardoner to
pick up their lamps, and then towed the precious flesh out of the
refectory and over the doorstep into the courtyard. The runners
squeaked when Emil had to pull harder to keep the balky sledge in
motion. If any brother lay awake and listening, please let him think
he heard bats, Emil prayed, and God did seem to smile upon this larceny. The pardoner dashed ahead to open the gate, and Theo somewhat wistfully pushed it shut behind them.

As their clean escape continued across the plaza, Emil was grateful but at heart incredulous, and a little bewildered that half-awake
brothers in their nightclothes weren't streaming after them, waving

harrows and scythes. That would have been more his kind of luck. In the uppermost row of windows, a flickering light offered the one sign that someone might be mindful of them. Emil couldn't tell if he were squinting at the heretic's cell or not. Well, what good in fretting over that?

Their only sounds were stealthy footsteps and the swoosh and groans of the runners over crushed vegetation and stone, till they neared the outermost village hovels.

"Where do we put him?" the pardoner hissed.

"You hadn't thought about that before?" Emil cast sidelong contempt at the pardoner without slowing down.

"The odor would give us away at Emil's or in the church," Theo warned, and Emil scowled again at this pathetic lack of foresight. He had also been veering away from village inroads, and cruising alongside the windowless back walls of houses, on gravel where the sledge left no trail. The pardoner demanded in vain to know where they were going. The priest followed quietly, with steadfast, childlike countenance, verging on adoration, toward the aromatic corpse, causing him to trip and reel for balance every so often. In a moment they were on the beach. Priest and pardoner were already starting to pant, and Emil grudgingly reined himself in.

"The shepherds have driven their flocks home for the winter. One of their summer huts isn't very far, and your saint and I will stay there," Emil declared.

"Good! If that is settled, I can return to your house now. I need the priest to build me a fire." The pardoner's rosy complexion was already faded and waxy.

"No. You need to learn the way to my shelter, and I want the priest with you, to make sure you don't get lost coming back tonight. You still have to bring me food twice a day. Take him with you if you decide I'll be too hard to find."

"I could stay instead of Emil and watch the saint," Theo volunteered, but nobody seemed to hear him.

"How long do you expect me to feed you?" the pardoner fussed.

"How long do I have to stare at an old foreign corpse?" And how far would tonight's business have gotten with the pardoner in charge?

"By today, the ship that brought me should be moored behind a headland to the north, and men will row out every evening to see if the catapult is gone. The day after it is, they will send in a boat for me. Can you not fend for yourself till then?"

"If you want me to believe you're trustworthy, keep showing up with my meals." Emil showed his teeth without elaborating on the backlash of losing his trust. Supplying food was the least the pardoner could do after devouring Emil's figs, irreplaceable for months till the new crop dried.

No doubt the pardoner, who did not default on the next two days' food, believed Emil stupid enough to base someone's trustworthiness on a steady delivery of table scraps. Emil also had a strong hunch that the pardoner's talk of a ship coming for "me" instead of "us" revealed more than a foreigner's shortcomings with the language. Emil had no desire to go west, but wasn't about to let an unaccompanied pardoner fence their stolen saint and cheat him out of some or all of his money, assuming the pardoner ever returned. And those shares due Emil and the priest were yet to be discussed, as were the arrangements to transfer sacred flesh to the Westerners' dory. Maybe, in light of the fantastic wealth lying in the subcellar, no such arrangements figured in the pardoner's scheme.

The pardoner that evening offered only one piece of information along with a ragged fistful of barley loaf and an exceptionally bony, greasy portion of goat. Abbot Clement had decreed tomorrow All Saints' Day, without causing visible confusion, though no procession and lottery had chosen an icon to load in the mangonel. It sounded to Emil as if Clement were on the verge of going through with whatever Theo had alluded to several days ago, and Emil harbored a suspicion of what that might be. It prompted him to follow the village-bound pardoner's lamp from afar, steering around obstacles by moonlight, and then navigating to the monastery by a glow in the same topmost window as last night.

Emil was aiming for the lit window with some of the heretic's near-fatal potsherds from around his feet, but had to dive headlong into the rubbishy ditch along the foundation as the gates started swinging out. He espied the priest poking his furtive, unlit way into the night, stopping on occasion to cough softly and spit, soon shuffling beyond the range of moonlight. The priest must have seen himself out; the gates yawned untended.

Emil groped through courtyard and up stairs to the corridor with one doorway open and bright, as if in readiness for him. Yet at his entrance, the abbot's eyes widened and his lips pursed in outward astonishment. "Have you quit working for me? Why are you here now?"

Emil might as suitably have put that second question to Clement, who was standing in the middle of a dark cell, with crabshell lamp on windowsill. Like a beacon? To see how many moths he could attract? Instead, Emil asked, "Did you tell the priest you were going through with it tomorrow?"

To his tentative relief, the abbot relaxed into an uncommonly mild, or maybe resigned, mood. "We repeat the sacrifice of a clay saint every year out of habit, but no one is satisfied. The sea still claims the lives of our good men, as perhaps it always has, on days without gale or thunder. The sea wants appeasement, as it did since long before the birth of our Savior. And we want to appease it, if that will persuade it to make sense, or at least stop killing us without explanation." He flapped a careless arm toward the left-hand wall and, presumably, the heretic on the other side. "His own people have abandoned him to us. Are we to keep him jailed forever? He has no life here. It is cruelty. And this is no hospice."

"So what you're planning for him is less cruel?" Any other time, such impertinence would have annoyed the abbot, but to judge by his melancholy smile, he welcomed this conversation. He'd at least temporarily misplaced any rancor at Emil's early return to the village.

"What would your conscience have me do?" Yes, Clement was asking for advice, and in all seeming sincerity!

"I know something that should carry some weight," Emil averred. "Of the two foreigners among us, you've confined the one who's harmless, despite whatever he's babbling. The pardoner is a danger to everyone here, and especially to you."

"How so?" Clement leaned encouragingly closer.

Careful, now! Whatever Father Theo had confessed, Emil needed a story that pushed him into the shadows, out of the glare of wrongdoing. "What do you know about the ship that will retrieve the pardoner?"

"I know it should sail into our waters in the next few days." The abbot's patience was verging on uncanny. So unlike him!

"The ship is already moored behind a headland, somewhere north of here. The pardoner admitted that to me." Emil was beginning to feel self-congratulatory, as if he and Clement were playing some aristocratic game with tokens and a board, and he was holding his own.

"And why would the ship go into concealment?"

Emil took a steadying breath. "The pardoner discovered where all the salvaged saints are. I can lead you to a shepherd's hut where he stashed one. He has even learned of the tunnel from the seashore to your cellars." Going by Clement's fraught new expression, Theo hadn't broken this last piece of news, and to be honest, Emil's may have been the only ears to detect echoing wavelets against stone. No matter. The candor of his words was far less important than their impact. "How many men will be rowing the dory from the ship to fetch the pardoner?"

"Six? Or maybe eight?" Clement's shrug belied any increased concern.

"It can hold more. And the ship certainly has more than one dory. If the pardoner can lead well-armed men to a huge fortune in holy flesh, do you think they will just come get him and paddle away?"

"How do you suggest we prevent such a calamity, if all is really as you say?"

"The pardoner is the only foreigner who knows where the saints are, or even whether there are any. No point in attacking us without him. Too much work, too much risk, maybe for nothing."

"Do you propose to murder an agent of the Church?" The abbot drew back a little, in obligatory dismay.

"As I said, you've made plans for the wrong man."

The abbot nodded slowly, gravely, tacitly accepting Emil's arguments. "But he is not likely to sit quietly in the mangonel bucket."

"The brothers have been harvesting figs. Can you spare me a bowlful?" Emil's request was pointedly casual.

"In the kitchen." Clement showed no sign of understanding what Emil had in mind.

"He'll be in your hands before afternoon prayers."

Clement replied with neither words nor a nod, as if lack of reaction meant he hadn't really agreed to Emil's designs. He plucked his lamp off the windowsill. In the fleeting brightness of the cell as Clement strode ahead of Emil, a cathedral chair burst into view, and over it was draped the cowled robe of the heretic, as if awaiting someone new to wear it. Emil couldn't help wondering who had been manipulating who, but why dwell on hopeless riddles?

Emil waited by Saint Basil in the refectory while Clement collected the figs. The abbot again refrained from comment as he handed Emil the bowl and Emil duly thanked him.

As they crossed the courtyard, the abbot confided, "Father Theo was loath to see us lose even one saint, and particularly to greedy foreign devils. He is in essence a sentimental old dunce, and it is said that sentimentality breeds homicide. But why would you not throw in your lot with the foreign devils and reap enormous riches?"

"I don't know," Emil stalled, words suddenly eluding him. "Whatever I'd have had to go through would have been too much, for riches or anything else." Emil's tongue was working ahead of his brain, but maybe he was inventing truth. He couldn't tell. "I'm too used to how things are, whether I like them or not, and everything is too uncertain elsewhere. I'd rather stay here and stop things from changing, if I can."

"Nobly put," Clement muttered.

The abbot ushered Emil through the gate, and while Emil paused to map out his course before the lamp withdrew and left him in treacherous moonlight, a stocky, distorted silhouette clanked toward them across the plaza. A soldier in armor? No, by the sulfurous air that preceded him, this had to be the smith.

"Ah, the one visitor I was expecting when I lit the evening oil!" greeted the abbot. "I was worried you might not finish in time."

The smith smiled, and a broad crescent of teeth shone against his sooty face and the murky night. He was soon in the lamplight, where Emil could ascribe the noise to hulking chains over musclebound shoulders, with links like kelp and locks like sea urchins, a scaled-up version of what enveloped the doll-sized icons on All Saints' Day. The smith still had nothing to say when he barged between Clement and Emil to enter the monastery, and the abbot said nothing more as he closed and barred the gate. Emil grimaced into the sky. He wasn't looking forward to the long, dim hike to the shepherd's hut.

The pardoner appeared at the shepherd's hut next morning with a couple of rye buns and a skimpy wedge of blue-veined cheese. The bowl of figs was centered on the sledge, which doubled as breakfast table upon the filthy floor. Sunshine through the doorway gilded the bowl amidst windowless gloom. Emil squatted behind the sledge, facing the door, and reached up for his meager rations with an appreciative nod. The pardoner sniffed at the syrupy fragrance rising directly under his nose, cutting through the bouquet of old come and garbage and dead saint on impromptu bier of half-charred firewood and brown-leaved branches. "What are those?" he asked, eyes fixated on sun-flecked green fruit.

"Fresh figs. They grow all over the hills," Emil informed him while chewing cheese.

"Are they good?"

"Next to these, the dried figs have no flavor."

"Really?" The pardoner sought to affect indifference, but impulsively licked his lips. "Can I try one?"

"Take the whole bowl," Emil offered dismissively. "I've had enough. They're on the rich side for me."

"Thank you very much!" The pardoner seemed to find Emil's generosity astounding. He bent gracefully, then snatched the bowl and took his hasty leave with a slight bow, lest Emil change his mind.

Squatting Emil gazed after him out the doorway until his knees and feet ached too much. The pardoner had already chomped one fig down to the stem, tossed the stem, sucked his sticky fingers, made equally quick work of another, and was tearing into a third.

Emil studied the inexpressive face of drowned martyr on and off till mid-afternoon, but was frustrated to distinguish nothing godly or benevolent in it. Maybe someone of a more spiritual nature, like Theo, could sense holiness beneath the blank surface. There had to be a pearl within the shell. Or else why would God so lovingly preserve that shell? Well, all theology was in Turkish, as Emil always said. He stretched the blessedly supple corpse upon the sledge again and embarked for the village.

Wine at these festivals was known to soften Clement's judgment. With luck, he would react to the spectacle of Emil towing a saint by awarding him the once-in-a-lifetime salvage fee, failing to recognize his own stolen property and forgetful of their transaction in the queasy morning after. God had smiled on Emil's larceny so far!

The day was cool when Emil re-entered village streets, but the handful of logy celebrants loafing on doorsteps or in windows seemed overheated. He smiled affably at more than one version of the slurry observation, "Look, Emil's got a saint for once! Smells nice! Too bad we can't use one today!" He stopped at home for a minute. The pardoner was gone. The bowl on the little scrapwood table was empty. The contemptible fool had gobbled a dozen figs! Not for nothing was gluttony listed in the deadly sins, as he should have learned firsthand by now.

In the plaza, people were swarming like flies around the three trellised barrels of wine that, based on the level of hilarity, must have been tapped around noon. Everyone had a clay cup in hand. Close relatives in clusters conversed or bickered as the wine impelled, and at least one member of each group was watching the monastery gates. Most of the elderly were sitting, and some were precariously snoozing, upon stools. Numerous children ran in packs on plaza outskirts, apart from those on all fours, retching away their likely first sick-drunks. On the jetty, Theo, gesturing grandly with his cup, was supervising burly fishermen who were almost finished winding down the mangonel arm into firing position.

A gangly, hiccupping monk leaning on a barrel noticed Emil and his freight negotiating the plaza, and hurried to knock in a spritely rhythm on monastic gates for him. The abbot himself opened up and beamed to behold Emil. "Here's a first! Emil with some flesh on his sledge!"

This sounded promising. Emil tried to frame the most innocent rejoinder. "Where do you want me to bring him?"

"Down in the cellar where you found him!" the abbot roared, and laughed a little louder than the jibe merited. He'd been drinking, but not enough, if ever he could drink enough when money was at stake. He pulled himself together, which only bared a vein of tension in his voice. "But for now, take him to the infirmary and put him on a cot. Not the one where the pardoner was. That one's going to need a lot of bleach."

Restless young men were gawking through the open gates, and Clement lurched over to narrow the gap, as if that would foil a mob's forced entry. Emil had started toward the infirmary, but the abbot stopped him. "I underrate you. The pardoner handed himself to us in perfectly submissive condition, apart from shitting himself inside out."

Someone commenced banging a rock on one of the gate's iron studs, at the tempo of a funeral march, and others soon followed his lead, in their own flurry of tempos. Was this a cue to inform Clement of mob impatience? The first rapping had been gingerly enough that the gates didn't even shake, and the rest had only made them tremble. But when Clement heaved the gates wide to reveal Theo and much of the village stepping clear, the priest dropped his rock, while everybody else held on to theirs.

Clement stood frowning in silence a few seconds. As best Emil could tell, Father Theo, in the heat of the moment, was hard put to remember his instructions, but finally shouted, "The heretic! This year, the heretic!" His flock joined in. None of them pressed forward, though all were waving their rocks over their heads. The outcry spread like burning oil across the plaza, and through the throng Emil caught glimpses of fishermen around the catapult baying with the chorus, fists upraised.

From the stables erupted a gang of the more rugged brothers, tugging someone in black robe and cowl by the loose ends of lead chains that pinned his arms to his sides and looped around his neck and over his shoulders. His clothes were messy with straw and horse dung, though his seaweed-and-sea-urchin fetters were spotless and shiny. He wasn't resisting, but seemed to be stumbling from out of a swoon, and as he regained his faculties he cramped up and convulsed as wildly as he could within crushing links and fig-induced delirium. In his violent throes, long yellow strands, stuck together with sweat, went whipping past his cowl. And whatever he was ranting, in a mix of village language and his own, sounded authentically heretical. As the crowd, with renewed cheering, made a path for the priest and the ungentle escorts and their hysterical victim, the alleged heretic's similarity to the pardoner gave nobody pause, as if all Westerners might look the same. Had any laymen except Emil even seen the heretic within handshake range?

The rest of the brothers, to a man, streamed out the gates with the restraint of water down a drain, and Emil sauntered after them, casting a jaundiced glance at the forsaken saint on his sledge, as a cloud of courtyard dust settled on divinely moistened skin. Halfway across the plaza, Emil grew uncomfortable with his own burgeoning eagerness to see the last of the despised Westerner, and turned a minute to the building that used to represent calm and order. It wasn't entirely abandoned. In one of the uppermost windows someone gazed out, and on his head was the pardoner's soft white hat.

A more scornful howl rippled from mouth to mouth, out of the plaza's center to its rim, and it seized on Emil's attention. The pardoner was gabbling on his belly in the trampled weeds, and the exasperated monks were dragging him by calves and ankles, letting the free lengths of chains trail in the dirt. Clearly his last spasms of strength had deserted him, and could he even breathe for the lead squeezing his ribs? But onlookers were treating this as a malicious attempt to spoil their one bid at placating a devilish, formerly predictable force of nature. Emil hated feeling sorry for this scoundrel who, in his fashion, would have done to the village what the village was doing to him. Might as well stare at the ground and hum a pretty tune!

Emil stifled urges to peek at the most savage uproars or find out whether the fishermen were scrunching the pardoner completely into the bucket or letting his legs dangle over, for all the difference it would make. Whatever they did was met with a breathless hush, broken in short order by the priest, bellowing more lustily than Emil would have deemed possible with those impaired lungs. Emil refused to watch him invest vengeful enthusiasm into the annual prayer that God make the sea content with a crockery saint, with the substitution now of "unregenerate heretic." "Amen," Theo wheezed, with the last bubbles of air in his spongy chest, as Emil pictured it. But everyone's "amen" in response overflowed with a ferocity that could only be curbed by the bass-note release of the trigger and the unreeling of cable, swift as a sneeze. Emil lifted his eyes only as the pardoner and his dangling chains windmilled high into the distance, falling as a speck whose crash into the sea went un-heard amidst the mob's sodden shouts of cold-blooded hope.

Emil went home and hung up his rucksack and found the par-doner's wineskin. One barrel at the plaza, after a little jostling, held enough to fill it. The gray robes and the priest had stolen off. Every-one else carried on with the accustomed singing and dancing and games, as if drink had dissolved the distinction between this and any other All Saints' Day. Emil took his wine home.

There was never any fishing on the second of November. Noon devotions were over before the groans of antique wheels and of head-achy men accompanied the catapult's return to monastic storage. In their wake Emil, with staff and rucksack, clacked into the courtyard and reclaimed his sledge, bereft now of precious corpse. A barrel-chested Georgian with a pink scar from earlobe to chin shooed him into the refectory, where Clement sat hunched at his head table, in the thin lamplight from the feet of Saint Basil. Puffy eyelids and splotchy skin bespoke his woozy condition, which he seemed intent on relieving by hedging his bets. On a silver platter were hardboiled eggs and artichoke hearts, and his two twitchy hands were pouring wine from a squat stoneware decanter into a jeweled chalice. "Using a wedge to dislodge a ledge?" asked Emil, indicating the chalice.

The underlying reason to pay him for beachcombing eight days in a row was as valid as ever, and he was banking on a nod and a wave to send him along. He had no wish to rub shoulders so soon with any of his murderous neighbors. Nor had he near or amiable kin among them, not since the Venetian plague.

Sadly, Clement in hangover was his testy old self, and Emil's lev-ity withered in the pod. "When were you last at mass?" the abbot demanded.

"At the southern end of my rounds, I always attend. Right after I buy the red bread to show you," Emil improvised.

Hangover seemed to have muffled Clement's ears. "You need to do penance. The other men, to atone for yesterday's sinfulness, are forbidden to go fishing tomorrow. Instead, they will sit in their boats, anchored off the jetty, until I judge they have achieved redemption. You will join them, with that lethal fencepost of yours."

This punishment struck Emil as lenient indeed for drunkenness, riot, and slaughter. How remarkable that Clement should live up to his name in this instance! More to the point, though, Emil advised, "If you're going to let your prisoner look out the window tomorrow, maybe you should take away that white hat with the picture of Jesus pinned to it."

"It's called a veronica," Clement enunciated with overbearing care. But his expression was thoughtful as he discharged Emil with a slipshod sign of the cross.

In the thick, dreary gray of pre-dawn, Emil awoke to a racket as of a hundred woodpeckers storming the village. He had realized what was under way, but was still blinking sleep from his eyes, when one of the brothers rushing house to house rapped on his door and barked simply, "Penance!"

Emil arrived on the beach as the last few of two dozen boats were embarking. The dinghy to which Father Theo conscripted him was soon floating at one end of a crescent-shaped formation, a porpoise-leap from the north side of the jetty, as the sun crept up over his shoulders and shone wanly on a single-mast cog, a furlong away on the black depths. It was by no means gigantic. More impressive Byzantine galleys and Arab caravels had sparked Emil's admiration during salvage journeys. The ship nonetheless had room for a crew that could lay waste the village, if provoked. Scanning the village flotilla, Emil couldn't find Theo among the sullen penitents.

Ten sailors were rowing a dory toward them, in silence as businesslike as the fishermen's. They stayed their oars out of spear range, but close enough to parlay without caterwauling back and forth. Nothing they wore was appropriate for shipboard routines. Some had tarnished breastplates, and a couple of others were in dented-up helmets. Otherwise, brown leather covered most of their bodies, and their skin was likewise leathery and tanned dark as beef broth. The slight clatter Emil heard when a wave rocked the dory must have been weapons under the benches. Yet for all their steel and padding, these were no more soldiers than seafarers.

The foreigner nearest the bow stood up. Adversity had ripped the visor from his helmet, and his sea legs were ungainly. "We have agreed to fetch the pardoner from here!" His accent was as clumsy as his stance.

In the heart of the crescent, the abbot hove to his feet almost as clumsily. "He is no longer with us! He has already put out to sea. He found other means!" Yes, Clement, so skilled at avoiding the truth without perjuring himself, was by far the best spokesman in this situation. He sat down heavily, while the Westerner stood slack-jawed, at a loss.

The foreign oarsmen mutely faced the arrayed villagers, and the unsmiling villagers faced them, and then, as if losing interest in this staring contest, casually inspected their fillet knives and hatchets and harpoons and even longer-shafted gaffing hooks, such that the metal gleamed in the rising sun. Discomfort began to prey on the foreigners, who fidgeted and craned their necks toward different horizons. The pardoner may have dangled irresistible luxury under their crow-beak noses, but no risk to life and limb was worthwhile without his involvement, and they knew it.

Emil tossed a glimpse at the monastery. The veronica was nowhere in sight, but on the battlements and in cupola windows, the industrious brethren were polishing bright, silvery farming tools and butchering cutlery. The man in the bow reseated himself and glumly bid his crew to dip their oars. They pulled away, and around noon when their ship weighed anchor, Clement proclaimed that all the village sinners were redeemed.

There were too few hours of daylight for a round trip to the shoals. The fishermen beached their fleet, perhaps to go home and sin again for want of other recreation. Did anyone besides Emil realize the priest was missing? Or was he? Most of the men were toting their makeshift armaments up trails through tall beach grass into the village. Some were strolling toward the dunes, and as the southern slope of the jetty came into their view they jerked thumbs at something there and joked coarsely and chuckled. The abbot, red-faced and winded, lurched toward Emil. "Let me lean on that staff, will you? I'm not accustomed to boats." Emil shook his head, crooked his finger for Clement to follow, and hustled onto the jetty.

Theo was sprawled face down on the rocks, most of the way out, where incoming tide soaked his outthrust right arm and right leg. A dribble of blood slunk wormishly from his mouth to the water. With Clement huffing well behind, Emil clambered down to

Theo's side, but had a surprising bout of squeamishness about touching him in case he were dead. The salvager did his awkward best to lever the priest onto his back and away from drowning, only to slip and accidentally thump Theo in the ribs with the staff, which made the priest fart. Emil, relieved at this sign of life, hauled him by the collar to safety, and supported him as he had in the noisome monastic cellar. The blood flowed lazily from a cut on Theo's lower lip. "The excitement this morning may have exhausted him," the abbot suggested, panting with fatigue himself, "or else he talked his lungs into giving out again."

Emil finally let Clement borrow his staff. Doubtful that the abbot was in real danger of collapsing, but why take a chance and end up with twice the weight to rescue? Theo's breathing, meanwhile, was gurgly and hoarse. He neither stirred nor opened his eyes.

"We'll see to him in the infirmary. I want him to rest on the cot where the pilfered saint lay overnight. He seems like someone it might do some good. And if it does, then who can say?" speculated Clement. "A blessed bed to heal the sick! Word of that might ensure we have the coins to pay you for the rest of your life."

Knowing what he did of the monastery's entombed resources, Emil suspected the abbot of trying to pick an argument, maybe to quash Emil's recent upstart familiarity. Emil hesitated as if about to disagree, but said instead, "While we speak of doing some good, I've been meaning to ask, might we not set the poor heretic free? Provision him and put him on a road away from here? The people have made their blood offering, and the prisoner is just one more mouth to feed, and cell to clean."

Clement sneered as if Emil had taken the bait after all. "And do you dream that their offering will be effective? And that next year, or any year, they will simply go back to clay icons? We would be foolish not to have a pardoner in readiness for them, a pardoner, that is, if clothes make the man. Or else they might want to test an abbot or a salvager." Clement had the smug air of a cat with a mouthful of sparrow, and Emil chose to gaze elsewhere. They had crossed the plaza and in a minute were in the shade of the monastery. Emil still had his qualms about condemning an innocent lunatic to a year in a vile, lonely cell, with or without summary execution next All Saints'

Day. Was there no other means to placate his neighbors?

A trio of bricks in rapid succession narrowly missed their toes, and Emil recognized them as the kind that might be pried from a cell wall by someone with many solitary hours. "God will damn you to hellfire for making sense!" The voice was booming from an uppermost window. Emil and Clement hastened to part the gates and evade the next volley. Dammit, Clement had to change that madman's cell for something more secluded! Theo was still limp and oblivious.

"After I put the priest to bed, may I start on my rounds?" implored Emil in the courtyard.

Clement nodded, handed Emil his staff, and tromped off without wasting further words. Judging by posture and unctuous smile, the abbot was well content with his salvager's old submissiveness. And Emil, after that last assault from above, was likewise content to let the heretic be Clement's problem, and to let Theo, if he survived, fulfill the spiritual needs of a congregation of wolves.

Emil couldn't leave soon enough. The longer he stayed at home, the less sense the whole world made. As for God, who hadn't resented the course of local events ardently enough to stop it, Emil couldn't believe the unhinged heretic was right. But that was the trouble, Emil reflected, as he lowered Theo onto the fragrant cot and raised an eyebrow as the priest's breathing instantly quieted down. Wrong as the lunatic was, who had a better claim to be right? Who the hell knew what God wanted? Unlike the lunatic, though, Emil at least had the sense to keep such heretical thoughts to himself. He eyed Theo enviously, now peaceful as a baby.

Passenger Bastion

Naturally they asked first in coach if anyone wanted to go up front and shovel. Their own guy had either fainted or died from overwork. No straight answer forthcoming as to which. And what reward was on offer for the game passenger? The plane stayed up in the air, that was all.

So far the engines sounded normal. No stirrings of turbulence or that uh-oh feeling of your stomach rising balloonishly. But loss of altitude was mere heartbeats away. Still, nobody spoke up. Our stewardess (can't stand the newspeak of "flight attendant") was already frowning aggrievedly. What kind of asses were we?

She didn't look old enough to remember when this situation could never have arisen, before jet fuel got too expensive. Reverting to the yesteryears of iron horsemanship, planes now ran on coal. Not just any old lumps, of course, but specially "enriched." No idea with what. Very few people know with what. In any case, "enriched" enough to keep commercial flight viable. Which is all anyone really cares about. Except that, just like any other coal, someone has to keep shoveling it into the furnace, from takeoff till landing.

"Please? Anybody?" My own sidelong once-over affirmed that nobody was giving her a chance to make eye contact. Go recruit up in first class! They had that much more invested in this trip. We were miserable enough as it was, between stale air and leg cramps and bad food, without adding hard labor. For that matter, in the event of a nosedive, the forward cabin was that much closer to the ground. As for other members of the crew pitching in, including our stewardess? Forget it. Absolutely against union regulations. She expelled a sigh of disgust and U-turned through the curtains, to appeal to our betters.

Meanwhile, the guy sitting next to me, who'd run off with his inhaler a minute ago, came back from the bathroom.

"What'd I miss?" he asked. "What's the flight attendant upset about?"

"Not much. Plane going down, that's all."

"What?"

I then had to catch him up in full.

"And nobody volunteered to go help?" Indignant tone and a certain spark in his eye ignited simultaneously. He gawked around askance, thick neck puffing adderlike up against close-trimmed beard. I knew what light burned in that window of his soul. The Right Thing to Do was manifestly at hand. Into the breach, like gas into a vacuum. And this was no idle assessment on my part. Hardly had we gotten aloft than he'd poked at a headline in my paper about a flasher and proclaimed, "Hey, I nailed a guy like that once. I was sittin' in a Denny's and I saw 'im exposing himself to some girl in the parking lot. I chased 'im down and told him if I ever saw him around there again I'd beat the crap out of him. Then I went in and saw a cop at a table and asked 'im, 'Did you see that?' I told him what had happened and he went out and arrested the guy, just like that."

"How was the girl dealing with it?"

"Huh?" He was at a momentary loss. Why would I ask about that? "She was laughin' at him in the first place, if I recall. She was like fourteen or so. And when the cop came after 'im, she took off like it might have been her in trouble. Imagine that!"

I kept it quiet that I generally felt sorry for flashers. I mean, if they wanted to abduct kids, they'd abduct kids, right? Instead of wasting so much energy making themselves conspicuous. And now this bastion of decency was saying, "I better go up there and talk to her."

"I'm not sure engine stoker's the best line of work for an asthmatic," I counseled. His fingers still encircled inhaler. "Wait and see if anyone's more civic-minded up in first class."

"Never," he averred. "They figure, for what they pay for seats, why should they have to do anything? I'm goin' up there."

Not just yet, he wasn't. We tilted forward, we dipped, my stomach rose in me like the aforesaid balloon. A mighty engine knock traveled the length of the plane, rocking Passenger Bastion into the aisle. He found his footing, though inhaler was missing in action. Another jolt sat him on the carpet again.

"We're losing altitude!" hollered the captain over the p.a. "Somebody get off their fucking ass and help!"

Even this lapse in professionalism accomplished nothing. Tacit consensus, despite shadow of worry on every face, was that what the captain wanted was simply not our job. First class must have shared our feelings, stewardess entreaties be damned.

Passenger Bastion was up again. His wide-set features aglow and fixed, as though his head were a purposeful jack-o'-lantern, he lurched forward. Those along his path pointedly ignored him or lifted apprehensive eyes as if their biggest concern were that he might pitch into their laps. Why couldn't he stay down like everyone else instead of creating a nuisance? The sounding of internal bugle had sped him halfway through the curtain before anyone heard, "Someone grab my inhaler for me off the floor, will you?" A few checked around their feet. Nobody reached down.

After that, each of us was a self-contained huddled mass. Wretched, withdrawn. Staring at magazine print but never turning a page. The plane bucked. A baby squalled. A mega-sputtering and chuffing came from everywhere and nowhere. An overhead luggage compartment popped open. The plane trembled as with fever. This went on long enough to seem as if it had always been going on.

Then the grosser perturbations spiked further and further apart, till it suddenly occurred to me there hadn't been any in a while. The ubiquitous trembling weakened by degrees to where I may or may not have been imagining it. In conjunction, the very fuselage was regaining strength, and by and by bore us with godlike ease again across the sky. Apart from the absence of Passenger Bastion, the life-threatening crisis had wrought no changes and was good as forgotten by the time we started our descent.

The curtains flew open. The stewardess was hard-pressed to support Passenger Bastion's tottering dead weight. Nobody lifted a finger on her behalf. Or applauded his heroic efforts. Into his aisle seat she dumped him, a wheezing sack of potatoes. Didn't buckle him in. Click-clacked away, dusting herself off. Body language fairly screaming, Thank God that's over with!

Passenger Bastion, like Pigpen in funny pages of yore, languished in a gray, cloying miasma of enriched coal. Even had inhaler been handy, he'd have been too spent to use it. His bulging eyes hove toward mine, and his mouth opened and closed, feebly miming a question. I didn't want to second-guess him or encourage worse overexertion. So I quickly averted my sight as if at some distraction. At next glance, he'd passed out. Better that way. Would he ever relax otherwise? And relaxing was the best thing for him right now, wasn't it?

Landing could have been smoother. Met with a smatter of clapping from the more habit-prone. Passenger Bastion opened his eyes. Couldn't have thought the acclaim was for him. But in dreamland, would that ideally wake him? Blinking away sleep, he asked me, "Was I out long?"

"Yeah. Long time," I assured him.

"Did the flight attendant bring me back?"

"From where? You've been asleep for hours. You having weird dreams?"

He goggled at me. "How did I get all covered in coal dust then?"

"Flying's not as clean as it used to be. Look at me. I've got it all over myself, too." That part was no lie. Of course, it had all billowed off him. "You can have some crazy nightmares at 20,000 feet."

The plane taxied to a stop. Mass release of seatbelts clattered like a hailstorm. Without waiting for flightcrew go-ahead, restive travelers were on wobbly feet and pawing at overhead baggage. I freed my briefcase from under the seat in front of me. Passenger Bastion, now thoroughly befuddled, stood up and gaped around, desperate for enlightenment. But within his turbid cloud, he couldn't tell if others were gray like him or not. Nor would anyone face him straight on, and so have to say something nice about his rescuing them. I could read their expressions like a billboard: clearly he wanted to be a hero, didn't he? Or he wanted something. Which exempted them from feeling beholden. Was I supposed to stand up on a seat and rant that he couldn't help being a good do-bee? Hell, I didn't like the guy either.

Would anything have earned him the gratitude of this crowd? Well, saving casualties from burning wreckage, I suppose. But we'd been nowhere near that point. We'd have come to that, yes, or maybe someone or something else would have intervened. Hard to say what. Didn't mean that Passenger Bastion wasn't self-seeking or toadying for stepping in when he did.

Funny thing about the inhaler. While Passenger Bastion was out of it, I was squirming away from him as best I could. In vain efforts to keep that blend of sweat and petrochemicals out of my nostrils. Couldn't shift to the window seat because someone was there, so fixated on the view as to leave no record in my memory. Literally faceless for all I knew. Anyway, my fidgeting jammed something against my backside. The inhaler! I'd been sitting on it all along. I sneaked it into Passenger Bastion's blazer pocket and wiped my knuckles on the upholstery.

And now, in a daze, he was wrestling his totebag from the over-head rack. People pressed by with no one begging his pardon. Acting more inconsiderate than they would have if he hadn't gone shoveling.

I got up after he disappeared into the milling exodus. He didn't get far. Ten rows maybe. He was sitting down again, fighting for breath. His profound confusion couldn't have made matters easier for him. Whose recent history was right, his or what seemed like everyone else's? I could have spilled the beans but, like the rest of us, didn't want to be on this plane a minute longer than I had to. And if this boiled down to taking his part or the rest of humanity's, I guess my answer was to keep walking.

Dammit! He caught my eye. "Hey! I lost my inhaler, didn't I?" he croaked. Stubborn fellow.

"In your dreams, maybe," I commented in passing. He'd be fine if he just let go of his own take on reality. I had so much as told him that the inhaler was safely on his person. I didn't look back.

Power of Midnight

"Every experience creates a new reality."—Bill Moyers

Craig wasn't going to make the same mistake twice. Two years later, he still smarted at the memory of finding that second Left Banke album in the cutout bins at the university bookstore. The record wasn't even a decade old at that point, but he'd never seen it before, much less heard of it, and within him broke that little wave of excitement at unearthing a rarity. Don't get too worked up, though! The cover was kind of bogus, with a bunch of masked guys posturing amidst craggy scenery, and none of the song titles were familiar. The baroque-and-roll classics like "Walk Away Renée" and "Pretty Ballerina" were on the first LP, and he was under the impression that the band had split under the pressures of success, without any follow-ups.

The artifact fascinated him. On the other hand, it might be unlistenable. Besides, he was strapped as usual, and wasn't sure he could afford the two dollars. It might not leave him enough for groceries, which had been painstakingly narrowed down of late to a quartered fryer, four big yams, and ten artichokes from the corner market, to get him most economically through the week. So he regretfully let the Left Banke go, to be snapped up by a better-heeled customer by the time he came back, after Voychek had set Craig wise to its auction value and cult appeal.

Mick Voychek was his big influence, mentor even, in the pursuit of knowledge and trophies of the last fifteen years in art rock and psychedelia. Today, though, Craig traveled alone. He'd learned the hard way that Voychek was primarily competition in these situations. Anyway, Mick would have turned up his nose at this little junket, so no need for Craig's conscience to act up. Public transit to a factory town on the skids, where a flea market occupied a defunct mill (the exotic-sounding Nyanza Mills, to be exact), simply wasn't Voychek's style. Nonetheless, in just such depressing environs was Craig likeliest to scare up cut-rate gems, and maybe the black album. And he always carried $20, figuring it should more than cover the priciest collectibles in these places.

Voychek, of course, had educated him about the black album, during an evening of joints and Stone's Ginger Wine at Mick's apartment. Craig had contributed the wine. And now, up the clanging iron stairs, through the stubborn glass door, and past the tough chain-smoking grandma who took his 50¢ admission, he surveyed aisle upon aisle of cultural detritus and leerily inhaled the industrial odor of dust laced with machine oil and noxious mystery chemicals, and thought, Well, why not here? After all, the odds were equally against him everywhere.

He strolled with studied blandness among the warrens and dens slapped together of toys and clothing and junk jewelry and paperbacks and household appliances, shunning eye contact with the unkempt, dumpy old dealers lest they accost him like carnival barkers. However, at any stacks or milk crates or shelves of vinyl, whether 33 or 45, he zeroed in with a generally unacknowledged sunny smile and hello. For the next hour he flipped through hundreds of LPs, and the way he paused to double-check every halfway black cover (despite a consistent 99% certainty of what he was looking at in the first split-second) verified that an idée fixe was at the helm. Craig took it in stride. As he'd told himself more than once in twenty-five years of life on earth, If a thing's really worth doing, it's worth obsessing over.

Anyway, this trip was not a waste. For a quarter each, he scored the second Troggs album on Fontana, the one with "I Can't Control Myself," and the debut album by banjo-and-primitive synth duet Silver Apples. They had both survived since the mid-'60s in pristine shape, and the Silver Apples still had the poster inside! So what if the songs tended toward monotony? It was a prize he could enjoy in small doses, and it reduced his letdown at failing once more to bag the black album.

On the bus home, only one random glance at the roadside marred the pleasure of inspecting his purchases. The woods opposite the dogtrack had been bulldozed. Yet another distasteful swipe by megalopolis at the shrinking wilderness! Fronting the devastation was a sign the size of a classroom movie screen, and it brayed "Condos Coming Soon!" What the hell were "condos"? Did it mean to say "condoms"? Were birth control products such a big deal out in the sticks? Joke as he would, everything seemed to be under a subtle but ominous darkness for a few miles.

The mood was right for bringing the black album to mind. Obviously, it wasn't called that. It was one of those cases where the band name doubled as the title, and because the band hailed from behind the Iron Curtain somewhere—Azerbaijan or the Ukraine or Bulgaria—the name was a matter of guesswork. Voychek translated it most often as Power of Midnight or Half Past Dead of Night. The material had been recorded on a two-track reel-to-reel in someone's living room or cellar or secret studio, beyond the ears of a regime with broad definitions of decadence and subversion. Only 500 or 100 or 50 copies had been pressed, and in the last couple of years, 10 or 25 or 50 had been smuggled to the U.S. via Helsinki or West Berlin. Voychek showed no signs of obsession with the black album himself, though it had somehow cropped up in several conversations after that evening of ginger wine. And in typical Voychek fashion, if Craig made bold to question the inconsistencies in place names and numbers and translations between descriptions, Mick went on the defensive. What, you don't believe me, man? Besides, someone Mick knew in New York had played him a cassette of it. Not a whole side, but sufficient to get the idea. Aha, Craig's stop was coming up.

Lorna was expecting him. It suited him to live in the historic district, a mile farther down the route, but her apartment was hands-down much cheerier. The bus dropped him at the foot of the hill called Mount Hope, for a climb that guaranteed a sense of accomplishment on even the most unproductive days. He passed turn-of-the-century tenements and Victorian homes converted to off-campus housing, and reflected on how lucky he was to have graduated in a town where it was so easy to be poor. And how could it be otherwise, with multitudes of students to accommodate? If only the slumlords kept these classy old buildings in better repair!

At the summit, he turned left onto Hope Street. His thoughts strayed inexorably back to the black album. The black album was utterly black. On that one particular, there was no doubt. A lot of releases had mostly black covers, except for the lettering that announced *Earthbound* by King Crimson, say, or Soft Machine 5. But in a fanatic purging of compromise, or fears of divulging personal info to the authorities, or obeisance to occult or more unguessable principles, the front, back, inner sleeve, label, and vinyl (naturally) were pure, unrelieved black. Whatever had impelled these musicians to express themselves, it wasn't crass fame, though they needn't have been idealists either. They may well have had a more sinister agenda than "art for art's sake."

Craig was halfway up the porch steps of Lorna's triple-decker. Better switch gears before he went in! He might never find closer approximation to the open-minded girl of his dreams, but she wasn't into the so-called "negative energy." He unlocked the front door while pressing the bell to let her know he was inside, as he had for going on two years. She was on the top floor. Apparently a manic spark in his eye and undercurrent of agitation when he talked about the black album made her uncomfortable. Only the bright side held any attraction for her. He'd given her *Hangman's Beautiful Daughter* by those highbrow hippie mystics the Incredible String Band, and she had gazed wistfully at the front cover's decade-ago crowd in motley robes and tunics and hats, and remarked how nice it would be if everyone felt free to look however they wanted. There in a nutshell was what was endearing about her. That, and her offhand way of sitting around with him watching TV or reading, and suddenly coming out with "Want to fuck?" A heroine of the underground comix in the flesh! And to think, when he started seeing her, she owned nothing but Judy Collins and Mary Hopkins and suchlike folk snooze.

Her apartment door was open an inch. He detected the aroma of bulgur-and-cheese loaf in the oven and hoped she wouldn't mind hearing the Troggs over dinner. He set his purchases by the turntable, found her in the kitchen chopping lettuce, and kissed her hello. He had turned her on to a ton of cool music and movies and books, and she sprang for most of the groceries they ate at her table. It seemed an equitable arrangement.

From her place, next morning's walk to work was twice as long, but what was a little inconvenience in the name of love? The self-professed "friendly" bank downtown, maybe in a tardy nod to the bicentennial, was rewarding big depositors with reproduction Colonial-era pewter, which Craig boxed up and mailed off or handed to walk-in claimants, keeping track of transactions on a multipage xeroxed list. A few wives of Marketing Division honchos assisted him part-time. The bank's corporate HQ occupied a gorgeous Federal-era commercial row, though he was relegated to drab, dusty basement. Fine by him. Better than having bankers around constantly, and they didn't make him dress up to toil in their dungeon.

He'd been yelled at once for answering the phone "Pewterama" instead of the ugly and cumbersome "Bedrock Savings Bank Pewter Redemption Center." Did they really expect him to take this job seriously? Today, another customer called to complain that his tankard had fallen onto a shag rug and the handle had snapped off and bounced across the room as if springloaded. Yes, he wanted a replacement, which in Craig's mind made him a two-time loser. Then one of the marketing guys came down to pester the missus for an hour or two, as often happened. Craig had no desire to eavesdrop, but hubby was too much of a blowhard to ignore. The missus wanted to go see the new David Bowie movie at the nearby art cinema, so hubby had to straighten her out.

"Anything to do with that Bowie character has got to be weird. I heard he goes around wearing a dress. If I were you, I wouldn't waste my time. I'm sure not going." Craig had to grit his teeth and focus on matching address labels to flagons or trenchers or whatever the hell they were. Wearing a dress was the essence of weird? He'd like to lock this buffoon in a padded cell with the black album blasting through hidden speakers and watch the fireworks. Or maybe the man was so dense that it wouldn't get to him, and he'd just be standing there scratching his news-anchor hairdo twenty minutes later.

For anyone else, suicidal madness was the alleged upshot of sitting through an entire side at once. Voychek, with atypical literary flair, had referred to the black album as the "*Necronomicon* of vinyl." He had also described it as "doom rock." Craig hadn't heard that one in years, and then only from Boston know-it-alls badmouthing downbeat "progressive" bands like King Crimson or Sam Gopal or Van der Graaf Generator. Portentous mellotrons, dramatic drum rolls, lyrics from the id couldn't have added up to the black album's dire effect. The marketing bigmouth would have shrugged all that off with an arrogant quip. Sometimes Craig wondered how conversant Voychek truly was with Power of Midnight, assuming it existed outside of a bad trip way back when.

Still, let's be fair. Some textbook "prog" bands reportedly created or attracted an obstinate cloud of juju. Take Van der Graaf. Their *Stürm und Drang*, and long excursions into shifting time signatures and colliding parts, put them in league with Genesis and Gentle Giant, but those groups weren't plagued by freak accidents and near-death incidents and riots trailing them from concert to concert. Something in Van der Graaf's music drew down a curse, or eldritch agency of some sort, upon them. Band members had flat-out admitted that to the British press! Craig, in contrast, had played their records incessantly to help him weather a harrowing breakup with an old girlfriend, so he considered them a positive influence. Then again, his life had reached a saturation point of misery, and the legendary Van der Graaf juju couldn't have made it any worse. As for Power of Midnight, at their implicitly higher order of magnitude, maybe the two-track was recording, or on playback for the first time, in 1968 when Russian tanks rolled past the Czech border and forced an end to Prague Spring.

Fingertip poked his shoulder, brusquely as if stopping an alarm clock. He shuddered and, while flinching from this invasion of personal space, plastered a crooked label on a box marked "Porringer." He turned forlornly to the suit-and-tie galoot literally breathing down his neck. "I'm taking Sharon to lunch!" he announced as if Craig were deaf. Craig nodded. No use saying anything. Nor was there anything to say. No, you can't take her? Run along and have fun, kids?

He resumed labeling boxes, and overheard marketing guy mutter something about "in a world of his own" on the way out. Which was ironic, because Craig felt as if this workplace were a fading world of dinosaurs, with their completely out-of-it values and attitude, whereas everyone in his circle knew better than to take the bullshit of banking or business per se seriously. There was so much more to life! And the waters were slowly but steadily rising in Craig's favor, weren't they? Possession of under an ounce was a mere misdemeanor in more and more states, and flag-waving jingoism was passé, and Jimmy Carter was saving millions of wilderness acres from development, and the revolution in Iran was finally telling Uncle Sam where to get off. On the other hand, in his co-workers' world, there was no room for weird ol' David Bowie, let alone a black album.

On the uphill hike home, Craig stopped in at Rimes, an underground record shop in both senses. It operated out of a basement in the commercial zone adjoining the university, and its specialties were punk singles in picsleeves, prog imports, a slew of cutouts, and best of all, import cutouts. Last month he'd snagged a Brit pressing of Pink Floyd's *Relics* for a measly $3! He also enjoyed shooting the shit with the people behind the counter, especially Bonnie and Cynthia, who were both superlatively cute in disparate Irish and Italian ways. He got occasional vibes that Bonnie kinda liked him, unless those were a trick of his wishful thinking. But the cheerful red-haired palooka known to the record-buying public as Jimbo Machine (thanks to a misspelling on a piece of junk mail) was on shift now.

New Arrivals filled a pair of bins on a table up front, so that customers could whittle them down before they had to be integrated with the rest of the stock. Otherwise this was a very industrious crew. Rimes was part of a co-op chain, and the wave of the future in Craig's view. The clerks were co-owners. They did the work, and they knew what was going on in the shop, so why shouldn't they call the shots and reap the benefits? They deserved to succeed.

Whoa! Craig hated how everyone these days reacted to the least little thing by braying "I don't believe it!" He would have joined them, though, had he been any less stunned. Amidst the New Arrivals, behind the umpteenth remaindered influx of *Propaganda* by Sparks (how goddamn many had they pressed?), as if it were nothing extraordinary, waited a solid black cover. Craig swayed a little and steadied himself by thrusting forth an arm to seize this dream come true.

"Hey! Craig, you all right, buddy? You look like you're gonna faint!" shouted Jimbo.

"It's okay," mumbled Craig, keeping his head down. He held his breath and slowly lifted and revolved his square plastic grail. The back was plain black too! There was shrinkwrap, but it was loose, crinkly, with a rough seam across the equator on the hindside. An amateur job, as Power of Midnight patently would be. Craig's eyes stole into the bin again. A second copy! He grabbed that as well. Foolish not to corner the market.

Through the cellophane he discerned a texture in the cardboard cover, like the barest shadow of topography, or like cured skin in close-up. Excellent choice for a "*Necronomicon* of vinyl."

Jimbo was right next to him, grinning good-naturedly. "You sure you're all right? You're lookin' pale. You want a cup of tea? Slug of whiskey?"

"What do you know about this?" asked Craig, holding the two copies together between the palms of his hands as if he were displaying framed artwork. Play it cool, man! The ordinarily compelling offer of free liquor registered only in passing.

"Your guess is as good as mine," Jimbo shrugged. "Distributor didn't say. Charged us for 'em, though. I got half a mind to return 'em as 'damaged,' if you know what I mean."

At the mention of sordid lucre, Craig checked the price sticker. Ow. $3.99 each, plus tax. Suppose this wasn't really Power of Midnight? He almost balked, until history tugged at his sleeve. Remember the Left Banke! And Jimbo's talk of "damaging" the goods had serendipitously upped the sales pressure. "I'll take both of these," Craig blurted.

"That's what I like about you! You're a gambler," Jimbo declared. Craig gave him the merchandise to ring up, with a twinge as the cash drawer clattered open. This outlay wouldn't have felt quite as onerous if he'd been shrewd enough to jump at that complimentary dram. Too late now!

Craig had the first floor of a gray, marginally Greek Revival house from the mid-nineteenth century. It was on a generally quiet corner, and its façade abutted the sidewalk. His bedroom was to the left of the front door, and its windows looked out on treeless street. The neighborhood was an oil-and-water mix of student and Portuguese and old-line WASP, and was pungent with nearby estuary when summer winds blew southerly. Craig had spent three years on the premises, two of them with a roomie who was now shacked up with a girl in Boston. Craig was managing as sole tenant, but money was tight.

A staircase in the front hall led to Daphne's half of the house. Her door beyond the landing was closed. Good. It had taken months to convince her he wasn't some species of fiend. In her first semester here at grad school, she'd remarked some curiosity about Ornette Coleman. So at her request, while she went about her business upstairs, he put on *Skies of America* at a volume to billow through her open door. He stood reverently between the speakers as the first glacial sheets of orchestral chords and discords clashed and flowed. Jazz ignoramus that he was, he still knew sublime (transcendent, even) when it hit him. He withdrew to the foot of the stairs and was about to call Daphne and ask if she wanted it louder, when her door slammed and made the walls quiver. The verdict he later coaxed from her on that particular *chef d'oeuvre* was "demonic." He didn't need to alienate her afresh with the black album.

Craig entered his domain through the door at the end of the hall and set to procrastinating. He went to the bathroom, picked up his mail on the side table back in the hall, and surveyed the kitchen cupboard for supper options. He stopped when his eyes happened to light upon the paper bag from Rimes among the clutter on the living-room table. All right, already! Five momentous paces across creaky floorboards, and he was slipping one album from the bag, and his thumbnail was slicing the brittle shrinkwrap along the mouth of the sleeve, and his thumb and forefinger were pinching the inner sleeve and about to pull, when the doorbell chimed. He couldn't decide if he were relieved or exasperated.

In the hall, hand upon doorknob, he heard Daphne from above. "Craig? I was wondering if—"

The door swung open while she was in mid-sentence. Voychek, hands in leather-jacket pockets, greeted Craig with a hearty "Hey, man!"

Daphne's door slammed. Craig she no longer believed dangerous, but his friends were destined to remain "hoods." Ridiculous, wasn't it? "Mods" was what they called themselves, equating that, aptly or not, with garish striped shirts, vivid scarves indoors and out, a clean shave, and rock star-length hair. Mick's was of the Prince Valiant variety and emphasized an eerie resemblance to Dee Dee Ramone. His bandmate Carl, whose blasé hazel eyes were fixed on something in the distance, had the mane and the stance to qualify as a member of Led Zeppelin. "We're goin' down to the Riverview," Voychek was saying in his resonant monotone. "You doin' anything?"

"Come on in!" Craig found himself exclaiming. "You have to see this. I was just about to put it on." Mick and Carl slouched in after him. Their shiftiness pretty much semaphored an aversion to dawdling here. Craig plucked his trophy from the table to show off, without actually letting it within their reach. "I don't know for sure, but I think it's the black album!"

"Whoa! The black album? I don't know, man." Hard to tell with Voychek if he were skeptical, or impressed, or apprehensive, or humoring him.

Well, pal, just you wait! Craig dashed over to the stereo, on the topmost of several cinderblock-and-plank shelves that braced his 500-odd LPs against the wall. He jabbed the power button on the amp and had the inner sleeve halfway into daylight before realizing his problem. He had his back to the others, who didn't say anything if they saw him slump.

The inner sleeve was white. A bad sign. Hence Craig was roundly disappointed but not surprised at the 8" × 11" insert that slid out with the record, to inform him he was holding *Air Fiction* by the Muffins. In any other context, he'd have been happy. He'd seen the Muffins once in Maryland. Arguably the best band in America, with the wry ingenuity of Zappa and the energy of The Who. But on the basis of prissy band name alone, the farthest cry from the expectations he'd raised. "False alarm," he sighed, killed the stereo, and resignedly faced his guests. "Sorry." He tilted the disk back inside its jacket.

Voychek had sauntered up from behind and snatched the album away. He upended the cover and gruffly tapped the black spine till the insert emerged. He ogled it in silence, then handed the package back to Craig. "Good one! You had me goin' for a minute."

"We oughta move," urged Carl. "I have work soon."

Carl drove a dented black '64 Catalina. Craig had the backseat to himself, cracked upholstery, empty soda cans and all. Voychek turned and proffered him the better part of a lit joint. Craig said thanks and indulged in a long hit as Mick spoke. "Hey man, I went into that record store the other day to pick up some 45s I ordered, but the picsleeves were missing. You don't know anything about that, do you?"

Craig automatically shook his head no, and relinquished the joint. Then his inner cogwheels began to mesh. A few weeks ago, a bunch of empty picsleeves had come in at Rimes, and Jimbo had given them to him insofar as they were worthless by themselves. Craig had received them with demure thanks. Someday, he bet, they'd be valuable! But that had happened at a much greater remove than "the other day." And the sleeves and contents wouldn't be sent separately, would they? That didn't make sense. Still, best not to say anything. Craig shook his head again, and Mick, whether 100% convinced or not, turned aside and gave Carl the joint. Jeez, Jimbo hadn't said anything to Mick, had he? Too late to worry about that now! Craig looked out the side window as the pot kicked in.

The Riverview was a greasy spoon with '50s décor and a view, logically enough, of the river, and of the derelict railroad drawbridge that had been left to rust pointing straight up. Craig, as he did every time he was here, thought the bridge a perfect subject for a postcard with the "Greetings From" sentiment, but in his reefer wisdom knew it was never to be. No love of humor in this town—that was its trouble.

They all ordered eggplant parm, as usual, because vegetarian Mick would denounce anything else on the menu as a "plateful of death." Over at Lorna's, Craig was a vegetarian too, but a carnivore at home. If civilization collapsed tomorrow, he wanted a digestive tract that could handle squirrels and pigeons.

Craig glanced up from his plate. Voychek was smirking at him. "Y'know, the second you showed it to me, I knew that wasn't the black album."

"So you've seen it then?" Craig tended to adopt British diction when being needled.

"You'd know it if you had it." Voychek seldom acknowledged yes-or-no questions as such. "It has, like, an aura that it gives off.

There's a feel about it. That thing you had didn't have the same presence at all."

"Is it supposed to be alive or something?" Carl ventured.

"Well, it projects an influence. It sort of takes care of itself. Once you've been near it, it can affect you from a distance."

"Is that so?" Carl's tone was less than deferential.

Expression faded from Mick's face. Mouth agape, he could have been deflating. He was slowly sinking floorward and listing toward the wall of their booth. It looked too dramatic to be real, especially after his talk of "effect from a distance" and Carl's thinly veiled sarcasm. Craig grinned broadly and told Mick to cut it out, and Carl scoffed, "Come on, man, that's too much."

Voychek's sluggish hand went to his brow. "Whoa. Why are you guys laughing? I was really about to pass out." He set his palms against the table and heaved himself back into upright position.

"We thought you were jerkin' us around." Craig's lingering smile betrayed a shadow of hope that Mick was still jerking them around.

"I'm serious, man." Mick eyeballed each pal aggrievedly. "That was the third time this month."

Craig and Carl were quick to mumble apologies, and Voychek advised they drop the subject.

Carl had retrofitted the Catalina dashboard with a tape player, and en route to dropping off Mick he popped in the newest mix of the band's three songs. Craig couldn't distinguish it from last week's version or its many forebears, but dug them all equally. They mixed a punk attitude with the overachiever drumming of classic prog, and the freakout synth of Roxy Music's wilder days, and wacky overdubs galore à la Todd Rundgren. To put it another way, they were like Devo with the superior chops of Yes. Plus, the stuff was catchy. Craig often had "Margie '86" stuck in his head for hours. According to Voychek, the lyrics had something to do with a sexy android in the dim future of 1986. The band had no name yet and no plans to play out, preferring to hone the perfect demo tape and sign a deal with the label of their choice. Craig waxed enthusiastic about today's remix rattling the flimsy rear speakers, but Carl and Mick listened in customary fussy silence. Craig was sure these guys could set the world on fire, if only they'd quit hiding their light under a bushel.

When they pulled up in front of Mick's, Carl looked Craig in the face and said he had to get to work. Craig took the hint and cleared out. He didn't mind an evening constitutional, and anyhow wanted to see Mick safely inside. Least he could do, after treating that seizure or whatever it was like a comedy routine. Huh! Suppertime already wore the patina of a hazy old past. A sign of quality dope.

They were in the building and at the apartment door before Mick noticed that Craig was with him. "You want to come in a minute?" The invite had a genuine, if unsteady, ring.

Voychek had a ground-floor unit among the two dozen studios behind a hulking mock Tudor exterior. His quarters were markedly gloomier and more constricted than Craig's, and their odor of incense and patchouli would likely persist for decades after he vacated. When the bathroom door was open all the way, it half concealed a window that would have let in afternoon sun, had it not faced a narrow alley and the neighbors' clapboard wall.

A burglar couldn't have asked for easier access, and last New Year's Eve a turntable and pair of speakers and television had gone AWOL. Mick gamely laughed it off. The turntable belt was busted, and both tweeters were fried. Their pawnshop value was zilch. But the thieves, whether to be funny or gentlemanly, had removed from the turntable and placed in the center of its dust-free former location a Beatles single worth a thousand dollars. The anecdote almost made up for the loss of the TV, which Voychek claimed he hardly ever watched anyway. Another break-in was a matter of time, but what to do except drill holes through the window sashes and insert three-inch nails as poor man's deadbolts? The landlord, who was too cheap to install screen or storm windows, plainly wasn't shelling out for steel bars over the window frames. And if he did, Voychek's place would end up looking even more like a cell. This wasn't security-fixated New York, not yet at least!

Voychek sprawled on the threadbare black sofa, and Craig dropped into an old red armchair that somehow led him to imagine he was sitting on an acanthus leaf. Voychek extracted a joint from a drawer in the beige lacquered coffee table between them. Craig asked if more pot was a good idea after the Riverview incident. In lieu of yes-or-no answer, Voychek requested Craig's lighter. Craig tossed it to him, and Mick lit up, took a hit, passed the joint to Craig, and said, "You know, man, your attitude earlier kinda bothered me."

"You mean at the restaurant?"

"No, before that, at your place. I don't know where you're comin' from sometimes. Are you having a competition with me over that Power of Midnight record?"

"No, no, of course not," wheezed Craig through an escaping cloud of smoke. He wasn't, was he? Wait, come to think of it, yes, he was.

"Because I wouldn't want something like that to come between our friendship." Mick took a long drag, and Craig reached halfway across the table as Mick passed the joint back. "You know, there are some things, when you win, you lose."

Craig couldn't tell if Voychek were pressuring him to stop hunting for the black album, or if he had a more metaphysical, oblique meaning, so he simply nodded.

"Anyway, I was wondering if you could do me a favor." He snagged the joint from Craig. "I'm still a little shaky after what happened tonight, so I thought maybe you could help me with an errand. It's on your way home." From the coffee-table drawer he produced an ounce bag. "Just pocket this and press the buzzer at a house down the street and give it to whoever comes down. I can trust you with this, can't I?"

"Sure." Burn a friend? Who did Voychek think Craig was?

Voychek held the roach end toward him, and Craig wagged a hand sideways. He needed no more. In fact, the first puff on that second joint had been a mistake. His happy high was subsiding into a morass of bubbling anxiety, jumpiness, foreboding. He had to kick himself for letting casual excess beckon him into paranoia once more. In his worsening state, he wasn't keen on making a "drug run," but how to bow out gracefully? Or was paranoia having its way with him when there was nothing, statistically speaking, to worry about? It was only pot, and half the people on the street might have been "holding." He decisively planted the Scotch-taped baggie in an inside pocket of his vintage green military jacket, repeated the address

Voychek gave him, and saluted good night as Voychek saw him to the door with a jaunty "Thanks, man!"

A block away, he spotted a shiny dime on the sidewalk, shoved it into hip pocket, and frowned at emptiness where his Bic should have been. He'd forgotten it at Voychek's. He lost more lighters that way!

Angst, meanwhile, stuck with him, weighed on him, dictated he cast a wary eye at oncoming cars and pedestrians and gradually pick up his pace, despite overwhelming odds that everything was fine. The weed had turned on him. That was all. His heart was racing, and there was a pounding in his ears. Familiar symptoms. He shot right by the address he'd been mouthing the whole time, and doubled back, to hesitate in front of a multi-unit dwelling with mansard roof and a hood with fancy scrollwork above the door. He'd been by here a hundred times and had never sensed anything suspicious or sinister. Till now.

He reminded himself that drug deals vastly outnumbered drug busts, and that Mick would be stupid to set him up, since the result in short order would be cops at Mick's door. Or was Mick stupid? His feet, while he'd been busy equivocating, had brought him up the cement walk and within reach of the doorside panel with its rows of buzzers. Let's get this over with!

He rang, paused at least a minute as best he could judge, and rang again. From the squawk box below the buzzers, a voice growled as if Craig had been leaning on the button continuously. "What is it?"

He followed the printed instructions to press the little black knob and speak distinctly. "Something for you from Mick!"

"Is that so?" The voice receded, and Craig heard muffled conversation and the insipid harmonies of the Carpenters in the murkier background. These didn't seem like Mick's kind of people at all! "Stay right where you are. We're coming down."

We? Why "we"? Scant seconds remained before the tide of panic bore him away. He pushed the black knob and announced, "I'll leave it on the stoop!" He yanked the baggie from his pocket and, halfway to the sidewalk already, flung it at the welcome mat. "Top floor, you bastards, please be on the top floor," he chanted as he ran. When he reached the corner, he headed left and slowed down. Less incriminating, he decided. Blend with the rest of the foot traffic. He was winded by then anyway, but luckily, nobody was giving audible chase.

Craig woke with the malaise that should have dispersed when the dope wore off, and it fluttered unabating in his stomach for days. Was rogue cannabinol loitering in his bloodstream, or was he failing to suppress fears of repercussion after that business with the ounce bag? He felt disinclined to phone or visit a potentially wrathful Voychek. Why not give any heated emotions a chance to cool down?

Bad enough that he was putting his foot in it wherever he went, as if the negative energy from last night were relentlessly jinxing him. Restrooms at work were adjacent to the "Redemption Center." One of the few conveniences of his marginal position! He seldom resorted to the cafeteria beyond the elevators. Too many bankers in there, and the secretaries were prone to join them in eyeing him askance. The suits were almost as unavoidable in the lav, and the exchange overheard today while he was in one of the stalls wasn't the first that would rankle till bedtime. They were grousing, in atrociously un-enlightened terms, about an old Afro-American gent on the next block who'd been resisting years of pressure to sell off his eight-eenth-century storefront, currently a junk shop. Handwritten signs in his windows, legible from across the street, contended that whoever the official buyer was, demolition for office block or townhouses would follow, and banners cut from bedsheets flapped between third-floor windows to proclaim his contempt for City Hall, corrup-tion in the Historical Society, and gentrification in general. The bankers were themselves contemptuous that "the law" hadn't con-trived to seize the property for the sake of "getting this street turned around." The art cinema next door was plenty of eyesore for one neighborhood!

Racism, elitism, hostility toward whatever obstructed the march of profit were inextricable, apparently, from the circuitry of the business mind. Scratch a pillar of industry, find a fascist! Sharon was still out to leisurely lunch with marketing guy when Craig returned from the bathroom. Why couldn't the financiers and developers just hurry up and die without issue, before they made it that much harder for everyone else to get along? Better them than the poor, besieged eccentrics. The disgust expanded and expanded in Craig's head till it had to spill out. "My God, bankers are pigs," he muttered to himself.

"My husband's a banker!" shrilled Sharon. Oh fuck, what was she doing in Craig's "world of his own"? And at her desk, too, the front of which was flush with hers, such that a pencil would roll smoothly from one to the other. The glower in her eyes should have melted the mascara off her cheeks.

"Your husband's not a banker! He's in marketing. He's an advertising man," Craig babbled. She wasn't having any. Baffling how her makeup hadn't melted yet.

"You should be grateful they gave you a job at all," she said more quietly, but no less venomously, as she got back to work. Well, they should be grateful for someone willing to do their chimp labor, he thought, but saw no use in carrying the discussion further. She wouldn't repeat his little *cri de coeur* to hubby and associates, would she? Yeah, good one! This was going to cost him. She pulled the silent act all afternoon.

Counting on a bit more warmth from Lorna, he walked in on her in the middle of folding paper bags from the market and stowing them under the kitchen sink. The trot from the bank in balmy Indian summer was thirsty work, so he opened the fridge, checked out the nice full shelves, and grabbed a bottle of apple juice and, for good measure, since he was peckish, some carob drops from a Tupperware cylinder. When he turned around, Lorna was glaring at him. "Please ask me first if you want to raid my groceries." Craig stifled a smile on understanding she was serious, though he'd never needed permission before. Maybe she was extra irritable after food shopping. Funny how her neck got long and scrawny and her face resembled Stan Laurel's when she was indignant. Not very attractive! Later she informed him that her yoga classmate Karen had family in from out of town and they were treating Lorna to dinner tomorrow. He and Karen never had much to say to each other, and he and her relatives even less, so he didn't care that he hadn't been invited. In which case, why did that nervous knot in his stomach tighten?

Then hump day, which was also Halloween, was upon him. At least Sharon never worked Wednesdays. All quiet on that front.

When he got home, he dialed Lorna every so often, waiting ten rings each time. No answer. Oh, right, didn't she have dinner plans with Karen?

At dusk, the hip-capitalist landlord showed up with a plastic punchbowl of wretched 69¢-for-100 lollipops. He summoned Craig and Daphne to the foyer. Last Halloween, nobody bothered doling out candy, and vindictive kids had egged the house. Raw yolk was conspicuous as hell on gray paint and a bitch to scrub off. So could they please see to it that the trick-or-treaters didn't go away mad tonight? Craig was of the opinion that placating vandals with the worst candy in the milk store was bound to backfire, but didn't care to prolong the landlord's visit by debating him. As for Daphne, Craig read her mile-long gaze and slight backward tilt of her shoulders as signs of feeling put-upon. But she too had the wisdom not to waste even more time wrangling. When she falsely believed no one was watching, though, she wrinkled her dainty nose at the punchbowl on the side table as if it were full of kitty litter.

Craig and Daphne glumly contemplated the front door after the landlord's exit. "This is not good." Daphne's tone bordered on sepulchral. "I need to concentrate on my thesis tonight. Interruptions are not good." Craig turned to find her subjecting the punchbowl to a forlorn look that entreated, Don't lay this on me now! He sighed. Oh, all right! He'd go greet the moochers, provided Daphne's door stay open in case he needed a break for whatever reason. She readily agreed, with spirits on the instant rebound. In retrospect, how laughable to imagine nothing would go wrong!

No sooner had he wolfed a can of chili and plunked the dirty plate in the sink than the doorbell rang, as it did without letup till he felt as if he were working a second job. By then, he'd devised the most efficient way to get rid of each clutch of junior blackmailers. When he answered the door he was cradling the punchbowl, and while the kids were still crowing "Trick or treat," he scooped up a handful of lollipops and chucked a few into one sack after another, hopefully too fast for them to see what they were getting. As he dumped whatever was left into the last sack, he bellowed "Happy Halloween" and slammed the door. Nobody's costume inspired compliments or a second glance. They might as well have been the

same dozen customers over and over: Star Wars or Disney characters, Wonder Woman, Superman, or generic hoboes, princesses, gyp-
sies, all redolent of Woolworth's.

After a short breather by the side table, he heard the phone, and
three paces along, the doorbell. "Daphne!" he hollered up the staircase. "Please get the door! Daphne!" No acknowledgment. He resorted to maximum volume. "Daphne! Get the door!" How could
that fail to roust her? The doorbell rang again as he ran to the phone.

It was taciturn Carl. This was a first. The damnedest things happened on Halloween. "Mick wanted me to tell you something."

"Okay. But why didn't he call me himself?"

"They only give you one phone call. He's in jail."

"What? In jail? Why?"

"Busted."

"For pot?"

"Listen, I don't wanna talk about it over the phone. If you can
understand what I'm sayin'." Boy, that Carl didn't need a lot of pretext to start copping an attitude.

"But he had a message for me?" When Craig came right down to
it, he didn't really enjoy chatting with Carl either.

"He said, if you wanted it so badly, it's on the bottom shelf, in a
box marked 'Auction.' He said, maybe better you than some other
people."

"Why me? What's he giving me?"

"You oughta have enough on the ball to know what he's talking
about."

"I don't have keys to his place. Do you?"

"He also said that shouldn't be a problem. He thought you might
have a hidden talent for snagging things." Jesus! Was that another
swipe about those bloody picsleeves?

"What did he mean?"

"That's all he said. I gotta run, man." Silence followed an un-
ceremonious click. And there went the doorbell again. Daphne had
abandoned her post in the hall, if ever she had occupied it.

Thankfully, the onslaught was tapering off, allowing Craig respites to plan his technically illegal mission. Once a half-hour had
elapsed without any little beggars on the stoop, he grabbed his

jacket, on the premise that he'd have the sidewalks mostly to himself now and could duck into shadows whenever he didn't. The fewer witnesses, the better, obviously. Questioning the rashness, the unsavoriness of this foray would have been blatant hypocrisy. Of course he was going, though he hadn't owned up yet to the influence of that particular obsession riding him for months. If he hoped to be functional at all, he had to focus exclusively on logistics. No eyes on the prize till it was literally in sight! He locked up apartment and house in soundless slow motion. Why spoil Daphne's impression that he was staying in?

He stuck with his prearranged route of most sedate and tree-lined streets and came no closer than two blocks to any other pedestrians. Would this have been easier behind the wheel? Hell no. Anonymity was his watchword, and unless he were to turn and find a telltale license plate fastened to his ass, he had to believe he was better served on foot. One more real-life scenario to support his (seldom voiced) contention that driving was for suckers!

He reined himself in as Voychek's Tudor pile loomed ahead. No one was around. His means of ingress had occurred to him even as Carl was gauchely hanging up without a good-bye. He checked for onlookers again and skulked down the alley on Mick's side of the building, past drawn curtains and lowered shades. Mick's window must have been open these last several warm days. With any luck, he'd neglected to reinsert the nails in the sashes. Bingo! Craig grimaced at some initial creaking before the window begrudged a gap through which to clamber hastily. If this was all there was to it, no wonder a life of crime was so popular.

He pushed the open bathroom door away en route to landing palms-first on the gritty carpet. Weighty green velveteen drapes on either side of the window startled him, as if they were towering in wait, forcing him to concede how skittish he was at heart. He stood up, shaking unclean particles off his hands, and listened. Nope, no concerned footsteps beyond walls or ceiling. His own steps in the gloom were tentative, and at relocating his lighter on the coffee table where he'd forgotten it Monday, he was acutely pleased with himself. Also on the table was a cassette, and by the glow of the Bic he read yesterday's date on it. Into an inside jacket pocket it went. Craig had long coveted a dub of Voychek's band, but the third time he'd asked, Voychek had gotten inexplicably pissed off. Now that the man was in jail, Craig might as well help himself.

In jail. A sobering image. The nonstop fluttering in his stomach for the last forty-eight hours worsened in sympathy. He hadn't stopped to dwell on Mick's plight till his surroundings, and a lungful of stale incense, called him to mind. How was he holding up? Were the cops browbeating him? Brutalizing him? Demanding names and threatening hard time? Was he cooperating? Could he say anything that would get back to Craig?

Breaking and entering didn't sit any better with the *gendarmes* than peddling dope. Maybe Craig should snag what he was here for and vamoose. Behind the acanthus-shaped red armchair, the record collection dominated the wall, floor to ceiling, as if it doubled as a load-bearing element. Craig had let the Bic flame die. Now he knelt and relit it and, on the far-right bottom shelf, found the cardboard box. It was of a music-industry design for shipping 25 units. He gingerly removed it from its tight fit beside the Zoot Money LPs. It was full. He held his breath and threw back the flap extending halfway down the front of the box, and brought the lighter to bear.

What the fuck? He held the flame as close as he dared. *Left Banke Too* was the title, all right. Was this necessarily his particular one that got away? The two-dollar sticker from the university bookstore was still in the upper right, though the cover didn't look at all the way he recalled from two years ago. That Voychek! Could this have been what he'd intended for Craig in a parting gesture of goodwill, before the court system swallowed him up? Craig pulled out enough of the next album to see it was pure glossy black, and sealed. He gasped. Voychek had also been sitting on this all along, had he? A month ago, he'd flatly denied knowing where any copies were. What the hell else was in the box?

That wave of excitement at latching onto rarities slammed into him and lifted him to his feet. Or was the thrill of avarice coursing through his veins? He didn't care to split hairs. Which of these two prizes was for him? He doused the lighter and bent over to lift the box. A fine lot of good any of Voychek's belongings would do him in prison, and if deciding what to do with them devolved upon the landlord, the dumpster might be their fate. The box was hefty, but Craig could manage it from here to home. Saving the *crème de la crème* of Mick's hoard was imperative, and this might be Craig's one chance. Someday Voychek would thank him.

The doorbell chimed. Craig hugged the box to his chest, and the trembling in his stomach escalated into handsprings. Diehard trick-or-treaters? Cops trawling for evidence or accomplices? Mick's presumably thuggish supplier, champing for his money? Craig still had the Bic between two fingers. He thrust it into hip pocket and lurched to the window, overturning coffee table onto worn carpet with a subjectively enormous crash. A tortured yelp was unavoidable. All bets were off! He swung a leg over the windowsill, which he straddled an instant before pushing clumsily into the alley, stumbling with a thud against the neighboring clapboard wall and nearly falling on his face. His grip on the box was still secure. That was the important part! He cast out a hand to lower Mick's window, as if that would throw pursuit off his tail, and stopped a hairbreadth shy of slamming it.

He staggered down the alley to the rear of the house, scowled at the palisade fence between him and the next street, and followed the fence to the far side of the brick tenement to the east, where he rushed up the driveway and halted, peeking toward Mick's building. Funny—no cars out front, or across the street. From his angle, the doorway was out of view. Someone had to be lurking under the portico, though, didn't they? Foolhardy to pass by, so he made a break for it in the opposite direction, scooted around the corner, and went north another block, well aware that he was heading directly away from his house. He then hurried east to the next street and finally started homeward, one block parallel to the way he'd come. Already the box in his arms had gained a few pounds.

For all his hustle, the return trip seemed twice the distance. Was this street curving insidiously farther and farther from his outbound route? The box was more sadistically leaden by the minute. He wished he could walk faster, or get home faster at any rate, but the odds of a friend driving by and picking him up were microscopic. Eventually his arms ached as if distended on the rack, and his fatigued legs were trudging on autopilot. He had panted and perspired all his angst away for the moment, and was almost fed up to the point of culling the best records in the box and ditching the rest. Thank God his obsessiveness was keeping him on track.

He was five minutes from home when some whooping idiots in a rumbling Trans Am overtook him and lobbed eggs. Reflex bid him twist aside and shield the precious cargo with his back, but they must have missed. He felt no impact, and the gleeful swine weren't slowing down to check their marksmanship. Craig tried to be philosophic. Easy to argue that completing his errand by car would have spared him pain and trouble. Yet weren't all bargains on some level devil's bargains? Ninety percent of the time, relying on bus or shank's mare posed no hardship, and if he joined the motorists his low-budget life of freedom would be over. To pay for gas, repairs, insurance, and fuck-all else, he'd need a suit-and-tie job, and he wasn't about to sprint into that open grave! His thirtieth birthday was still half a decade away, for chrissakes.

Meanwhile, why was the back of his leg cold and damp? The idiots' aim hadn't been so shoddy after all. The wallet in his back pocket had absorbed the brunt, but not the Rorschach blot of egg white slowly seeping through the denim. Goddammit!

On the bright side, he was in the home stretch at last. And close enough to survey a naive action painting in eggshells and goo across the front of the house. Damn that oblivious Daphne! But what to say to her that would do any good at this stage? More dauntingly, what to say to the landlord? Was it too much to ask that cleansing rains fall before he came back over? The fluttering in Craig's stomach revived with a vengeance.

For days, the knowledge that Power of Midnight was in a box on his dining room table made for exhilaration enough. He didn't need to open the box and marvel at it, and truth to tell, the idea of giving it a spin was too intimidating. But what shame in that, inasmuch as Voychek, the "hood" himself, had never even punctured the shrink-wrap? Next to the monumentality of the black album, whatever stood behind it abjectly failed to stir his curiosity, and *Left Banke Too* was fine where it was. As for those two copies of *Air Fiction* from Rimes? He might play the one he'd opened someday; the other, so far, was still in the bag on the table, somewhere behind Voychek's cardboard box. Meanwhile, independent of any suspense about the landlord's next visit, gut-level anxiety tainted every moment with presentiments of axes due to fall.

The one new musical acquisition that piqued Craig's interest was the cassette of Mick's band, when he remembered it in his jacket pocket, though thoughts of Mick induced a pang of loss, as if he'd been wearing an orange jumpsuit for years already. He might as well have been, for all the good Craig could do him. Where was Mick exactly? City jail? State prison? Carl knew, but Craig didn't have his number, or last name for that matter, even if he wanted to endure further snotty attitude, which he didn't. On an extra somber note, this tape constituted the band's swan song, unless they regrouped after Mick made parole.

Come what may, "Margie '86" was in his tape deck, thanks to his quick wits at Mick's. He had that to be glad about, or so it seemed before the opening bars strummed in and he collapsed onto his tatty plaid couch as if poleaxed. Where were the boisterous drums, the ballsy synths, the edgy overdubs, the imagination, the vision, the fun? Why the overhaul? A misguided stab at commercial potential? At "cleaning it up," at "getting to the point"? Like using a lobotomy to "straighten someone out"? Maybe they were aspiring to open for Graham Parker or Dire Straits or Billy Joel, for godsakes. For a minute, Craig couldn't even tell which song he was cringing at. He definitely wanted nothing more to do with Carl now, after this travesty, this artistic seppuku. His sympathies for Mick were drying up too. Not that he was wishing incarceration on the guy!

As the week lumbered by, and the inevitable axes refused to fall, Craig's dread accumulated. At suppertime Thursday, he was pulling the bedroom shades just as the landlord was parking his yellow Karmann Ghia across the street. Craig watched him emerge from the car and then yanked the shade down to the sill, clenching his teeth and listening. Ten minutes later, the landlord had yet to enter the house. Craig squinched through the slit between shade and window frame. The car was gone.

That, however, was no more reassuring than the last two-fifths of his workweek. Sharon was a no-show. If she were calling in sick, nobody told him. Nobody hassled or assisted him. He dealt only with the tight-lipped receptionist upstairs, who handed him each morning's list of addressees. No loss of camaraderie saddened him, but at the same time, languishing forgotten didn't sit well. Nor did the telephone limbo that engulfed Lorna. No calls from her, no answer when he called, for two days. Friday night, he debated popping in on her, but wasn't keen on a half-hour walk to learn she was out.

He reached her on Saturday morning. She sidestepped the niceties and asked if he'd like to go camping for the weekend. With Karen and her relatives. He'd have to be ready in half an hour. Her lukewarmth implied that she expected, and hoped (given his history of grumbling about "weekend woodsmen"), that he wouldn't be up for it. He obligingly begged off. Short notice, and not his idea of fun, with or without Karen's clan. So where had she been the last few days? Busy. With Karen's family. He couldn't pinpoint why that sounded like an evasion, but it did, and it heaped fuel on his jitters.

He overheard some mealy-mouthed guy in the background asking what the holdup was. That would be Karen's cousin Cliff. Ugh. They'd met briefly at an outdoor wedding reception. A corn-fed, glad-handing jock, brimming with unearned optimism. Curly blond hair that came across as permed, whether it was or not. And he actually wore a puffy blue ski jacket, ubiquitous symbol of today's dullard collegiates who snorted at "doing your own thing" as uncool '60s jargon. What a tool! Lorna said they were running late. Talk to you Monday!

Craig settled in for a lost weekend. Best friend in jail, girlfriend off freezing in the woods, no one else to hang out with on the spur of the moment. He toyed at catching up with reading, on writing overdue letters, even resorted to light housework. He saw himself as becalmed, marooned, with only his unquiet nerves for company. Bad sitcoms and worse dramas on his 19-inch TV atop the bedroom dresser were no comfort. Come Sunday, he drifted deeper into torpor. Did this qualify as depression? Yes or no, it was becoming a royal pain in the ass, and he had to find something to snap him out of it. Not the 6:30 news. There was an election Tuesday? How had that snuck by him? He shambled into the living room and twisted the dimmer for the plastic chandelier all the way up.

For the better part of a week, Craig had treated Voychek's box of records as invisible, while letting slip he knew it was there by steering compulsively around it. To escape his quagmire of a mood, he wrote off all that behavior as neurotic and, to coax himself forward, zeroed in on the innocuous scribble "Auction" on the front flap of the box.

Ridiculous, how that one formidable item had been standing between him and the enjoyment of everything else in the box. Enough with the moping. He impetuously flipped the box open, and with two fingers, avoiding contact with the "*Necronomicon* of vinyl," nimbly lifted what lay behind it. As he let the LPs slip one by one back down, bewilderment mounted. High Tide? Moving Finger? Plastic Cloud? Forest? July? Touch? International Harvester? He fancied himself a connoisseur, an initiate into the secret history of musical groundbreakers consigned to the margins by an apathetic public. These names, these covers, so unfamiliar as to seem unreal, might bounce him back to square one if he let them. Something about them had to be flawed, untrustworthy, or condignly minor-league, or Voychek would have introduced him to them in the last three years. Craig unhanded them, and they sank back into the box.

No, the black album alone merited his attention. That *Left Banke Too* likewise paled in significance. Time to start clearing up the hype. Even if Voychek hadn't been feeding him the contradictory, overwrought lore of an acid casualty, Craig ought to be fine as long as he raised the tone arm every so often.

He felt the boredom lift from his shoulders, and the tingle of forthcoming revelation in his fingers, as he took up Power of Midnight as if it had never fazed him. The shrinkwrap was tight. Fortuitous of him to come along before it warped the vinyl. The cover was of sleek European stock, and it mirrored Craig's face as in a deep, cold pool. He was unaware of feeling as grim as the cover portrayed. He tried to grin instead, but the mockery in his reflection was even ghastlier. It rattled him into hastily revolving the cover ninety degrees, and apprehension flared up as he watched himself surgically wield a thumbnail to split the cellophane seal at the top corner of the jacket and slice downward carefully, to prevent any little crumples in the cardboard edges. Holding his breath, he widened the opening with gentle thumb and forefinger and clamped down on the coarse parchment texture of the inner sleeve. Impossible to tell by his thumping heart if he were poised upon culmination or ruin.

Glass shattered. Then, a pregnant silence. Had a tumbler, perched high in the drying rack, toppled into the sink? Or was a burglary in progress? The kitchen was dark. Outside, below its window, were a tarpaulined woodpile and the fenced-in driveway. Busting in would be easy. Getting from window to floor without bumps and scrapes would not. He leaned the black album against the box and stood rapt, straining his ears till he had to exhale. Maybe the culprits had busted the window by mistake and turned tail. With a wary pause between each footfall, he slowly advanced to the kitchen. He steeled himself at the doorway and inched his hand toward the wall switch. "Piss off!" he shrieked as the room burst into fluorescent brilliance, in half-assed bid at the element of surprise, with no inkling of what he'd do if anyone were there.

Fortunately, he blinked alone. The window was broken. But no glass in, or around, the sink. He craned on tiptoe through fragmentary pane and found a glinting arc of shards across the tarp. Somebody had made a forced exit? That was nonsense. And he was afraid the police, and the landlord, would say the same, after he conceded being home since Friday. He felt like a cosmic fall guy: the rules had changed, and now glass flew outward when punched in, as if to victimize him for the hell of it. His intrepid moment for spinning Power of Midnight had passed. Fuck it. Something on television might soothe his nerves.

Work on Monday entailed seven more hours of isolation, apart from a slick little official in olive sharkskin whom Craig found sizing up his office after he'd gone for a Snickers bar in the cafeteria. The guy continued ogling the space from different angles long after Craig smacked his purchase onto the desk and directed hairy eyeball at him. Finally Craig roared, "May I help you?" The guy acknowledged him with the merest glance and a mirthless grin. He'd be out of Craig's hair in a minute, okay? His tone was somehow both patronizing and feral. A coming man in his own mind, for sure, who despite Craig's harshest glare left in his own good time. An air of dislocation, of unreality almost, lingered in his wake, and Craig wondered in passing if he'd hallucinated the whole encounter.

In any case, it flung a troubling stone into the already choppy waters of his psyche. All this weirdness at work since last Wednesday must have stemmed from that comment about banker stupidity, and waiting for backlash to spring into the open was becoming more and more torturous. A stopover at Rimes generally cheered him up. They were closed, but the lights were on. Jimbo, Cynthia, Bonnie, and a couple of well-dressed strangers were sitting around a card table in front of the counter. Jimbo ambled over after Craig caught his eye. "Sorry, pal!" he exclaimed through the muffling glass. "We're havin' to reorganize. Old lease is up. Lookin' into a change of address. If we're lucky."

"Best of luck, then," Craig replied, very earnestly, and Jimbo hustled back to his meeting. Bonnie raised her eyes doorward. They were swollen and didn't seem to see him. She looked ashen.

Craig's knees wobbled as he climbed cement steps to the sidewalk. Two beefy lawyer-types were resting their butts against the iron railing over the stairwell. They paused in their deliberations to gawk at Craig as if he were a Neanderthal rising from a glacier. Right back atcha, you atavistic heels! Before turning at the next corner, he tried to shoot a parting glower at them, but they must have moseyed.

Ignoring the weakness in his legs, he did his best to remain upbeat about Rimes. Nobody was throwing in the towel yet. Other storefronts had to be available. Switching from basement to street-level might bring in more business. It might be providential in the long run. And there let the matter rest, before his thoughts followed the tracks full-circle into despair.

Home again, and none too soon. Lorna had no Kelly Girl gig or resumed ed classes today, as far as he knew, and by now should have recovered from her nature ordeal. She said they'd speak Monday. So he called, and at the sound of her hello, started wishing he hadn't. She claimed today was bad for going into things. Had she led him to believe differently last Saturday? Sorry, that was then. Huh? Since when had she adopted the usages of shallow trendies? A horrible understanding dawned on him. He demanded to know if that lunkhead Cliff was with her. She didn't see what that had to do with anything, and he was only showing how little he knew Cliff, who was a very nice person. Craig took all that for a Yes. Another big rock landed with an angry, destabilizing splash in his psychic waters.

He had no stomach for setting eyes on Cliff. But neither would he forfeit Lorna without a struggle. He told her he'd be over sometime next day, and they could talk then. She didn't answer right away. He hung up before she could put together the words to deter him.

The phone rang before he made it to the kitchen. Lorna, obviously. Only it wasn't. The landlord had to meet with him and Daphne tomorrow. He didn't sound mad. He exhibited no feelings at all, which was worrisome in itself. Craig suggested 7:30, and the landlord asked him to go inform Daphne. He agreed, though it promptly slipped his mind once he was off the line.

He was in for an abysmal night's sleep. Foregone conclusion. The loaded words of Jimbo and the landlord and the jerk in sharkskin assailed him in medium rotation as he rolled over every other minute on his mattress on the floor, and each replay contained graver implications. But the heavy rotation was reserved for his contretemps with Lorna. As girlfriends went, to be bluntly realistic, she was the best he'd ever do. Whatever about him had been sowing discontent, she had to put it in plain English, give him a chance to change. They'd been going out a long time, so she owed him that. Or was she the girl he'd assumed she was, someone who valued individuality, who wished people were free to dress and live according to their unique potential? If so, how could she be attracted to that wanker in a puffy blue ski jacket and curly blond perm? Losing her to him, that would be insufferable, a hundredfold worse than being dumped for someone whose appeal he could understand! It just didn't make sense, he shouted at the wall beside the bed, and didn't care if passersby on the sidewalk heard him. Anyhow, time to get up and go to work.

The laconic receptionist, instead of forking over the day's address list, sent him in to see decrepit Mr. Melrose, in Personnel. God, did she ever blink? Yeah, Melrose. He'd interviewed Craig for the job, and classic pulp illustrators had come up somehow, and Melrose had let on that Craig's favorite *Weird Tales* artist Hannes Bok had sketched a cat on a napkin for him back in the '40s. Melrose said he'd bring it in, but when Craig asked a week later, the old man hemmed and hawed about accidentally throwing it away. Craig still winced to think of something so wonderful rating such short shrift, and braced himself to be discarded with the same doddering indifference.

At least Melrose wasted no energy beating around the bush. "Please," he murmured, gesturing at a hard plastic chair in front of his desk, and with his next breath relayed that the bank was suspending its incentives for depositors, effective immediately. Hence Craig's period of employment was at an end. His final check would arrive by mail. Nothing in the old Philistine's phlegmatic wheeze hinted that Craig had brought this on himself through word or action. It was like getting fired by the mechanical fortuneteller at a penny arcade. But wasn't there anything else Craig could do for Bedrock Savings? Temporarily at least? No, the bank had no openings for him in the foreseeable future. That was that. Finality of a key rasping in tomb lock. Nothing more to say. Stunned Craig retreated from Personnel without a word or look of farewell. Just because he'd always disliked the job didn't mean he was immune from that *mal de mer* when crisis, or serious inconvenience, struck.

On a hunch, he took a detour through the basement on his way out. Yup, there was Sharon, at her desk as usual. And she needed the money a whole lot less than he did! She saw him in the doorway and bit her lower lip. Hey, he wasn't supposed to be down here!

He smiled impishly. The words, ill-advised or not, tumbled forth like water down a flume. "Chimp work suits you."

"What?" Before she could process that and start screaming for hubby, Craig was loping up the stairs and into the lobby. Had he said something shamefully ugly? Only if he let himself think about it! Uh-oh, what was that? Somebody in peripheral vision seemed to be bearing down on him. He bolted for the revolving door and glanced backward as it spilled him onto the street, but marketing guy was nowhere in sight.

He caught his breath a block away, unable till then to shake the impression of being followed. Even while gasping for air, he never stopped putting one foot ahead of the other, as if some wind of destiny permitted him no rest. It propelled him away from home (which was fine because his bum mood would only coop him up there all day) and toward Lorna's. Also fine. With the day already in ruins, he might as well go for broke and have it out with her. He hadn't specified when he'd be by, so technically he was playing according to Hoyle, though running a bigger risk that the abominable Cliff was still around. Trepidation dogged his steps but couldn't slow them down.

He finally paused on the stairs to her porch. That bygone era when he'd ring and go on in and show off his flea-market finds was scant days ago! Which reminded him, she still had his Troggs and Silver Apples records, and he wanted them back. He pressed the doorbell hard and counted to three. Then he waited. Impolitic to use his key today, he wagered. No response. Twice more, he pressed and waited. Aha, feet pounding down the stairwell. If she'd delayed any longer, he'd have given up and left. Foolish girl!

She frowned at him through the dusty pane of glass in the locked door. What was he doing here at this hour? Her voice carried poorly from inside, and the dark landing reduced her to a smudgy charcoal sketch. Well, he said he'd be over sometime Tuesday. She fell back upon insisting that it wasn't a good time. Why, because *he* was up there with her? That had nothing to do with it. Craig had heard that line recently too. It was up to her to decide when he saw her, she asserted. All right then, what was a good time? She didn't know. She'd call later.

No admittance this morning, obviously. Still, the trip needn't be a total washout. He was on the brink of demanding she go fetch his two LPs and then he'd go away, but who was that standing beside her in the shadows? "Is that him?" Craig demanded, in his agitation misjudging the distance from the window as he raised a hand to point inward. He realized, even as knuckles plowed into loudly splitting glass, that it was only his own reflection. "Accident! Freak accident!" he shouted after her, to no effect. She had fled from sight, and chances were nil she was rushing to get him a Band-Aid. Or his records, dammit. He'd best clear off. In her present state, phoning the cops might not be beneath her.

Against such worst-case scenario, he rambled home via side streets of rickety tenements and woodsy vacant lots, and lanes too narrow for police cruisers. He wrapped a handkerchief around his hand to avoid leaving a trail of blood, and dabbed his wounds clean in the privacy of a vacant lot's towering stand of Japanese bamboo. Thank God for municipal neglect! And thank God as well that the damage amounted to one cut fingertip and two gouges on the back of his hand, and no embedded slivers of glass.

Bad enough that he owed for a new window an hour after losing the means to pay for it. And blowing it irreparably with the girl-friend at the same time. He wearily rewrapped his hand and got a move on. As for the landlord tonight, how could that portend any-thing good? Especially once he'd seen the kitchen? Craig's first of two broken window in as many days! It was also first in his series of débâcles, the first in that row of axes so slow to fall, and it happened the minute he cut the shrinkwrap on the black album. But was there a connection, with the outlook on work and romance unsettled for days in advance? Voychek had likened Power of Midnight to the *Ne-cronomicon*, and never to Pandora's Box. Or should Craig move the goalposts and trace the first of his troubles to egg stains on Hallow-een, upon taking possession of the black album? Funny how one lit-tle soupçon of the occult muddied the clear flow of cause and effect.

Back home, the hours till 7:30 yawned like an impassable desert. Why not dial Daphne? Suggest they grab a coffee or maybe lunch? Might be good to talk with someone. Just because he'd never pic-tured her as a confidante didn't make it a bad idea. She wasn't in, ap-parently. One of those hoity-toity new answering machines picked up. He overcame a stammer at being taped for posterity and invited her for coffee, and as an afterthought broached the impending get-together with the landlord. Then he frittered away the afternoon chasing through government listings for someone at Unemployment to explain his benefits, if any, and through the Yellow Pages for a glazier, with thoughts of pacifying the landlord by a display of initia-tive. No dice, on either score. Who knew there were that many an-swering machines in the world?

Frozen mac and cheese was the most he had it in him to do for supper. He watched it bake behind steamy oven door as a Zen exer-cise in self-composure. Daphne came down ten minutes early; the landlord barged in twenty minutes late. In the interim, Craig brewed a pot of coffee. The landlord declined a cup with a curt "No thanks."

Nothing hip about his capitalism this evening. Any mask of personality or humor or warmth would only get in the way of bloody-minded business, Craig reckoned. The landlord sprawled in an armchair as if not only the house but all its belongings were his. Okay, the leases expire in December. Craig and Daphne ought to start looking for a new place. The landlord could be getting a lot more for these apartments. He seriously doubted they could afford what he'd be asking. Or he might convert the place to condos.

The rocking chair Daphne occupied was as still as a boulder. She had a hand to her brow, evidently nursing a headache, and seemed more resigned than surprised. Craig had the temerity to ask, "But why raise the rent at all? Aren't you doing all right as it is?"

How dare this piss-ant tenant dispute his right to maximize income? "This house is my investment. I'm losing money renting below market rates."

"You're not losing money. It's just money you're not making. There's a difference, isn't there?" Daphne was goggle-eyed as if he were waving a red hankie in Pamplona. What the hell, they were already out on their asses, why not get his two cents in?

"Are you trying to tell me what to do with my own property?" Wow, the avaricious bastard was really hot under the collar now, like a bishop attacking heresy.

"Look, just because you can do something, doesn't mean you should. You're only sidestepping the issue of being greedy or not by saying you're following common sense."

This erstwhile hip capitalist, whose car still bore the remnants of a Jimmy Carter bumper sticker, had daggers in his eyes and might have taken a swing at Craig if Daphne hadn't been there. He stood up scowling. Craig and Daphne kept their seats, Daphne with eyes to the floor. "End of December." He jerked his thumb over his shoulder umpire-style. "Be gone by then." After the front door slammed, Daphne sighed. She said she had to go, and Craig nodded weakly. The confrontation had fatigued him. Good thing he hadn't squandered meager funds on fixing that window. Cardboard could stop the cold for the duration.

He sagged listlessly in the dining-room chair he'd pulled out from the table and rested achy eyes on Power of Midnight. It was still propped against the shipping box. It had become a trenchant mirror of his black mood, his gutted spirit, the hole into which his life had been blindsided. One short day had deprived him of job, girl-friend, and roof over his head. Plus, he'd gored his hand and was liable for a window and could kiss his damage deposit here good-bye. Ill luck, bad choices, or both had deposited him at rock bottom. Worse in store was inconceivable. Why not play the album? Maybe like Van der Graaf Generator during his previous nadir, Power of Midnight would be helpful, a positive influence on his attitude, despite its evil reputation. Even if ripping the PVC seal had precipitated his woes. That damage was done!

Only one way to approach this, he resolved. He made his mind a blank as he heaved forward, submitting himself as a conduit for the black album to put itself on. So what if he was buying into arrant nonsense, crediting five ounces of plastic with the power not only of self-defense but of controlling human flesh? Ah, but the means justified the ends. He was blinking down upon the black album spinning on his turntable, the needle easily surmounting the slightest of warps.

The grooves were silent long enough to raise suspicions of a surreal hoax. An inaudible record in an inscrutable package. Gradually a midtempo pulse impinged on his awareness. It was free of reverb or flanging or any studio gimmickry. Then why couldn't Craig tell what instrument or instruments were involved? It was also, strictly speaking, not a pulse, because it lagged almost subliminally, or came in infinitesimally early, or reverted to regularity. A pattern might have surfaced if the erratic flow had allowed him to concentrate, but he grew queasy trying to anticipate when the next tone would fall. He fancied himself a victim of prog water torture, but in the interval it had taken to form this idea, everything subversively, unaccountably changed.

The whole band was going full tilt, a standard lineup of bass, drums, and two guitars, but with an abrasive, unorthodox, overwhelming onslaught, as if Craig were being flushed down sonic rapids. He fought for inner balance and won to the extent of achieving some idea of what was buffeting him, though its momentum remained irresistible.

From measure to measure the band flailed between order and chaos, a function, he apprehended, of how he was listening rather than of what he heard. Each instrument careened along in its own rhythm, its own time signature, its own key, and the gestalt was grating, brutal, yet unified, a juggernaut of interlocking rotors to which he had to readjust his ears repeatedly as instruments one by one arbitrarily changed rhythms, times, keys. The world's first and only non-Euclidean rock music! Impossible to arrive at this complexity via anarchy or improv. Craig was agog at the genius or geniuses behind this score, while sensing afresh the divide that could gape between benevolence and intellect. God help Daphne if her door was open now! The "negative energy" cascading from the speakers had the makings of a baneful presence that might quite plausibly walk and jeer and inflict bodily harm by the end of Side 1. But as if Craig's will were sand in an hourglass, he began to let his misgivings go, let the black album transport him, without regard to destination.

Habit, good old obsessive habit, restrained him. He had cultivated an ear for the larcenous "homages" that all too many musicians paid one another, and it homed in on the bass line. How in the world could that sound familiar? He had hardly begun to rack his brains when the answer struck like a blast of gritty wind. Oh, right. The bass line from "Margie '86." He was dead-set against figuring out what that connoted, now and perhaps ever. He flicked the Eject toggle on the turntable, and after the tone-arm rose and retracted, he warily resleeved the vinyl.

The phone rang. Lorna, ready to talk it over? Finally wise to what a chump Cliff was? No, it was Daphne. Had Craig been rapping on her door a minute ago? Nobody around when she went to see. She could have sworn . . .

So her door hadn't been open while the black album was on. That was the good news. As for who, or what, was knocking? Coincident with his musings about a baneful presence? Craig strove to come off as low-key. Nope, he hadn't been upstairs. And no callers at the front door, or he'd have heard. Sometimes the pipes banged when heat started up toward the radiators. That must have been it, she agreed, and their chat ended short of having nothing to discuss but eviction. Power of Midnight had wrought no harm, it seemed, even if Craig was profoundly creeped out. Lucky he'd lifted the needle when he did.

An early bedtime commended itself. Today had been the worst in his life. The sooner it ended, the better. He heaped his clothes between him and the wall, for easy access tomorrow, and got under the covers, vowing not to think, but that coffee at 7:30 ordained otherwise. The best he could manage, between tossing from left side to right to left again, was an unstable mantra affirming that nothing else was going to happen, he'd bottomed out, and things had to get better from here.

The glowing clockface atop the bedside fruit crate was a few minutes shy of midnight. He began to drift off, mumbling that he had nowhere to go but up, till knocking on the apartment door reinstated his tension in full. Daphne had better have a damn good excuse for spoiling my sleep, he thought, while from outside, squealing tires and brakes sounded awfully close. He had been peering at the bedroom doorway, listening for anything further from Daphne, when a bomb went off next to his ear, and the wall around the doorway brightened. He rolled over, to gape at a headlight six inches from his face, as a chalky-tasting cloud billowed over him and made him cough. He didn't scream until a second later, on realizing that if he'd been much nearer the wall, this intruder would have run over his head.

He lurched out of bed. He had to act immediately, or the sons of bitches would most likely pull a clean getaway. His clothes were stuck under clapboard and plaster debris. He grabbed whatever outerwear first met his fingers in the closet. Oh crap. It was a long, quilted, lavender smoking jacket from the '30s, inherited from an uncle of uncertain orientation. No time for second thoughts, though.

The culprits had already backed into the street when Craig dashed forth, waving wildly and yelling, "Hey! Where are you going?" He had a good head-on view of Jersey plates on a big late-model Chrysler. Spoiled little Ivy Leaguers, no doubt. And in a flagrant miscarriage of justice, not a scratch on the hood!

"We're just gonna park out front," called someone from behind the windshield.

Craig stood with hands on hips while they did, and after the engine cut off, made it theatrically obvious that he was memorizing the license number. "I'll be right back!" he shouted at the car and ran inside.

He dialed zero and beseeched the operator to connect him with the police. Emergency! To the desk sergeant he reported a one-car accident with destruction of property; please send someone to this address! No ambulance necessary. Then he tried Lorna's number. In the teeth of this calamity, she'd have to give him a break, show him some love, let him spend the night, what with his own bedroom demolished. She harped on the lateness of the hour and didn't believe his crazy yarn of someone driving into his building. Couldn't she tell he was in shock (which, in truth, maybe he was)? He overheard conversation on the sidewalk and hung up.

A squad car was parked up past the Chrysler. A patrolman was already jotting notes and nodding as the two housewreckers presented their version of the crash. They were, as Craig had surmised, pudgy, short-haired undergrads, perfect puffy blue ski-jacket types, and the cop wasn't appreciably older, if even Craig's age.

The cop gave Craig's bathrobe a disapproving once-over. Hey, let's not forget who's the victim here! The cop dutifully scribbled Craig's statement. Craig emphasized the damage and the nearness of his brush with death.

"But you're all right, aren't you?" the cop demanded.

Craig had to admit he was in one piece, yes, as opposed to his home. The cop, with professionally modulated delivery, recapped the kids' story that they'd swerved to avoid a dog. Nobody's fault. Craig eyed them skeptically as they studied their shoes. So they missed a dog but couldn't help hitting a house? How could that not sound fishy? Furthermore, he'd been standing in their vicinity long enough to smell what he'd bet was beer. "Were you going to give these guys a breathalyzer?" Eminently reasonable question.

"Are you tryna tell me how to do my job?" the cop barked. Craig shook his head and backed off from this distinct subtext of threat. Fucking rookie! What words, or interactions, had gone down between these trust-fund twerps and the cop before Craig had come outside? The cop strode over to his cruiser.

"You musta been scared, huh?" ventured one of the young bribesters.

"Is that your idea of an apology?" The twerps clammed up after that.

The cop returned. "All right, I have more important things to do. Can you get this car out of here?"

The kids nodded.

"But what about the hole in my wall? My room is exposed."

"Insurance'll cover that. Stuff some cushions in it for now. A lot of people tonight are worse off than you." What the hell had happened to "Serve and Protect"?

People and vehicles dispersed. Craig gazed ruefully at the wall. Daphne was framed in her lamp-lit bedroom window.

She met him downstairs. She saw what had been going on, and he could stay on her foldout. He thanked her and hoped she understood that if his responses seemed aloof, it was because he was in shock. But why, offhand, hadn't she come outside too? Well, he'd been kind of a loose cannon today. Ouch. Okay then. He bleakly contemplated the punchbowl with its inedible dozen-or-so lollipops. Would it languish in the hall till next Halloween?

By the time he was settled in, and waiting for his paltry allotment of sleep, two insights had become manifest. Henceforth, he should never, ever say, or think, that things couldn't get any worse. And echoing a thought from earlier, lucky he'd silenced Power of Midnight when he had, or he might no longer be part of this mortal coil.

He awoke to a pleasant semblance of normality. Daphne's living room was sunny, and eggs were sizzling in the kitchen. He donned flamboyant robe, took the liberty of using her bathroom, and then shuffled in to say good morning.

"How are you?" she greeted him, in what resembled genuine concern. At last, someone who understood that he'd been through the wringer!

"Surviving," he joshed and gratefully accepted a plate of fried eggs and toast. Coffee was coming right up. She was really pretty nice, wasn't she? Or very nice, in fact, to tolerate his fashion selection without comment.

Craig squinted at a trade paperback on the table. A preppie handbook? What? "Oh, a friend of mine wrote that," Daphne explained. "It's an advance copy. You should take a look at it. It's funny."

Craig flipped through it, but couldn't get past the title. Was there really a demand for a thing like this on the planet where Craig had grown up? If it was supposed to be mining the same vein as *Animal House*, its humor was devoid of anything sharp, or nostalgic for that matter. Granting it was meant as a joke, it reeked of the sort of joke that too many people were going to take seriously, to the detriment of progressive society. A disturbing air of unreality surrounded it. What next, college frats making a comeback?

A portable TV on the counter had been tuned to news the whole time. Hey, didn't an election happen yesterday? He asked Daphne if she knew who'd won.

She became significantly less chipper. "Reagan."

His eyes widened incredulously. Ronald Reagan? That ham actor? Red baiter? Second fiddle to a chimp? Laughingstock candidate throughout the '70s? "Are you kidding me?"

She shook her head morosely. He wondered again what planet this was. His appetite was down the tubes, but he didn't want to spurn her generosity, so he toughed it out to the final crumb.

He washed the dishes. Least he could do. Did she kinda like him, possibly? Bigger issues cried out at the moment. He surveyed the damage downstairs, cleaned up the mess, stuffed the splintery gap from the inside with spare pillows and blankets, and envisioned minimal repairs on the landlord's dime during Craig's tenancy.

In the living room, he caught his blurry reflection in the black album, propped against the shipping box like an invader lounging in plain sight. "All right, I'm convinced," he reprimanded it. "Things can always go from worse to worse. The pit is bottomless. I get it!" Or did he? The relative positions of cause and effect in the realm of the black album would not stay fixed. By breaking the seal, by sampling the contents, did he release something, or did he only act in tandem with changes under way in the world anyhow?

He warmed up the TV on his bureau. He had yet to shed all his disbelief, as if his own set, unlike Daphne's, wouldn't dare offer fake election results. Second opinion, however, was touting this victory of the absurd as a "landslide."

The aura of dislocation persisting for days, this morning's heightened perception of waking in the wrong place, might bode nothing but imminent crackup under many stressors. To conceive otherwise delved into madness as much as a quantum leap of inspiration, but helped account for a lot. If his feeling of "transport" while playing the black album denoted more than inner turmoil, perhaps it indicated what the black album specifically did, the nature of its diabolical curse. Going by subjective impressions and the upshot of local and national events, did the music have the power to shift the hapless listener into a different, parallel, defective world? He couldn't go along with that wholeheartedly and number himself among the sane, but couldn't help harboring the idea in the back of his head, and sometimes front and center, as time wore on.

Power of Midnight had certainly portended a new reality on the horizon, whether in Craig's native dimension or elsewhere, and he found less and less in it to like. Short-term, he'd been accurate in predicting no repairs beyond two boards nailed over the hole in his wall. Later that winter, he was sloshing down the block where dear, departed Rimes used to be and spotted Mick and Carl across the street, bucking the tide of student foot traffic. Should he intercept them or leave well enough alone, considering that untidy business circa Halloween? Ulp! Voychek had Craig right in his sights, but gave no sign of knowing him, of ever having seen him before. Then they were out of view, and out of Craig's life, for good. Mulling the incident somehow sent him down nonlinear paths to theorize that the more of the black album someone played, the farther from his proper reality it rerouted him. In any case, he now resided in a world where Voychek and Carl were strangers.

In the long run, no invisible knuckles knocked on his door, and no peripheral phantoms (or equally unverifiable dogs) bedeviled him, after his "election night surprise" with the Chrysler. That may have marked the extent of what he'd incurred by acquiring Power of Midnight and playing as much of it as he had, but to ponder it too much made him antsy. Why tempt residual juju?

Getting rid of the black album never crossed his mind. It accompanied him through subsequent romances, miscellaneous jobs, and ramshackle addresses one step ahead of gentrification, concealed in closets in its cardboard box and flanked by Mick's marginally less obscure rarities, unlucky by association. The idea of inhabiting a parallel world sounded ever crazier in the course of years, but what harm in hedging a bit? On the off-chance that he could brainstorm some way to reverse Power of Midnight's effects, say, by dubbing it and playing it backwards, or by doing something for which no technology existed yet, then he retained that gossamer hope of going back where he belonged, though he never carried this project beyond the occasional daydream.

Meanwhile, his every sensible expectation landed in the wastebasket of history, whether about decriminalizing pot, or safeguarding the environment, or knee-jerk nationalism, or equitable rents. Optimism about the tenor of life in postrevolutionary Iran was especially misplaced, but what the hell, the old regime did have it coming.

Hopes for the future nonetheless died hard. Years elapsed, and one night he was doing mushrooms with some of the guys in his roommate's band. The psilocybin at first ushered him under the aegis of what he characterized as a laughing god. Never had his outlook on life been so jolly, all his silly knickknacks and souvenirs a cause for such merriment. Then suddenly he was on the flipside, in the grip of his most intense sorrow and paranoia ever. The guys gave up on him after a weepy half hour and went to a club, correctly advising him to sleep it off. As for whatever divine message the mushrooms were customarily held to convey, the single phrase to haunt him the next day was the directive, "Take a night class in financial planning." That's when he knew the jig was well and truly up, no matter which planet he was on.

The Men at the Mound

A fitful breeze carried early-autumn chill through eyelet windows into the hall, but lacked strength to fan the guttering fires in the central trough or in goblet-shaped iron lamps on trestle tables. Thin howling from out on the fens may have been wolves or else stiffer winds, audible now only because the lyre was silent. The attentive court poet had nodded at the lift of royal eyebrows and performed "Gudrun's Lament," as customary at evening's end. Best to break up a gathering when men were subdued and logy, or else for some reason the quiet provoked moody words and then fistfights. Those bygone lawgivers were wise who forbade weapons where bold men convened and drank.

Raedwald, king of East Anglia, overlord of all the English people, friend of the Ynglinga kings in far Uppsala, caught his adviser Hereward's eye and signaled him to stay while the others rose ale-weary from benches. After the household guards had retired, Raedwald spoke low to his wisest friend, within sniffing distance of each other's bitter breath.

"I went riding at nightfall, to put the day behind me. I rode on the grass between river and grave field. At the foot of a burial mound, I saw ten men or more. They were squatting or lay on their stomachs, with their backs to me, and were watching something closely. They were dressed very drably, in short coats and loose leggings. I took them for foreigners or slaves. Impossible to mistake them for warriors. I hailed them and demanded they account for themselves, and finally shouted threats, but they pretended deafness. So I rode back a little, to come galloping and frighten the insolence out of them. But when I turned to face them, they were gone. They went without sound, and all the more uncanny, I never heard words pass between them. Could these have been spies?"

"They were behaving like no spies I've known." Hereward was at a loss to offer better in his late-night condition.

"Could they have been spirits?"

"They don't sound like any spirits I've seen," Hereward confessed.

"Was our bread made from bad wheat that breeds visions?"

"No one else has taken ill." Hereward had followed Raedwald through battles and feuds and religious strife, with worse on the horizon perhaps, and could not understand why this flitting mirage would make such an impression. He counseled postponing discussion till morning, when their thinking would be fresher. And as he'd hoped, the king refrained by light of day from broaching nocturnal imaginings.

In the days ahead, affairs of state dispelled thoughts of mere figments. The new kings of Essex and Kent had backslid into the faith of their fathers and had hounded Christian clergy back across the Channel, to refuge among the Franks. One morning, pagan envoys arrived for assurances that Raedwald, as English overlord, would side with those kings when churchmen, with Frankish ambition lurking behind their vestments, tried reclaiming a foothold. Then that afternoon, runners had announced a Frankish boat a day downriver, no doubt bearing envoys who sought conflicting assurance of Raedwald's loyalty to Christ, for he had freely received baptism and given Christians free rein in Anglia. Here was the kind of diplomatic headache that had already flared into war during Raedwald's reign.

After a long, trying day equivocating with heathen petitioners, Hereward looked forward to ale and songs in the hall, even if the obnoxious petitioners were to be guests there. He'd had supper and a nap at his own farmstead and was passing the temple as the first bright stars poked through the twilight. Raedwald emerged from gable shadows to beckon him over and retreated inside.

The light from candles on the altars was flickering and murky, but Hereward saw Raedwald's milky, stricken face all too well. The king was no longer young. Whatever had aggrieved him would do his laboring heart no good. Hereward wanted him to sit down, but the temple contained only the two altars side-by-side, one Christian, and one heathen at the behest of Raedwald's wife, herself a priestess. Here was a compromise that pleased no one! Members of the old religion grumbled because the altar that Thunar, Tiw, Frige, and all their kin shared wasn't good enough for the new god from Rome, who had to have one to himself. Meanwhile, the culprit was still at large who had switched the communal chalice and the sticky sacrificial bowl. This had sowed hotter anger among the Christians because the trick had gone unnoticed in temple dimness till the pungent bowl had taken part in Mass. Hereward couldn't stifle a slight smile. Well, it was a good joke on the damned humorless Christians! But the king's words called for more solemn demeanor.

"I rode along the river again at dusk, to clear my head of Kentish accents, and of Christ and Woden. The strange gang had regathered at the mound. Their backs were to me as before, and they were deaf and speechless still, though now they were standing. This time I spurred the horse right up to them, to as little effect as I had had on them before, and from my vantage in the saddle watched over their shoulders. They were inspecting a collection of things, passing them from hand to hand with a wonder that heightened my sense of eavesdropping on foreigners. I was startled to find a woman among them, and dressed like them in leggings and short coat—a perversion that marked her, and by association them, as outlaws. Then came the shock that almost knocked me to the ground, for these people were handling the nested silver bowls, my baptismal gift from the former bishop in Canterbury. You know them, I am sure. The bowls with the little crosses stamped on the bottom, which my wife keeps hidden in the linen chest."

They had been hidden too long for Hereward to preserve any memory of them, but he nodded obligingly.

"At the idea of these felons ransacking my home, I became bleary-eyed with outrage, and dizzy, and for an instant all was blackness. When my sight returned, my heart was thundering, and the strangers were already gone. I breathed deep until my heart was quieter, before racing back to the hall. The bowls were under bedclothes, as they had been for years. Now I am even more anxious to understand these trespassers. Were they thieves, as they seemed?"

Hereward shrugged, but the answer was easy. "They stole nothing."

"Were they Christian devils, taunting me with those souvenirs of my lapsed conversion?"

"If they wanted to torment you, they were not nearly persistent enough, to go by the preaching I have heard."

"Maybe they were Christian angels, sent to impart a message?"

Hereward shook his head. "Did they fly all the way from heaven to impart a message so poorly?"

Raedwald's look was searching and dissatisfied, and he was gripping his adviser's wrist, as if to help him maintain balance. To no healthy purpose, he wasn't about to give up so easily on framing the question to unlock this riddle. Hereward would have to wait it out.

His eyes were more accustomed to the gloom, and they traced the forms on tapestries that graced the walls. The weaver had alluded to the exploits of the English gods and noble ancestors, all the way to divine progenitor Woden. The priest who had installed the Christian altar had started to demand these coarse idolatries be ripped down, but had shut his mouth at meeting Raedwald's killing glare. One of the king's prouder moments, in his adviser's opinion, and a pity that more hadn't been there to enjoy it.

Helith, goddess of wisdom, finally smiled on Hereward. "The queen is a priestess. Have you consulted her about these visions?"

Raedwald sighed. "If she knew of them, she would only use them as a sign to side against the Christians. She must never know."

Hereward agreed, grateful that the man of state was taking over from the afflicted witness of mirages. "As I see it," he added, "these strangers will appear to you again if they signify anything. Otherwise, you will forget them soon enough."

The king unhanded him. "We have dignitaries in the hall to entertain." Hereward was reassured so long as Raedwald put more stock in dealing with fleshly nuisances than imaginary ones.

In the coming days, East Anglia upheld its neutrality. Another compromise that gave no one joy! Raedwald piled the emissaries from Essex and Kent with gifts and with promises to lend the Frankish missionaries no support, and put them on the road a short while before the Frankish delegation rowed into view. The Franks also went away with rich gifts, and his promise to hinder no missionary work in neighboring lands. Raedwald had secured his kingdom a moment's peace, grudging as it was, and in his most carefree mood for weeks he went riding along the river, anticipating all would be well this calm evening.

Hereward was sitting on his porch steps, chewing an apple, listening to the last hardy crickets of the season. At the sound of pounding hooves, he guessed who was in earshot without looking up. He stood and brushed off apple seeds as the king dismounted. Raedwald's hands upon the reins trembled, the horse snorted and pawed nervously, and the king needed respite to let blood flow back into bleached-out face. "At dusk when I rode by the river," he rasped, "I sighted one stranger in front of the mound. He wore their usual peasant clothing, but was turned my way, for once. My horse cantered up within a spear's length of him. He was empty-handed and unarmed, like a man who has no business being where he is, but means no harm, either. Though his lips were open, no sound escaped, and when our eyes locked, I felt a bolt strike my heart. He was goggling at me as at someone who did not belong in his world, as if I were a hundredfold more foreign to him than he was to me. And no matter how outlandish his manners and bearing, upon studying his features I felt he looked as English as you or me. Yet he was petrified at the sight of me. I could withstand his expression no longer and sped the horse away. By the time I dared glance back, he was gone." Raedwald shook his graying head. "These beings make no sense. They are thieves who steal nothing, and foreigners whose place is here."

Dwelling further on these phantasms would serve no one's peace of mind, Hereward decided. "Words will solve nothing tonight. I suggest we wait for light of day, and stroll to the mounds, and seek for some sign of these people, and then begin to talk." And again, with any luck, by breakfast these illusions would fade like any other dreams.

Hereward won his brief reprieve, but at dawn the king banged on his door, intent on chasing the truth. On their way, skillful Hereward gave the king no chance to brood, but steered their speech down a commonplace path, through repairs to the hall, the harvest, the weather, the cost of brewing ale.

Conversation ceased at the edge of the grave field, and the farther they trudged beside it the more ill at ease and confused and agitated the king became. Hereward paused as Raedwald stopped and backtracked and returned and paced ahead, with ongoing grimaces and a darting survey all around. "It isn't here!" he shouted. "The mound where they met on those nightfalls is gone! I'm certain I couldn't have ridden this far. We should have passed that mound already, but we haven't. It seemed as if it had always been here, and I'd known it all my life, but now I see it would fit nowhere in the lay of the land. What has been visited upon me?"

"Maybe it is as the Christians have said," remarked Hereward, generally unimpressed with what they said, but happy to exploit a useful grain from their mountains of chaff. "This life is like a bright hall at night, and what happens before and afterward is in darkness, and the soul is like a bird that flies in through one window and all too soon out another. If only we understood the language of that bird!"

"Whatever the Christians may claim, they cannot tell us where that bird goes any better than our own priests can. And so I am convinced to think as my wife does, that we should not forsake the old religion. If we did, our dealings with all those friends east over the sea would have to end, for the Christians forbid commerce with nonbelievers, and no good would come of that, I suspect." The king had drawn from the riverside mysteries what meaning he could, and thus could be done with them, and Hereward admired him for it. If these visions had plagued Hereward, he might have lacked wit to dismiss them so nimbly. But even if Raedwald never spoke of spectral strangers again, he also avoided re-entering the burial ground, at least till funeral procession bore him in a magnificent boat with his silver bowls and more opulent freight, to the site where a new mound would rise to enclose him. There would never be another pagan display so splendid in all of England.

The professor pondered the foamy remnants at the bottom of his glass and voted down another pint. Christmas lights lent the pub extra cheer, the end of semester promised time to relax, and this nook resounded with simpatico colleagues and students. The moment shamelessly enticed him to order another, except that he was on the unmistakable verge of turning voluble, and he liked himself better, especially in the morning, when he stopped short of that. Then the decision was out of his hands along with his empty glass, and another brown ale was thrust upon him. Oh hell!

He indulged a sporting sip, even as he heard a tipsy grad student venture, "Any other time of year I might not have the nerve to ask, but since it's the season for that sort of thing, I've always wondered, when you consider all the violence and history and death it's seen, has anyone ever heard whether Sutton Hoo is haunted or not?"

Well, the horses were out of the barn now! The professor, with a drinker's helpless detachment, regarded himself disapprovingly as he cleared his throat and scraped the chair too loudly away from the table to get more air.

"Whether it was a ghost or something else, I can't pretend to say, but toward the end of excavation one year at Sutton Hoo I went out in the evening to stretch my legs. It wasn't too cold yet for the crickets, but their chirping was pretty lackadaisical. My path skirted the burial field, on the side toward the river, and my mind was elsewhere, so I can't really say they came out of nowhere, but there they were, a horse and rider bearing down on me. I was taken aback, as you can imagine, and since I didn't stand a chance of escaping, I stood my ground and waited, forced to take it on faith that the man wouldn't run me down."

The professor caught his breath, swallowed some ale, and noted with mixed feelings that the whole room was paying attention.

"He did pull the reins at the last second, and I got my first clear look at him. His clothes weren't modern. I'd never seen anything exactly like them, so I couldn't place the period, but it was the basic kind of costume someone might've been wearing any time in the last four millennia. Even more remarkable, although his expression may have held a thousand words, he said nothing. And his horse, balking a little for some reason, was visibly whinnying and panting, but without making a sound. I was too dazed at that point to form any coherent idea of what I was looking at. It was more than enough to realize that he could also see me, and something about seeing me was deeply upsetting to him. I had the strong impression I didn't belong there as far as he was concerned, and nothing about me made any sense to him. We stared at each other, until he apparently decided enough was enough. He flipped the reins and the horse charged off, and I only discovered then that I'd been holding my breath. As soon as I exhaled, it seemed to break some kind of connection or circuit or what have you between this phenomenon, let's call it, and myself. I must have blacked out an instant, and afterward I was disoriented and falling-down dizzy. The horseman shouldn't have put much distance between us yet, but he was already back wherever he'd come from."

And that was that, let the chips fall where they may. With any luck, nobody tomorrow would remember he'd admitted to seeing a ghost, or at least wouldn't take it seriously. As the grad student had said, this was the right time of year for that sort of anecdote, wasn't it? When he lowered his glass, though, everyone was watching him, as if expecting him to say more. He sighed, and after every blink seemed to be looking through a vaselined lens, and the silence dragged on.

"But who was it?" an intrepid undergrad finally asked, over by the doorjamb. "Did you ever figure out who it might have been?"

"No! I never did! I had no way of finding out!" He was astonished at the amount of emotion in his voice and hoped others sensed it less sharply than he did. He excused himself and hastily squeezed his way out of the crowded nook, holding back tears with a maximum effort. He rushed into the men's room, where they probably assumed he was heading for the usual reasons, and he wanted to give them every reason to leave it at that. He locked himself in a stall and cried for a while, as quietly as he could.

Maybe one ale too many was having its way with him, but suddenly his inability to name the unearthly rider had flared up into the biggest failure of his life. Other equally appropriate questions, about the basic nature of his experience, or about why the rider had appeared at that hour and only to him, were easier to discard because they belonged to metaphysics or parapsychology or something even fuzzier, and outside his jurisdiction. But for an archaeologist to grasp nothing in what he glimpsed of a past that nobody else would ever be privileged to see—that was mortifying. And it was the damnedest thing, but for the first time in his memory of that ancient face, he perceived a shadow of failure there too, as if the rider, whoever he was, had also contended with one abiding challenge he had not over-come, or ever could. It was a resonance with the past that gave the professor no comfort.

With sangfroid restored, he flushed for the sake of verisimilitude and wiped his reddish eyes dry in front of the restroom mirror. To his relief, the crowd in the nook was entrenched in other matters, and he regained his seat without having to field additional questions about phantom horseman. He was more confident than ever that he'd met something other than a ghost, but a ghost it may as well have been, for he appreciated now that it had haunted him ever since, and likely always would, at near or farther remove from the conscious surface, just as he may well have haunted someone in the impenetrable past.

Three Ounces over Advent

They ran out of gas in front of a laughably dumpy house. They wouldn't have, of course, if they hadn't had to hightail it down back roads with no filling stations. And they wouldn't have had to hightail it had the sheriff not been bound to find their walk-in closet full of grow lights and pot plants. Nor would the sheriff have ousted all the tenants on half an hour's notice had the bastard landlord made any mortgage payments. What more could anyone in their position do beyond cramming paper A&P bags with clothes and miscellany and exiting under the steely eyes of the law? Nicky and Jess generally paid their rent the month it was due, so this descent into craziness was hardly their fault. Furthermore, dealing pot would never have been their career choice had the job market offered better opportunities. Nicky, for the fifth time today, identified the root of all their evils by breaking smoldery silence to roar, "Fuckin' banks!"

Jess nodded loyally, lending an inappropriately cheerful bounce to her brunette bob cut. She graciously regarded the shanty on their left as "unprepossessing." A trailer could have occupied the site with no loss of prestige. The first story was encased in dull pink tarpaper shingles, with upper half-story in brown brick-pattern tarpaper. An undersized chimney, more in keeping with a backyard barbecue pit, coughed occasional wispy smoke. Fearsomely off-balance Norway maples crowded around the house, their bare December boughs casting a mesh of chilly shade.

Hopefully the folk inside had gasoline to buy or freeload. If not, the fugitives were royally screwed. No other human construction stood the mile or so behind or ahead of the hairpin bend that enfolded house and frost-blackened front garden.

"Nicky honey, try and take some deep breaths," Jess cautioned as soon as they were out of the car. "If you're more relaxed, you'll make a better impression on these people. And then maybe we can take a medical break." Nicky nodded, but that bulging vein on his temple wouldn't settle down till it was good and ready, and Jess herself used to be scared of that nervous tic in one eye, before she realized he was really a lamb deep down.

The name stenciled on the mailbox was "Alborg." Didn't sound like hillbillies! Swedish perhaps? A man in murky silhouette at a table was squarely framed in the window beside the door. The door was flimsy, and the length of one rectangular panel was split. Sky-blue paint set off smudged, loamy handprints around an old-fashioned doorknob of multifaceted glass, ordinary enough between dining rooms and parlors, but a sore thumb somehow in the fresh air.

Jess raised an index finger as reminder for Nicky to knock with gentle restraint, and while they waited she traced a rank scent around the corner to a cubical bin of scrapwood slats. Under the green tarp, she concluded, must be compost. Nicky applied his knuckles more smartly. Still no reply. He tried the knob, and as the door wobbled open, he called, "Hello?"

They entered cagily. Mr. Alborg's profile remained intent on a pot of beans simmering on the gas stove across the kitchen. As they circled the table to confront their suspicions directly, Jess offered a last half-hearted "Hello?" But the blockish head with shameless comb-over and white chevron mustache didn't budge, and the gray eyes bore straight through Nicky and Jess at the pot of beans.

Nicky sniffed guardedly. "He doesn't smell yet."

"Do you think he can still hear us?" Jess felt small and childlike next to the overwhelming finality of a corpse.

Nicky picked up the spoon next to Mr. Alborg's waiting bowl and gave the inert shoulder a tentative poke. The body as a unit shifted minutely. "Stiff! How long does rigor mortis take? An hour? A miracle his lunch wasn't incinerated."

Jess, through long experience, could easily read Nicky's subtext. She scurried over to turn off the flame and slide the pot off the burner lest he started fussing at her about it.

"This is good, actually, this is good," Nicky announced, and tossed sullied spoon into a tublike sink, to gouge one more chip into porcelain already rife with rusty flecks. "We need somewhere to hang out till the brown shirts get sick of looking for us. Even if we find some gasoline, I think that's safer." Again, his subtext was plain. Nicky had reason to worry. His next arrest for possession of weed, his third such strike, would land him behind bars for a decade, pursuant to state mandatory sentencing. "Look at the stains and crud on this guy's shirt. I'm willing to bet he wasn't expecting guests to pop in, ever. We can have this place to ourselves as long as we want."

"Not quite all to ourselves," Jess demurred, nodding toward Mr. Alborg.

"Yeah, we'll have to get him out of here," Nicky conceded. His lack of enthusiasm quickly darkened into a despairing frown. "But I think I need to improve my coping skills first."

They also had to push their old Corolla out of sight. "Dammit!" Nicky bristled as they stepped outside, as if this complication had completely slipped his mind. On the bright side, a cinderblock garage, almost as big as the house, hunkered past the curve in cracked blacktop driveway, among the leaning maples. Plenty of room inside next to a beat-up two-cylinder Saab!

Nicky extracted a glass pipe and three ounce bags from under the false bottom he'd cleverly installed in the glove compartment, while Jess fetched their other worldly remnants from the backseat. "Let's go back in and cope," he urged. Fine with Jess. Cold was already seeping into her feet from the cement floor, which was slick with raunchy old oil.

To her admittedly foolish disappointment, Mr. Alborg was sitting exactly where they'd left him. Past a door that opened halfway and then clunked against the stove was a parlor benighted by bulky drapes. It was creepy in there, but less so, they agreed, than lighting up in front of a dead guy. Jess's fourth hit was, as usual, one too many, but what the hell. The stress had been nonstop today, and more was looming. For now, inner reorientation was absolutely what the doctor ordered. Her focus on Nicky slipped away, as she realized it was ten degrees cooler than in the kitchen and unhealthily musty. The contents of the parlor hadn't registered on her yet, and wouldn't while she had a corpse through the doorway to contemplate.

How preposterous this situation would have seemed first thing this morning! A smile began sneaking across her lips. Ah, she was turning into her old self again. And her old self believed in a sense of humor come what may, because the more you could laugh at, the happier you'd be, right?

Fascination drew her toward the deceased. No longer intimidating. More like a challenge. An exercise in problem-solving. Then Nicky was beside her, and he appeared reconciled to staring death in the face from their table's length away. Coping accomplished! "The old Swede had a compost bin by the door," Jess heard herself saying. "Planting him in there ought to be a lot easier than digging a grave in the frozen ground." She revisited what she'd just said. Swede? Wasn't that another word for a kind of turnip? And she'd proposed planting him? At the image of miniature Alborgs sprouting next April, she had to laugh. It was her customary robust, cascading laugh. Nicky's look was questioning, but he didn't ask what was so damn funny. She let the subject wither in silence. How to dissect the joke without killing it? Oh, good. Nicky's curiosity had lapsed into resignation.

"So are we gonna do this?" he wanted to know. "This" Jess understood as her cue to make the first move. She put on coat and gloves, and he followed suit. She gripped the back of Mr. Alborg's black straightback chair and jerked it backward an inch, and Nicky gripped it from his side and jerked, and when they had clearance enough to shift Mr. Alborg, she tilted the cadaver toward her by tugging at soiled beige flannel sleeves. Did Nicky appreciate how she was letting him carry the less unpleasant lower extremities (apart from soggy blotch at crotch level) that swung slowly into his hesitant grasp?

"Hold on good!" she warned, and swiftly kicked the chair out from under the cumbersome, sagging body, flexed like a question mark, arms extended like a stuffed bear's. They were already winded as they tottered out the door with their miserable load. Thank God no traffic was passing! Bad enough she had to lower his head to the ground and get rid of the rocks holding down the tarp, and fling the tarp aside. Hurry, before Nicky freaked out at holding an upside-down corpse by himself!

They managed to heave Mr. Alborg into the compost, and then had to lean in and scoop dead leaves and coffee grounds and carrot greens and damp earth onto the body because it scarcely sank on its own. At least he'd died in a posture that fit in the bin without grisly adjustment. Jess was replacing the tarp when a Chevy station wagon with a punctured muffler rumbled by. Jess and Nicky couldn't help but eyeball its deafening retreat. "Shit, you think they saw us?" wheezed Nicky.

"They didn't slow down or anything. They had their own issues with that muffler. Who knows? Maybe the cops are after them too."

"Should we say a few words for the old codger?" Nicky's eyes ranged nervously up and down the road.

"Like what?" Sometimes when he got skittish like this, Jess was tempted to holler "Boo!" Or would that be too mean?

"Oh, I don't know." Nicky's roving gaze lingered on the tarp as he improvised, "This is the way he would've wanted it?"

A single cackle escaped her. Was Nicky taking a stab at humor, or was he just too scared and wasted to know what he was saying? Either way, her reaction derailed the eulogy, and she had to giggle some more as they hustled indoors, where she toted the fallen chair to the corner, left of the parlor door. Obviously a seat of last resort, since dead Mr. Alborg had sat there most recently.

Making themselves at home dictated more ambitious measures, and the sooner the better. No telling how long they'd have to stay. But first they had to repel an attack of the munchies. The beans on the stove comprised their course of least resistance. Nicky gingerly transferred Mr. Alborg's bowl from table to sink, and that effectively dispelled their qualms about scarfing a dead guy's lunch. Hey, they hadn't eaten all day! The beans were a cheap brand with a tomato-based rather than molasses sauce, and benefited greatly from generous squirts of the no-name ketchup in the archaic Kalamazoo fridge. Once they were full of beans, as Jess whimsically put it, they felt up to a house tour.

Soon they were sharing the wish that they'd broken down in front of some other dead person's hovel. Warmth emanated solely from a measly vent near the base of the gas-on-gas stove. No use even re-entering the parlor, where skunky smoke thickened the stuffy atmosphere.

In the furnished attic that passed for a bedroom, they saw their breaths. Yet the freezing air couldn't suppress an odor, as of mung sprouts and ripe socks, from the jumbled sheets and quilt on the mattress. At the foot of the mattress was a white dresser, and from one of its drawers, adorned with folksy blue-winged, red-breasted birds, they rummaged clean sheets and blanket. The mattress they wrestled down the narrow stairs and pitched, fresh side up, in front of the stove.

The cellar, redolent of damp plaster, contained a freezer, washer, drier, and shelves of nonperishables, but was accessible only by a bulkhead wedged between the rear of the house and a side of the garage. In a layout where elbow room was sorely lacking, the kitchen and cramped bathroom, to the left of the front door, added up to the only habitable area. How cramped was the bathroom? Someone on the toilet could turn on the shower without a serious stretch. There was no sink.

Nonetheless, thanks to the buzz dulling their critical edge, Nicky and Jess saw fit to dignify their haven as "cozy." After all, they had to "make virtue of necessity," a phrase Jess often recalled from a survey course on English poetry, with no memory of who had written it. Apparently Mr. Alborg was out of sight and out of mind as far as Nicky went, though Jess sometimes caught herself hoping he was "all right" out there, and wondered what she meant by that.

At second glance, they were relieved to learn the old man hadn't been a total hermit, for a digital converter box sat atop the old red portable TV on the counter, in the recess beneath a cupboard. Nicky voiced surprise that such an ancient shitbox actually had the connections for a converter. Cable wasn't in the cards, but they could pull in some local channels. There was nothing on the five and then six o'clock news about pot growers on the lam.

Next to the television, Jess discovered an absurd candle in a likewise absurd holder. Stamped into the white wax of the candle was a column of green numerals, from 4 at the wick down to 24. Each number was underlined, and bracketed within tiny holly leaves. The holder was a wooden block covered in crinkly plastic turf, from which sprang rusty wire approximations of a moose head and legs. The legs straddled a flatter, turf-covered lozenge of wood.

Holding the candle by the green moose torso, she pretend-flew it between Nicky and some pregnant weathergirl's seven-day forecast. "Look, it's a 24-stage candle!" Jess exclaimed.

She paused it at arm's length from Nicky's face until he drily commented, "That's weird."

"Yeah, I'm not sure what Advent is exactly, but that might be what this is for." She put the candle on the table as a centerpiece. Christmas was the last thing on their agenda, but the season was upon them. Why not take advantage of this little festive touch?

They foraged mildly wilted salad fixings from the Kalamazoo's vegetable crisper and made Russian dressing with the ketchup and some mayo. Officially spent for the day after last-straw effort of dining, they gave up on prime-time viewing and yielded to the habit of making love. To encourage a more romantic mood, Jess had lit the candle, but the minute workmanlike Nicky satisfied her, Jess couldn't keep her leaden eyelids open, through which still flickered a warm orange glow. She awoke at sunny half past eight, according to her Swatch, and noticed that the candle had burnt down only to the line above the number 5. Nicky was in the bathroom, and when he emerged, she thanked him for snuffing the flame in the dead of night. He glumly denied responsibility. Must have been a helpful draft, then.

Nicky's chunky glass pipe played a major role in staving off restlessness those first days. To venture this early from their hideout would have been rash unto suicidal, assuming Mr. Alborg's Saab had gas to siphon. Might as well be resigned to eating, sleeping, smoking, changing channels, and fucking for the unknown duration, in what amounted to a womb for grownups, tight but with amenities. They discreetly piped down when the mailman shoved a bill or catalogue through the slot in the door, but that only happened two or three times a week. As for trash pickup? Garbage can, next to the compost bin, was far from full. Ditto the kitchen wastebasket. Some morning, Jess believed, they'd just toss off the covers and know they were good to go, wouldn't they?

On their third day, though, Jess was already worried about devolving into a slug. With Nicky, it was harder to tell low-key baseline from lethargy. No matter. She had to snap out of it and rise to the occasion through the psychoactive haze.

A change of clothes was long overdue. Excellent start! Jess had neglected their bags from the apartment since dropping them under the row of coat hooks next to the door. Transferring bags to table, she pawed around in one for a colorful ensemble, and tangled up in a red satin blouse was a ridiculous plastic Santa. Of all things to be among the saved! Someone had foisted it on her at a party, and it was so awful that she'd kept it. First off, it was long and skinny. And it was leering psychotically. Its limbs and spine were reinforced with wire for posing it. Another chance to perk up their grim surroundings! She bent its arms and legs to hug the vertical portion of the tin chute that fed stove exhaust into the flue, and she twisted its head to goggle across the kitchen. On the mattress, Nicky looked up dourly from filling the pipe. "Why did that piece of shit have to follow us here?"

"Please, Nicky, let's try to make the best of this."

He opened his mouth but said nothing. She stripped down and changed by the warmth of the stove, leaving her dirty clothing on the floor. Nice that he still gazed longingly at her naked body, three years into the relationship. He handed her the pipe and lighter. "Maybe this'll help you chill out a little."

Four hits later, an urge to tally what else was in the bags overtook her. So much for chilling out. Incredible that all the rest of their stuff was lost forever. The stereo, the toaster, the sofa. Granted, it was entirely crap, but that was hardly the point. Ah, thank God for the blunted affect of chronic drug use! When she dug out her shocking pink slippers with the fluffy poodle heads, they entranced her to the exclusion of regrets about everything MIA. Nicky was studying her with a raise of eyebrows. It made her fidgety, and the silly slippers reminded her of a joke to restore more genial vibes. How did it go again? What kind of shoes do you make from bananas? Right. So she literally thrust shopworn punchline at him and asked, "All right, Nicky, what kind of fruit do you wear on your feet?"

Oh shit. He was gawking at her as if she were crazy. With surprising harshness, he went, "Haw!" And rather than expanding on that, he took a sloppy swipe at her thigh. "Come here and do something I like, why don't you?" Well okay, seeing as it was sometime after dark, and she didn't feel like eating. Only first she lit the candle and made an anxious wish that they could always be outlaws in love, writing their own rules, laughing in the face of authority.

Bright and early, a whiff of molten plastic woke her. She sat up gasping, to blink at skinny Santa on all fours between the stovetop's back burners. Heat from the pilot was releasing toxic fumes, but hadn't stuck bulbous fists and clubfeet to the enamel yet. Jess bounced up, dragging along blanket and sheet, and smacked Santa to the floor with a pink slipper from the bedside. On her way back down to the mattress, she glimpsed the candle, only a fraction shorter than it had been last night.

Nicky pulled displaced covers up to his chin again, peevish in the limbo between dreamland and cognizance, mumbling in what might have been a foreign language. As Jess thumped butt-first beside him, he grumbled, "Whaddya foolin' around for?"

"Nicky, did you get up in the dark and put out the candle? Did you accidentally knock that stupid toy off the stovepipe?" And why the urgency invading her voice from out of nowhere?

"Maybe a big truck drove by and shook the house." No further comment. He'd be cranky and uncooperative till it sank in that sleep was a lost cause. Better not to bug him. En route to the toilet, she inspected the candle more closely. The flame had consumed it to the line above the number 7, which incidentally was today's date. Huh! That would mean the beginning of Advent was December 1. Good to learn something new every day.

Nicky also spoke of learning something new. The hour had come to "size up our options," he proclaimed, and gestured at her with his breakfast of flimsy whole-wheat toast and margarine as if it somehow illustrated his point. Then in the same breath he demanded, "Lemme see your cell phone." She dug it out of her beaded handbag on the counter, and he stuffed it in his left hip pocket. "If you turned this on, they could trace it here. We can't risk it. One slip and we're screwed."

What the hell? Did he really consider her such a space shot? As if she was going to crack under the isolation and commence babbling at everyone on speed dial? She shut her gaping mouth. Smarter to wage battles over more pragmatic issues. No matter how galling the principle of the thing. Plus, Nicky was on to his next order of business. He whipped on vintage blue peacoat, shut the door softly, and skulked by the kitchen window toward the garage. Later, Jess heard him through the checkerboard linoleum, clunking around in the cellar.

She watched the 700 *Club* to jeer at the holier-than-her hucksters, wishing she were high but not daring to light up without Nicky. He burst in with a hefty cardboard box and asked if she wanted the bad news first. She shrugged. He forged ahead. Siphoning gas from the Saab to their Corolla might not be doable, even though a mile of garden hose hung in loops on the garage wall. They needed a key to the gas cap, and with their luck, the old man had gone into the compost with all his keys on him. Striving not to sound superior, Jess broached the obvious. Why not hotwire the Saab, drive to a gas station, and fill a jug with gasoline? Nicky's arching brows implied that maybe she was missing the obvious. Could she drive a stick? No? Back to square one, then.

As for the good news, Nicky had rustled up canned and dry and frozen goods down cellar, and resolved to slave away all afternoon fixing them a gourmet feast. Or die trying, Jess mused cynically. Before any of that, however, Nicky proposed an additional mission. "I don't know about you, but I'm feelin' kinda cooped up in here. Maybe we oughta give the parlor a second chance. Expand our elbow room. The gas-on-gas might be able to warm it up some."

"Do you want to smoke?"

The question seemed to throw him. "I can't decide. I got us a surprise for later. It might make a nice change from gettin' stoned."

"That's later," Jess argued, plucking pipe and near-empty baggie one-handed from the table. "How about now?"

So they were somewhat off-focus when they slunk into the drafty, dusky parlor. Nicky waved a hand around till he connected with a pull cord at room center. Harsh light broke over them from a single bulb encased in moonfaced paper lampshade. Nicky had almost banged his shins on a coffee table whose surface was a laminated art print of an old-fashioned girl and a tuxedo cat in front of an unkempt flower garden and red farmhouse. On the far side of the table was a Victorian loveseat.

Wow! With all the junk in here, it could have been a museum of the Old Country. Or a shrine. The sun must have brightened this space once upon a time, because it had bleached the blue and yellow from a framed Swedish flag, and the legibility from a map of Sweden, that shared one wall. High-rise glass-and-wooden cases from IKEA lined the remaining walls, and one of them contained a cavalry's worth of monotonously similar red horses, from matchbox dimensions up to something a Barbie doll could ride. A few were blue or white, but all wore the same multicolored saddle and reins. They reminded Jess of indigestible pastry. The next case swarmed with crude goats of straw and red ribbons or occasionally wood under green paint, in the same range of sizes. Why would anyone want even one of these?

To either side of the ponderous draperies were more cases. One glinted with souvenir drinking ware, a miniature martini glass with a moose decal, stunted goblets, shot glasses stamped with *Playboy* bunny or Swedish flag, narrow-necked glasses with bulges suggesting breasts and hips, midget drinking horns that might have been earrings. Good grief!

Jess inspected one more display, of insipid red-clad elves or gnomes perhaps meant as Christmas tree ornaments, cobbled out of cotton puffs and felt and Styrofoam. For all the cash and effort invested here, everything was so cheap and ugly! Grody, as Jess's mom used to say. If this had been old Alborg's lame-ass idea of Swedish culture, he must have been a big fan of that Swedish Chef on the Muppets.

"This could be nice," Nicky was muttering. "There's a lot of potential in here, don't you think?"

That was a hoot! Maybe if they burnt everything and then fumigated, yeah. "What are you talking about?"

"I don't know." Was Nicky a shade irritable, borderline resentful? "Even before we came here, I've been feeling kinda spent. Like there's not enough in me to go around. I can't really put it in words. It sounds mental, I know it. But I don't feel as empty in here. I'm more at home."

What the hell was going on with him? She could tell he was getting worked up by that throbbing vein on his temple. He needed a distraction. In everyone's interests. "Nicky lamb, I'm freezing. Come on with me," she pleaded, and slowly folded her fingers over the back of his hand, stroking it, then drawing him like a sleepwalker toward the mattress. In passing, she pushed the parlor door shut with her toe.

Afterward, Nicky sprang up and started rattling utensils and clanking pans, and it was irritable Jess's turn to mope in bed. Nicky was making himself a nuisance showing off his new, unjustified enthusiasm, and he'd only be bumming worse than ever when it ended in grease fire or diarrhea.

Might as well get dressed and straighten up the place! First step, rescue skinny Santa from the floor and blow off the dust bunnies. Reposition him beyond the bend in the stovepipe, where it ran horizontally into the wall. She slapped toy onto warm metal with a force that made her realize she was acting on a grudge, that she had some need to prove who was boss. She raised the grinning face to survey the kitchen, as it had before, only now Santa seemed more like a figurehead on some prow intruding from their abandoned world.

She might have finished more housework, had she not wavered all afternoon between staring contests with Santa and self-consciously averting her eyes from him. She also kept turning on the television to fend off pangs of worry and guilt that only bit deeper with each view of life outside till she switched the set off. Their overlapping circles of friends and customers must have been upset at Jess and Nicky's road trip into thin air. She missed people and hoped everyone would understand when they heard what had happened, and was tempted to poach back her cell and sneak a call or two.

Or wouldn't old Alborg, recluse or not, have a landline in here somewhere? And if she could find it, why not touch base with trusted associates when Nicky was, say, in the shower? In the course of wiping down counters, a comically obsolete phone came to light, behind some Deco aluminum flour tins that still contained stale treats for absent pets. It was evidently one of the first touch-tones, shaped like the hefty antique in Grandma's attic, save for the square keypad instead of a dial. But Nicky, damn him, was a step ahead of her. No cord between phone and wall! He was still futzing with ingredients on the other side of the sink. If he were simultaneously gloating at her, she didn't care to see.

She also didn't care to watch him fumbling at cookery, but did kill moments gauging each new smell, nose in the air and eyes on the ceiling, amazed when nothing scorched or curdled. By sunset, when he clanged spatula against mixing bowl in lieu of dinner gong, she had succeeded mostly in stirring up more dust than had gone into the wastebasket and in transferring piles of clothes and miscellany from underfoot to less trammeled corners. Mr. Alborg's odds and ends, like the salt and pepper shakers in baffling crayfish form, wound up on his chair, as if his morsel-by-morsel reconstruction were under way. His Advent candle on the table was an exception, and she took a lighter to it before uneagerly sitting down.

Supper was a revelation. The flavors of onion soup, beef strogan-off on egg noodles, creamed spinach, and apple cobbler all lived up to their enticing aromas. Unbelievable! The third time she marveled at his culinary expertise, he scolded her, "You don't have to sound so shocked! Sometimes you don't give me half the credit I deserve. Before I met you, I did plenty of cooking on my own."

There went that tic again. Jeez, the defensive Nicky was a new one on her. No idea he was so bad at fielding compliments! She nimbly flipped his indignation back onto less surefooted terrain, by asking what had happened to that surprise of his. Nicky swayed gently as mental wheels spun in midair a minute. Oh, right!

From a shelf in fridge door he retrieved a half-liter bottle. "Found this on top of a meat freezer down cellar." The contents were pale autumnal yellow, and according to the label's fake runic font, were called Pors Brännvin. Below the name was what seemed at first a cartoonish Viking, with upheld drinking horn, greeting a dragon-prowed boat full of cookie-cutter brethren. But nobody's helmet had wings or horns, so Jess couldn't peg who these people were supposed to be. More importantly, though, the bottom left corner of the label boasted, "38% VOL." And hurray! Nicky's tic had subsided.

Just as well he hadn't unscrewed the black metal cap yet because, he opined, this unpronounceable liquor had the aura of a *digestif*. A fifty-cent word, Jess reflected, for aftershave with a dose of sachet, as based on a wary sniff at the four fingers sloshing into her tumbler. Nicky raised a toast to nicer destinations down the road, and they drank, and she made a face and busted out laughing, and he did the same. This shit tasted as bad as it smelled! Well, what did Jess expect from a bottle that couldn't get Viking helmets right? Yep, it was one awful beverage, agreed Nicky. And a bigger shame that it was the only alcohol in the house! Suppose they stuck it in the freezer, he suggested. Might that blunt enough of the flavor to make it bearable?

What a relief that Nicky and Jess were on the same wavelength again, joking around, facing a topsy-turvy future together.

Jess couldn't recall the last time they'd exchanged such a longing, open look. And as she began to beam at that, the candle midway between them went out by itself, as if snuffed by callused thumb and fingertip. Darkness took charge till her sight adjusted. Were her own pupils as dilated, her expression as stunned, as Nicky's? He laughed at her through the thinning spiral of smoke, in implicit answer.

She bowed her blushing face toward the candle, away from taunting mirth at her expense, and found something to draw attention from herself. The flame had gone out after consuming today's date, as it had on previous days, she informed Nicky. She couldn't fathom how, but ingenious Swedes must have invented a wick that stopped burning at set intervals. Nothing eerie going on, or funny in any sense. Nothing here but advanced candle technology.

He nodded indifferently, as if he hadn't just mocked her, as if they hadn't shared a tender interlude a minute earlier. He got up and tugged hard at the Kalamazoo's freezer door. It opened with a dull pop, to divulge the sad white mouth of an ice cave, too constricted for accommodating much of any food, with scant room to spare after Nicky slid in the bottle. From the faux humidor of a breadbox by the TV, he broke out the second of their three baggies. Back to their usual. Fine. She'd have to sleep on her side to alleviate the stomach-ache from that Pors whatever-it-was.

Sometime later, Jess was strolling on a misty beach. The tide was lapping in and cast an icy paw at her feet. She skipped aside, onto drier sand, but another little breaker leapt at her ankles. She altered course once, twice, multiple times more, but waves kept rushing in to harass her. And no getting used to the frigid water. Meanwhile, her nose told her she was nearing the site of some chemical fire or oil spill, but no signs of disaster were visible. At her next breath, the fumes gained choking potency, and her feet became iron, too heavy to dodge the mounting surf or turn away from whatever spiteful power stank in the fog. Help!

She awoke with her feet toward the fridge instead of the stove, and Nicky was lying at the same right angle to normality. To short-sheet themselves this way was rude enough, but her legs below the knees weren't even on the mattress. What the hell had they been thinking at bedtime? The freezer door was open, and the ice cave was halfway reduced to a cascade down the front of the fridge, and a puddle numbing her heels. That bottle of icky booze was on the counter beside the fridge. And the toxic odor had followed her from the beach.

Santa, for the second morning in a row, was facedown on the stove! But worse, he crouched squarely atop a pilot, and tiny points of flame were winking on and off along his limbs, spewing smudgy puffs of smoke. Jess screeched and scrambled over snoring Nicky, still up to his eyes in his own dream, from which he grumbled, "Where's the fire, lieutenant?"

A dishcloth was hanging off the oven-door handle. She whipped it free and bunched it around Santa and scooped him up. She bit her lower lip as inspiration struck. Stumbled to the open freezer door. Luckily the plastic wasn't melting yet. Bad enough that brief flare-ups on Santa's spray-coat of red paint had sowed a crop of gooey black blisters. She shoved Santa in the freezer, withdrew the dish-cloth, and slammed the door. Let's see you flop onto the stove now!

Peals of merriment transformed her agitation to rancor. Nicky was propped up on his elbows, grinning like a dolt. "Yeah, that's better. He'll be happier in there. More like the North Pole." It sounded like an imitation of a quip she might have made, except she was a lot wittier.

"What did you mean putting him on the stove like that, you jackass?" she exploded. "You wouldn't be laughing if the house was on fire!"

"Whoa, whoa! You got that wrong!" If Nicky sincerely wanted to protest his innocence, he should have controlled that goofy smirk first. "I'm not the one who hates that piece of crap with a passion." Curious how he'd emphasized "I'm," as if lodging a counter-accusation against her. Or somebody else.

"Who, then? Mr. Alborg? Is that who also got up to drink some Swedish aftershave and forgot to shut the freezer? Gee whiz, Nicky! Do you suppose he wasn't actually dead when we chucked him in the compost?" She didn't like lobbing sarcasm at him, but he was asking for it.

Obliging Nicky, without a word, rolled out of bed, shrugged one of Mr. Alborg's windbreakers over his nakedness and stomped outside in untied sneakers. She stood breathless in neutral gear, not knowing what to think. A minute later he trudged back in, stooped to wipe grimy hands on the discarded dishcloth, and said, "It's not a problem." Again with the cryptic phrasing! She was the one with the sense of humor. He really ought to stop trying to be funny.

Uh-oh! Nicky lurched over and leaned on the counter as if dizzy, and gazed across the kitchen as if unaware of where he was. "I don't know how it got to the stove again. It was lying flat on the stovepipe, wasn't it?" Jess arched her eyebrows. As far as the record of Nicky's memory went, someone had apparently set the needle back a few grooves. "I'm gonna go hang out in the parlor a while. It's too full in here right now."

Too full? Jess was about to discourage him on account of the cold and the unsavory vibes, but what the hell, let him go. He was acting a little too pathological for her to be into him right now. When he came out later to medicate himself, she partook too, of course, as she did at subsequent junctures when he left his new sanctum.

During the next few days, amidst frequent recourse to cannabis, their strained relations eased. The bottle of rotgut stayed put behind a cupboard door, and so did Santa in the freezer. As for Nicky, there was no guessing when, and for how long, he'd retreat into the nasty parlor, and erratic as his behavior was, Jess was grateful for the extra breathing space. They ate together, but nothing on a par with Nicky's haut-cuisine extravaganza. With energy at a bloodshot premium, why waste it on mere food? They'd only get hungry again. Jess summoned the gumption, at least, to light the Advent candle every suppertime, primarily for the gag of seeing it extinguish itself. This never failed to raise a titter, and she read that as a sign that her gift of robust humor was on the rebound. Once they were away from here, she trusted, she and Nicky would make a hundred percent comeback as an affectionate, copacetic couple.

Or maybe the world should come to them. They had a rent-free roof over their heads, potentially forever. They'd sidestepped the narcs' radar. Did they have airtight reason to go elsewhere? These considerations dawned during a reality show where C-list celebrities helped build new homes for disaster victims. Nicky would have given her grief for watching anything so weepy, but he was busy communing with the rubbish in the parlor. She enjoyed a couple of tokes in his absence. Against protocol, but give her a break! They still had a whole ounce and a half.

Yet sometimes factors beyond her ken and control recast the fickle weed as a bringer of gloom rather than jollity. Gushing sentimentality on the small screen clearly bore part of the blame. Those people on TV had each other, had life coursing around them. She and Nicky had been forced to maroon themselves apart from the human race. They were dead to the world, and while they lay low here, could they prove to themselves that they were alive? Could they be ghosts and not know it? No, there was something to be done, she had it a minute ago, think back!

There, she had it again, and then Nicky emerged from the parlor. Perfect timing, while her thoughts were in order. She cut to the chase. "Nicky lamb, now that we're all moved in, why don't we get the business up and running here? We can put grow lights and hydroponics in the cellar. We can pay the utility bills with money orders or something. Maybe we could make this our home for good!" She anticipated kneejerk sales resistance and tried feeding him that soulful pout to melt his heart and stir his libido.

Nicky paused golemlike as if waiting for the light to stop hurting his vision. He slowly raised his eyes to hers and erupted, "Are you out of your skull? Do you have any idea what that would really be like? We can never have this place to ourselves!"

"Nicky, you're scaring me!"

Nicky wasn't listening. His tic was pulsing. His nostrils flared. He sucked in air. Held it for analysis. Bellowed, "And take it easy on the stash, goddammit! We're down to a bag and a half." Done with words, he undermined his point, or maybe unmasked it, by grabbing pipe and baggie off the table and stuffing the bowl. Took deep, vindictive puffs. Neither offered any, nor rested eyes on her.

"All right, Nicky." Her words bounced off predictably deaf ears. Just so long as he chilled out! She hadn't given up on reopening shop here, not by a long shot. But she had all the time in the world to work on him. He tromped back into the parlor. Slammed the door. In absentia, became a child in her mind's bleary eye again.

How to make their new home livable for Nicky? Not as thorny a riddle as that of how to reverse his burgeoning personality crisis. This would be the worst hour to lose her capacity for seeing the lighter side. In furtive silence, she refilled the pipe and tiptoed out, for another three fortifying tokes while she studied the compost bin, with no handle on what it made her feel.

Why try so hard to deny it? Fragile Nicky was struggling. He simply lacked her resilience when it came to ditching their stuff, hiding from arrest, fighting cabin fever. Especially after those sojourns in the parlor, he was in a daze where words came slowly. She might chalk that up to hypothermia. But when they screwed, he watched her with a vigilance that made him seem like a stranger. Or else he shuffled around like an old man, refusing any help with finding what he'd evidently mislaid. He really needed to lighten up. She'd said that a lot lately, hadn't she, but what to do about it? The compost bin, despite her piercing stare, withheld any hints on how to get through to him. And the bowl was played. Why was she still out shivering in the dark?

Nicky was in the kitchen. Open parlor door was creating a fuggy draft. She hurried by and closed it. He was oblivious. Down on his knees. His rapt face practically inside the cardboard box formerly full of dinner ingredients, and forgotten ever since, on the floor by the table. Gripping stubby Advent candle by its green lozenge base, he tilted it to illuminate one stray item, shaped like a can of tuna fish or chaw. Nicky carefully hoisted it by fingertips to the tabletop. "What do you make of this?"

The can was a vivid red and yellow. On the lid, a howling wolf was depicted above some illegible scrawl. More straightforward print below stated "Surströmming." That lid and the bottom were so convex that the can balanced like an egg on the table. Yet Nicky was perversely chipper, inches away from a likely holocaust of botulism and shrapnel. "What do you suppose this was doing in the box?"

"Preparing to go off like a bomb, maybe? Jesus Christ, Nicky!" Later she could be compassionate about Nicky's guttering sanity. Right now she was hugely pissed at him for stupidly endangering their lives. Most likely based on his stoned weakness for a pretty color scheme. Someone had to be proactive around here. She cupped this Swedish-style grenade in both hands and screamed at Nicky to let her out. He complied like a sleepwalker, damn him to hell! She scurried to the compost bin and laid the can like a napping baby upon the tarp. Her wish had come true. Nicky had chilled out, though she felt more than ever like killing him. He was in the shower when she returned.

After staying out of each other's way for the balance of the evening, they bedded down together as usual. But minus any good-night words or kiss. In the dismal small hours, Jess awoke with remorse at missing the candle snuff itself. Something she'd never ever see again after the 24th. The candle was a nub of its former self. They must be on the cusp of Christmas. Rustling bedclothes signaled Nicky's equally restless night. Should she try and normalize relations while drowsiness softened any grudges? The mattress shuddered. Jess rolled over. Nicky was up and headed for the bathroom. No, he was slipping out. What the hell? Was he deserting her in this wasteland after three years through thick and thin? Her gaze was fixed upon the drop-panel ceiling, but it was no more forthcoming with answers than the compost had been.

She must have listened and waited long enough to doze off occasionally. Didn't want to count how often the ceiling rushed back into startling focus. The dark and the silence formed a single oppressive medium, till a muffled click alerted her to Nicky at the door. She quietly rotated her head on the pillow, to spy on his progress toward the sink. What could be motivating him to affect both stealth and that elderly shuffle? Was he sleepwalking now for real? She discerned a faint clink as he placed something under the faucet and trickled water onto it for a minute. When he turned off the tap, he left the mystery item behind and let his coat drop from his shoulders as he doddered back into bed. His skin gave off cold like an open fridge, but even beyond that, Jess felt averse to touching him and took a flustered while drifting into sleep again.

Unrested, grumpy, she consulted her Swatch in gray soupy light. After nine? Honestly? The rain clattering at the windows and drumming on the roof accounted for the dawn ambience. Nicky was in the bathroom. A golden chance to scope out what he'd stowed in the sink. She wasn't particularly shocked at finding the red and yellow can next to the drain. Nicky opened bathroom door to face the acerbic question, "Is there some reason you brought that hazardous waste inside last night?"

"What hazardous waste?" His bewilderment rang genuine enough. "I was in bed all night. Weren't you?"

She wouldn't dignify that with an answer, but short of calling him a liar, one explanation remained. And she couldn't very well hold his sleepwalking antics against him. Infuriating or not. "Look, I'm going in the bathroom, if you're done in there. Guess we won't get anywhere fussing. Do me a favor though, okay? When I come out, I want that can to be out of here. Please?"

Without awaiting his response, she barged past him and shut the door more or less in his face. The can was indeed gone when she came out, as was Nicky. She hadn't heard him leave the premises and deduced he was in the parlor. With his dumbfounding choice of fetish object? Her shrewder judgment told her to pause for breath. Maybe she had been a mite high-handed. She sure wouldn't want to brave that downpour herself. She filled a conciliatory breakfast bowl, knocked on parlor door, and trooped in. No point letting on she'd had to unseal the last of their three ounces. Meager light through gaps between drapes imposed a funereal feeling.

He accepted the peace pipe listlessly. His posture in the loveseat suggested that his inner man had suffered a cave-in, while the outer man reminded her of whitish putty. His look and voice alike bespoke a crushing burden of going through some trauma that had somehow escaped Jess's notice. Their eviction? His two priors for possession? Were those still eating at him? To Jess they felt like lifetimes ago. She didn't realize he was talking for a couple of seconds. "If you want us to stay here, I guess we can give it a shot. I don't want to fight. I'm not winning any fights these days. Here, there, what's the difference?"

"Okay, Nicky." Best to be demure in victory. She also refrained from harping on the grass going to waste in his limp, absent-minded hold, but delicately retrieved the pipe and inhaled till the red in the bowl faded to black.

Yeah, that was better. She weathered that transient wooziness, as when plane wings dip during a course change. Funny how a lungful of mere herb revamped her priorities. Despite local dearth of Xmas spirit, the holiday loomed, and though the gewgaws in here were plainly Yule-related, they were so dreary and depressing behind dusty glass, so devoid of seasonal cheer. Her mood to decorate was finally in recovery, after those setbacks with Santa melting on the stove. The right dose of levity just might redeem this rainy day. And coax Nicky from his stubborn funk.

She tentatively pulled at teardrop-shaped knob on the front of one glass case. The door opened smoothly. She removed some straw goats that arbitrarily appealed to her, but then felt mysteriously obliged to ask Nicky, "All right with you if I take out some of these things and put them around?"

"Why should I mind?" Of course he shouldn't. But his probing expression fairly dared her to tell why he should. Or did it? At second glance, that must have been overanalysis under the influence. Meanwhile, she covertly sought in vain for the whereabouts of the swollen can. After several trips to and from the parlor, she left Nicky to his own devices and contemplated her chintzy array upon the table. Bringing it out into the open had perked it up considerably. A pattern was hiding in the disorder and whispering to her. It provoked a grin, a decisive "Hah!" and a gale of amusement.

She worked at the speed of inspiration. Like an artist, she fancied. Sparing mental energy only to beam psychic command into the parlor, Don't come out till it's ready! She'd been steadfastly admiring her handiwork for an indeterminate time when the swinging parlor door clanged against the stove.

"Check it out!" Still fixated on the tabletop, she gestured expansively. Larger specimens of straw goats and red horses brought up the rear in a procession that curved gracefully from the edge of the table toward the center, where the humblest animals, including salt-and-pepper shaker crayfish, were first in line to adore a Holy Family whose Joseph and Mary were a pair of red-felt elves, smiling above a tiny elfin Jesus in a shot-glass manger filled with straw stripped from a goat. A Viking ship embellished the shot glass. Jess hadn't come up with versions of angels or shepherds or wise men yet, and crude as the present results were, they were no less charming and colorful for all that. Why wasn't Nicky heaping her with praise and delight? "It's a Nativity scene!" she exulted. "Isn't it great?"

As her patience frayed and she turned toward Nicky, he leaned over the tableau and backhanded it with one spasmodic swipe onto the floor. The vein in his forehead stood out like a plump red worm. He shook as if a motor were overheating inside him. His unblinking eyes bulged. His lower jaw twitched from side to side. Words were stuck fast in some interior logjam.

She was too upset at his misbehavior to fear his inarticulate wrath. If ever he laid a hand on her, he knew damn well she'd whack him with a skillet the instant his back was turned, and if he revived, he'd never see her again. She shrilled, "Since when were you religious?"

The logjam broke with a loud outburst. "Where is your respect?"

Huh? The question was so unlike him that she goggled speechless as he re-entrenched himself in musky den. Slamming the door.

Sulky Jess collected all the victims of Nicky's violent ill-humor from the floor. Taking slender consolation in the shot glass's unchipped survival. Leaving everything jumbled on the table, at the foot of tacky candleholder.

All quiet in Nicky's refuge. That bothered her, as if the silence were conducting his bad attitude right through the door at her. She turned on the TV out of self-defense. Even if he was teetering on breakdown, even if he wasn't acting deliberately, she could see what he was doing. Her sense of humor was under assault. Her better nature, her joie de vivre, were at stake. She wouldn't sink to his joyless level! She had to stay afloat. The baggie was on the counter, but where was the pipe? With growing dismay, she paced the kitchen from end to end, glowering when parlor door was at perigee, striving to think, reeled in every so often by infomercial come-on for science's mildest depilatory, until memory resurfaced. The pipe was still on the coffee table in the parlor. Fuck!

No use kicking herself. With clenching teeth, she marched straight in. Too perturbed to knock. Swooped down on the pipe. Unerringly, despite its concealment within tabletop scene of a child's garden. She mumbled, "Forgot this in here." Avoided eye contact. Steeled herself for more shit from Nicky.

None was forthcoming. Fine. She had one foot through the doorway. Elated at clean getaway. A twinge of worry stopped her. Was he okay? Slowly she turned. Nicky was regarding her through droopy eyelids. He sat slumped in the loveseat. Powerful emotions had receded to expose the spiritual equivalent of a tidal flat. He seemed even more strung out and debilitated than when she was in here last time. Her heart went out to him. His boorishness now trivial.

"Nicky lamb, what's up?" She strove to downplay her concern, lest she alarm him into worse condition.

"Nicky lamb, Nicky lamb," he repeated. Rolling the words around, as if debating after all these years whether he liked them or not. As if they were new to him. He raised his hands in front of his face. To cover it? No, he was inspecting his palms. Consulting his fortune maybe. "I had a little life left, not so long ago. Where is it now?" Such a mournful tone.

"Don't worry, Nicky. We'll get past this." The ongoing strain of his weeks here, self-inflicted or not, explained all his aberrant behavior. It had to. She had to convince him she was on his side!

He looked at her, though, as if she were thick. Or beneath him.

"In here like this, it's been like living on a submarine," he muttered. An ironic observation, insofar as they were high most of the time. She suppressed a smile. Best not to make light of anything Nicky said for now.

"We didn't have a whole lot of choice, Nicky. We're lucky to have this old shack."

Again with that look. Oh, he must have been referring to the parlor, and not the house in general, as a submarine. That did make more sense.

"You don't have to stay in here, you know. Not all the time, like you have. You ought to come out more." She attempted the most fetching expression possible under the circumstances. "Be with me. Personally I don't see how you put up with the dust and everything. I don't think it's healthy."

A wry smile stole across his features, the first in ages. That was a good sign. Or was it? "You have to stop resenting dust. I've learned it's like resenting yourself in the long run."

Was he putting her on? Messing with her head? Pretending to be a wreck, for some deranged joke at her expense?

"You smirk at me. You think what I tell you is funny?"

Crap, she hadn't meant for anything to show. "I'm sorry, Nicky." Playing along seemed prudent. "You're not usually this philosophical. Would it be better if we moved somewhere else soon, like you wanted? Where we weren't so dead to the world?"

Nicky's brooding smile broadened. "People eventually want to die because the world becomes less and less the way they like it."

Now he was just bumming her out. Intentionally, no doubt. Or trying to spook her into backing off? Well, it was working. "I'll be in the other room, Nicky." Quietly she closed the door on him.

Man, that one little conversation had taken a toll. She'd be damned if he was going to capsize her precious conviviality. Leastwise, as a squint at Advent candle confirmed, on Christmas Eve. Whether white Christmas or wet Christmas was in the offing. The pipe in her hand was a godsend, wasn't it? She tapped out the ashes and crammed in a guaranteed restorative bud, which in five deep breaths was ashes itself.

Oh dear. Traipsing back and forth by the sallow light of the blaring TV was making her dizzy. She had to sit down. Was it possible she'd smoked too much? Rumor had it that heavy users never came down with colds and suchlike bugs. But was she susceptible otherwise? To something she couldn't define, or resist, that took advantage of altered nervous system? That assertion, however inchoate or ominous, was preferable to conceding she'd inhaled more than she could handle. Whatever was responsible, she was succumbing to it. Darkness swallowed the candle stump, and her chin bumped the table as she nodded off.

She sat up, no longer high at all, and looked around. The TV was off. That was good. Nicky must have come out and taken care of it, but where was he now? He was gone. Why did she put it that way, she wondered, when he was simply in the parlor as far as she knew? The candle was gone too. Then she noticed muddy shoeprints heading from the door, toward the table. She swiveled around to get up and screeched like a monkey. Old Mr. Alborg was towering over her, dirt and garbage on his heaving breath. He clutched the candleholder by its furry green torso and jabbed a finger at its wire head and antlers and railed, "It's a gräslig älg! It means grassy moose. It also means ugly moose. It is a joke! You like jokes! Laugh! Laugh!" His singsong voice was gurgly and raw.

She woke up blinking spastically in the kitchen with TV blathering and candle on the table and no shoeprints on the floor. Only a dream, of course! She drew a grateful breath, and the room spun mercilessly as she gagged. She had to marshal utmost self-control not to puke. The worst putrescence ever had hit her like a sucker punch, threatening her balance as she staggered to her feet. Whatever the hell it was, it also contained some familiar strand, yes, of industrial virulence, from that other nightmare, many days ago, about a beach. She gaped at parlor door, fearing the unspecified worst. She reeled forward as if crossing a storm-tossed deck and flung the door wide. Its crash against the stove made her jump a little.

The stink was radically stronger in here, which she'd hardly thought possible. Nicky had smuggled in a can opener as well as the distended can, whose sawtooth lid now stood straight up. He was on the loveseat, swigging from that bottle of Swedish aftershave. He plunked it on the coffee table, next to the can, and, wagging a finger at her, he lectured, "Never put this in the freezer! It destroys the complex bouquet!" And with reckless aplomb, he dipped his fingers into the slick black-and-silver strips of fish inside the can and tucked one in his mouth, sucking it in like a gangrenous tongue. Judging by the glistening oil on his cheeks, this morsel wasn't the first. "Stop it! You'll kill yourself!" she screamed.

He smacked his lips and sported a smile half-smug, half-contented. "It's not a problem."

"Not a problem? We have to go to the emergency room right now!" She lunged over, daring to gulp only shallow breaths, loath to touch his slimy hands, pulling him up by the wrists. Nicky let himself be led without protest through the kitchen and into the rain. Jess did love him, as this panic at the risk of losing him attested, and she was terrified to picture him dying in convulsions on the floor of that foul shanty, even if hauling him out into public ended in police custody. At least he'd be alive! They had to reconnect with the world to some extent soon anyway, since they were running out of pot. Not until they entered the garage did she remember that the Corolla was out of gas, and the Saab had no keys.

She was groping for the best way to break this to Nicky, but he was digging in hip pocket where her cell phone still languished. "I found the keys." First she'd heard of it, but fine! He brushed by her and unlocked the driver's door of the Saab and planted himself behind the wheel. "I'll drive," he offered affably. But brooking no argument. Okay, so long as they got going before it was too late!

They were out of the garage and cruising down wooded road, and Jess had to take it on faith that their heads-or-tails choice of direction would lead to a hospital sooner rather than later. Miles had rumbled by before something else occurred to her. "Nicky, I didn't know you drove a stick."

He chuckled. "No, he can't, but I can."

What? An unwanted realization, long overdue or not, was creeping up on her. Nicky's jaw was set with atypical firmness. But whose firmness was it?

"There's a lot you don't know." An accent uncomfortably like that of the Swedish Chef from the Muppets was gaining ground. Yes, quite the joke on her! One way or another, a little Alborg had sprouted, months and months ahead of spring. He took his eyes off the waterlogged view too long and too often and scrutinized her coolly, as if ending up in the morgue were not an issue. His breath reeked of compost as much as rotten fish and booze. "Have you ever thought about being humble?" he demanded.

Then his demeanor brightened and he paid the road more heed, and minus accent, he babbled about the beauty of this second chance, as if he weren't flirting with hard time or in immediate need of a stomach pump. But was a dead man walking with Nicky's borrowed legs? Or was impersonating old Alborg Nicky's way out of his own personality crisis? Or did both cases apply?

Jess no longer hazarded to guess who was talking, and wished mainly she'd had the presence of mind to grab the rest of their stash on the way out. And dammit, she'd also forgotten to turn off the TV. But the TV nattering on by itself in the empty house was funny in its own right, wasn't it? Her eyes followed the swishing windshield wipers as a raucous laugh escaped her.

During his past 35 years as a writer, JONATHAN THOMAS has also worked as factory hand, artist's model, manager of a recycling center, postal clerk, concert promoter, library technical assistant, comedian, and copyeditor for medical journals and the Providence Art Club. At Brown University, he was a student of Lovecraft scholar Barton L. St. Armand. He has written comics scripts for *Eerie* and *Vampirella*, music journalism for the *San Francisco Weekly* and other newspapers, and lyrics for performers Angel Dean and Sue Garner, Shackwacky, Fish and Roses, Escape by Ostrich, Video Aventures (in France), and scumCrown (in Sweden). He has written liner notes for the French band Etron Fou Leloublan and the US/Italian band Barnacled. His fiction has appeared in *Fantasy Macabre, Ballpeen, Radio Void, Resister, Symbol, HunterGatheress Journal, Studies in the Fantastic, PS Magazine*, and the anthology *Black Wings*. Radio Void Press issued a collection of short works, *Stories from the Big Black House*, and Hippocampus Press published the collection *Midnight Call and Other Stories*. He has composed and played keyboards and miscellaneous percussion with the Amoebic Ensemble, the Panic Band, and Septimania (in collaboration with musician/producer Frank Difficult). Thomas lives in Providence and is married to artist and singer Angel Dean.

www.ingramcontent.com/pod-product-compliance
Lightning Source LLC
Chambersburg PA
CBHW051523050726
47503CB00014B/1117